I0891454

GRINDING OF THE SOUL

Naum Prifti

Translated by Peter Prifti
Edited by Rafaela Kondi

EAST EUROPEAN MONOGRAPHS, BOULDER, CO
DISTRIBUTED BY COLUMBIA UNIVERSITY PRESS, NEW YORK
2009

East European Monographs, No. DCCXLVIII

Copyright 2009 by Naum Prifti

ISBN: 978-0-88033-641-3

Library of Congress Control Number: 2008938730

Printed in the United States of America

To my grandson Eri Tare

Peace be with you...

Contents

∞ Tears at the Wedding ∞

In the cellar you could hear, better than anywhere else, the rhythmic stomping of guests who were dancing in the room above. Along with the sound of feet pounding the floor, you could hear laughter and shouting, the clinking of dishes and glasses, and the tunes of the musicians. Rising above all of that was the muffled and confusing din of a wedding party. The hullabaloo and mirth of the wedding shattered the serenity of the autumn night so that those neighbors who had not come to the wedding found it hard to sleep. The house seemed to rock like a boat, and made you think that at any moment the floor was going to cave in, and all the people above would come tumbling down, yelling and shrieking, but still engulfed in the merriment that had inundated them.

"What a wedding!" said Chef Pandeli in a tone that suggested amazement at what was going on upstairs. With his gray eyes, bordered by deep wrinkles, he looked at Aunt Mara, the lady of the house, and shook his head, unable to find words to express properly the pleasure he felt in his soul. Being the chef, he had been given a white apron to wear, which still showed some creases from the ironing; and every so often, whether he was busy or not, Pandeli wiped his hands on it, as its unspoiled whiteness had made him feel uneasy. Leaning over the stove, a short man with a large spoon in hand was sautéing something in a pan, and squinting to keep the smoke from getting in his eyes.

Speaking in a weary voice, as if she had either not heard a word that Pandeli said, or as if his words had made no impression on her, Aunt Mara exclaimed:

"I'm worn out… from running around the whole blessed day.... My legs have given out on me. Thought I'd come down here and rest a bit."

"That you should! A wedding is no picnic." Pandeli brought out a little wooden seat, placed it against the wall, and in a pleading tone of voice said to her, "Sit down here if you like."

Aunt Mara sat down with the sort of pleasure one feels at the end of a long trip in blistering heat, and looking at Pandeli she said in a soft, apologetic voice:

"I'm dying to sleep. Last night I didn't catch a wink. Went to bed at two, got up at five."

Pandeli had strewn dry grass and fern leaves over the cobblestone floor of the cellar, which had been turned into a kitchen for the duration of the wedding. The aroma that came from the soft layer of grass and fern, the pots simmering over the fire, and the loaves of white bread piled up in stacks, had all changed the look of the cellar. It no longer seemed gloomy and forsaken, even though its walls were unplastered and the exposed, age-old stones had been blackened by grime and the passage of time. The cellar had now taken on the appearance of rooms in newly built houses still lacking the finishing touches, but whose owners were in such a hurry to move in that they paid no attention to the things not yet in place.

Aunt Mara put her elbows on her knees and rested her head in her hands. Over her black kerchief she had placed a scarf with white fringe, as was the custom to indicate that there was a wedding in her home, and joy in her soul. She had put the white headscarf on as soon as the bride had crossed the threshold, and had not yet taken it off. But while she was dozing, the scarf slipped out of place, as if the wind had just blown it there whimsically.

Ordinarily a symbol of mirth and happiness that white piece of cloth was a stark contrast to Aunt Mara's long, painful mourning, for in this poor mother's heart, there was little room for celebrating.

In and out of the cellar went those who catered to the wedding guests. They brought in empty plates, and took out dishes filled with appetizers. They put the platters of food on big trays and hurried out, ever eager to serve the guests as best they could. And with those trays, they brought word of what was happening above.

"The godfather drank seven toasts, one after another."

"Thomas is dead drunk. He wants to get up and dance, but his feet won't hold him up. He's reeling all over the place."

"The best man threw a handful of money at the musicians."

The cooks each listened with a grin, as if expecting something funny to happen so they could burst out laughing. Even if what they heard was quite ordinary, they went on grinning, pretending to be having fun. From time to time, Pandeli would ask insistently:

"What about Stefan? Is he drunk yet? He's quite a card when he drinks."

Hardly anyone was paying attention to Aunt Mara resting in her seat and unconsciously picking up scraps of conversations swirling around in the cellar turned kitchen. Her mind goes drifting into a whirlwind of clamor and the noisy bits and pieces of the day's events. As her eyelids begin to droop, she suddenly sees there before her, a throng of in-laws escorting the bride into the courtyard, tables full of relatives and guests emptying glass after glass of *raki*. Some guests are laughing, shouting, dancing, moving about, and then someone starts singing. All of these fragmented visions become clouded and soon melt away as Aunt Mara finally surrenders to sleep.

Looking at her, Pandeli wiped his hands on the apron once again, and smiled innocently. No one could blame the exhausted woman for dozing off on the night of her son's wedding. He stirred the embers in the fireplace and watched the sparks fly up the high chimney. Aunt Mara trembled in her sleep and crossed her hands in front of her.

"My son...."

Pandeli turned around at once and, with the fire tongs still in his hand, asked her in a troubled tone:

"What's the matter?"

Aunt Mara sighed with dismay and fatigue.

"I just saw my son in a dream."

In her heart-wrenching dream, her elder son had appeared and was standing at the front gate, as if he did not want to disturb those who were singing and dancing joyfully. Only his mother had noticed him standing outside. Speaking in a weary voice, as if he were in pain, he asked:

"What about me, mother? How is it you forgot to invite me to the wedding?"

"My dear son,...do come in."

He just stood there, reflecting, as though he could not make up his mind, like a stranger in his own home.

"Come in, son! Come in!..." Aunt Mara said, and rushed to take him by the hand and bring him in. As she ran toward him, she caught herself saying: "Oh dear God, he is dead; how could he come here?" For a moment, she stood in the courtyard as if frozen. She realized that she was dreaming, and her entire body quivered like a plucked string, afraid she might wake up before she embraced her son. She dashed ahead with open arms to hug him tight, kiss the thick locks of his hair, and quell the longing for him that had festered in her for fourteen years. She ran as fast as she could toward him, but the front yard kept getting longer and longer, and she was not able to reach him...when suddenly, she awoke.

Aunt Mara wrenched with longing for her son.

"You came to me in my dream, my son! 'Why didn't you invite me,' you asked me..." Aunt Mara became even more distressed, as she thought of her son. "My dear, dear boy!" she wailed, and her grief became a knot in her throat, her jaws tightened up and tears streamed down her face. "How could we invite you, my precious? Where could I find you, dear heart...?"

Her face changed at once and turned pale, her eyesight dimmed, the tears kept rolling downwards. She could no longer contain herself.

"Here I am, rejoicing at the wedding, while you, my son, are wasting away in the ground below. 'You have forgotten me,' you said, my precious! How can my aching heart ever forget you, my son...?"

Pandeli went over to her and, taking both her hands, sat down by her.

"Now, now, take hold of yourself! This will not do at all," he said sternly to her.

Aunt Mara ignored him and went on weeping quietly with an anguished heart.

"You came to me in my dream, my beloved son, and stood at my door like an orphan. You who belonged at the head of the table...!"

As she looked around the cellar through her tears, people and objects seemed formless and lifeless.

In a short while, four women gathered around her, and tried to console and quiet her. Overwhelmed by her emotions, she wept incessantly but still worried that if the guests would hear her, the wedding would be ruined.

"Today would have been your wedding day, my son. Instead, you are rotting in the ground. How can my heart endure this?"

Those who came over to console her were moved by her tears and the memory of Paskal. Many of them were family relatives, and at a time like this, when a wedding was in full swing in the house where he once lived, they felt a certain sorrow and emptiness in their hearts. This was also their grief so they too wept freely. Just like that, in the midst of the festivities, sorrow had walked in and would not let joy swell unhampered. With its silent presence, it demands: "Make room for me, too, my friend. If it were not for me, you would not be as much appreciated."

The women and girls who had gathered in the cellar around Aunt Mara wept in silence, wiping their tears with their aprons or with the backs of their hands, and trying, at the same time, to give heart to the grieving mother.

"Pull yourself together! You can't go on like this; it's just not like you."

While they were crying in the cellar, those above were singing and dancing. Pandeli found himself in a tight spot. The cellar had suddenly taken on a heartbreaking ambiance. He seemed lost and did not know what to do. He swore at the women a couple of times under his breath, and then stepped out into the yard.

A woman of large build with big sad-looking eyes came into the cellar.

"Is Aunt Mara here?" she asked the moment she stepped inside the door.

"Yes, she is here," one of the women answered, "but she needs to be alone now."

The woman with the sad-looking eyes walked into the throng of women.

"Come on over, the bride is about to dance!" she said to Aunt Mara.

"Wait, her eyes are full of tears," a girl said to her. "She can't go out looking like this."

Only then did the big woman notice that the eyes of the other women, too, were bright red from weeping. On the cheeks of some of the women you could see the trails left by tears as they glided down.

"Shame on you all! What's the matter with you, crying like this?" she said in a tone of astonishment and irritation. Then, turning to Aunt Mara, she said: "You should thank your lucky stars that you're still around to see Andre wed."

"It's easy for you to say." Aunt Mara retorted, sighing, "What about my other son? Where is he? He has ripped out my heart. Only I know how that feels." Saying that, she stretched her arms forward in pain, and then placed them over her breast.

"Brave men do get killed in battle," said the big woman. She spoke with such firmness and boldness that you could not help but respect her. At that moment, however, she looked at Aunt Mara compassionately, not as an elderly woman, but as a little girl in need of guidance and support.

"Come, they're waiting for you!" she said, taking her by the arm. She lifted her up from her seat, motioned with her arms, carved a pathway through the circle of women and girls, and stepped out into the courtyard.

At the head of the stairs, there was a kerosene lamp, but the upper part of the glass was so blackened by soot that the lamp shed only a faint light that barely lit up the stairs. The courtyard itself was left in twilight darkness, except for some flagstones that were illuminated by a small shaft of light that came from the window. In this part of the courtyard, the shadows of guests came and went like strangely shaped phantoms. Off in a corner, a lilac bush was in bloom with flowers that hung like a small cluster of grapes. Yet, it stood there silent and drooping, like an orphan witnessing the celebrations of the night from a distance and apparently longing to draw nearer to the window and watch the festivities inside the house.

The wooden steps of the staircase creaked under the weight of the two women. When they reached the top of the stairs, Aunt Mara glanced at the soot-blackened lamp, but was unaffected by its dingy appearance. When they stepped into the dining room, a wave of hot and heavy air washed over them.

Though the guests were still dancing, curiously the rhythm of their feet seemed to dissipate somehow, so that nobody was even conscious of it. Here one was interested only in the steps, turns and theatrics of the dancers. Those who sat at the tables, however, just went on drinking oblivious to what was going on in the room. The bride in her white veil sat by her sister-in-law and, in a gesture of affection, had put her arm around her, and from time to time spoke to her in a soft voice.

"We want to see the bride dance!" some young men cried out.

"We want to see the bride dance!" joined in the other guests, as they began clapping with excitement and impatience. The bride got up with an embarrassed look on her face and was joined by the proud groom and close relatives of their families. The guests watched with curiosity as the bride stepped out to dance. Blushing somewhat, she almost tripped on the carpet and everyone burst out laughing good-naturedly. Some of them yelled out to her: "Careful, don't you embarrass us now!"

The musician who was playing the accordion was so eager to demonstrate his skill and musical virtuosity that he stood up and began to sing, opening his mouth from ear to ear.

Our bride is dancing,
Oh, how she's dancing,
Dance on, and do not stop,
You're shining like a star....

He sang with all his might, but his voice was hoarse from too much liquor, and however much he tried to raise the rafters, he could not do it. He sounded more like a croaking old rooster. Around the table, those drinking from the outset began another round. When the groom sat down at one of the tables, some of the guests began urging him to drink.

"Here's to the groom. May you be blessed with children and a long life!"

"Same to you!"

"To your health!"

The groom did not feel like drinking much and went over to sit by Dane Bregu who had come from a distant village. They had seated Dane at the head of the table, as the most honored and valued guest at the wedding, and not without reason. His brother, too, had been killed on the same day and in the same battle as Aunt Mara's son. They had fought side by side against the Nazis, and had died very near each other.

The man who played the accordion got up on his feet again and started singing:

Our bride is dancing,
Oh, how she's dancing,
Dancing with the mother of,
the mother of....

Dancing hand in hand with the bride, as was the custom, Aunt Mara began to lead the round dance. The old woman's feet moved in time with the music, but her mind was not on the dance. Her face showed none of the happiness one should feel on such an occasion; her ears were still ringing with the words: "How could you forget me, dear Mother...?" She felt the timid look of his eyes behind her back, and turned her head. No longer mindful of her dancing, Aunt Mara looked at Dane, who was leaning toward Andre and swaying with jerky, drunken movements. With tears in his eyes, he was pulling the groom by the sleeve and pleading with him. His voice nearly broken with emotion could be heard clearly.

"Andre! Let me hug you once, for my brother's sake."

Andre looked at him with distress. Troubled by the memory of his own departed brother, he gazed at Dane through his own tears.

"Let me embrace you." Dane pleaded, "You know, just like brother…with brother."

Aunt Mara, who was leading the dance, stopped in her tracks and peered at this scene. Something ran through her body like a heat wave. She felt uneasy. Her chin dropped, her lips trembled and she burst into tears. But then suddenly, she began to move her feet again, and as she danced she wiped her tears away with the same handkerchief that she was waving merrily in the air when she first led the dance.

A few of the women were moved and began to sigh.

"Her heart is broken, poor soul!"

"Oh, the suffering a mother endures in this world."

"Ah, this damned war," sighed a young woman.

Getting her sister to lead the bride's dance, Aunt Mara broke away and stepped aside. The tune went on as the relatives started to take turns dancing with the bride.

Slipping unnoticed through the crowd, Aunt Mara went out to the front yard. She could not take her mind off the dream she had. What if Paskal had really come back? She wanted to take one more look at him, just long enough to quell her longing for him. That's all.

"Could he be at the gate waiting for me? Why don't I go and look?"

She ran over to the gate in a single breath. She looked around, but there was no one there. Disappointed, she clenched the iron bars and rested her head between them. High up in the sky the stars of autumn flickered brightly. From the house the wedding guests could be heard dancing and the voice of the accordionist rose up beyond the portals of the gate.

Our bride is dancing,
Oh, how she's dancing,
Dancing with the aunt of,
the aunt of....

ꕤ Weeping Pines ꕤ

The alleys to the west side of the city were the most difficult to cross illegally at night, since that area was more carefully patrolled by the militia and the police patrols. Aware of the danger Marion Kapshtica walked cautiously, with his eyes wide open, so as not to be surprised by a police patrol. The sudden flight from the city left no doubt whatsoever that he intended to rejoin the National Liberation Movement. While in the city, he felt as if his feet had been caught in a trap whose iron teeth were grinding down his shinbones. Would his luck hold up long enough to reach the liberated areas, and reunite with his comrades, from whom he had been separated a few weeks earlier? Fortunately the alleys in the outskirts of the town were unpaved, so his footsteps made no sound at all. He came to a plain field with log cabins that looked just like a village. The cabins were surrounded by fences and meadows, and stood far apart from one another. This area was inhabited by "sharecroppers," gardeners who produced and sold spices and vegetables.

As soon as he passed the last cabin, Marion took a deep breath and started to run, raising his arms skyward and shouting "Freedom! Freedom!" He realized that uttering such yells could be dangerous. However, he could not restrain himself. He felt that even if he was shot and killed now, he would die a free man. "A Free Man!"

Who could better appreciate the value of those three simple words than a prisoner sentenced to death? After weeks of torture in the cells, he felt the freedom he had just won in every part of his body, every neuron of his brain. His was overwhelmed that the plan had worked out marvelously. He could just imagine the anger and the disappointment of the Investigation Unit to find out that he had slipped through their fingers and escaped. Marion had indeed signed a statement saying that he was withdrawing from the armed struggle, but he doubted that this stratagem would succeed. Believing that he was lost anyway, he figured it was a gamble worth taking. He was surprised when four or five days later, they opened the iron door of his cell and let him go. Thinking that the police would keep track of him, Marion decided to limit to the utmost his contacts with anyone in his hometown so as not to compromise them. He would buy a soft drink from street vendors, and drink it as he walked, without going into cafes. As for a place to sleep, he went back to Aunt Pandora's, where he had stayed prior to taking off for the mountains. Pandora welcomed her sister's son warmly. She was glad to see that Marion came back.

"You're in your own home. Don't worry about a thing," she said, in an endearing tone of voice.

She also promised to find a nice bride for him, if he wanted to marry. Smilingly Marion replied that when shells are exploding, the violins cannot be heard.

After a dreary week that seemed ever so long, Marion decided to return to his military unit and rejoin his comrades-in-arms. He grabbed a pair of old pants and said he wanted to alter them. He walked into the shop of tailor Van Grabovari downtown. He knew that the tailor looked after his own affairs, without getting mixed up with the Liberation Movement or the Nationalists. After placing the pants on the counter, Marion said to the master craftsman:

"Van, you have been and still are one of my closest friends. But..."

"I am the same as before," Van assured him.

"I have to ask, because I know that we have different political viewpoints," Marion added.

"Couldn't be helped," Van retorted with a chuckle. "You're a bachelor, I am a family man. You hang up your backpack wherever you drive your stake, while I have to strain my eyes, working with a needle, to feed and clothe my wife and kids..."

"Van, you are a practical man, which is why I've come to consult with you," Marion whispered, glancing toward the door to see whether some stranger had come in who might hear their conversation.

"Go on, I'm listening." Then he added sarcastically. "Do you think I'm smart enough to teach educated people?"

"Yeah, big stuff, two years in High School and I didn't finish the second year," Marion said disparagingly. Wasting no time, he came straight to the point. "Van, you know what happened to me..."

"Yes, I do. As a matter of fact, I felt sad. All the time I thought of you, locked up in that prison. Who knows what suffering he's going through, I kept asking myself, and how they are torturing him... I would not feel more hurt, if it had happened to my own brother." He sighed, as if to relieve himself of his pent-up anger. Then he said, "But your affidavit, Marion, it astounded me, and not only me, but the entire town." He looked him in the eye. "I always thought of you as a resolute man. So much so, that secretly I envied you; that is, I did not want to believe what you did. Why you did become a turncoat? That's not what was expected of you..."

"I wonder how much they cuss me..."

"Especially those on your side." Van informed him. "Was it because you couldn't stand the tortures, or what? There are also those who say that you did the right thing. After all, if you can't enjoy life when you are young, when can you?" Van noticed Marion grinding his teeth. He reckoned that he had hurt him, asking such a question.

"I am as I was," declared Marion.

"I don't understand," Van said, fixing his gaze on him.

"Very simple. I fooled them, and they believed me," Marion explained. "I have not withdrawn from the war, nor do I intend to sit on the sidelines. I want you to put me in touch with a contact, so that I can find out the whereabouts of my unit. You know them; at least some of them."

Van did not respond immediately. He ran his hand over a three-cornered ruler, as if he were going to decipher a secret message there.
"I can take you wherever you want, but..." he halted before completing his thought.

"But what...?" Marion prodded him.

"Do you think they will want you back after what happened?"
Marion felt as his chest had been run through with a red-hot iron rod, when he realized that his fellow fighters had misgivings about him. Perhaps it was not their fault. Some of the men had been broken under torture, and had spilled to the enemy whatever they knew, or worse still, had placed themselves in the service of the enemy. Therefore, Van's reservation was understandable.

"How can I unravel this mess?" Marion asked broken-hearted.

"Very easy. There's no need to wander here and there. Go to Kondili's family and ask them if they want to send something to Jasmine, like a letter, a pair of shoes and so forth," suggested the tailor.

"Even if they don't know where the unit is located, they can find out."

Marion thought about it, but said not a word.

"You don't like the idea?" Van asked him.

"No way, and you know the reason," Marion replied.

A year before, it was rumored that Marion was going to be engaged to Jasmine Kondil. For that reason, he did not want to step into their house, as that would only add to the misunderstandings. Uncle Van knew quite well that those rumors were spread by his niece, to find out how Marion felt. To say that she liked him would be an understatement. Whenever Marion's name was mentioned, her face lit up, her eyes flashed, she was all smiles, and as sweet, as could be. Van said that Jasmine would not have left home, if Marion had not joined the Resistance. Still bashful but driven by her romantic passion, she took to the mountains only to be close to her idol. "It's gone to her head; there's nothing you can do," Van would say to his sister. Turning to Marion, he said:

"Fine, I'll be on my way this afternoon."

"Thank you for your help."

"Don't mention it," said the tailor. For a moment, he stood there pondering, as if something gnawed his insides. "Marion, I wanted to keep it to myself, but I can't," Van said, as if talking to himself. "If I were in your shoes, I would not go back to the 'Faik Tabani' Battalion."

Another arrow pierced Marion's heart.

"Why? Where could I feel more at home than among those who know me, and whom I have known for months?" Marion objected unsuspectingly.

"But what if someone should remind them of what happened? Wouldn't you feel hurt? Better join some other unit, no matter where."

"I promised myself in prison that I would rejoin my comrades, and I see no reason to change my mind." Then, changing his tone, he said, "Shall we meet at eight in front of the Majestic cinema?"

"Done," Van replied curtly.

* * *

As soon as he learned that his unit was somewhere between Opar and Voskopojë, Marion decided to leave town that very night, by sneaking through the alleys, unnoticed by anybody.

The darkness was thinning out in the East. The stars were becoming scarce, and the contours of the Morava Mountain came into view over the horizon, even as Marion raced through endless space, breathing clear air and treading on ground sprinkled with dew. Shortly after, the sky brightened gradually, as the weak morning light brought into view trees, shrubs and fences, amid the sublime stillness of the new day. Conscious that he had miraculously evaded the jaws of death, he ran as if his body was weightless. Already, he envisioned Jasmine, her eyes shining with joy; saw himself shaking the lumpy hands of Commander Luto, felt the warmth of chubby-faced commissar Misto Panariti, the cordial embrace of Dino Elmaz, the warmth of the prudent old man Uncle Mersin and other comrades in arms. Even the unit commander Vait Hekurani was going to be pleased that the ranks of the squadron did not suffer another loss.

The first rays of the sun found him climbing a hill covered with spruce and pine trees. The blades of grass on embankments and prairies, the petals of flowers, stones, pine trees – everything, were tinted with fresh colors. His nostrils felt the sweet and tangy aroma of the resins that evaporated from the barks of pine trees and the needles of the spruce trees. He felt the warmth of the sun softly massaging his neck, shoulders and the palms of his hands.

"I'm running like a dog off his leash," Marion said to himself, recalling a popular expression. The analogy made sense, he thought, since he himself had been bound with chains. Still, it could be that the troops in the Battalion had not missed him since they had plenty of company around, while he thought of them day and night, in and out of the cell. The tortures in the prison had steeled his will and the desire to fight to his last breath, to liberate the Fatherland from the Fascist occupation.

* * *

They were traveling from Vithkuq to Kamenicë, on a mission to meet a contact in that area. They walked carefree, with the rifle slung over the shoulder, just like the troops in the liberated zones. However, during the night, a militia unit had blocked the road, close to the highway. Looking through his field glasses, the militia commander detected two armed men advancing toward him, and ordered his men to hide behind the bushes. Marion and Kliton heard a call: "Drop your weapons! You are surrounded!" Thinking that this was a practical joke of some comrades of theirs, they kept walking. But the black barrels of the rifles in the bushes, and the eagles on the caps of the militia, gave them to understand that they had fallen into a trap. They could not flee or resist. After disarming them, and tying their arms with rope, the militia men put them in a truck and drove them to prison. After torturing them savagely, the military tribunal asked them to sign a statement renouncing the civil war; otherwise, they would be sentenced to death. Kliton refused, and two days later he was shot in the prison yard. The memory of the prison buddy, the black-and-blue eyes and the scars of tortures grieved him even more now that he was a free man. How he wished that both of them had returned together. He considered it a noble duty to avenge his partner's death. Only in this manner was he going to lessen the pain he felt about the executed fellowman, as well as the other fellows who still suffered in the Fascist prisons.

* * *

A shepherd he met just outside the village told him that a few infantrymen were in the vicinity of the Monastery. As Marion started walking towards the Monastery, he recalled an event that had occurred sometime ago, and he smiled. Father Ilia, an old gray-bearded pastor, continued to live alone in a bare room of the medieval monastery, without caring what was happening beyond his locality. But the war came to the monastery, as well.

One day Father Ilia came out of the church, walked into the midst of the unit men who were resting in the church yard, and asked them who was their chief. They pointed to Luto Kabashi. The pastor took him by the arm and went inside the church, as if he were going to tell him a secret. When he brought him in front of the Lord's icon, he ordered him to kiss it. On impulse, Luto drew back.

"Are you a Moslem?" the pastor asked. "It doesn't matter. God is one and the same for everyone."

Luto looked at him as if he were joking.

"Listen, Commander. You must understand that this one here is greater than you or I. We come and go. We're here today and gone tomorrow, while the Lord – his blessings be upon us – is everlasting," Father said.

Feeling the heat, Luto pretended to kiss the icon. But when he came out of the church, he began to throw barbs at the pastor, for forcing him to kiss the icon. Marion envied Father for his devotion to religion and God. Perhaps he was the living image of believers of every faith.

As soon as he drew near the monastery, he sensed the aroma of the resin that came from the pine and fir trees, as they warmed up in the light of the sun. Bursting through a pass, a huge billy goat appeared before him, and looked at him with glass eyes that seemed to stand guard over some mysterious vision. A little farther, he found the Partisans seated in a semi-circle formation, on a grassy meadow in the middle of the forest. Facing them was the Commissar, who was holding some sheets of paper in his hands, reading out loud the last communiqué from the war fronts all over the world.

Marion opened his arms, quickened his steps and shouted:

"Greetings, fellows! It is so good to see all of you!"

Shouts of joy and surprise burst forth from all sides, when they saw their comrade. The enthusiastic welcome warmed his heart. It was just as he had expected. Marion wanted first to great the Commander, and afterward the others in turn. He walked over to Luto Kabashi but he didn't even bother to get up. He held out his hand slowly, with the haughty air of a Turkish *aga,* while his gray eyes looked at him with disdain. Marion however did not mind. Luto was like that, an undemonstrative man, when it came to expressing his feelings. As for his failure to get up, that could be ascribed to his age. He and another fellow were the oldest in the unit. Marion walked away from him quickly, to greet the Commissar. Unable to restrain his emotions, he embraced him with both arms.

"Careful, there, you'll crush me," he rebuked him pushing him away with the hand holding the typed sheets of the memo. "Sit down with the comrades, and don't interrupt the reading session!"

The fidgety reception dampened somewhat Marion's enthusiasm. He regretted bursting in on them impetuously, without asking anyone's permission, and worse still, in the midst of the political update session.

He should have waited until recess. Discipline must be respected everywhere and by everybody. At any rate, his comrades were aware of his state of mind, and were not going to hold it against him. He sat down, greeting those nearby with a nod of his head. Then he looked over the fellow Partisans seated in the semi-circle formation, hoping to encounter Jasmine's blue eyes. But he saw no trace of her and his heart sank. Had she been killed, while he was away?

The squadron Commander gave him a fleeting smile, when their eyes met. Then, as if he regretted it, he broke contact and his face darkened. Some of the men in the unit were trying to avoid eye contact with

Marion. Only Dino returned his greeting with cordiality. The cold reception of a few of them, made him stop and think. Had the unit suffered a terrible setback, which he knew nothing about it? Had a ranking comrade been killed or seriously wounded? Like an intoxicated man, he had walked into a funeral, not realizing that his joyful demeanor would hurt them even more. He had been immature, even egotistical; so he decided to apologize for his ill-natured behavior.

He was in no mood to follow the Commissar's lecture. The sense of guilt that had taken hold of him pained him without let-up. Crawling on his buttocks, so as not to attract attention, he approached Dino Elmaz, and whispered into his ear:

"What's happened, Dino?"

"Nothing," he replied, almost as if he was sorry that he could not satisfy Marion's curiosity, by telling him about some dreadful event. Even as he spoke, Dino focused his eyes on his sandals.

"Do you know how much I have looked forward to this day?"

"I understand you, Marion. I understand very well," he assured him. "Let us talk a little later," he suggested.

"I don't see Jasmine," he whispered in his ears, so as not to be heard by others.

"She was here this morning," Dino said.

He felt a sense of relief for a moment but was not sure why Dino had said that they "talk later." Why later? Had he made a mistake to come without prior notice? Should he have obtained a letter of recommendation first from the Party Committee of Korçë? That did not make much sense.

As soon as the news update session was over, quite a few men greeted him warmly, and were glad to see him again in their midst. The Squadron Commander Vait did not budge. He began to clean his rifle, as if that were the most important chore at the moment. Meanwhile, he whistled a tune that sounded terribly like a mournful chant. Marion suspected that he only pretended to be busy, just to avoid meeting him. Was he holding a grudge against him for surrendering without a struggle, or because he returned unarmed? Marion felt like saying to him "If you had been in my place, you would have done the same thing. We didn't have time to take our weapons off our shoulders... They jumped us unexpectedly."

Vait's conduct troubled him so much that he was unable to concentrate. His chat with friends slowly stopped. Just then, he recalled the advice the tailor had given him, and concluded that Van was right. He should have gone to another detachment in Skrapar, Mokër or any other place. A fellow from Korça asked him, just for the sake of conversation, "What's new from the city?"

Marion got the notion that the guy was not serious, and turned on him nervously, saying, "I did not get to see the city, anymore than you who weren't there. As for the prison, I know what that is like. And I tell you now, it's a hundred times better to die fighting in battle, than to fall into their clutches."

They were waiting for him to tell of incidents that impressed him, and show them the bruises and scars from the tortures. He answered that he did not want to recall that time. The silence that ensued was so heavy; no one knew how to break it. Fortunately, just then Jasmine pulled into the lot, dragging a horse by the halter. The Partisans shouted gleefully, "Food! Food!" and rushed over to unload the sacks.

Jasmine embraced Marion, putting her arms around his neck, and he felt the locks of her hair tickling his neck. Her body exuded a potent aroma, which Marion inhaled ravenously, as if it were the most delightful scent in existence.

"I'm all sweaty," she said looking at him tenderly with her blue eyes.

"Doesn't matter," Marion said. This was just the way he had pictured their meeting, and he was not disappointed. It was the first time that they were embracing in front of others, like comrades in wartime, without any danger of being misunderstood. In fact, they had promised each other to marry, after the liberation of their country. Although they took care to conceal their feelings, their love for each other was obvious from the happy look on their faces, whenever they were near each other.

Because of the peasant composition of detachments, plus the gossip that Nationalists spread around zealously, claiming that female Partisans were whores, lovemaking was considered immoral, and the "guilty" ones were put to death. While Cupid pierced the hearts of young people with golden arrows of love, the Partisan command posts pierced their chests with volleys of bullets.

"Did you escape?" Jasmine asked him, with the eagerness of a child who could hardly wait to hear the reply.

"They let me go..." Marion answered casually.

"How come?" Her surprise betrayed a certain doubt.

"I put one over on them," Marion told her, ready to relate the deceptive scheme he had deployed.

"What about Kliton?"

"They shot him ten days ago...." The memory of his friend brought tears to his eyes. "I signed a statement alleging that I'd quit fighting, and oddly enough they believed me..."

"So, it' true, after all...," Jasmine said with dismay, eying him with a sorrowful look. She felt a cutting pain in her bosom, as if the happiness she had looked forward to had been blown away forever. "How could you do this, Marion?" she scolded him regretfully.

"Why, what's wrong?" he asked naively.

"I think a letter has come from the District Committee, or the Joint Chiefs of Staff, I'm not sure which," she informed him.

"About me?" Marion asked astounded. "That's odd, because I did not ask for any letter of recommendation."

"Well, Vait told me, in a roundabout way. You know how he talks, in enigmas," she said. "I did not like it, when he said 'That comrade of yours shamed us.' 'Why, isn't he your comrade, as well?' I shot back... Around here, they say that you..." She wasn't able to finish, since just then, the Commissar clapped his hands to signal to all to sit down in the meadow enclosed by the forest.

"We are now going to discuss another matter..." he began, pushing his briefcase aside, to emphasize that this was not a bookish subject. He motioned to Marion and Jasmine to get closer to the group. "You know what happened to two of our comrades some weeks ago. The enemy captured Marion Kapshtica and Kliton Nasta en route to Kamenicë. The situation was critical. They were unable to resist and they surrendered. In the town prison, they were tortured by the Fascists, to get them to talk and pressured them to drop out of the National Liberation Struggle. The information we have is that Kliton stood firm to the end, and was executed by the Fascists, while Marion Kapshtica was unable to endure the torture. He feared death and agreed to give up fighting. Comrades, how do you judge his action? What stand should we take, now that Marion has come back? Can we still accept him as a comrade?" he asked. "So let everyone speak his mind."

All looked at Marion, who stooped as if the weight of their bodies was pressing down on him. More than anything else, he was hurt by Commissar Misto's question whether he still deserved to be considered their comrade. The Commissar took a few steps back, as if to make room for anyone's thoughts. Marion felt at ease when he reflected that he had chosen the most reasonable road, to uphold the ideals he had sworn to fight for. No doubt, his comrades would understand and approve his action.

Sitting in the glade among the pine trees, Tosun was the first to raise his hand. He was a peasant from Devoll, with such a large build that, even when he seated, he topped all the others. The Commissar gave him permission to speak.

"Allow me to put my two cents in. The Commissar here asked us to discuss this matter. Frankly, it looks like a 'trial' to me. As the Commissar himself said, they did no wrong to surrender, for to be killed in vain is no bravery. My grandfather used to say, the living, even when they get lost, can find the way again. The dead cannot. Had anyone of us been in their place, we would have done the same too. True enough, it's shameful to be captured, but Marion is not proud of that. Look at him, seating there with his head bent down. As long as he did not desert, as long as they did not walk away from here of their own free will, I say they did no wrong. You don't sell a horse just because he stumbles once. Marian is still a comrade. We're no better than he is, no braver. That's why I say, let us pardon him."

Shouts of "Pardon him! Pardon him!" came from the crowd.

"Don't all talk at once. Let everyone speak his mind," the Commissar broke in, so as not to let the matter come to a neat and quick conclusion.

Next Maqo asked to be heard.

"Go right ahead! We're listening," said the Commissar. Maqo was quick to grasp the nuances of a situation, and correctly understood the Commissar's intervention as a demand that they denounce Marion's deed. Maqo was not known for bravery, but he had a glib tongue.

"We're dealing with two different issues here," he said, thrusting two fingers in the air. "The surrender and the statement. Why they surrendered and how they were captured, we know quite well, so there's no point in discussing that anymore. As for the statement, I condemn what Marion did. That was a mistake; indeed, a serious mistake. We shouldn't forget that the Fascists use the most heinous, most inhuman tortures, and as a result, he was broken.... Who knows the circumstances? ... That's all I wanted to say."

Murmurs and expressions of approval were heard simultaneously.

"Well said! You hit the nail on the head!" The praise came from Mersin Metko, a villager from Opar. "I'm telling you, these guys with schooling are sharp. They can split a strand of hair four ways. I say again that you don't sell a horse just because he tripped one time. Marion tripped, too, but I'm sure he regrets his error. Why do I say that? It's common sense, comrades. He came back because he wants to fight side by side with us." Nearly all showed their approval. "That's why I say, let's pardon him and congratulate him for returning to us in good health."

The calls for pardon came from the crowd in the semi-circle. The scales had tipped markedly in favor of pardoning Marion.

"It seems to me that you are making rush judgments," observed the Commissar. "You condemn his actions and you also pardon him. But how do you reconcile these two? How can he be condemned and pardoned?"

Seeing that the Commissar did not want to close the matter, without some form of punishment, a young fellow asked for permission to speak.

"I say that we ought to penalize Marion for his mistake. So, I propose...." He stood there, lost in his thought, not knowing what to say next.

"Go on !" the Commissar goaded him.

Everyone was waiting to hear the reprimand articulated by his tender lips.

"Deprive him of his rifle for one month!" he said.

"Deprive him of..." intervened Luto. "Look here. The only thing we can deprive him of, is the belt of his pants. He has no rifle...."

The quip of Commander Luto provoked laughter, which relaxed the tense court atmosphere. Suddenly, the gathering heard the silvery jingle of a bell, and soon a billy goat thrust his head between the bushes, as if he wanted to see what was going on in that meadow.

"Get out of here!" Mersin yelled, and went after him. The billy goat stood his ground unafraid, until he got close to him.

"Why are you upset with him?" the Commissar chided Mersin.

"He brings bad luck," Mersin replied.

"May I have your attention," said Squadron Commander Vait, as he got up on his feet. "Comrade Marion has been in my squadron so I know him well. He is resolute, brave and friendly. But I cannot swallow the filthy dung he let drop. He should have been in the same spot where his comrade was executed. He abandoned him to save his own neck. He panicked. Comrades! I will not take him back in my squadron. I have no use for men who take to their heels when they're in danger," he said angrily, as he wound up his argument.

A heavy silence fell on the meadow.

"I agree with Vait," said Antigoni Terziu.

A skinny girl with a bony face, high cheeks, tiny eyes and skimpy hair, Antigoni resembled the witches in fairy tales. Lacking eyebrows, her forehead was bare like a desolate pasture. She eyed with envy and enmity any closeness between young people. Indeed, she could not endure even anecdotes that were somewhat off-color. Feeling neglected as a female, every joke that had a bearing on sex, seemed to her indiscrete, if not sinful. The morals of the Partisans had to be held high and untainted under any circumstances, because this was not a time for petty love affairs, but for heroism and sacrifices.

With her feminine intuition, she had sensed that Marion and Jasmine liked each other, and enjoyed being together and having a good time. Therefore, she followed them stealthily, hoping to catch them *en flagrante.* Convinced that they had an on-going love affair, she thought that their example could spread like a fire on a dry prairie, and ruin to the morale of the Partisans.

"Marion has put a stain not only on himself, but also on the whole unit. So, I say that there is no place for him here. Let him go somewhere else," said Antigoni.

"If he is not worthy to be here," someone said, "why would he be worthy somewhere else?"

"Because they would not know him," answered Antigoni.

Her naïve argument prompted laughter in the crowd.

An elderly Partisan, with a dense, bushy moustache, chubby cheeks and ruddy complexion, got up and stood still, as if he didn't know how to begin.

"Brothers and sisters, hear me out. If I had tripped, or someone close to my age, you would be right not to pardon us. But young people are reckless sometimes, just like our boy here, who rushed things. It was a first for him, that's all. We should not make a big fuss over it. We should overlook it, I say. He came back to fight with us. What more can we ask of him? Even if he did slip up with those papers, of whatever they're called, seeing that he returned to fight, I forgive him. Because war needs fighters, not words. That's all I wanted to say."

"Pardon him! Pardon him! Let him be!" voices rang out from around the semi-circle. They wanted an end to the trial. Even without putting the matter to a vote, the sentiment of the majority was in favor of closure.

Commander Luto Kabashi stood up and tightened his belt.

"It seems to me that you are not considering this matter seriously, but rather lightly. The majority decides, but I have to get off my chest what's boiling in there," – and he struck his chest with his fist – "or I will find no rest. Two of our men were captured by the enemy and tortured. One of them stands up to the adversary. The other takes a pen and signs a paper renouncing our war. Kliton defied death like a man, and was cut down by their bullets, while the scary cat saved his neck. What about principles? Don't blame it on his age, because he is not a child." Then pointing at Marion, he said, "He is a de-ser-ter, and should be punished for desertion, because he defiled us all…" As usual, Commander Luto expressed his opinions in a categorical manner.

In the abrupt silence that followed, a sudden wind that blew among the pine trees, sounded like a wailing whistle.

"The Commander is right. Marion committed treason."

"You're going too far…"

"There's no other name for that sort of thing."

"Do you know the meaning of 'traitor'?"

"I think you don't know it." "I don't expect to learn it from you." "You'll do well to learn it." "You should stop to think, before you speak." "Do I need to ask for your permission?" "You can't accuse comrades for no reason." "You call one of us a traitor?" "You don't make sense…" "suppose you were in his place…" "…were you there?" "a traitor would not have come here…" "Let him go back where he came from." "…talk gibberish…" "for principle" "good" "a mistake" "I'm telling you" "an obligation" "—in vain" "—the leaflet" "—twisted…"

The Commissar clapped his hands and raised his voice to bring order over and above the clatter of loose words and phrases that flew about in all directions.

"You're gabbing like Gypsies. Whoever wants to speak, must ask for permission."

Jasmine could see that, after the remarks of Commander Luto Kabashi the discussion took a different turn.

"Comrades! We're not thinking calmly," she began in a quiet voice. "We are burdening Marion unfairly, saying things about him that he doesn't deserve. We have heard about a statement that he supposedly signed. We still don't know whether the statement is his, or something the Fascists fabricated to discredit our comrade. I am astounded that up to now, none of the comrades thought to ask Marion what's what, what really happened. That doesn't seem right to me, at all. Why should we believe the Fascists, instead of our own comrade? Marion is right here. So, let us ask him how this all came about, if indeed it did happen. I have no doubt that he will tell us the truth. The information we have could be wrong, or a maneuver of the enemy… I'm finished."

Her words met with approval by all. They were simple and sincere words spoken from the heart. It wasn't as if she were defending him. She just wanted to know the truth. Why had Marion been ignored, as if this was not about him, at all? All eyes were upon Marion, as if to beg him to speak.

Marion got up on his feet. His unsettling state and pale face bore witness to the turmoil he had lived through.

"I will not hide anything," he began. "I will tell you the truth, just as it happened. After all, this is a second lease on life for me." He took a deep breath, and then continued. "I understand that I made a serious mistake. I await with a clear conscience any punishment you see fit. I did sign the statement." Sighs of "Oooh!" in protest or sympathy came from the crowd. "I did it not because I was not broken under torture, not from fear of death, but because I decided to avenge Kliton's death…."

"Coward!" someone said.

"You feared for your hide…," thundered another.

"Let him speak, for God's sake! We asked him to speak up, now…"

"Continue, Marion!"

"What did you say? I was afraid for my life?" Marion said, turning toward an unfamiliar face. "I did not fear for my life. I wanted to fight for our men, shot in prisons by the enemy. I knew what would happen, the moment I fell into their hands. You've heard about the Fascist tortures. But it's one thing to hear about them, and something else to go through...."

"We don't need any excuses," intervened Vait.

"I'm not trying to make excuses. I am saying that I decided to sign when I realized I had no reason to be truthful with enemies. Who would have benefited, if they shot me in the prison yard, the way they shot my comrade? I made my choice. I lied to the enemy, so they would let me go, even though I didn't think they would. While in prison, I had made up my mind to find you and reunite with you, if I survived. They can do what they want with my statement. I have come to the mountains to fight to the last breath until we liberate our fatherland. Did I choose the right path, or the wrong path? I don't know. Good or bad, it's up to you to decide."

The breeze whistled among the needles of the pine trees, like a melody played by a multitude of lutes.

The candid remarks of Marion made a good impression. There was no pretense or guile in his words. He opened his heart without trying to make excuses or to justify what he had done. Whatever was dubious was clarified. His great drive to return to the unit and his comrades motivated his actions. He had fooled the enemy, and he deserved credit for being smart. Now those who had insulted and denounced him looked upon him with sympathy and approval.

Dino Elmaz found it opportune to say what he felt at that moment.

"Comrades! Marion's sincere confession made a great impression on me. He revealed his feelings and thoughts without the least hesitation. I wouldn't think of questioning anything he said. How can you not believe a fellow who opens his heart to us? Someone might say that he did not choose the right path. I say he did not have many choices. Did he get out alive? Yes. Was the goal a good one? Yes. Well then, what more can we ask from him? His intensions were good, and that is what we should be looking for here."

Jasmine smiled at Dino from afar, to show that she agreed with him. It seemed that logic had prevailed and the trial had come to an end. The scales had tipped yet again. This time in favor of Marion.

In such situations the life of the defendant was delicate. There was no code, nor bylaws to determine the verdict. There was no established procedure, nor a jury. Everything depended on the mood or the general opinion at a given time. The verdict was simplified in the extreme: Death or Pardon. The person on trial passed from life to death and vice versa, after each discussion, depending on whether it was favorable or not. It was hard to say whether one would be pardoned for a serious offense or pay dearly for a slight mistake. A number of extra-judicial factors like personal grudges and sympathies, jealousies and friendships, ambitions and patriarchal mores, were constantly in play. It sometimes happened that the command first spelled the verdict then conducted the trial.

Commander Luto Kabashi stood up holding a newspaper in his hand. He stepped in front of the crowd then began to speak.

"And what shall we do with this? How can we dispose of it?" he asked, shaking the paper in the air, and calling attention to a square box on the front page, by jabbing it with his finger. "The statement of comrade Marion Kapshtica…." He regretted calling him a comrade, and immediately followed up by saying, "Some comrade! The Fascists put the declaration right on top of the first page, and boxed it, the better to catch the eye. In this own words, he says that he had made a mistake, that he was deceived by the Communists and that's why he is quitting the war. What's more he appeals to others to abandon the ranks and ditch the war…"

"That last line…, they tacked that on themselves," remarked Marion. "I did not agree to make appeals to anybody."

"What did you expect?" Commander Luto turned on him. "Did you think you were dealing with fools, who would treat your statement like an amulet and keep it in a drawer, or that they would publish it the way you signed it?" His tone was fraught with fury and sarcasm. "Even without that addition, it's still the same. Your statement is a call to abandon the war. It's desertion. There's no other way to read it. So, tell us. Who does it serve, and what label shall we put on it?" He asked angrily, raising his hand.

Jasmine sensed that his intervention had shaken up the opinion of the audience. To redress the situation, she felt that she needed to speak up again.

"It seems to me that comrade Marion explained things quite clearly. He signed the statement to fool them, and he did. If he wanted to turn traitor, he would have stayed in town, or gone back to his village. The fact that he came back to us, should make us all glad." Some people murmured and others exchanged smiles that alluded to her feelings for Marion. She felt all of that, but did not back down. "Let me ask you this.

Why should we care about those worthless rags of Fascism? Haven't we always said that they are filled with lies, which nobody believes? The people will learn the truth soon enough about our comrade...."

The argument of Commander Luto was somewhat discredited as vengeful, without logic and contrived. Jasmine's point met with approval by the majority. The Commissar felt the blow and decided to intervene.

"Not so, comrade Jasmine. I do not accept your reasoning." He paused for a moment to note the reaction, and then continued. "Why? Because Marion has handed the enemy a powerful weapon—the weapon that brings on repentance and disbelief." Raising his voice, he went on to say, "How many young people, who were ready to take up arms and join the Partisans, were discouraged by this statement and are now standing on the sidelines? We don't know the number, but we think there are many. With this declaration, Marion has dealt a heavy blow to our cause and our anti-Fascist propaganda, as well as defiled our high morals and ideals. You said that he is sincere, but I don't see how I can believe him. Was he truthful when he signed the statement or now that he is trying to excuse himself and pull the wool over our eyes? This is hypocrisy."

The Commissar continued to weigh in on the damage done by the statement. The day before, a confidential memo from the General Staff had been circulated, along with a copy of the paper which ran the declaration. The Staff advised that Marion Kapshtica be denounced as a deserter. Further the command was advised to locate Marion and ask the guerrilla units to execute him, thus setting an example to all those who desert the ranks. Orders from the Staff could not and would not be discussed.

The Commissar concluded his remarks in a firm tone.

"I tell you pointblank, comrades, that we're all badly disillusioned with Marion Kapshtica. As far as I'm concerned, he is a deserter; there's no other name for him. So, speak up. What do you think he deserves? To be pardoned or to be punished?"

Incited by the words of the Commissar, the extremists shouted, "Punish him! Punish him!"

When he felt that he had turned the situation around, he asked,

"What kind of punishment does he deserve?"

"The firing squad!"

"A bullet in the head! The bullet! The bullet!"

There was no need to put the matter to a vote. Upon hearing the closing argument of the Commissar, the majority of the unit had already sentenced him. There would be no appeal, since there was no higher court in the war. The Commissar asked formally if anyone was opposed to the death sentence. There was no point in challenging the sentence, after the majority's approval.

And yet, although no one expected it, Mersin, the oldest soldier in the Battalion, requested permission to speak. Using his rifle to support his weight, he got on his feet. Though he was actually in his mid-fifties, to the younger soldiers he seemed old, more like a grandfather. Therefore, they respected him for his age, but paid no attention to his ideas, since for him both Communism and the Koran taught the same things. Like the date of his birth, his viewpoints, too, belonged to the previous century. What could 'grandpa' with a worried look on his wrinkled face have to say?

"Now, boys, I have only one question. Where do we go from here? One comrade was killed by the Fascists. And now we want to get rid of this one. But how can you kill a man, on account of a scrap of paper? Because that's all that is, a scrap of paper, no matter how you turn it and twist it… I just don't get it. My heart cannot accept it," he protested.

"You think about things like in the old days," commander Luto rebuked him. "But we are not outlaws."

"Well, I'll say one thing about the old days. They did not execute a defenseless man," Mersin retorted angrily, as he sat down with his hand resting on his rifle.

The Commissar thought it was useless to discuss the views of a sentimental grandpa.

"There is no compassion for traitors," he said firmly.

The sound of a bell came from the forest, as if to signal the conclusion of the court session. The head of a he-goat jutted again from the pine trees. The goat looked at the crowd with eyes that shone with an enigmatic light. The animal swayed his head as if to approve the verdict that had been rendered. Mersin turned on him angrily:

"Get away from here!" he yelled, hurling a pine cone at him. "He just won't let us alone today, the cursed creature!" he snorted.

"What have you to say?" The Commissar asked, addressing Marion, without mentioning his name.

At that time the condemned was allowed to say his last words, before the sentence was carried out. From time immemorial, statesmen, generals, revolutionaries, rebels, kings, artists and criminals, distinguished leaders or common villains, have expressed their last wishes, left mandates, called out their ideals, revealed shattering secrets, cursed their tormentors, repented or begged God to have mercy on them, pleaded for liberty and justice, religion and homeland. What was Marion going to say? What was he going to express, and what legacy would he leave behind?

Marion stopped to think. What was it that he had not yet said? What could he ask of his comrades? At this point, he too viewed what he did in a different light. True enough, he had fooled the enemy. But his action was imprudent and immature, and had inflicted great harm on the common cause.

"Comrades, I realize that I made a serious mistake, and the sentence passed on me, is entirely just," he said calmly, without emotion, as if talking about someone else. "I just want you to know comrades that I did not realize that I could seriously hurt our movement. Life has no meaning for me, after all that happened, because I don't deserve it. Go ahead and shoot me, comrades. I shall welcome the bullets. If I erred, and I know that I did, forgive me. I came here because I wanted to join you and be with you, and I still do. I ask only one thing of you. I ask that you allow me to embrace you one by one, and to part as friends."

No one expected him to express such a wish. With a few simple words, he erased the line between his conscious awareness, and the damage he had unconsciously caused by his behavior. In his heart he would be their comrade forever.

He turned first to the fellow Partisan closest to him. At first, he hesitated, and only shook his hand. Then, as if he regretted his hesitation, he put his arms around Marion and squeezed him tight. To part like this, while still drawing the breath of life, was painful. Dino embraced him vigorously, and held on to him for some time, while trembling with emotion. As soon as he let go of him, he lit up a cigarette to calm his nerves. When Marion stood next to Jasmine, she heard him say: "It's time to part, Jasmine. So much for our dream!" To the great surprise of those who were watching them, she maintained her composure, until they parted. Then, she ran toward the monastery. It was obvious that she did not want to see Marion killed by the bullets of his comrades.

Commander Luto and the Commissar Misto shook hands with him with their arms fully extended, so as to keep him at a distance. It was a tangible manifestation of disregard. Then Marion approached Vait, the Squadron Commander, who gave him a contemptuous look. Without budging from where he sat, Vait struck the barrel of his rifle with the palm of his hand to gesture Marion's fateful farewell that soon awaited him. The cynical jest prompted a few suppressed chuckles. Turning toward the pines, Marion took a few steps and then turned around to face his comrades. Vait selected a few from the ranks by pointing to them and saying, "you, you, you." The weapons were cocked, and then a battery of gunshots boomed briefly over the meadow. The echo was repeated by the surrounding slopes like a shrilling wail until it rested down into the ravines.

And every summer the hollows on those bullet-struck pines fill up with crystals of white resin that look like big teardrops frozen with pain.

The Rusty Container

He resembled greatly Chekov's "man in a sack." He went about in a black beret, which he pressed down to his ears. His jacket, all wrinkled and dirty, was much too long for his short body and made him look contemptible. The corners at the bottom of the jacket dipped to his knees, distended by all the junk he carried in his pockets. In the back, the hemline curved upward like an arch. All around the year, he wore a pair of rubber boots, and they did not fit him, either. In the winter, he carried an umbrella in his hand, while in the summer he switched to a kind of walking stick. His picture would not be complete however if we neglected to mention that sticking out from his mouth there was always a half-charred pipe.

He had a face full of wrinkles; a thin, drawn, pale nose; and small eyes with the cunning look of a marten that emitted a greenish light. Only the gleam and movement of the eyes indicated that there was life inside that body.

Nonetheless, within himself there churned unpredicted forces and curious passions. Despite his look, he had made every effort to be with people and chat with them. They tired of his presence and scorned him. It seemed that once they ran into this little, insipid, pitiful creature, they could not resist the impulse to tease and taunt him. Being on the receiving end of the mocking, the scorn and the abuse, he suffered even more.

Slowly greed started growing in his soul like a cancer, causing all other traits in him to atrophy. He craved fine clothes, a big house, money, especially money. He thought that money was the key to life, and that if he had money he would climb up at once in society, and he would no longer be picked on and teased. He would not be the Joti Petsi whom people of the little town ridiculed.

He grew up with two other brothers, one older and the other younger than he. The older brother was weak and for that reason, their mother tried harder to please him. She gave Topullah the best food, the biggest loaf of bread, and the best of everything. Joti didn't like that. Sulking, he would say to his mother,

"I want the same thing you gave to Topullah."

When his mother had nothing to give him, he bided his time and at the right moment grabbed the food from the hands of his brother and dashed outside as fast as he could.

The older brother did not live long, and when he died Joti curiously did not grieve for him. He was sick for as long as Joti had known him, so he had come to accept the idea that his brother was going to die soon. With the older brother gone, he expected his mother to lavish upon him all the care she had lavished upon his sibling. However, his mother, too, died soon after his brother. Perhaps it was just as well for everyone….

After a few years, when Joti thought of himself as a grown-up man, Mehdi Bey[1] the town's vice-mayor, liked to tease this gutless man. He always played the same joke on him. Wherever he happened to be, whether in the coffee house or in the town square, the moment he spied Joti he would call out to him,

"Joti, come over here."

"At your service, bey."

Small and curled up within himself like a hedgehog, Joti would drag his feet and stand before him without daring to look him in the eye.

"How are you, how's it going?"

"Fine, thank you."

"Joti!" the bey used to say with a sly grin.

"What?"

"Say, 'at your service,' you swine."

"At your service."

"Do you still have it, or did the cat eat it up?"

Joti would hang his head.

"Come on; speak up, because I've heard that the cat ate yours up."

Those standing about would start to snicker and make insinuating remarks.

"Come on, unbutton your fly," the bey would say, "or else I'll order the officer to do the job."

Joti's hand would reach down and slowly unbutton his pants…. The whole crowd would scream with laughter. The bey also laughed heartily, his hands at his sides; then opened his purse and threw some change at the feet of Joti.

---

1 *Bey*, a Turkish honorary title, commonly associated in Albania with the proprietors of landed estates.

"You still have it, Joti. Now take this and get going."

Joti would pick up the coins amid the malicious laughter of the crowd, and walk away with his head bowed and his spirit crushed. He was not surprised that the bey threw his money in the streets so liberally, for it was rumored that his father had left him barrels of gold.

Angry over the degrading way he was treated by the bey, a couple of times he had refused to do his bidding. That only amused the bey all the more, because he would then order three or four men to go after him, and the result was the same... the pants were unbuttoned.

Because of the humiliation he suffered in public, Joti's feelings dried up: he did not know the meaning of sympathy or compassion. Moreover, he lacked the resourcefulness to do something on his own. He was drifting when the war broke out, but even then he did not wake up. During the wartime, he set up a stand where he sold all kinds of knick-knacks, but since he has no idea how to run a business in wartime, he sold most of the stuff on credit, and expected that he would be paid back with interest. Although he ended up with very little, he kept the credit register hidden some place, along with the money he had saved.

Later he earned a bit of money from the sale of lottery tickets for the Red Cross, and old religious literature. At the beginning of the New Year, he went about peddling religious calendars that were based on the Hegira,[2] which put the world back 580 years, and according to which we were in the year 1379!

Although he was often seen carrying books, he never read them. He valued them only as items for sale that would bring him some money. The only literature Joti read were obituary notices that were posted on bulletin boards throughout the city. Whether he read them out of curiosity so he would have something to talk about, or simply for the fun of it, it is difficult to say. At any rate, whenever he read such notices, he would say with a certain satisfaction,

"Another one gone! Another one has bid us farewell!"

Whatever bit of news he picked up, he spread it around with great zeal. He got a big kick out of telling others things that would startle them and cause them to worry. He was a messenger of defeatist slogans.

---

[2] Hegira denotes the flight of the prophet Mohammed from Mecca to Medina in the year 622 of our epoch.

"This is going to be a bad year. A dervish at our teqe[3] has said that this coming winter is going to be so severe, all the livestock will starve to death."

He generally was full of glee when others turned gloomy and silent, as if he were taking revenge on them for all the ills they had caused him.

In his pockets, apart from his tobacco pouch, a few buttons, glass beads, beat up dice; he kept anything that his sharp eye spotted in the streets. He believed that everything in the world had its value, and that the day would come when it could be put to some use. One thing, however, he did not do, and that was to steal. His most endearing habit was collecting money, for he yearned to be rich some day, and he told no one about the money he hoarded.

The town's officials had sent for him several times, because they pitied him and wanted to give him a job so he would have a regular income, but Joti had always resisted.

"Please, don't mess me up; I'm afraid I won't be able to do it," he would say, and walk out feeling glad that he did not take the job.

Clearly, he had done some math and knew that he earned more as a peddler than as a town's employee. Besides, he was at the head of the list among those who benefited from state welfare aid, whereas if he were on a regular payroll, things would be different.

Joti's table manners were particular. He wouldn't hear of setting two separate tables so the children could not eat before or after their father. Everyone in the family had to sit down and eat together. When the family sat down to eat, he would watch wild-eyed to see how the meat pieces were given out. It seemed to him that one of the children got a bigger and better chunk of meat than he. Right in the middle of the meal, he would reach out across the table and grab the chunk of meat, saying,

"Hold it; your piece is bigger than mine. Here you take mine."

Then he would regret it, because he felt that he had given away the better piece of meat. And he watched enviously as the other ate up his piece of meat, and angrily scolded his children as good-for-nothing scamps.

---

3 A *teqe,* pronounced teh-KEH, is a Moslem monastery of the Bektashi sect, which is part of the mystical wing of Islam.

It did not help that his wife tried her best to please him by giving him larger portion of food. His avaricious appetite took over him. That's why the family ate lunch in peace and with pleasure when he did not eat with them on the market days when he bought and sold pieces of junk, and lunched out somewhere.

On that day he felt that he had turned a couple of things in his favor. He had deceived a peasant by selling him an out-of-date calendar. Better yet, he had kicked his younger brother out of the house.

His brother who had gone off to the capital about seven years before, and had not been heard of since, all of sudden, returned home. When Joti came home that evening, he found him seated by the fireplace in the living room.

Although not pleased with that sight, Joti wanted to be sure of his brother's intensions. He figured that his younger sibling had been fired from his job, or else he had quit his job and perhaps had come back with the sole intention of selling their home, taking his share of the money and vanish. He asked him in a roundabout way whether he had brought back anything for the house. When he learned that he had come back with empty pockets, he had no doubt about his purpose, and got up and pointedly took the stick that was behind the door and walked to the middle of the room.

"Tell me, what brings you here?" he asked, shaking the stick.

"I've come home," his brother replied from the place of honor in the house.

"What home?"

"My home."

"This is not your home. The old woman left the home to me, because I was by her side when she died."

"I'm your brother, isn't that so?"

"No, you're a scoundrel, not a brother. You played around in the city to your heart's content, and now you tell me you've come back to your home. Get out of here, and don't let me set eyes on you again! Some brother you turned out to be, always on the lookout to grab something. Out of my house, I say."

His wife said it was shameful to chase him out like that, when he had barely set foot in the house, but that did not trouble Joti Petsi at all.

He figured that if he let him stay for a while, he would grow roots in the house; so the sooner he left the better. He was quite happy with himself for having done what he did.

As he walked down the street, he spotted a broken pocket knife. He bent down, picked it up, flipped it in his hand a few times, then slipped it in his pocket. Farther, he stopped again, emptied the ashes of his pipe unto the palm of his hand, then wiped his palm off on his jacket. After filling the pipe with fresh tobacco, he waited until a man with a lighted cigarette came by.

He stepped in front of him and said,

"May I have a light?" It was his standard phrase on such occasions.

When he finished with that routine, he sauntered over behind the town hall's building to smoke his pipe in peace, amid the ruin left over from the war. Oddly enough, this desolate heap of rubble that was bare of any beauty appealed to him a great deal, perhaps because it resembled his soul. He felt good in that forsaken place, but what his thoughts were over there nobody knows.

There he was, sitting on the remnants of a wall and dangling his feet like a kid. His boots, warmed over by the hot sun, smelled of rubber mingled with the heavy odor of sweat. A little farther, some children were playing among the ruins. They had set up three stone slabs on one side, and three others on the opposite side. After dividing into two teams, they struck the targets with stones they picked up from the ruins. The team that knocked down the slabs of the opposing team first, won the game, and had the right to ride piggy-back on the backs of the losers. The children quarreled, laughed, and shouted, filling that deserted spot with cheer and life. Joti saw them without any interest. Among the kids in the group he noticed Reshat, Nik, and the son of Nuzman, the wandering Gypsy, for whom Joti nursed a grudge because he called him nicknames in the market place.

In the past, there was a row of shops there, dominated by the house of Nexhmedin bey, which rose like a castle amid the shops. During the war, English warplanes raided the city one day, and their bombs fell on the shops. The fire from the air raid finished off what was left standing after the bombing, and so the place known as the Bazaar quarter turned into a heap of rubble. The raid also snuffed out the lives of Nexhmedin bey and his family. Looking at the ruins of the bey's house, Joti felt a sense of quiet, subdued satisfaction. It warmed his heart to see his house reduced to rubble. He felt that he had been avenged for all the misery and humiliation the bey had inflicted on him. Perhaps that was the secret reason he liked going there. It was as if he were saying,

"You made fun of me, but I got my revenge. Now you lie under these stones and I stand here with my pipe."

When he heard that the bey had died in the house, he rejoiced that a malicious jokester and prankster was gone.

Strangely, Joti felt a peculiar respect for death. "Death wipes out people without asking any questions. It doesn't care whether you're rich or poor, young or old, with or without position." That is why he admired death silently, and thought it was the only force that did not take sides, a force before which everybody trembled in fear. In its sight, he felt equal to others.

He tapped his pipe against a stone to empty the ashes, and then put it in his little pocket as if it were a pen. The children had stopped playing and the commotion had died away suddenly. They were huddled at the foot of a ruin and looking at something. Joti's skilled ears picked up their conversation.

"We better not tell anybody."

"Let's show it to the school teacher."

"What if it's empty?"

"Lemme see… is it heavy?"

Obviously they had found something, and that rose Joti's curiosity.

Slowly he got down the wall, and stepping carefully over the rubble, he drew close to them. He had made his way over there without a sound, like a cat. Standing directly over them, he noticed that Nick was holding a small, round black container. Reshat took it from him and weighed it in his hand.

"What if it's got gold coins in it?" There was an unusual look in his wide-open eyes.

The other kids looked at him with marvel and wonder. Joti was thrilled and crouched like a marten ready to pounce on its pray. His green eyes lit up with bright sparks. What if the container really had gold coins? The very thought of the precious metal caused a lump in his throat. Strange visions floated before his eyes. The veins in his temples began to pound hard.

How was he going to wrest the thing from the kids? How could he trick them? Suppose he offered to give them those trinkets, he had in his pocket, would they fall for that trick?

"Let's just open it up," said one of the boys.

Joti shuddered and every muscle in his body tensed up. If they opened the container, he would never get his hands on it. His happiness was suddenly bound up with that container, his yearning to be rich, and his hope of bidding farewell to this little town – covered in dust in the summer and plastered in mud in the winter.

His instinct told him to gather his wits quickly and distract the kids' attention from that container they found by chance in the ruins of the bey's house. Speaking calmly, as if he were advising them for their own good, he said,

"What are you doing with that? Put it back where you found it!"

"Why? What's it to you?"

While gazing at that cylindrical, slightly elongated black object, Joti said:

"Leave it alone, I say. Who knows? A devil may be inside, because they hang around ruins," he said cunningly to frighten them.

The kids laughed.

"Oh, yeah, devils! There ain't no devils, not anymore. They tell us in school that there ain't no devils."

"Let me have it. I can use that, Reshat" Joti pleaded with him.

"Why? What would you do with it?"

"Make a tobacco box out of it," he said, like one who spoke with the voice of experience.

"You can't use it for tobacco. It's all rotted."

"Don't worry. I can scrape off the dross."

He thought of jumping down and snatching the container from them. He eyed the distance carefully because he had to grab it as soon as he hit the ground. He could not afford to miss it. The kids were already suspicious that they had found something of value and Joti's failed attempt would make the kids guard the container at all cost.

"I'll give you a penknife and a steel cube for it," Joti said in a childish tone.

"Where are they?"

"Here, in my pocket."

"Lemme see them."

Joti thrust his hand in his pocket and took out the penknife he had found in the street, a few stamps, a steel cube and several others trinkets.

The boy eyed with curiosity the objects that glittered before his eyes, and gave in.

"Okay," he said, and stretched his arm to trade articles with Joti.

At that instant Nik grabbed the container from Reshat's hand, and said roughly to him,

"You wanna give it to him. It wasn't you who found it, in the first place."

"Don't worry. I got something for you, too," said Joti.

"I don't want nothing."

Joti realized that Nick was in that stubborn mood that sometimes takes hold of children, when they want to have their way, and would not trade the worthless thing they have at hand for the world. His fortune was slipping through his fingers, and he felt as if he were a little round rock rolling downhill into the ravine. He had to grab that container no matter what. He waited until Nik was off his guard, and like a cat leaped and grabbed his hand. Yet Nik wouldn't let go of the container. Joti then sank his teeth into Nik's hand, forcing him to let the container down into his palm. Nik was so angry he yanked Joti's beret off his head. All of this took place so quickly the kids didn't know what was happening. This was the first time they had seen the sluggish, good-for-nothing Joti move with such speed and determination. This was a revelation to them.

Nik retreated a few steps and amid tears shouted,

"What's the big idea? That's not yours."

"Sure it is."

"How come? You didn't hide it down there."

"Sure I did. You went and uncovered it. Wait till I tell your father; he will beat you to a pulp."

Nik looked at him skeptically and would not believe him.

"Oh, yeah? Don't gimme that."

"I tell you it was me. Wait till I tell the police that you loiter around these ruins.... And the school principal, too, is going to hear about this."

Aware that he was powerless to act on his own, Joti always appealed to the authority of a third party to save his honor, or at least to scare the kids so that they would let him alone. The names he used most often were: the policeman, the school principal, and the boy's father.

The kids were downright angry because the trophy they had found was about to be taken away from them unjustly. After stepping back, the Gypsy kid began to throw stones at Joti, yelling,

"Bean-head Joti! Bean-head Joti!"

The other kids joined in, shouting in unison and with great glee, "Bean-head Joti!" The growling rumble of a bulldozer rolling along the road stopped them on their tracks and they took off like a flock of birds after the bulldozer.

Left alone, Joti reached into his pocket and with his fat fingers fondled the rough metal surface of the rusty container. Did it really contain gold pieces? Well, why shouldn't it? Didn't everybody say that Nexhmedin bey was loaded and that his father had barrels of gold in the cellar? Sliding his fingers under the container, he weighed it in his hand. It was quite heavy.

His heart began to beat fast. Slowly he drew back about fifty steps, as he searched for a quiet hiding place where he could not be seen by anyone. He crept behind a heap of ruins and nestled among some rocks. Then, he took out his pipe, pressed some tobacco into it and lit it up.

He raised his head. The sun was scorching hot. The sky was a clear, clean blue. He heard the silvery chimes of the church clock, which afterward were devoured it seemed, by the infinite vastness of the sky. Shortly after, from a loud speaker came the sounds of Radio and then a southern popular song. Joti listened carefully. It was afternoon and the road was usually quiet at that time. He did not see the hands of the clock, but he figured it must have been close to three.

He put his walking stick aside, and took the container out of his pocket. He thought he noticed the bright gleam of gold inside it. Then he weighed it once more in his hand and tapped it lightly against a stone. He heard a muffled, muted sound which made him feel uneasy. Instinctively he looked about him once more, to make certain no one was around, and then took out his penknife. He could hardly wait to pry it open with the blade and see what was inside. He held the container with his left hand, while with the right he pressed the tip of the blade into the metal. Finally, he pierced it. The tip of the blade went deep inside....

Instantly the flame and the smoke scorched his eyes, and the force of the blast dashed him against a pile of rocks. The pipe flew from his mouth like an arrow, and he saw a sea of red and yellow rings. The rings changed into coins, and Joti sliced the air with both arms trying to collect them. Strangely, however, they slipped through his fingers like water or a liquid matter, no matter how hard he tried to hold on to them. He had the sensation that he was being pulled down along with the coins and with incredible speed into the abyss.

* * *

The police said that the device Joti snatched from the kids was an old rusty bomb left over from the war. It didn't look like a bomb, because the strap had rotted away and the white aluminum cover had been eaten away by the elements.

Hardly anyone felt sorry for Joti when his body was brought to the hospital. The people of the town said that greed had consumed Joti. But they did not know that his greed had saved the kids.

The Ambulance Driver

The ambulance driver had settled down in the bar with a couple of friends and was drinking *raki.* He had downed three or four glasses and was in a good mood. His eyes smiled, his spirits soared, and he wanted to express the joy he felt with a song. Frankly, there is no better way to enjoy drinking. So, Milo cleared his throat, then burst out singing:

What's all this talk, my pretty one,
That's going around the town?
It's not true, my pretty one,
It is all just spite.

His friends sang along with him oblivious to everyone around. The waiter walked over to them and told them, in a faint and apologetic voice:

"You can't sing here, Milo. You know there is no singing in the bar."

The driver turned toward the waiter and pushing him gently, said:

"Leave us be, will you? Don't spoil the fun."

Milo's tone was mild and subdued. It expressed merely the wish to be left alone.

"I know my friend, but it's the boss's orders. What can I do about it? If it were up to me, I'd say go right ahead."

"You go and tell that boss of yours not to bother us. Where in the world did he get such an idea, anyway? When guys get together for a drink, they're going to sing. What does he think this is, a monastery? Go 'way, now, and if he says anything to you, tell him, 'I told 'em, but they don't listen.' And if he likes, he can come over himself."

The waiter gathered up the empty dishes, put them on an old tray and went back behind the counter.

Milo started singing again.

Oh, you mountains, covered with snow,
Oh, you mountains,
Have a care for my troubles,
Oh, you mountains.

One man of short build and hunched back, with small, oval-shaped eyes, winked at him and said,

"And what have you got to worry about, except running out of booze?"

"There ain't nobody without troubles, no," sighed Milo. "Do you know that I ain't got no tires for my car? That's why for the past three days I been here at the bar from dawn to dusk."

"Drinking, huh?"

"What else is there to do?"

"Look for those tires till you find them, that's what."

"Well, ain't you smart!... My job is to get behind the wheel and drive, that's all. Is it my fault if the Chief of health division isn't smart enough to keep a couple of spare tires? I got to let him know when I'm short of somethin' or when somethin' breaks down. If he don't bother, so be it. Don't ask me how the job it's going to get done, 'cause I don't care. I get paid just the same."

He tipped his cap over one eye in a smooth, habitual gesture. It was his way of saying that it didn't matter to him one way or another.

The other one laughed and reckoned there was no point in carrying on any further. He turned to the guy beside him and nudged him with his elbow.

"Ain't you had enough to drink, Lazi?" he said. "If your wife saw you like this, she'd beat you up."

"I'll say," Milo added, picking up the jest. "That woman of his, she is nuts. Even I am afraid of her."

Lazi pretended not to hear what was said about him and his wife. What mattered to him, as usual, was that his glass should not be empty; so he didn't even bother to reply to them. He emptied the glass of brandy quickly into his mouth, swirled it around so that his cheeks bulged out, and gulped it down. Then, like a lost soul, he looked outside. From the bar's wide window, you could see the town's only fountain, the main street, and a part of the square where open market was held every Friday. If you spent any time at all at the "Big Bar," (the town had a smaller bar), you could see everything that went around town.

Kumesh was just a small village like the rest of the villages in the area. Unlike them, it acquired its dignified status, thanks to its favorable geographical position. Since it happened to be at the center of the district, it was upgraded into a 'town'.

To a stranger, the little town seemed quiet, sluggish and boring. No one hurried in the streets. Indeed, when somebody did run, it was either because of some great sorrow or great joy; otherwise nothing disturbed Kumesh. The days just dragged and the sluggishness of the town had settled in the townspeople's lives. Curiously, however, they did not feel this way at all. To them everything was ordinary, familiar and indeed dear. They could spot one another from afar, without having to see the face. It was enough for them to glance at a corner of the coat or the hat one was wearing to tell who that was. They were familiar with habits. They knew who liked to tell jokes and who had a hot temper; who smoked and who never had a drink; who suffered from ulcers and even who bought meat every day. Like everywhere else, their lives were filled with certain small and insignificant details that are an inseparable part of the human existence, and without which life would be unintelligible in its deepest recesses.

As usual, Leksi walked down the street with his hands clasped behind his back, and all the while whistling a tune. A naive and hard-working young man, who was the town's jester. Then, Nasho, the baker's helper, headed for the fountain with two pails in his hands. Nasho lacked the thumb in his right hand. Often he waved his crippled hand in the air and announced publicly: "I was born to be a baker; look at my hand, it's like a paddle, perfect for mixing flour." Across the square, the doctor's wife was shopping in the market place, and flaunting for all to see that red wicker basket of hers. Up the street, the butcher was carrying the meat packages to the store.

The town's high hills seem to dance around Kumesh in a circular formation and mock its small size and feeble existence. The defiant patches of snow on the mountain peaks in the summer were a reminder of the long and hard winter that the town had lived through.

"Summer's here, at last. The peak will be taking off its snow-white cap and the hills will be turning green, " said Milo gazing up.

Four peasants passed by. They carried a stretcher that was put together hastily out of fishing nets. One corner of the red blanket on the stretcher was dangling and swaying back and forth like a banner. Some town kids in wretched clothes followed the stretcher that moved silently through the center of the town. Trying to catch a glimpse of the patient in the stretcher, Lazi asked:

"Nasty kids! Who can that be?"

"These peasants wait too long without giving any help to the ailing person, and after that, they rush them to the clinic. What can the doctor do? He can't breathe life into the patients!"

"They got thick skulls, them peasants," Demir said.

"Not smart like you, huh!" Milo retorted.

"Look, look; the Chief just came out of his office," Lazi said, pointing at the doctor who was walking down the street, deep in thoughts.

"Watch him head straight for here," Milo said, laughing. "It's his way. He's got to make a visit to the clinic, then stop by the bar, otherwise he can't do nothing."

True enough, the Clinic's Chief took a turn and headed for the bar. He was a short man of chestnut-brown hair, dressed as usual in a velvet jacket and a pair of light cotton pants.

"Enjoying your drinks, Milo?" he asked purposely the moment he got near the bar.

"You bet, I am. How 'bout you, want a drink? Why don't you come out and say so, instead of beating around the bush?" Turning to the waiter, Milo called out: "Get the Chief a drink and put it on my tab."

The Chief fixed his eyes on the waiter while he poured; then, after taking a drink, he held the glass in his hand and kept fondling it and eyeing it avidly. Milo called out again,

"Hey, Chief, come over here and have an appetizer with your drink. It's the godly way to drink."

"No, no; I'm in a hurry. I better drink it here, on my feet."

"Oh, yeah, your work load is killing you. You are afraid that if your boss walks in here and catches you drinking, you'll be in hot water!"

"You think it's a joke? It's not easy to work with that cripple. He's got a bum leg and a sharp tongue."

Milo nudged his buddy with his elbow and whispered something in his ear, then said aloud,

"Funny, I never thought of going over to him to complain 'bout you for leaving me with no tires. How come I never thought of it before?"

"What! Don't you do that! I am telling you. That's all I need. He's got it in for me already."

"I swear to God, I'm gonna tell him…"

"Is this how you treat me to a drink? Damn you, Milo! I wish I hadn't set foot in here."

Milo turned his head away and eyed the Chief angrily.

"I'm going to stop by the clinic," he muttered.

"Go ahead, 'cause they miss you. In fact, they asked me about you. If you see him, they said, tell him to come over."

Judging by the tone of his voice, it was not clear whether Milo was serious or joking. His drinking fellow scrutinized his face to see if he might detect an ironic smile there, then said to him,

"You were very crusty with the Chief."

"And why not? I'm not afraid of him. I don't need nobody, that's why I don't fear anybody. You know I don't flatter nobody. My father was that way, too."

"To speak nicely, don't mean you're afraid."

"So you want me to talk fancy, is that it?"

"Well, yes, if that's what you want to call it."

"Forget it. That's not me."

"Come on, fellows, drink up," Lazi said cutting in, and quickly downed his glass.

* * *

The medic whom the town people called "Big-Head Dhosi" came by riding his bicycle, an old, rickety thing whose tread had lost their elasticity. This kind of bicycle was used by the postal service of the Italian army, and was left behind after the war ended. Its decrepit condition made you wonder what force kept it from disintegrating altogether. Dhosi propped up the bicycle against the wall and hurried into the bar. He looked around and as soon as he spotted Milo, he let out a sigh of relief.

"Ah, there you are, Milo. Man, am I glad to see you. I've looked for you everywhere."

"Take it easy, take it easy. What's the hurry? You're running around like the Germans were on your tail."

Milo's two drinking buddies burst out laughing. It was clear from the way they were looking at Dhosi that they were eager to see what he had to say. But Dhosi paid no attention to Milo's taunt.

"Never mind me. Come quickly; the doctor wants you."

Milo winked slyly.

"And what does doc want me for?"

"An ill woman is in urgent need of transportation to the center."

The news did not shake up Milo in the least. Dhosi was stunned, since in the past, whenever he had called on him for a job of this kind, Milo was on his feet right away, and then would say, "Is the patient ready? Let's roll," and he would drop whatever he happened to be doing. This time he didn't budge an inch. Had he had too much to drink?

"You and doc can go to blazes. My car has broken down, and here you are asking me to go on an urgent errand. You bullhead, haven't you seen my car? How am I gonna transport the woman? Do you expect me to carry her in my arms?

Just then, Dhosi remembered that the ambulance had been parked in front of the clinic for several days. The car flashed back in his mind: a vehicle covered over with an old waterproof cloth, and supported by two logs that had been placed under the disks of the front wheels.

"Don't ask me," the medic whispered weakly, as if cornered. "It's not my idea… It's the doctor's order. If you want to come, fine; and if not, well, it's up to you."

"I'm not coming," Milo said firmly, just short of shouting. "That's all there's to it."

"You won't? Then don't… now or ever! What a mule-head you are, you wretch. If I were in their shoes, I would fire you on the spot. I'm gonna tell the doctor that you don't want to come."

"Go right ahead!" Milo said curtly.

Dhosi didn't know what else to say, but he was burning up inside and did not want to just get up and go. Finally, he muttered some insults and left. As he was walking out of the door, he almost collided with a beautiful woman who walked into the bar.

"Watch where you going, Dhosi!" Milo called out to tease him, grinning all the while.

Dhosi stepped out, got on the bicycle with the worn-out treads and sped away. Milo didn't even bother to look. He was following with lustful eyes the lovely woman who just came in. In this respect, he was no different from fellow drivers.

"That's what I call a beautiful woman," he said, swaying his head and sighing like a passionate lover. "Look at those legs, look. Boy, oh boy. Give me a beautiful woman, a home, a glass of brandy, and the world can go to blazes, for all I care."

* * *

The doctor of Kumesh was walking down the street, stooping, frowning and thinking. He had thrust his hands into the pockets of his white frock, even though it was not cold. His eyes were riveted to the ground, and it was clear that something was troubling him. He didn't bother to greet back the people along the way. Indeed, he wasn't aware of them, at all.

He was an old doctor. On this particular day, he was not wearing a hat, and his bald head glowed in the sun. A few strands of gray hair clung around his ears and on the back of his neck, forming a gray wreath of premature aging. He had been working for twenty-two years as a district doctor, and glory to him seemed like an empty yearning and an adolescent dream. There was a time when he dreamed of both glory and wealth; but as the years passed, he gave up those dreams and now, out of all his former passions, there remained only one – to play backgammon at the Hunter's Bar.

As soon as he saw the doctor, Milo sensed that he had done wrong to disregard his order, and suddenly regretted it. He was in just that kind of a mood at the time, and behaved in like manner. He had no reason to disobey him and felt ashamed of himself. As he looked at the doctor, he was thinking.

"Instead of me going over to him, he gets up and comes over to me. Poor man, he can hardly walk."

He waited calmly for the doctor to blow up and swear at him. Since he felt guilty, he had no intention to respond and defend himself. "Let him say what he likes; he has a right to," he thought.

The doctor drew close to him, but said nothing. It did not even occur to him at this point to ask why he had not obeyed his order. It seemed that something bigger and more important held him in its grip, and the incident with Milo was rather insignificant. Pushing his chair back to make way, Milo got up and put the cap on his head.

"I know what you want me for, doc, so don't even bother to tell me," he said, waving his hand. "But how can I help you? You know the ambulance can't go anywhere."

"I know, I know; but I also know that she has to be driven to the center. If she doesn't get there in two or three hours, it will be all over." The doctor rubbed his hands to add strength to his words that whatever was to be done had to be done within a few hours.

Milo shrugged.

"What do you want me to do?"

As if he hadn't heard, the doctor went on,

"Two lives will be lost..."

"The woman is expecting?"

The ambulance driver was shaken up. He now recalled the stretcher those peasants brought in, and the corner of the red blanket flapping likes a banner.

"Is it that woman they brought in about an hour ago?"

The doctor nodded his head. Then, gazing at Milo, he went on as if speaking to himself.

"This is a very serious case. It's not a normal birth, you see. Only one hand of the baby has appeared. The only thing that can save her is an operation."

The doctor stood still. His aged eyes with their clouded look focused hard on the sturdy face of Milo, pleading it seemed for compassion and hope.

"I can't help her. I'm not a surgeon. I don't even have any surgical instruments," the doctor went on. He had a very troubled look. After pausing for a moment and squinting his eyes, he said, "Right now, Milo, the life of that woman depends more on you than on me."

Milo held his breath and trembled. He looked with respect at the round and fatherly face of this man of science, and felt close to him, like son to father; so much so that he wanted to embrace him and say to him, "You've got a big heart, doc!" He had reached that state of elation and energy when one is ready to do anything, make any sacrifice, and never regret it.

"Tell me what to do, doc! Tell me and I'll do it!" he said, much moved.

"Just that, drive her over to the main hospital, that's what I want."

Milo sighed and smiled wryly.

"Please doc, don't kill me with words. How can I drive her over there? Just tell me! Find me a car and I'll get here there in no time."

There are some people who cannot be won over with malice. Such people are "vanquished with kindness," as the saying goes. Threats and insults do not impress or daunt them. But if you speak a kind word to them and touch a sympathetic chord, they are ready to tackle anything with endless energy, too. Milo was one of those people. The doc's sincere words that the life of that woman depends more on you than on me had hit the spot and made him think.

"I have told the Chief over and over," Milo began, his temper rising. 'Don't leave me high and dry, but try and get me those tires.' He just don't care. C'mon, let's go find him and tell him off."

The doctor's face darkened, and in a tone that brooked no opposition, he said,

"Forget it; this is no time for telling him off."

*   *   *

They were walking along a narrow paved street, lined on both sides with eucalyptus trees that had been planted years ago. At this time, they were full of leaves, and their musk-like fragrance pervaded the street. All around, everything was light, fragrant, fresh and soothing. Kumesh wallowed in its sluggishness. Milo could not get it out of his head that he had to do something; only he had no clear idea what that might be.

"Doc, you put me in a tight spot, you did." He seemed to be speaking more to himself than to the doctor. Then, as if he suddenly remembered something important, he stopped and in a hopeful tone asked the doctor,

"Did you call the main clinic and ask them to send over a car? Let's go over the post office to check."

He slipped his hand under the doctor's arm, as if to prod him to run with him over the short distance, but the doctor didn't budge.

"I already... There's no help from that end of the road. They have only one car in good condition, and that's on the road somewhere. They said that they don't even know when it will be back. Besides, there's no time," he added, shaking his head.

"So what are we gonna do? Why don't we go over to the local party office?"

"What for?"

"To ask the secretary for a car."

"You go ahead. There's no point in me coming."

"No, no; you come along, too, 'cause it's better to go together. Besides, whom is the Secretary going to listen to, a driver like me or a doctor? You have authority, while me…well, who cares what I say?"

On the way to the party office, the doctor still wondered how the villagers had brought her to Kumesh and how many hours were they on the road. He felt uneasy that he had spoken harshly to the ill woman's husband, while he replayed in fast-forward mode the events that had led up to that moment. The doctor was about to go home when they informed him that they had in an ill patient. He recalled vividly the face of the young woman, pensive and exhausted from the pain. Her face mirrored all the suffering the wretched woman had experienced. Her big eyes, wet with tears and bordered by black circles, had a weak and tired look. Her brow was pale and sweaty, the cheeks sunken, and the lips thick, swollen, dried up and cracked like parched land, and all sliced up from the bites of her teeth, as she labored in vain to give birth to the baby. After examining her, he came out to the door looking very stern and distraught.

The four men who had brought her from the far-away village were sunning themselves on the steps of the clinic. They were chatting about routine matters while smoking, like people who had done their duty and waited quietly to hear a good word, before they could go back to the village. As soon as they saw the doctor at the top of the stairway, they all stood up. The youngest of them hid the cigarette behind him then threw the butt on the ground putting it out with his foot. They did not like the worried look on the doctor's face.

"Which one of you is the husband?" the doctor asked, jutting his chin forward.

"I am. Name's Kosta."

A tall man stepped forward. He had a calm and quiet look, and a pair of thick, black, arching eyebrows that gave him the look of a man who was perpetually astonished by all he saw and heard. The doctor noticed a thin silver earring dangling from his right ear, a sign that he was the only child in his family.

"You are her husband? Good. Come inside a moment."

They went into a narrow room, paved with white and red marble slabs.

"Tell me, how long has she been in this condition?" he asked.

"Well, since yesterday, just as the sun was going down or maybe a little before."

The doctor made a despairing gesture with his hand, the kind of gesture people in his profession make at desperate times to connote, "What blockheads!"

"Why didn't you bring her sooner?" he yelled at him angrily, his broad forehead turning red all over.

"We just didn't… We thought she was going to have the baby up in the village."

They stood face to face and eyed each other like enemies. On one side the patient's husband standing with bowed head and a heavy heart; and on the other side the doctor looking fierce and irritated.

"We are a long way from here, doctor," Kosta said. As if to excuse himself. "Five hours on foot. We set out a little after sun-up."

The doctor looked at the wretched peasant, who was twirling an old cap in his big hands, and suddenly felt sorry for him. No doubt, the peasant was waiting to hear a good word from the doctor, something like, "Don't worry, she will be all right…." The doctor's heart softened. With a compassionate look, the doctor drew close and placed both hands on the peasant's shoulders. He gazed at those eyes under the arching eyebrows that seemed to view everything with astonishment.

"It's not your fault," doctor said, letting out a sigh, and rounding his lips as if he were blowing out tobacco smoke.

Those words soothed Kosta. In a tone that showed his distress and the love he had for his wife, he asked,

"Please, doctor, tell me. Is she going to make it?"

He waited anxiously for the answer knowing that these were the most critical moments in his life. Moments that can age a man ten years and ruin him! Moments that fortunately for us come only seldom in one's life! Unbearable even for the most patient and even-tempered! All at once Kosta had the feeling that the room was bending out of shape; the doctor's features seemed gigantic; his forehead looked big enough to dig with a plow…. Kosta snapped out of it only when he heard the doctor's voice.

"What can I tell you? It's like this: we have to send her over to the next clinic center to be operated on. I sent a medic to look for our driver and the moment he arrives we will have her on her way."

Kosta felt a fever-like wave go through his body. His arms hung listless and powerless. He leaned against the wall to keep from falling down. His worst nightmare stared him right in the face! Why did things always turn out this way? Whenever he feared something, it was sure to happen. On the way to the clinic, he thought to himself: "My God, what if they don't keep her there and tell me that she has to be sent over to the clinic center? What I am going to do then?"

Kosta shook his head hopelessly as tears welled in his eyes.

"Don't be childish. We'll get her in our ambulance and on the way in no time."

Just then doctor remembered that the ambulance was out of service for some days. It was idly standing outside the clinic building like a piece of junk.

The expression on the doctor's face changed at once. Anxiety replaced hope. He bit his lower lip and slowly took his hand off Kosta's shoulder, the way he did when he unwrapped a bandage off a wound. There was sadness in his eyes.

At that moment a nurse passed by with a bouquet of flowers and a water pitcher.

"Kristine," called the doctor. "Get some camphor, penicillin and glucose right away to the woman that was admitted just now. I have to go somewhere, but I'll be back soon."

The doctor thrust his hands in the pockets of his smock and slowly headed for the door. Kosta remained standing in the middle of the room. He looked thoughtfully at the red marble slabs on the floor, but didn't know why. The doctor stopped at the door, as if he remembered something, and said to Kosta,

"What are you doing there? Come along..."

Kosta tried to join him, but his feet resisted. He thrust his arms forward and pleaded,

"Fine, doctor, but ... could I see her one more time?"

"Sure!" The doctor pulled the door behind him and went out.

* * *

The office of the Party Committee was not far. As soon as they stepped into the courtyard, Milo stopped, glanced at the garage and muttered,

"We wasted our time, doc. The car is not here."

Being Saturday afternoon and way past closing time for office workers, they found only the guard on duty at the building of the Party Committee.

"How you doin', Petro? How's it going?" Milo asked him.

Petro closed the book he was reading and somewhat ill at ease stood up. He straightened out his belt and his hat and asked the visitors to sit down.

"No, thank you; we're in a hurry," the doctor said.

"Is there something you want?"

"We like to talk to someone in the Party Committee."

"There's nobody around. They've shut down for the day," answered the police.

The doctor rubbed his chin thoughtfully.

"Where is the Secretary?" Milo asked.

"The Secretary is out of town. He left yesterday to attend to some business in the capital."

"Is he coming back today?"

"I doubt it. But even if he does, it will be at night, or else tomorrow."

"We can't wait till then," the doctor said, as if talking to himself.

"Why?" Petro asked. "Is something troubling you, doctor?"

"Yes, something is troubling me," the doctor said glumly.

"Tell me and I'll help you out," the sergeant said.

"There's nothing you can do."

"You never know. Sometimes you can get help from those you don't expect."

"Well, I need a car to go over to the main hospital..."

"I got no car, doctor. But if I had one, I would let you have it, no questions asked."

The doctor had gone over there in the hope of finding Stefan Xhiku, Secretary of the Party. And if he had found him, he was certain that he would have been rewarded for his pains. He would have listened to him attentively, as was his custom, and in the end would have said: "Very well, doctor, take the car; there it is."

Now the doctor forgot all that the district Party Secretary had done for his benefit and convenience. The Secretary had seen to it that the clinic got the best food available. Indeed, he once rebuked the President of the Executive Committee, in the doctor's presence, for ignoring the clinic and habitually allocating choice meats to the restaurant. Nor had they ever denied the clinic the funds he asked for. Yet all these things seemed trivial to the doctor now. There he was, with a critically ill patient on his hands to be transported urgently to the hospital and the Secretary was not around to help him out.

He went there fully expecting to find the Party Secretary and discuss the matter together and come up with a solution. But as luck would have it, he was not there that day, and this disoriented the doctor.

"What are we going to do now?" he asked stupefied.

"Try the Office of the Internal Affairs," suggested the sergeant.

"What for?"

"To look for a car. If they have one, they won't keep it from you."

"By golly, Petro's got something there," Milo said.

They bid him "Good day" and left.

On the way to the local office of the Internal Affairs, Milo Shkembi was boiling inside and yearned to let off steam.

"How long can you expect an ambulance to last, anyway? Three, four, say five years; that's about it, while our ambulance has been around for seven years. I've told Spiro time and again: 'Look, Spiro, why don't you try to sweet-talk the Ministry into giving us a new car? The one we got is way over the hill. She's like an old woman with one foot in the grave.' But you can't talk to him. 'I know my job,' he says 'I don't need anybody to tell me what to do.' Moreover, the tires – I been telling him about 'em for two weeks."

The doctor listened wearily convinced that such talk was useless now. He knew that it getting a vehicle was not as easy as Milo imagined.

There was no car at the Interior Affairs, either. A short lieutenant, whom the doctor did not know, welcomed them with much formality and listened to them attentively.

"I am very sorry that I can't help you in this situation. Our car is in the garage in the center. We're expecting it back at any moment. As soon as it gets here, I'll talk to the Chief and we'll gladly let you have it."

"Well, it can't be helped. Even God can't make something out of nothing," Milo said, as he shook hands with the lieutenant.

There was nowhere else they could go to ask for a car. All hope was now gone.

* * *

They took the road to the clinic. The doctor was weary and sad, while the ambulance driver was boiling with anger. As they walked, Milo gestured with his hands as if he were quarreling with someone.

"What is the matter?" the doctor asked.

"Two tires... and we can't find them. Damn this place!" Milo swore.

Impelled by something they weren't even aware of, they made their way back to the rear of the clinic where the ambulance was stranded. They had been all over town, and now ended up where they began. Never before had they appreciated that car as much as at that moment. They walked around it the way a peasant walks around his horse when it dies on the road, and looks at the creature with both sorrow and anger.

Milo was about to give the car a kick, as if it were alive but too lazy to move. But then changed his mind and spit on it instead, and cursed it.

"What the hell am I gonna do with you?"

"In short, it's all over? There's nothing more to be done?" the doctor said slowly. Believing that he was talking about the car, Milo hastened to say,

"What can you do with it? You can't drive to the main hospital without tires."

"Hmm! This has never happened to me before," the doctor sighed, putting his hand over his brow.

Someone called out to him.

"Doctor, they are looking for you."

"Who?"

"They're waiting for you at home, for lunch."

"Lunch? All right, all right; tell them I'm coming... No, better tell them I ate at the clinic."

Milo stepped aside and lit a cigarette. Nearby were the four peasants, who not knowing what to do, had stealthily drawn closer to the doctor and Milo. The doctor went over to Milo and grabbed him roughly by the arm.

"Do you understand that the woman has to be taken over to the hospital?" he shouted as if his wits had left him. "What are you going to do, Milo? Speak up, man!"

Milo restrained himself as never before, and answered him in a mild voice, but with a trace nonetheless of resentment.

"Why blame me, doc? It ain't like I had a car and I refused to take her."

The doctor felt embarrassed for losing control and promptly let go of Milo's arm. One of the peasants, a swarthy fellow in coarse felt clothes approached the doctor.

"It's no use, doctor, there ain't no car around. But it don't matter... Let God's will be done. We will carry her over there, if you give us a good stretcher."

The doctor looked at him with amazement, not understanding at first what he was saying. But when he grasped his meaning, he raised his eyebrows in disbelief and shook his head.

"It's far... it's far... 50 kilometers," he whispered.

"It's all right, doctor. God willing, we might find a car along the way and..."

All the anger that distressed the doctor melted away now, and he felt a great and powerful affection for these peasants of clean, sincere and compassionate heart. Their love touched him, for it was a simple and innocent love, like that of children. It led him to the realization that the love people have for one another is far greater and more precious than any glorious accomplishment.

"It's far... It is far," the doctor muttered to himself, and looked up toward a window on the second floor of the clinic. It was from there that the moaning of the expectant mother came.

* * *

Milo was sitting on a stone, with his back resting against the wall of the clinic, and smoking with great relish. The doctor had gone away, and so had the peasants. Only Milo remained, and the disabled car. Both of them were silent, pitiful, abandoned. Who cared about them? Ah, yes! The woman who was still groaning. Laboring. Weeping. Screaming. Perhaps the wretched woman felt sad to depart so soon from this world. Milo was aware of all that. How nice it would have been if he didn't hear anything. But where in the world could he hide to get away from her wailing? He got up and for a moment thought that maybe he should go over to the highway and wait there to see if a car might come by, and then the matter could be taken care of, for sure. At first he liked the idea, then he thought it was laughable. The isolated village of Kumesh was located deep in the hinterland. All the main routes passed by it.

The town had very little traffic. The bus from the city made one trip a day to bring mail and passengers, and that was it. Things were different in the summer season, though. For about three months during the summer season the trucks drove back and forth to load up with lumber from a sawmill about 15 kilometers away. This was the town's only industrial enterprise. Some time ago, its inhabitants envisioned the town alive with auto traffic and noise and jobs, because coal had been found in a nearby village, and it was rumored that a big mine was going to start operations there. But their dreams never came true. Owing to the meager coal reserves, the mine was never built. And Kumesh remained what it has always been.

Milo thought of all these things unconsciously. Then he massaged his brow with his hand, as if to drive away a nagging thought that wouldn't leave him alone, and stood up.

He could not stay still. He opened the rear door of the car, and examined once more the tires he had carelessly thrown back there, tires with pieces of rubber that hung like tongues.

"No, these tires here won't run on them rubbers," he said loudly. "Look at 'em, they're full of holes, like sieves. Wait till I get my hands on you, Spiro!"

Just then Dhosi came by in back of the clinic, riding that notorious bicycle of his. Milo eyed him with envy and said to himself: "This guy don't have to worry none 'bout breakdowns on account of his tires. Lucky dog! Wouldn't it be something if a car had tires like that?"

The moment he said that, an idea flashed into his head like lightning, and he grasped it at once.

"What if... what if I stuff them? Stuff what? The tires? But would they hold up? Well, why shouldn't they?"

He latched on to that idea that came to him in those difficult moments, and like a lunatic rushed over to the clinic. He gave a push to the door, but the door, as if to spite him, did not open. He then shattered the glass pane with his elbow, and reached inside to open the door. Shortly after, he emerged with a mattress under his arm. He dashed the mattress to the ground, ripped it open hastily and scooped out a pile of straw. Next, he took the tires and began to stuff them with straw and rags. He was totally wrapped up in the task at hand. His hands and fingers were bloodied up, but he paid no attention. When he couldn't get hold of the threading wire with his hand, he grabbed it with his teeth and held on to it so tenaciously and with such intensity of feeling that you would have thought he was tearing apart his worst enemy.

He had no idea how long it would take to do the job.

After propping up the car on jacks and placing in one of the front wheels, he stepped back a little to examine his work, and shrugged his shoulders. Would they do? Could he drive all the way to the next hospital on such wheels?

* * *

At last Milo fastened the other wheel, and with his heart in his throat, he was ready to test-drive the 'fixed' ambulance. There was extreme anxiety on his face as he focused all his thoughts on the single task at hand. He turned the ignition on. The car shuddered, the engine started, the fender began to shake rhythmically, and Milo released the brake and stepped on the gas pedal. The car started to roll. It could run! It shook more than usual, like a vehicle driving over a rocky terrain, but it ran nonetheless. Milo's heart leaped with joy, like the time he first got behind the wheel, and drove around the clinic in a single breath.

Hearing the sound of the engine's car, the doctor looked out the window and was surprised to see the clinic ambulance crawling along. Seen from above, the car did look like a crawling creature.

The car came to a stop at the entrance of the clinic.

"What's going on, Milo?" the doctor shouted out.

Instead of replying, the ambulance driver waved his hand the way chauffeurs do just before they start swearing, then got out of the car.

"Is that our ambulance?" the doctor asked.

"You bet it is!"

* * *

Within five minutes everything was ready. Just then, as if sent there expressly, "Saint Leksi" came by. And with an air of naïve surprise, he asked:

"Where did you get those tires?"

"Oh, I patched them up with bits and pieces and some wire," Milo replied gravely, without bothering to see who posed the question.

"Will they hold up, you think?" Leksi came back with another question.

"I'll say they will."

"But there's no telling when you will get to the next clinic… with those tires. Tomorrow I reckon."

When he saw who was talking to him, Milo decided to kid around a bit.

"Why? You think wheels is all I'm gonna use to get there? I'm gonna put wings on the car, too."

"Did you say wings?" Leksi said, open-mouthed with wonder.

"Yup, wings; like an airplane. The car is gonna fly… You'll see."

"You're kidding… Where's the wings?"

"They'll bring them over from the carpenters' workshop. Ndreko came by and took the measurements. It's no big deal, you know."

"You don't say!" said Leksi, amazed. "How did you ever think of such a thing?"

"Well, it just came to me."

"Can I come along, too? I ain't never been in a plane before."

"Don't get mad now, but you're really a moron, you know? How can you fall for such a fairy tale?" Milo said with a grin.

Leksi wanted to say something, but had no time, because just then the door of the clinic opened and out came the stretcher with the woman in labor.

As they were getting her into the ambulance, her husband Kosta bent gently over his wife lying there as if he was going to kiss her.

"How do you feel, Rina?" he asked.

She shook her head in distress. Her swollen lips trembled and her eyes became moist with tears.

"I beg you Kosta, don't leave me alone. I'm afraid."

"No, no, don't worry."

* * *

Milo felt someone grabbing his arm with a vice-like grip. Turning his head, he saw the worried face of the doctor and that piercing look of his that went right through you.

"Are you going to make it? What do you think?"

"She will get us there, for sure!"

Milo spoke with such conviction he surprised even himself. To tell the truth, he feared the uphill road at White Pine, but he didn't breathe a word about that to anyone. He did not want to admit that even to himself.

The car started moving. Milo and Kosta sat up front, while the doctor sat in the back close to the patient.

They drove through town. When they passed by the bakery, Nasho came out and, as was his habit, greeted them by waving his paddle-like hand.

After driving two kilometers, apiece of the right front tire came loose, and every time it hit the ground it went "flap, flap, flap," brushing the dust off the ground and leaving its mark along the way, like a measuring rod. That telltale sign stretched from one town to the next, like a victory memento on the great road of human love.

The car sped along, leaving behind a trail of fine dust, which afterward settled slowly on the wheat that had just begun to sprout, and on poppies that seemed like drops of blood scattered over the plain, and on the blue flowers of flax plants.

Here and there, along the foothills, villages came into view with houses built of stone and roofs of red tile, while farther away there arose the high mountains that encircle the town of Kumesh. It seemed they were all watching with some anxiety the green ambulance that drove through the wheat fields, leaving in its wake a trail of light smoke.

Milo knew every foot of this road. He had driven on it hundreds of times. The bridge where a car over-turned this winter. Over there were the charred remains of the tank that was put out of action during the war, and was now covered with grime from the elements. A little farther was the wild pear tree with its dome-like form. Next was the narrow wooden bridge. Milo could drive over this road eyes closed. It always seemed so short to him. Not that day, however. It felt like the road was stretching endlessly.

Milo turned his head and glanced at Kosta's silver earring that kept moving to and fro. It was only that earring that made Milo feel that the ambulance was still running.

The path where the car drove was strewn with bits of straw that fell from the tires. No one there seemed to pay any attention, except for the birds that flew after them.

After crossing the White-Pines pass and reaching the Great Plain, Milo floored the gas pedal. His soul was in bliss and every muscle in his body was taut like an arrow on a bow ready to be shot.

Milo had never known such contentment before. In his line of duty, he had transported many patients and people in need of medical help, but had always remained distant because of the nature of his job. He was there to drive the ambulance, nothing else. The health and lives of the patients were the responsibility of other people, not his. Whereas on that day he, had done something out of the ordinary.

At about five o'clock in the afternoon, they reached the hospital with its iron fence and green banisters. The ambulance wobbled into the hospital's courtyard. The aide attended to the expectant mother out of the car. Soon she was rushed into the operating room. Milo drew close to the doctor, took him by the arm and asked him a question that had been bothering him all along the road.

"Is she going to pull through, doc?"

The doctor shrugged his shoulders.

"I don't know, but she ought to pull through, she ought to." The doctor almost went on to say: "Milo, you did an extraordinary thing to-day." But for some reason, he didn't tell him that. Instead he just shook Milo's hand warmly.

Milo didn't think that it was heroic to stuff tires with straw and rugs to transport a patient. After lighting up a cigarette, he put his hands on the wheel and began to think about buying some presents for his children. Since he had come to the city, he might as well get something for them. He just didn't know what presents to buy.

☙ Summer Day at Dock No. 3 ❧

The Soviet ship "I.V. Michurin" anchored at dock No. 3 in the port of Durres had been unloading for four days. This freight ship of medium tonnage made regular runs between Odessa and Durres. It was an ugly, run down cargo ship, built in the previous century. Its rusty color tone seemed even more somber against the blue expanses of the Mediterranean sky and the waters of the Adriatic. The container's engines ran on steam power. Two hefty metallic smoke stacks belched thick puffs of smoke and coal soot into the air. The age of the ship could be reckoned from the rust on the hull below the water line and the peelings of paint on the sides. It was as if the ship were suffering from an incurable skin disease. Each time the waves slammed the freighter against the rubber cushions on the wharf, one could hear rasping sounds like cries of pain coming from an old beast on the brink of death.

When the ship unloaded at the port, the crew reclined on the deck and basked in the warm caresses of the Mediterranean sun. Sochi of Crimea and Odessa, the southernmost points of the Russian plains and the favorite vacation resorts of the Soviets, could in no way compare with the deep blue skies or the greenish azure waters of the Mediterranean. The Adriatic Sea was usually so calm that its ripple-free surface seemed like a gigantic mirror. A few people could be spotted on the pristine beach that stretched for miles from that port all the way up to the rocky Cape in the south.

The arm of the crane oscillated from the merchant ship to the lot on the wharf. From a distance, the crane resembled a huge stork that pecked at the ship's hold with an insatiable appetite. As they stacked up the crates from the ship's hold, Tole Ramadani and Sherbet Nala, two dockworkers, cast glances at the deck where the Soviet seamen sunbathed in reclining chairs made of switches. Tole spotted a man with a white cap who appeared on the deck holding a balalaika in one hand, and a bottle of Vodka in the other. Tole thought, "If only I could have that bottle, right now!" After preparing lunch, the head cook took some time off in the afternoon and stepped out on the deck. As if to ask permission to sit down on a wicker chair, he bowed slightly before the portrait of

Generalissimo Stalin, which blanketed nearly half of the smoke stack. After sitting, he put the balalaika on his lap and began to play. The sounds of that instrument brought on the deck the aroma of Russian steppes, filled with melancholy and delight. To maintain a high level of inspiration, he sipped Vodka from the bottle he kept by his side. And up above there was Stalin's picture posing in his military uniform with his right hand thrust beneath the lapel of his overcoat, much like Napoleon. Even his portrait appeared to be smiling with pleasure upon looking at the Mediterranean landscape around him and listening to the balalaika.

The head cook disrobed from the waist up, even as he continued to draw on his repertoire of songs and melodies. When he started to play *Kazachoku* – a popular Russian folk dance tune – he could no longer stay put and got up to dance. The others on the deck kept him company by clapping. At that moment, it seemed as if Generalissimo Stalin himself was going to jump out of the picture frame and join in the *Kazachoku* dance on the deck.

"Now, that's what I call living it up!" sighed Tole with envy, weary from the heat and the long hours of work.

"Never mind them! They get paid even when they loaf," Sherbet said to calm him down.

The two longshoremen stuck to their job and only rarely talked to each other and to the crane operator when needed. In general, their vocabulary consisted only of verbs: lift it up, push it, let it go, hold it, line it up; and occasionally an adverb, like slightly forward, sidewise, leftward, closer. A hot vapor rose up from the cobblestone lot with such boiling intensity that it seemed as if the heat originated from the bowels of the earth, rather than from the sun up in the sky. After they loosened up the ropes, they signaled to the crane operator in the cabin to raise the hook. It looked like a big question mark in the air, turned upside down. Two other members of the team, Irfan and Bashkim, worked deep in the hold of the ship. But nobody envied them, for down there it was unbearably dusty and sultry.

Kozma Veisiu, the checker, who kept the tabs on the ship's cargo, sat cross-legged on a keg of tar near a stack of crates, and jotted down the number of crates and sacks that came off each load of the crane. At the end of his shift, he would meet with his Soviet counterpart, who stood at the edge of the ship's hold, checking his numbers. Although they only met briefly to see if their numbers matched, those meetings gave Kozma an excuse to say that he performed duties of international significance. Tole and Sherbet made fun of his bragging.

Matish Rodoni, the crane operator, worked nonstop for eight hours. Indeed, he needed to ask the supervisor for permission even to go to the restroom. With full concentration, he kept his eyes on the control panel, and his hands on the levers. Matish was aware of the danger spots where the crane load could collide, such as the brink of the ship's hold and the pile of crates in the lot on the wharf. So he was even more careful when he moved the loads close to those points. If the load was damaged and it was his fault, he would be held responsible and liable.

The dockworkers were always in high spirits when they unloaded food containers, because then they could get something from a sack chewed up by mice, a broken crate or a cracked vat. A week earlier, while unloading a freighter sailing under a Panamanian flag, they noticed rice pouring down as soon as the crane load came up from the ship's hold. The two longshoremen rushed over to the cascading rice, and started dancing and jumping with joy like children. Matish watched their dance from the crane cabin and laughed, not caring one bit to lower the load, in spite of Kozma who made threatening gestures at him with his fist, from the ground below. The comic scene continued for some time to the delight of the crowd on the wharf. As soon as their shift ended, the two dockworkers ran quickly to collect the rice that had spilled on the ground. Kozma Veisiu reprimanded them, saying they were making away with someone else's property. Standing on a mound of rice, Tole growled at him:

"Don't be an ass, Komi. Why let the seagulls and the sandpipers eat this stuff, when our children can enjoy the rice?"

"That rice is the people's property!" Komi retorted, wagging his finger at him.

"What about us? Ain't us part of the people?" Tole shot back, scornfully. Suddenly, he softened his tone and said, "Come on over and get a load. There's enough here for you, too."

Kozma did not budge.

"Guys, who wear ties, feel ashamed to scrape up rice from the ground," said Sherbet to tease him.

The two longshoremen stuffed the pockets of their jackets and pants with so much rice that they looked like circus clowns, when they started walking.

"I'm telling you once more to let the rice where you found it. You're making off with socialist wealth," Kozma warned them.

"Shut your trap, man!" Tole protested in the typical Durres jargon. "Scram, will you? We've had enough of your sourpuss claptrap."

Short of build, muscular and swarthy like all stevedores who roam the ports of the Mediterranean speaking sundry languages, Tole worked at the docks ever since the freighters were loaded and unloaded on the backs of longshoremen. Kozma on the other hand got in thanks to the introduction of mechanical gadgets. With his skinny body and a spine that curved like the contour of an egg, he couldn't carry even half a load on his back. That's why Tole couldn't stand him. He felt that Kozma was a parasite that did not deserve to be paid. For his part, Kozma could not bear Tole's boorish tongue and vulgar ways. In his view, Tole's looks revealed that he was a Gypsy with a shady family tree. Kozma thought that the Devil alone knew the sailor with whom Tole's mother had conceived him. Once in the heat of an argument, when Tole called him "a snail," the sophisticated Kozma could not restrain himself and let out all the resentment he harbored against the Gypsy.

"You don't have a drop of Albanian blood in your veins. You're a sorry Indian-African hybrid, that's what you are!" he yelled.

"Your mother is a hybrid!" Tole shot back not knowing what Kozma meant by t.hat word.

"He meant to say that you are a half breed, that your mother got pregnant with you by shacking up with some foreigner," Sherbet cut in to explain.

Instead of defending his dignity as Kozma expected, Tole only sneered. He was glad to be called part of another race. Besides, he took no interest whatever in anything immaterial that could not be measured or weighed; and he couldn't care less about them.

He befriended the Soviet sailors only for the sake of a bottle of Vodka, a can of meat, or a loaf of bread. Like all other stevedores in the Mediterranean, he had mastered the hodgepodge of gestures and words that made up the naval international language.

The Soviet seamen were allowed to step out into town day or night. They could go into restaurants, rotisseries and shops that sold grilled meats, and try out the drinks and appetizers. They praised especially "*Skenderbeu*" not the feats of Albania's national hero, but the golden-hued colored cognac in half-liter bottles. September had been proclaimed Albanian-Soviet Friendship Month. In honor of ‘the seamen friends’, High Schools and work centers in town performed artistic and musical programs in the afternoons. The evenings began with poetry readings, music and songs, and ended with fistfights with jealous husbands or boyfriends. Apparently, the Soviet sailors were inclined to broaden their contacts only with the female portion of the population. Such differentiation caused much disappointment among Albanian males. Thanks to the evenings of Albanian-Soviet Friendship, the seaport town of Durres, known since Roman times as the “Tavern of the Adriatic” was enriched with new scandals with each passing year.

Viola Prespa, the central figure in the most notorious scandal involving the Soviets, showed up at the quay carrying a bundle of newspapers under her arm. As an employee at the International Club, she distributed the daily press to subscribers and work teams at the port. Scantily dressed as usual in somewhat transparent garments that revealed nicely the charming contours of her body, Viola swayed coquettishly as she walked, conscious that curious and lustful eyes were following her at every step.

“Your ex-sweetheart is here,” Tole whispered to Sherbet.

“I dated her but she was not my sweetheart,” Sherbet said, resentfully.

The moment he spotted her, the head cook of the Soviet freighter invited her on board.

“Viola, ljubima moja, idi suda!” (“Viola, honey, come over here.”)

Viola replied with a smile and told him in Russian come meet her at the International Club that evening.

“Dirt-bag! He wants to f--- her,” Tole burst out.

In the meantime, Viola got close to the tar keg where the checker was seated.

“Uncle Kozma, I’ve brought the papers for you.”

“Leave them there,” he ordered her, without raising his head, for fear that he might be seen talking to her.

From atop the pile of crates, Sherbet chided her mildly, saying,

“Viola, there’s other guys around here, too.”

“What do you want, you devil?” she asked.

“For now, just a cigarette, if you got any. I beg you; I’m dying for a smoke.”

Viola opened her handbag, and threw him a pack. Sherbet took out two cigarettes, and was about to hand the package back to her.

"Keep it," she said, "I've got another one."

"Where can I see you tonight?"

"At the International Club."

"Wow! You've gone up in the world," Sherbet said with sarcasm.

"Naturally! Got to keep in step with the times!" Viola retorted, as she walked away.

Sherbet turned to Tole and whispered,

"There's no soul more generous than Viola! Have you noticed?"

"Whores are known for their generosity. You still keep in touch with her?"

"No. Who said that I am?" Sherbet said defensively.

"In that case, why do you want to see her?" asked Tole.

"I need a couple of packs of *Kazbek* for some friends," explained Sherbet, "and Viola can purchase them for me at the Club."

"It beats me how they keep a woman like her at the Club," Tole wondered.

"If you ask me, Viola deserves an award for strengthening the friendship with the Soviet Union. That poor girl has put everything she has in the service of the Soviet sailors. And do you know what they say about her? They say she's the most honorable whore in Durres, because she don't take no money from them—only presents to keep as souvenirs. Stuff like blouses, nylon socks, scarves, gloves and things like that. But I happen to know that she sells the presents so she makes out better this way."

"Get out of here! She's a clever cookie," Tole said with grudging respect.

* * *

Viola Prespa, a small-time hooker, became notoriously known after a scandal with the captain of the soccer team and star of the town's soccer fans, Sopoti Angjeli. The scandal gave Viola the image of a courageous target, but opinions about her were divided. Some called her a whore, while the majority saw her as a victim of male jealousy and savagery. Even at a tender age, Viola was disposed to welcome the attentions and flatteries of any male, regardless of their age or complexion. When she met Sopoti, she swore to him that she would be faithful, that he was the man of her dreams, renowned and handsome. And she was true to her word, as long as Sopoti was close by. But when he was out of town with his soccer team for several days, she would cuddle up with some other man, just to keep from getting bored.

During the fall playoffs, the cigarette factory held an afternoon of entertainment as part of the program in honor the Albanian-Soviet Friendship Month. That evening Viola put on a dazzling performance, twisting and turning with her dancing partners. The Captain of the Soviet ship proposed to Viola that they continue the celebration in his cabin. Since she had never before set foot inside a ship, she accepted gladly. She was curious, moreover, to find out how Soviet men made love, and what sort of sweet talk they used on women. It was the dream of many Albanian girls to have an intimate relationship with a foreigner, even though they did not dare to say so openly. Such relationships usually aroused the jealousy of other girls and hurt the feelings of the young men.

Viola was astonished by the luxurious cabin of the Captain, and even more by the selection of beverages and food in his refrigerator. Afterward, her visits became more frequent, since the freight ship had other cabins besides that of the Captain.

Stung by Viola's unfaithfulness, Sopoti's friends informed him that his darling girl was betraying him, by keeping company with Soviet seamen. The star of the soccer team did not believe the story. Nevertheless he told his friends that he would be on the lookout, and if what they said about Viola were true, he would avenge himself in such terrible fashion, no woman would ever again dare to betray athletes. And, of course, he did not have to wait long before he witnessed Viola nimbly climbing the narrow steps that led to the Soviet freighter.

The following evening Sopoti invited Viola to the hotel where they met habitually, after he slipped some cash underhand to the bellhop. They went to their room. Viola undressed and slipped into bed first. While she waited in bed to enjoy the act of love-making, Sopoti, instead of using the traditional equipment for the act, took out a surgical knife and tried to cut off her genital organ, the part that's visible to the eye. Sopoti figured that with a couple of rapid incisions, he could it cut like a slice of melon. But Viola screamed with pain, and gave Sopoti a kick that flung him out of bed, then ran out into the street, with her hand down to her genitals. A kind driver took her immediately to the hospital. The doctors at first thought that she was one of those unfortunate females whose had an illegal abortion with the aid of untrained women, and was in danger of dying because of a torn uterus. But when they put her on the operating table, they noticed that the blood was coming from a surface wound. They were greatly puzzled. How could she get wounded in such a well-protected place? They cleaned the wound, sutured it and assured Viola that no damage had been done to her sex organ. The doctors' second puzzlement was Viola's utter frankness about the medical aspects of the incident. She related in detail how Sopoti attacked her, while they were making love in bed.

"He tried to cut it with a knife out of jealousy. But why should he get upset? After all, they are both Captains." That was how Viola summed it all up.

The town doctors had heard in lecture halls about females wounding and cutting off men's sexual organ, but were not aware of any recorded cases of any man severing of the female genital organ. The news of this extraordinary event was spread by the doctors, and quickly reached the farthest corners of the town. Both the hero and the victim became well known in and out of their town's area. Speculation and comments about what Sopoti had in mind continued for a long time. Did he intend to put Viola's privates on a plate and take it home with him? Who was the object of his rage? The Captain of the Soviet ship or Viola?

After the incident, Viola was also known as "the one with the lacerated strings." All acknowledged that the anonymous author of that second name had come up with an apt analogy that described the violin, the female organ and Viola's first name. Apparently whoever coined that phrase had a poetic vein that was hard to be denied. After that scandal, Viola was sought after even more eagerly by naughty young men, who wanted to see with their own eyes the famous surgical scar.

Strange to say, some ordinary crimes escalate disproportionately when toned with political coloration, while the Sopoti-Viola scandal was terminated precisely on account of its political nature. A local official of the Party Committee advised Viola not to file suit against her ex-lover to keep the rumors from getting worse. Viola replied that the gossip didn't bother her one bit. Then the official told her bluntly that going to court would drag the name of the Soviet sailors as skirt-chasers and that would besmirch Albanian-Soviet friendship. In return for her understanding, the authorities promised to find work for her right away. The buzz about the scandal died down. To the delight of soccer fans, Sopoti remained captain of the soccer team. As agreed, Viola got a job as a cleaning lady and courier at the International Club.

* * *

Viola walked back to dock No. 3 after distributing the newspapers.

"So, I'll come by around 9, okay?" Sherbet tried to confirm.

"Fine, whenever you like," replied Viola, walking past him.

"I don't think you'll make it. You should have told her much later than that," Tole said to Sherbet.

"Why?"

"Because we have to finish unloading by 10 tonight," Tole explained.

"How do you know that?" Sherbet was interested to find out.

"I heard it from Vuxhi, who was talking to Kozma today at noon."

They could not leave before the last load was out since there was no later shift to follow theirs. If they finished unloading ahead of time, they were free to go. This was the order from the supervisor.

Tole focused his eyes on the deck of the freighter. How was it that none of the Soviet seamen thought to toss a bottle of Vodka to the longshoremen, who were sweating to unload their ship? What kind of friendship was this?

He asked Sherbet:

"How about if I went over to those guys, who are sunbathing out there on the deck and ask them for a bottle of Vodka? My throat is parched!"

"Wait till Kozma leaves; otherwise, he will report you to Vuxhi, or someone still higher, and then we'll never hear the end of it. Komi is bound to go and piss sooner or later," Sherbet said.

More than once, Kozma had accused Tole of lowering the dignity of Albanian longshoremen, with his beggar's ways. Tole, for his part, could not see what connection there was between his belly and that muddled word "dignity," that Kozma liked to use a lot.

"He's not budging from that keg like his ass is stuck on the tar," Tole said over and over again with disgust.

The crane cabin began to rotate with scraping noises, like a child that whimpers for no reason. The ropes of steel, which up to that point were limp and entangled, began to firm up until they formed two parallel lines that cut absurd geometrical figures across a portion of the ship and the sky. Matish maneuvered slowly and carefully until the load was over the deck. Once the load was out, he swung the arm of the crane quickly toward the lot. If the swing's pull were too hard, it sweeps the load past the pile of crates. Whenever that happened the longshoremen had to wait for the load to stabilize before they could continue working.

"Looks like Matish is going to mess up badly today," Sherbet said. "He's carrying on like he is not all there."

"He's got to go to a wedding tonight, that's why he's in a hurry," Tole explained. "He asked the supervisor for permission to leave a couple of hours early today, but Vuxhi turned him down. 'You won't leave your cabin,' he told him, 'until "Michurin" is unloaded. We cannot afford to violate our work schedule. The Port Authority will fine us. But if you get done sooner, then you can go to the wedding or to the moon, for all I care,' he told him," Tole said.

At the port, the week depended on the schedule for loading and unloading. The longshoremen got Sundays and holidays all together at a stretch, when one ship unmoored and another was set to dock.

"The supervisor is right," Kozma butted in. "You can't walk out on government-paid job to go enjoy yourself. No reason why the ship should stay anchored, because Matish want to go to a wedding and drink himself into a stupor."

"But, Komi, the wedding is a one-time thing, while merchant ships come and go every week," countered Sherbet.

"The sooner the goods get to the clients who ordered them, the better for our economy. But to understand that, you need a head on your shoulders, not a block with seven holes."

"Komi, I have a request," Tole started politely. Then added, "You're busting my chops!"

The eloquent form of the request and its gross content did not go hand in hand. But that was the highest level of etiquette Tole had inherited from his family.

"Why? Did it bother you?" Kozma goaded him, pointing the tip of his pencil at him.

"We get enough whining from the rusty winch. Go and talk a hole into someone's else head not here. I don't need it."

"You most certainly do," Kozma insisted.

"Do not! It's my back that bears the weight of the merchandise, and my ass that sweats, not yours! Who is unloading this ugly freighter right here, you or me?" Tole snorted.

If someone else referred to the freight ship as "ugly," Komi would have denounced him as "an anti-Soviet." But to take a Gypsy to court was not worth the bother!

"Are you blind? Read it for yourself!" Kozma fumed and pointed to a sign on a tin sheet that hung from the crane, which said: "Socialism cannot be built without the aid of the Soviet Union." The poster was meant to unmask the revisionist viewpoints of the Yugoslavs, who claimed that they were building socialism outside the Socialist Camp. It appeared on billboards alongside roads, in the courtyards of plants and factories and in towns all around the country.

Seeing that sign again made Tole think that no verbal reply was necessary. While facing Kozma, he twirled his thick lips and blurted out sounds that mimicked those that normally come out from the rear end.

"Idiot!" shouted Kozma. "Scum! The proletariat, too, has its trash and you are it! Your mind is only on booze."

Tole slapped his hips with his hands, furious that Kozma would not let him alone.

"What a pest! My ears are splitting...," Tole carried on, as if talking to himself. Moments later, his monologue turned more explosive.

"Get lost, you skinny runt! It is not bad enough that my butt sweating from the heat, I got to put up with your breathing down my neck."

Seeing the wild look in Tole's eye, Sherbet signaled to Kozma to lay off, before the quarrel got out of hand. Then, he slipped his arm around Tole's to calm him down and told him.

"Get moving! You're holding up Matish and us."

"He goes on and on...clack-clack-clack," Tole continued, with his head turned toward Kozma, "even when you tell him you don't want to hear no more."

Tole knew since the first time he saw 'the tab's guy' that he was turned off even by Kozma's looks, his sloping forehead, the small beady eyes and the moustache *a la* Hitler.

"This mug of his reminds me of someone, only I can't put my finger on it," Tole said.

One day, as if out of the blue, Sherbet said that Komi resembled the mole that digs tunnels underground, and only rarely comes up on the surface. Tole got all excited by the cunning similarities and shouted with glee,

"You hit the nail right on the head! That's exactly what he is—a mole."

The nickname stuck since a few years earlier Kozma had told on someone at work. Suddenly, the nasty argument of that day gave Tole an idea.

"Hey, mole; are you going to report me, like you did Guli?" he asked Kozma sarcastically. "Go right ahead. You are good at that."

"What if I do? Do you expect me to ask your permission?" Kozma said.

"You even went to the trial to testify...." Mockery and anger mingled in Tole's voice.

"All the more to my credit! I denounced an enemy...."

"Oh, sure, right. Whatever you got to say to yourself.... You know that Guli did not lie. At the trial, he was blunt and he told the truth. 'The date of the product is stamped on the chassis of the wagons. If you don't believe me, then appoint a committee to investigate on site,' he said."

The first passenger train from the Soviet Union arrived in Albania in 1948. It had small unsightly wooden-frame wagons, the likes of which could not be found anywhere in Europe. The longshoremen marveled at them. They sat on their sturdy wooden seats, they opened and closed the windows, and they posed for photographs in and around the wagons. One of the dockworkers was Guliem Marku, whom everyone called Guli. He got down underneath the train to take a look at the chassis' structure. He said that the wagons were manufactured in Sverdlosk in 1874. He was not aware that his finding constituted a political offense. It meant that the wagons were junk, a collection of antiques from the time of Tsar Alexander, which had traversed the Trans-Siberian railroad for three quarters of a century. After some fast reconditioning work, the wagons were given a fresh coat of paint and sold to Albania as brand new. Guli's discovery circulated freely in the port as a matter of curiosity. Kozma, however, gave it a political nuance, alleging that was intended to discredit the fraternal aid of the Soviets. A few days later, the police showed up at the port and arrested Guli. Handcuffed and ghostly pale, he walked among his fellow workers with his head bent down. The demonstrative manner of the arrest in broad daylight had an opposite effect from the one that police expected. Tole Ramadani said that if he were arrested instead, he would have walked with his head up high. The People's Court sentenced Guliem Marku to seven years in prison for anti-Soviet propaganda.

"Too bad it did not make for a stronger case," Kozma continued. "Today no one can get away with prattling against the Soviet Union. The dictatorship of the proletariat lays handcuffs on you and puts you in your place!"

The crane load was moving fast toward the pile of crates just barely above the heads of the longshoremen, forcing them to duck instinctively to avoid getting struck.

"Hey, have you gone completely insane?" Kozma yelled at the crane operator, tapping the temple with the butt of his pencil.

Matish leaned slightly beaming with delight and held one hand out the window with four outstretched fingers. That meant that after four more loads, they were free to go home!

The dockworkers unhooked the load, untied the ropes, removed the crates and began to stack them.

"These small crates are heavier than the big ones," noticed Sherbet. "What the hell is in them?"

"If you're not invited to a meal, what difference does it make if the food is served hot or cold?" commented Tole, as he watched the arm of the crane speeding toward the belly of the freighter. "I envy Matish tonight," he continued. "I can almost taste the whiskey flowing like a river at the wedding, the tables full of food and ice-cold beer. While us wretches will go home to fight with our wives and kids."

"Matish is mad at you," Tole said to irritate the checker. "Watch out he don't drop a crate on you, 'cause then your head will sink down to your belly and you'll look like a turtle without a shell."

Sherbet liked the image and laughed derisively as he pictured Kozma walking around with just arms and legs.

"What do you expect, when you're dealing with ignoramuses?" noted Kozma. "Instead of handling crates like glass he brings them out of the freight ship as if they're cabbages.... Why? Because he is thick-headed. He's got his mind on the wedding. He doesn't realize that anyone of those crates is worth more than his head, and yours, for that matter. They have valuable stuff while your heads are empty. Thanks to the Soviet aid, we are becoming an industrial country.... This is vital for us. The aid...."

Kozma Veisiu would have carried on his political lecture, but he noticed that the crane load was coming over fast and low and stopped. To save time, Matish executed two maneuvers simultaneously. He rotated the arm of the crane while lowering it steadily. Only this time, his calculations were off and the load crashed against the pile of crates on the wharf. All of a sudden, one of the crates flew up into the air and then dropped to the ground with a loud bang, cracking the frame.

"Simpleton!" screamed Kozma, pointing his fist at Matish. "You shall pay damages for your carelessness."

Sherbet and Tole jumped off the stack of crates and ran over to the damaged crate on the ground. Matish lost all his enthusiasm for the wedding that evening. He started to hurry down from the crane cabin. Tole stared at the broken crate with a puzzling look. It contained only pieces of metal all shaped like the number 8. Each had a threaded metal pin in the middle and a screw on one end. Tole bent down, grabbed one of them and began turning it around.

"What are these? Do you have any idea?" he asked Sherbet.

"Maneta," replied Sherbet.

"What's that?" Tole was not familiar with that foreign word.

"Handcuffs!" shouted Sherbet and then crossed his hands at the wrist to illustrate the function. "These days they are called 'bracelets'."

"For real?" Tole exclaimed with amazement. "But why so many of them?" He pointed to the stack of crates.

It was a naïve question and Sherbet did not bother to answer. Just then, Kozma showed up, terribly upset about the damage that had been done. His small mole-like eyes burned with anger. Matish was getting close to the stacks of crates. Tole was still twirling the handcuffs in his hands.

"Here, take them! They're ready for Matish."

Kozma instinctively took a step back. Tole threw them at his feet. The handcuffs clanged as they hit the ground. The longshoremen looked up and their eyes met with the Stalin's portrait in his Generalissimo uniform smiling on the deck of the "I. V. Michurin."

ꕤ The Trial of the Kulaks ꕤ

"I've never witnessed a more extraordinary trial," was Aziz's opening line at the round table where fellow magistrates were polishing off a bottle of whiskey. They were seated at the veranda of the restaurant at the downtown park across from the dried up fountain. Still, the view around was pleasant, the minced meat omelet in the earthenware casserole was delicious and the humor at the table admirable.

Aziz Merolli was part of a generation of magistrates that had graduated from the Law School. Unlike most of his colleagues, however, he was not a conformist or hypocrite. He told pointed anecdotes, which he embellished with personal comments. The son of a well-known war veteran, he felt at ease narrating whatever interested him, without worrying about 'compromising' the Party. His verbal excursions beyond the designated ideological boundaries appealed to his friends, who did not dare to tell such stories in coffee shops, either because of a built-in self-censure mechanism, or because they were conditioned to conform. Yet, they did not hold back from asking Aziz for fresh anecdotes. If he shrugged, they tried to coax him to retell old stories.

"I will not mention the name of the town where the trial was held. I just happened to be there on duty. As I was sipping my morning coffee, the district court clerk, approached me and asked if I wanted to attend the trial of a kulak at the courthouse. 'Gladly,' I said, since I had plenty of time on my hands, and didn't know what to do with it that morning.

"On the right side of the courtroom, sitting between two police officers was the defendant. On the left side was the district attorney, dressed in a suit and sporty tie, as if he was going to a wedding. Next to him was a secretary with glasses and across from them sat the Presiding Judge with two of his assistants. As soon as the prosecution read the charges, the courtroom burst out in applause. The attorney expressed his appreciation by nodding. He seemed pleased with himself, believing that he had drafted an exemplary Bill-of-Indictment, packed with an irrefutable body of evidence. In reality, the charges were a hodge-podge of slogans and propaganda."

The presiding Judge addressed the defendant, an adult on the threshold of old age, who looked stuck between two officers.

"Do you plead guilty to the charges, defendant Qerim Sinani?"

"No, no! There's no way I can plead guilty," objected the defendant. "How can I be guilty of 'confederating and conspiring against the state', when no one in the village even speaks to me?"

His brisk rebuttal was so logical and frank that those who had come to see him crucified, murmured words of approval.

Holding up a sheet and pointing at the bottom of the page, Judge asked:

"Is this your signature?"

"Mine, your Honor," answered the defendant.

"Why did you sign the confession, if you were not in agreement with the contents?" the prosecutor jumped in.

"If I hadn't signed, I wouldn't be here today...," the defendant replied.

There was laughter in the court.

Somewhat shaken by the uncomplicated reply, the government attorney launched a fiery discourse on the role and services of the national security, which the defendant was trying to besmirch by claiming that they got a confession of guilt from him by using force. That proved once again that the defendant was a sworn enemy of the state.

"Who would know better about the confession, you or my back?" asked Qerim.

Again, laughter broke out in the court, causing the prosecutor to gnash his teeth in anger. The presiding Judge came to his aid, by calling the first witness to take the stand.

"State calls witness Mevlan Tahiri!"

The wing of the half-opened door was pushed out, and in came a dark-complexioned man with a big head, hooked nose, and broad buttocks. He hunched and limped, as he made his way between the rows of benches in the courtroom. His cane struck the floor with a steady rhythmic sound. It looked as if he would keep on walking through the courtroom without knowing where to stop.

After establishing the identity of the witness, the Judge asked,

"Do you know the defendant?"

Witness seemed surprised.

"If I did not know him, why would I come here?"

"How long have you known him?" the Judge continued.

"Since the time of the Austrians," replied the witness.

The murmurs among the audience prompted the witness to clarify the time, by saying:

"All right, then; I've known him since the First World War, when we used to shoot birds with slingshots. Our villages are close and we are also distant relatives."

"We are not interested in your ties," the Judge intervened. "Can you tell us when the defendant started to confederate and engage in propaganda against the state?"

"Since the year they called us *kulaks*," witness answered holding up his cane.

Laughter erupted in the courtroom, since no one expected that the main witness for the prosecution would be also a kulak.

Then the witness turned to the defendant and asked him,

"Isn't that right, Qerim?"

"So, it's a partnership of kulaks," observed the Judge.

"Yes, Sir!" said the witness.

More laughter in the courtroom. The District Attorney scowled and scribbled something on his note pad. The trial that was meant to unmask a kulak for engaging in hostile activity against the state was turning into a farce.

Apparently, the Judge felt the prosecution's discomfort, even without seeing the angry sparks shooting from the attorney's eyes, and proceeded in a more formal judicial mode.

"What do you know about the actions of the defendant?" he asked, seeking to direct the witness. "Where did he stand, politically? What were his intentions?"

The witness realized that he had to confront Qerim, which meant violating his trust.

"This fellow here...," began the witness, pointing his cane at the defendant, who looked at him with a quizzical grin.

"What do you mean by 'fellow'?" protested the prosecutor and frowned at him.

The witness put his cane by his side.

"This kulak fellow...," the witness corrected himself, but was unable to continue, as loud laughter swept the courtroom. Even the members of the jury began to chuckle over the unheard of oxymoron "kulak fellow." Mevlan, for his part, couldn't figure out where he went wrong.

"Continue, continue!" the Judge ordered.

"Well, when we went to the depot to turn in our grain production, Qerim said to wait and we stopped over at the coffeehouse and ordered coffee and cognac. Well, God's truth, he didn't let me pay. 'What is your quota?' he asked me. 'Three hundred kilos,' I replied. 'Mine is five hundred,' he said. 'It's a heavy quota,' he said, 'too heavy for my back,' he said. 'After I deliver my quota, I don't know if I will have enough left to myself. How am I going to make it through the year? In the old days we used to complain that the quotas were high. Nowadays, it's four parts for the state, one part for yourself'..."

The government attorney leaned forward and made a notation on his pad.

"Then do something about it, I said. Complain to the authorities. 'Nobody listens,' he said. 'They slap heavy delivery quotas on us on purpose, so we wouldn't be able to meet our obligations, and then they can put us in the clink. There's no way out. I have to buy bread in town to feed the family. To think that even in the time of the Turks, or Italians, the government did not tax us on meat, wool, eggs and butter. It looks like the quota is leaving out to dry."

"What do you mean?" inquired the district attorney.

"I mean, we are left penniless," the witness replied. "Then Qerim said to me, 'Why don't they take everything we have, once and for all, so we and them can out our minds at rest' "

"You mean to say that kulak Qerim Sinani was opposed to the government economic policy to levy taxes on produce," intervened the prosecution. "And as if that were not enough, he confederated to get others to oppose the government."

"That's right," agreed the witness. "Did I have the guts to stop the deliveries? I handed over to them everything they asked for."

"No one used force on you," said the Judge.

"No! Except the notice they handed said, 'Obligatory' explained the witness.

The hilarious murmurs in the court caused the government lawyer to intervene sooner than he had planned.

"Do you see now, defendant Sinani that you have carried out propaganda against the state, inasmuch as you were opposed to the regulations in force?" The prosecution thought that, with that incriminating accusation, he had the defendant with his back against the wall.

"No, sireee! I told him my troubles like a friend," said the defendant. "Mevlan told me that I was right."

"Members of the jury! Fellow citizens! Look at the defendant before you! He pretends to be a simpleton. He does not admit guilt. Yet, all the while he was spreading his poison in small doses." Pointing his finger at Qerim, who seemed to be in a daze as he sat there between two police officers, he said: "The Party has repeated pointed that the kulak is a sworn enemy of the people's government. And here you have the proof of it. Kulak Qerim Sinani is opposed to the delivery quotas on produce, which were established by the people's government, complying with the teachings of Lenin. Instead the defendant praises the collection policy of former governments."

Then, he charged that the kulak sought to break the alliance between the working and the rural class, which constituted the foundation of the state. At that point, the defendant asked the Judge.

"I don't understand. Is he talking about me?"

"That's right," Judge said, angrily.

"I met my quotas down to the last one, because I knew what was in store for me, if I didn't," said the defendant, in self-defense. "There were others who didn't turn in a strand of wool, or a grain of wheat, and they got away with it...."

"Who were they?" asked the Judge.

"Those who pretend to be poor. After a couple of years, they were exempt."

Seeing an opportunity to intervene, the council said that the government valued much more those who did not fulfill their quotas, than those who delivered out of fear, like the *kulak*s.

The Judge cast a pulverizing glance at the attorney who indirectly was affirming that the state authorities privileged the shirkers and the violators of the law, and charged as enemies those who made regular deliveries.

"What else did he tell you?" the Judge asked the witness.

"At a common relative's wedding, Qerim approached me halfway through dinner, and said to me: 'We can't marry off our sons, because people don't want *kulaks* for in-laws. See if you can hook up some kulak's girls from your village. Help me, I beg of you!' "

The attorney jumped to his feet and prattled that the defendant desired the overthrow the regime. He was way off, since there was no reaction in the courtroom.

"One time," the witness continued his testimony, "he grumbled that the store had no olive oil, so he returned home with empty hands."

"Do you admit it?" the Judge asked the defendant.

"That's common knowledge," Qerim said. "The delivery truck broke down, and the store couldn't get groceries for a week. If you don't believe me, ask others. I told him no lie."

Again, the government representative intervened to say that the clay pots of the defendant were full of butter, and therefore he had no cause to complain.

"My good man, have you ever heard of anyone eating salad tossed with butter? Not me."

The courtroom rang with laughter once more. The distraught attorney silently rebuked those present, who were amused by the remarks of the *kulak*—an action that constituted a political error.

"Anything else?" an assistant to the Judge asked the defendant.

"About a month ago, I was on my way to the market, and I ran into Qerim. We chatted quickly and he asked me if my village had become a state-owned farm. 'Yes,' I said. 'Did they let you join?' he asked me. 'No,' I said. 'Me neither,' he said, 'just as well. At least, we are still farmers that own our land and estates.' "

"No, Mevlan, it's you who said that. Don't tack that one on me," objected Qerim.

Mevlan found himself in a tough spot. Not knowing what to say in self-defense, he turned to the right, turned to the left; then began to rub his nose.

"He said that, to find out what you thought," interjected the Judge.

"Yes, that's it," Mevlan said, relieved.

"And you approved," the Judge said, addressing Qerim.

"You bet, I did! They did not let us stay outside the fold, but dragged us in, anyway," remarked Qerim.

The Judge asked the defendant if he wanted to question the witness.

Qerim stood up. The court waited to see what he was going to do. Since his trusted friend had talked to the police, and revealed the conversations held in confidence, he was going to try to turn the tables on him.

"The wealth I have now, I earned with hard labor and sweat," Qerim said. "I worked night and day on my farms, together with my sons. While others relaxed in the shade, I broke my break working. Now, I'm told I did wrong. I don't get it. I have not taken anything from anybody. I've given plenty, with both hands...."

"Never mind the long tales," the Judge broke in. "Get to the point. Do you admit that you have engaged in propaganda against the state? Are you in agreement with what Mevlan Tahiri said in his testimony?"

The defendant looked at his chum who sat leaning on his cane, in a slightly crooked posture.

"Well, now, your Honor. When two kulaks meet, what are they going to talk about, except the troubles that are busting their brain? Right, Mevlan?"

"Yes," agreed Mevlan, "that's what I thought, too. Someone from the Internal Bureau"—he pointed to the bench where several officers in uniform and civilian clothes, were seated—"told me that our conversations were propaganda, and had to be brought out into the open. So, cane in hand, I used to go over and tell them everything we talked about. That's all, I swear!"

* * *

"Did they sentence him, or let him go?" inquired Fatos, sitting across the table from Aziz. The others were looking at their glasses still immersed in the story.

"The district attorney asked for eight years in prison for the *kulak*. The jury gave him ten," answer the narrator wryly.

"This blows...," remarked Fatos. "Yet, I wouldn't dare to say that in public."

"As I said, it was an extraordinary trial since our own brand of justice and penal code are equally outlandish."

ꕤ Target Practice ꕤ

As soon as I reached the clearing between the sheds, I saw a hand waving at me to come closer. I couldn't make out the face, since all uniform soldiers look alike, I thought that the signal was meant for someone else. I turned around and saw no one near me.

"Over here," I heard someone shout at me. "You idiot with a High School diploma. Come over here. I got some good news."

I recognized the voice of Berti and ran toward him to find out what the news was all about. Perhaps the military command had granted him leave to visit his family, and he was delighted that for a few days he would be freed from the boring routine of the two-year military training.

"Zana is coming over tomorrow," he said, rubbing his hands. "I have no idea how she arranged it. I will ask her when she gets here. Let's go over to the bar. I want to treat you."

Zana Bandilli was his fiancée, so he had good reason to feel good.

The bar of our military post was an ugly shack used to store coal and other junk. Its limited 'menu' would not permit you to spend much there, even if you tried. Anyone knew that soldiers were always broke. Nestor, who worked the bar as bartender and coffee man, did not know the first thing about business. Once a week, when he went to stack up and would come back with several kinds of sweets, of the sort that would keep for a long time, some hard biscuits, some black cubes of halva that you couldn't bear to look at. Once in a while he would get pastry with icing on top. Yes, this country bumpkin was not cut out for that job. In that forgotten corner amid the mountains, the city pros did not set foot, because business there was too slow for them. Nestor, however, did not mind, since he was paid by the month. Although the wages were low, they were still three or four times higher than the money he would have made working on the farm. In the summer season, he would bring bean pudding and cider, which were very popular with the soldiers and officers and sold out quickly.

"Maybe will be lucky to get some boze," I said to Berti. "I much prefer to drink that than those flavored lemonades with colored citric. Besides, it's our traditional national drink."

"It's just fermented corn professionally brewed," Berti said scornfully. "If it was a real good beverage, Europe would have gobbled it up."

We stepped inside the bar. Behind the counter, built of rough wooden boards, lay some darkened shelves and the electric burner which Nestor used for the Turkish coffee. Gossip had it that an officer, who was known as a connoisseur of coffee, once said to the bartender: "I know that I cannot ask you to put more coffee in the pot. Could you at least use less water, so as to make a decent cup of coffee...."

"Well, this is no time to celebrate with cider. If Zana got wind of it, she'd be mighty upset. She'd think I don't much care for her."

"You don't have to tell her everything," I remarked.

He looked at me with an air of disdain, as if I were giving him bad advice.

"She's my fiancée, man!" he reminded me in a chastising tone, as if I didn't know. "Do you realize what it means to be engaged?"

"Of course. It's not hard at all," I replied.

"You can't know, if you're not engaged," he retorted.

You could not get mad at Berti, no matter how he chided you. He always spoke without malice, like a child. There were no hidden thoughts in him.

"If I kept secrets from her, then I must be willing for her to keep secrets from me.... Then what happens to marital trust?"

It was a pointless question, for I knew that he neither wanted, nor was able to hide anything. He expressed himself openly about everything.

I had seen his fiancée in the neighborhood because her house was just two blocks away from mine. In grade school she wore ribbons in her hair, that she tied in two bows. After finishing high school, she went on to college to study languages. Getting in that college involved not only a high grade average, but also clean background and powerful friends. At any rate, she pursued her studies there regularly. That particular department was envied by all the young people who hoped to get a job with the foreign service in some embassy, or as a translator, or else secure a cozy corner in the offices of the foreign trade sector. Then, one day we heard that she was engaged to a young man who worked as a mechanic in the capital. Afterward, it was rumored that her parents had arranged the engagement, since she was their only child, and they absolutely did not want her to leave the city after college. Coincidentally, Zana's fiancé and I became friends at the military training in a camp in the city's outskirts.

"You go ahead and sit on that keg over there," Berti said, pointing to a nook. That spot was the favorite watering hole of the riffraff in our unit, because it filled the imagination with intriguing pirates' stories.

Berti approached the counter, reached over to Nestor, then returned holding two cups.

"I took care of it," he said. "Got four shots.... That's the way to handle that huckster. We will have to drink the cognac out of coffee cups, so that nobody suspects anything. Cheers!"

In fact, everybody was in on the 'secret', but went on pretending. This way, it looked like the regulation forbidding alcoholic beverages in the detachment was being respected.

"You know I haven't asked you how you met her?" I had to satisfy my curiosity.

The story he told me is rather comical.

Eager to learn some lessons in the area of romance, Berti had asked a friend of his who was reputed to have a good score card with females, about how he arranged dates with them, what approach did he use, what words did he say to them? His friend told him that the method he used was simple and practical. First, he winked at a girl, and if she smiled, he took her aside and set a time and place to meet. The rest followed naturally. There was nothing to it. Berti went ahead and casually tried to wink, but every time both his eyes would shut down simultaneously. His friend burst out laughing, He lost no time telling his friends, that Berti could not wink to save his life. To avoid more teasing, Berti started to practice at home before a mirror. He tried several methods. Sometimes he covered the right eye with his hand, and sometimes the left, but all in vain. Finally, after much pain and toil, he hit upon the idea of shutting down one eye by putting a band aid over it, to prevent the eyelids from moving together at the same time. After achieving the success he desired, he told his friends that he, too, had mastered the art of winking. Even so, he did not put it into practice for fear of being embarrassed. He thought it was bad manners and crude to wink at a girl you did not know.

"I fell in love with Zana the first time I saw her...."

"So, it was love at first sight," I cut in.

"No, no, it was not the typical love-at-first-sight, like seeing her in a park or a stroll downtown. We were introduced through my aunt

Marina. Well, not exactly a matchmaking deal, you understand. One day she invited Zana and me to her house. If we liked each other, then we would go to Zana's family and I would ask to be engaged officially. The moment I saw her, I was struck by her beauty, and lost all hope that she could care for me. As soon as Zana left, my aunt asked me what I thought of her.

" 'You better ask her. Do you think she liked me?' I felt stupid and worthless. Why would a lovely girl like her want to join hands with a boy in overalls?

" 'Why shouldn't she like you? Is there something wrong with you?' she asked me.

" 'Yes, everything,' I replied. 'No higher education, no profession to speak of. While she, on the other hand, she is a college student, knows a foreign language....' "

"Why did you feel unworthy? You have a lot going for you. You're good looking, serious, well built...."

"You know what bothered me?" Berti tightened up. "My last name. Who would want to marry a man with a last name like mine, Qafoku?"

I chuckled over his naiveté.

"What matters is your background," I argued.

"The last name, also. You know what I told Zana when we got engaged? If you like, you can keep your last name. I would not mind, since yours is better than mine. You know what her answer was? 'I would love you, no matter what your last name is.' Isn't she special? I love her so much. I dream that maybe someday I will have the chance to save a child from fire, or someone who was drowning—something like that.... It's all I think about."

"Well, it's enough that you are honest and sincere. There's no need for heroic deeds."

"I want Zana to be proud of me. I don't want to hear any gossip that she married me just so she could stay in the city.... Refills? It's all paid for," he said. Winking at me, he walked up to the counter, and returned with the cups filled with cognac.

We drank a toast to Zana's health.

"When Zana and I got engaged, it was winter, so we went to the movies a lot. Soon as the lights dimmed, we petted a little bit. Doggone it, some tramp sitting close to us, would start whistling and yelling: 'Check it out! Wow! He is squeezing her like he is going to suffocate her.' My father would not let me take her to my room. 'She can come to visit, yes, and as often as she likes,' he said. 'I cannot allow you two up in your room, because I have other children in the house.'

"Her own parents are more liberal, and always invite me to lunch or dinner. They have a two-story house, and they usually stay on the ground floor. We wanted to be more relaxed, so we went upstairs to commit our little sins. The door stayed wide open though and her mother would bring us snacks, like fruits, sweets, cake. She climbed the stairs without a sound, like a cat, and burst in on us unawares. Once, she found us in an embarrassing position, not terribly embarrassing, but bad enough. I had Zana on my lap and I was kissing and petting her so much, her face flushed red. Just then, her mother walked in with a tray in her hands. As soon as we saw her, we separated, both of us with downcast eyes like two guilty souls. She, too, stood still and didn't know what to say. Quickly, I collected myself and spoke up.

"Why do you come up here like a thief?' I said to her in a nice way. 'Are you worried about what we're doing up here? Well, we're not doing anything more than what you and your husband did, when you were engaged. Just so know, I'm gonna tell you one more thing. Zana is mine and some day you might find us holding each other real tight.' From that day on, she climbed the stairs audibly, so you could hear her coming half a mile away."

Berti's stories stood out for their naiveté and humor.

"Do you know how eagerly I look forward to tomorrow? I think I'll ask the commander to grant me leave for a couple of hours, so I can go over to the Geology Club. I don't want to hang around here with Zana. The guys would eat her up with their eyes."

"Well, you're a model soldier and he has taken a liking to you."

His eyes lit up with joy.

"Zana told me she's coming over just because she misses me. Isn't that something?"

Then he made a naïve request.

"Give me some interesting topics I can use to fire up my conversation with her. Come on; your noodle is more fertile than mine. You read books, too."

Jokingly I suggested that he talk about extra-terrestrial beings. A moment later I realized that it was an idiotic idea.

"You are no help," he retorted. "I want something down-to-earth, like: Which are prettier? Bedrooms of cherry wood, or maple? Personally, I like cherry, because of the red reflexes. We will wed as soon as I get my discharge papers, but we have to put in an order for the bedroom in advance, because there is a long waiting list."

A little later, he surprised me when he said:

"Could there really be people on other planets? It would be neat, if they came down to earth to tell us that neither capitalism, nor socialism are worth much." Then, he remembered to caution me. "Don't mention this to anyone, or my goose is cooked."

Later that night, I felt a hand on my shoulder and heard someone tell me to pick up my weapon for target practice. It was the platoon Commander. The time might have been around three in the morning. A military Chinese jeep was waiting with the motor running. I climbed on board, behind me got in Berti and Sadik. We made ourselves comfortable in the back seats. They have never driven us to the shooting range. The platoon commander swerved his pistol up front, so it would not hurt his back, then settled down in his seat. The car's headlights pierced the darkness and light up the brush by the roadside.

For four weeks in a row, our unit did target practice, following instructions, both theoretical and tactical. The same exercises day in day out, week after week: take aim, press the weapon butt against the shoulder, hold your breath until you pulled the trigger. Then, a dry, empty crackle. Target shooting got to be habitual, or more exactly a bore. We could hardly wait for the day when we could go to the range, to demonstrate our skills in actual practice.

Then, word spread around that we were going to do target practice at night, shooting at objects that are illuminated only a few seconds, and might even move. It was said that this kind of target practice is ten times harder than the usual. All of it made us feel somewhat uneasy.

The driver did not take the turn that led to the practice grounds, and the rusted and battered road sign that said "Military Zone", remained far behind us.

"Hey, driver! Are you still asleep?" Berti needled him. "Didn't you see the turn in the road?"

The driver did not bother to reply. He had his eyes on the road, and pressed the gas pedal as he held on tightly to the wheel.

"Where are we going?" Sadik asked the platoon commander, tapping him on the shoulder.

"To do target practice with live ammunition," he replied. "We told you before, so keep it mind. We didn't pick you for nothing."

He mumbled something about our backgrounds. The connection between the family biographies, and the target practice at night seemed feeling. Yet, soldiers don't tax their brain much, and we were no exception. The jeep made several turns over unfamiliar roads. The darkness was faintly dissipating over the hills covered with yellow oak brush. We had not arrived to the rifle range. It was plain that we were heading toward another camp, on some mountain slope.

The army barracks were no longer contemporary. All army detachments are spread out to increase efficiency in case of war. It was all based on the experience of the Israelis, but nobody would say this out loud or admit it, for fear of being misunderstood or worse. Yet, thanks to the Israelis' military experience, I had the chance to become well acquainted with friends like Berti. Our jeep pulled over a slope covered with brush, below there was a precipitous creek, and across from it another stretch of barren land. In the purple predawn light, we heard the rumbling sound of a military truck. The sound died down. We started eyeing the scene around us for some typical sign of a target ground, or at least some path that led to it. There was not even a goat trail.

We heard e melodic whistling sound, like the hurried twitter of a bird in hiding. Our platoon commander answered back, as if he were mimicking it. He scanned the barren meadow on the other side of the creek, and turning to us, ordered a line up.

"Ten steps forward! March!"

That sort of line-up exercise made no sense at all, just like many other things in the army. We marched ten steps.

Berti stood in the middle, between Sadik and I. The unit commander reached into his jacket pocket, took out two ammunition clips and handed three bullets to each of us, just as regulations called for, regarding target practice. He ordered us to load our rifles, then pointing to the other side of the creek, ordered:

"Take aim! There are your targets!"

Only then three targets without the pattern of rings on them seemed to have appeared out of the bushes. The color and shapes were unusual. Standing on two humanlike feet, the target in the center was higher and not quite square-like. Its corners seemed angular. The other two missed one corner perhaps shattered by bullets in the years of target practice. To our astonishment, the targets moved.

"Commander, they are people covered with sacks to look like targets," Berti yelled and instinctively stepped out of line, unable to stand still. He looked anxiously at the commander, so that he might stop in time, and avoid making a tragic mistake.

"They are your marks for shooting practice. Shoot at the one directly in front of you." The order fell on the prairie like discrete chunks of ice. The air chilled at once, making me shiver.

Berti was right. Across the creek, there were clearly three silhouettes, whose torsos were covered over with a sack. Why would they be made to seem like marked targets? Madness. I doubted anyone would agree to this type of exercise voluntarily. The sack over the target in the middle must have been used over and over again, since a corner of it hung limply on the side. The hands of the people inside those sacks must have been tied behind their backs.

We were the execution squad. I trembled at the thought. Why were we trusted with the execution? What execution? The platoon commander assured us that they were only marked targets.

Berti's hands trembled badly; his weapon even more. He had a hard time trying to load it. The bullets kept falling down on the ground, under the ferocious and impatient gaze of the commander. The distance to the targets was less than a hundred yards. We can hit them without difficulty. I wonder how many points we were going to get. What am I thinking? Who could have drawn the circles on the sacks and lines with numbers? What if the 'targets' can see us, as we load our weapons to take them down. How horrible! Perhaps looking out of the fabric of their sacks, in the bluish light of dawn, will make them think that the scenario is happening on another planet.

To the right, Sadik took aim and pulled the trigger. I also fired away, but without taking aim. I had a capricious desire to waste the first bullet, and let the sack stand for a few seconds longer, allowing the poor soul to take a few more gulps of the morning air, even if it didn't make any sense. What good were a few more seconds to anyone in that condition? To my astonishment, the two figures on the sides crumpled to the ground. One collapsed into a heap, the other was twisting all over. Sadik smiled at the commander, content with his skill at shooting. Berti's weapon was shaking violently. The barrel kept moving up and down, as if to slice the horizon in two. He pulled it together and managed to shoot. The target however did not fall. Instead, it took two steps forward.

"It's coming this way!" Berti screamed with terror, while looking at us with bulging eyes and a starkly pale face.

"You have the rifle in your hand, you moron!" shouted the commander. Then, turning toward us, he ordered us to shoot again.

All three of us took aim at the only remaining target, and before the smoke of the gun barrels dissipated, we saw it come down.

"Splendid!" said the commander.

Since we did not use the third bullet, the commander ordered that we hand it over to him. Not only did we score at target shooting, we had also saved three bullets for socialism.

Back to the jeep, the driver was as silent as when he drove us there. Sitting between, Sadik and me, with his rifle between his feet, Berti gripped the barrel of the weapon so tight, the knuckles of his hands turned white. His eyes seemed bigger, and he barely blinked. The pupils of his eyes reflected a deep daze, from which he could not tear himself away. He nudged my side with his elbow and whispered, "What was all that about?" Not knowing what to say, I made a gesture that meant, "Just forget about it". A little later, I felt another elbow nudge to my side. He drew my attention to Sadik who was sleeping, his head bent over his chest. We continued the rest of the trip back in silence.

Around 8 o'clock in the morning, we had returned to the training camp. The sleeping quarters were locked up, because regulations forbid soldiers to remain inside during daylight hours. Even those who are on sick leave or ill, have to go to the infirmary near the arms depot. There had been several burglaries that had taken place. Soldiers raided the personal handbags of their comrades, and took whatever they pleased, all the way from shaving razors, pocket knives to ballpoint pens.

The platoon commander approached the officer on guard duty and talked to him. The officer took out a bunch of keys to unlock the door of the shed. I could guess what the commander said to him: "These three did target practice last night. Let them in. They need some sleep."

Before moving on, the Commander said to us:

"You've done your duty for the day. Now you are dismissed."

"What duty?" Berti asked. His voice intimated a crazy yearning to talk, if not to quarrel.

The Commander smiled uneasily.

"The duty that was assigned you. Or better yet, the duty assigned to us. Now, go and get some rest!" With that friendly advice, he put an end to the discussion. Then he drove away in the Chinese jeep, perhaps to report somewhere the completion of the mission, or to stop by the bar for a drink.

Without saying a word, we put the weapons back in the armature, and then each went to his lot. In fact, they were not beds, but rather two rows of planks, like those in Nazi concentration camps. We had no desire to talk about that morning's target practice. Fortunately our cots were far apart. Berti in one corner, me at the opposite corner, and Sadik in the upper middle section. Each wrapped up in the whirlpool of his own thoughts.

Our unit was gone to the shooting range. They waited their turn to go in three bunkers, and then from the gun ports, fire at the marked targets on the hill. The instructors inspected the targets and evaluated the trainees. The high score booted the moral and the ego of the soldiers, who are confidently expected to shoot just as accurately at the enemy. They are praised by their superiors for their readiness to defend the fatherland, even though they have only shot holes in carton targets.

Sadik's snoring filled the quarters. He could sleep at any time and in any position. Sleep was his passion and his greatest pleasure. I could sense the puffing up of his cheeks, every time he took a breath. Covered over with only a bed sheet, I tried to read my novel, which proved to be an impossible task. I read mindlessly. Then realized that it made no difference whether I had the book open or not. None of the words written in the pages was able to make the transition to my brain. They got stuck somewhere on the retina of my eye, because the entire space of the brain was occupied by the image of live targets, of people covered with sacks, to serve as marks for target practice. The color of the sacks was similar to the color of the leaves, as if to blend in with the background. Those sacks could not be used anymore, since they had bullet holes in them. Besides, there would be blood on them. Those who will bury the bodies would get to see whom we shot early that morning. Did the sacks prevent the 'targets' from seeing the execution platoon or was it the other way around? Who were they? The question perplexed me for hours. Who could we have shot at? Criminals? Thieves? Villains? Treacherous politicians? Politburo members? The former Minister of Defense and his aides? Early this morning I shot the Minister.... No, I didn't shoot anybody. The platoon commander told us that we did our duty.

Was it our duty to kill people? We shot at targets that we were told were our marks, nothing more. Yet, we saw them move, not because someone in a ditch was manipulating them, or because they were being pulled sideways with a rope. We saw them walk on the prairie. We heard the rumble of the military truck behind the bushes but we did not see the truck. Maybe someone put the sacks on them in that truck or in prison, so they wouldn't know where they were taken. They ordered them to go to the prairie for the daily prisoners' walking exercise. I wonder if someone told them that three soldiers with fine backgrounds would come to execute them. Would they protest if soldiers with less suitable credentials would shoot at them? I was delirious. I had to stop thinking about what happened. Where would they bury them, I wonder. Over there in the prairie? Was there a designated lot for prisoners who are shot dead? My mind was obsessive stuck to a reoccurring thought. I had to get off that subject.... What happened to my book? Ah, there it was, in my hands. I wanted to get back to my novel, but thought that I should go over and see Berti.

Lying in bed, wrapped in covers, he was rubbing his forehead hard with his fingers, causing the skin to wrinkle from the temples to where the eyebrows meet. It seemed he had a headache, which he was trying to suppress by inflicting a greater pain on himself, with his own hands. I asked him if he needed an aspirin or analgesic. He gestured nervously, as if he couldn't stand my presence. I was hoping he would calm down by the time Zana came. It would be painful if she found him in that condition.

The unit was still out at the shooting ranch. Sadik woke up and sat on the bed. He tapped his wrist with his finger. He didn't have a wristwatch, but I knew what he meant. He was asking if it was time for lunch, so we could go to the mess hall. I motioned to him to go and get Berti, but he drove him away with the same unsavory gesture he used on me. I didn't feel hungry and was not in the mood to eat that early. Yet, I went along with Sadik, just to be civil.

"We're the first ones here," Sadik said, winking at me. Today we deserve a double ration."

He wiped his plate clean and rubbed his belly. I could not touch the food on my plate.

"Do you think they're going to reward us for this service?" he asked.

"Oh, they might put our names on the bulletin board of the marksmen," I said.

That kind of reward was not to Sadik's liking.

"The best thing is to get several days leave, or a reward of some kind. I love to take a trip down south."

We returned to our quarters. Sadik went to sleep with his clothes on. Berti kept massaging his forehead in silence with a ferocious anger and haste, as if he were trying to pluck from his brain something that was hurting him, but the skull prevented him from thrusting his fingers inside, and as a result he suffered terribly.

In the afternoon, it seemed as if he had calmed down. He sighed often but had stopped rubbing his forehead and temples. With his hands placed on the back of his head, he was meditating, but had trouble keeping his eyes shut. His breathing was hard, like a runner after a long run.

The unit returned from target practice, and our quarters hummed like a beehive. A minute later a guard called out Berti, and said that Zana was waiting for him by the entrance. Berti didn't move. I neared him and told him again. He got up from his bed with his hands outstretched. I thought that he was going to give me a hug for bringing him such good news. Instead he pleaded in an anguished voice to tell Zana to leave.

"Please tell her to go away, because I can't see her, you understand? I can't."

His plea was humble and distressingly sincere.

"Are your screws loose? Come on out quick. Your fiancée can hardly wait to see you," I scolded him.

Berti came out of the quarters, dragging his feet. As soon as she saw him, she rushed over to embrace him, without worrying that all eyes would be upon her. Berti thrust his arms forward, as if to protect himself.

"Please, don't come near me, don't! I am a killer. I have killed a man…," he said, pathetically.

She froze on the spot, not knowing what to do. In hopes of finding out something about the shocking incident, she turned to see if she could ask someone. The unusual scene had already gathered around a few soldiers, all set to have some fun.

"I see you don't believe me. You think that I am making things up. I do not lie. I shot someone today, I saw him fall down.... Why doesn't someone tie me up?" he said and crossed his hands in front of him, waiting to be handcuffed. The tired and flabby muscles on his face made him look so miserable.

"Take me to court, though I'm not guilty. They ordered me to shoot, and I took the shot. I shot...." He could not go on. He ran out of breath and collapsed on the ground.

I ran to him and slipped my arm under his shoulders to lift him up. His body temperature and the incoherent talk were indications of a seizure. Then, I whispered to him:

"Please, pull yourself together. You haven't killed anyone. You are our buddy, our brother. We've been together everywhere. Let's go to the bar."

Berti broke away from me and shouted:

"I am talking about what happened this morning. I am a killer. Why did I shoot him? Why did I take his life?" He spoke again in a voice full of anguish.

"They made me a killer," he added.

With teary eyes, he looked at her and said:

"I love you so much, Zana, but I am not worthy of you. I am disgusted with myself."

He fell on his knees, and began pounding his head with his fists. His comrades looked at him with pity, not knowing exactly what was troubling him.

Suddenly, commissar Tahir stepped over to the crowd.

"What's going on here?" he asked. "Can't you see that he has suffered a nervous breakdown?" Then, turning to Zana he said, "You will do well to return to the city. We'll look after him here. There is a car waiting, so you better get going. Will take Berti in the infirmary, until the ambulance arrives. The rest of you disperse! You heard my order—'Disperse!'" he shouted at the top of his voice.

I escorted Zana to the car, without telling her what had happened. I expected that Berti would soon recover from his nervous breakdown.

In the afternoon a green painted ambulance drove in the compound. Several paramedics dressed in white blouses took Berti to the car, despite his protests that he was not ill. He was admitted to the military hospital. After a week a team of doctors concluded that the patient was suffering from neuropsychosis, so he was transferred to the Psychiatric Hospital. Since then, I lost all contact with him, and knew nothing about his fate.

About a year after my discharge from the army, I chanced to run into Zana. Her face had lost the radiance of her youth, but she was still beautiful.

"Do you remember me?" I asked her.

"Yes," she said.

"Where is Berti now? What's happening with him?"

"You don't know?"

I gathered from her question that something tragic had happened to him.

"He committed suicide while undergoing treatment at the hospital. He protested constantly that he was not ill, that they were restraining him for no reason, and that the story he was saying was true. The doctors asked for a report from the military. The reply indicated that no killing had occurred during the term of Berti's service. Afterwards, the hospital's diagnosis on him was auto-suggestive mania. The doctor referred to Berti's condition as a classic case of psychomania without cause. He even related to medical students that the patient, tortured only by own his conscience, was driven to say that he had been forced to shoot at someone he didn't even know. As you may know, Berti insisted on saying that one morning at target practice he was ordered to fire at people half covered with sacks, instead of shooting at the marks with a pattern of rings on them. When his doctor tried to give this story a comical twist Berti's response was resentful and straightforward.

" 'It's the doctor who's telling fairy tales. What I am saying is the truth!' he cried.

"Berti felt that he had been twice dishonored; first he was ordered to kill like an ordinary criminal and then he was labeled a madman. The last time I saw Berti at the hospital; he told me that the stigma of being a mental patient would stay with him for life. Then he begged me not to visit him anymore. One night he jumped from the fourth story to his death."

I asked her if she believed Berti's story.

"Yes!" she replied. "You know that Berti could not tell a lie. That was what I liked most about him. He was so pure a man! After what happened, he could no longer live with himself. At the hospital he used to say to me: 'You must understand that it's because I love you so much, that I'm asking you to stay away from me.' I did understand him very well, and felt sorry for both of us," she said in tears.

I walked away without knowing what to tell her. It seemed pointless to say anything.

ꟈ Dardan's Dilemma ꟈ

A heavy lead-colored sky loomed over the city like a huge cupola about to crack. The dull gray slabs of pavement became infinitely long and sad after the rain of the night before; and it felt as if the swelling weight of the sky would squash everything beneath it. The leaves had already drifted from the trees, and the trunks with their branches resembled withered arms that prayed in silence for something incomprehensible.

The sidewalks retained the cold of the rain. Now and then, a car that had lost its original color, due to age and use, drove down the street. A few people, isolated, silent and enveloped by the vapor of their own breath, walked at a distance from one another. Slabs of concrete, sidewalks of stone, gloomy houses made of liver-colored bricks and crooked walls of adobe gave the city the appearance of a place that suffered from a long and incurable illness. Was the city always like this, or did it just seem that way to him after his father's death?

A Mercedes-Benz drove by, its dark blue color in stark contrast to the glittering chrome of its fenders and door handles. The curtains were drawn so that the government official sitting in the plush seats in the back would not be disturbed by onlookers. Only the faces of the chauffeur and the grave-looking bodyguards across from him could be seen by passers-by.

Dardan checked his wristwatch. It was a quarter to one. Still another forty-five long minutes to go before his appointment. He did not want to sit and wait on the long brown benches in the first floor reception room where petitioners, wrapped up in their problems, wait to be called in. Some impatient claimant would begin right then and there to air his complaint and protest against the injustice done to him, hoping to convince any listener that both fact and reason were on his side, and that the entire matter had been subjectively distorted by some local official. He'd go on ranting even if his poor listeners could do nothing but lend him an ear.

Dardan decided to spend a few more minutes on the bridge over the Lana River by the wide boulevard, watching the stream that flowed underneath between the two banks seemingly undisturbed. His life, which until then had been mostly worry-free, was turned upside down by the death of his father, the first in the family to die. Apart from the emotional upheaval, his father's passing shattered the family materially.

Dardan's thoughts on that bridge streamed along the lines of life and death. Father worked hard to provide for the family. He was a modest man, without pretenses, whims, or excesses. Sometimes he came home happy, other times sad, but he was always in control of himself. He joked and laughed and filled the house with cheer. But after a brief illness, the sun had set quickly on his life. Nobody imagined that he would die so young. How was it possible for a man so strong and powerful in the family to end up like nothing? What is the meaning of death? What does it mean to 'die'?

The finality of death had troubled his young mind. Although he knew quite well that he was not going to resolve the enigma that had puzzled mankind for centuries, he felt inclined to ponder the subject, which had perpetually remained as familiar as it was elusive.

Being a medical student, he had studied the anatomical aspect of death at the university clinic and hospital. His professor had said that birth and death are the two constant poles in every individual's life cycle. Dardan accepted this approach as a philosophical concept, but when death struck his family he could not contemplate it calmly and neutrally. The pain dispersed the venerable philosophical theories, leaving him with unbearable perceptions of loss.

Life had been easy while father was alive, so much so that the cares and woes of those days seemed inconsequential and trivial. But, his father's passing had brought real burdens upon the family. Indeed, he would not be on his way to the Central Committee Building today had his father still been alive.

Heavy in spirit, he walked away from the bridge and headed toward the massive building that dominated the entire side of the boulevard. At the reception window, behind a half-opened glass pane, was the same icy, bland face typical of every secret service member apparently thinking that a stern look added weight to the job. The man at reception looked at him with clouded eyes and indifference. Without actually speaking, his grim expression asked the usual question: "What do you want?"

"I have an appointment with the deputy director, Comrade Refik Kaptelli. I filled out the appointment form yesterday."

The receptionist glanced at a stack of papers on his desk. He leafed through them slowly and indifferently. Bored stiff with those endless petitions for help, he was just about to say that the student's form was not among those in the stack when he got to the last sheet. He took his time looking at it.

"What did you say your name was?"

"Dardan Krasta."

"Your identity card!" he demanded.

After formally verifying the information on the card, he closed the window, dialed a three-digit internal extension number on the phone, and muttered something. Then slowly, in a crooked handwriting, he filled out a sheet on a book perforated in the middle. After tearing out one half of the page, he handed it to Dardan, saying:

"Room 84. Third floor."

The reception cubicle smelled of tobacco smoke and boredom.

As he climbed the stairs, the student asked himself, "Why do these government employees behave like this? Who has robbed them of their smiles and good manners?"

He walked up the marble steps and came to a long corridor faintly lit by thick, cream-colored globes that hung from the ceiling like distant constellations. He could not even hear the sound of his own footsteps because they were muffled by the dark cherry-colored carpet. At every turn there were guards who routinely asked to see the permit sheet. After noting the number of the room, they pointed in the direction he was to take. Silence reigned, as in an ancient temple where mystical rituals were being practiced. The whole setting compelled one to talk either quietly or in whispers, so that no sound at all would reach the office where the Chief was working. He was not to be distracted from his profound thinking; nor should one cloud the refined Marxist train of thought that he was generating at that very moment. Dardan had heard someone say that people telling impromptu jokes in the hallways had once so enraged the Chief that he burst from his office full of anger, scolding the culprits with a piercing scowl. Afterwards, an order was automatically implemented in the Central Committee Building and nobody in that vicinity dared to laugh, or talk in a loud voice. Indeed, people made sure that they even turned the doorknobs gently, so as not to disturb anyone.

In the last corridor – he had lost count of the hallways he had passed through – an officer got up from his chair, looked at Dardan's sheet of paper, and then accompanied him to Room No. 84. A cold gold-colored knob flashed brightly on the heavy brown door. Dardan knocked gently on it, but no invitation to enter came from within. He then dared to knock a little harder. The heavy door seemed to open by itself, and Dardan found himself in front of the very person he had asked to meet. The man got up from his armchair and reached out from his desk to shake hands.

"Please sit down," he said.

The student sat.

The official put his elbows on the desk, and his chin on the arch formed by his arms and crossed fingers. His eyes were of an indefinite color – somewhat gray, somewhat green, but somewhat murky, like the waters of a cold sea; his thin lips were pursed on a pallid face rarely seen by the sun. He had big ears like those of a bat, which were strangely yellow with bloodless earlobes and triangular cartilage. As a medical student, Dardan had never seen such ears before. These features sat well with an exacting and scrupulous government employee, one who took his responsibilities very seriously. There were two phones on the desk, one black, and the other cream-colored. On the reddish marble slab on top of the desk, there was a cup with a few pens and sharpened pencils in it. Nearly an entire wall was filled with glass-enclosed shelves of books, along with a few art objects of alabaster, porcelain and colored glass. At the center of the bookcase was a space left for a television. But in that space instead was the imposing bust of the Chief. Its sculptor had poured all of his talents into portraying a statesman, a deep thinker with wrinkles on his brow, and eyes that looked far into the distance to emphasize the Leader's determination and revolutionary optimism.

"Go right ahead, I'm listening."

The young medical student, whose eyes had been fixed on the bust, was so startled by the director's words that he stood up at once, as if he were in lecture hall.

"It's quite all right; you can speak sitting down. We're not in class here," he said in an official neutral voice, neither cordial, nor cold.

For a moment, it seemed senseless to involve this member of the state in such a maelstrom of student woes. Moments later Dardan felt that such behavior would be regarded as neurotic, and he did not in any way want to leave the deputy director of the Department of Education and Culture with a negative impression. He reminded himself that he had pinned all his hopes on this meeting, following the useless runaround to numerous offices in various institutions. He had endured so much just to get to this office under the highest of cupolas. As in the old tales, he had reached the last boundary of hope. Farther than this, he could not go.

"Two months ago," the student began, "we had a great misfortune in our family. My father died. Death is always painful, and naturally parents go before the children. But father died before retiring on his pension."

Looking at the face of the official, he wondered whether the man was listening. Dardan began thinking: "There's no reason why he should be sad about my father. How can he feel sorry for a man he has never seen? It's the same as if someone told me that an Eskimo had died near the North Pole."

Dardan continued his story. "The loss and pain will always stay with us. But apart from that, he left us in a very difficult financial situation. Mother's a homemaker. I'm a student in my final year. All along, we had to pay for boarding school and tuition because I was not eligible for a scholarship. Plus, I also have a younger sister."

The official acknowledged this with a nod.

"As things stand now, I'm not at all able to continue my studies, since, according to the law, my mother is entitled to only half of her husband's pension, and that's all we have left to live on. Father provided my monthly allowance, which included school, books, boarding and incidental expenses. But now the family can't put aside any money from his pension..."

"What does your sister do?" asked the man behind the desk, as he unlocked his arms and put his right hand on his forehead. His long, thin, cream-colored fingers were the same color as the plaster-of-Paris bust behind his back.

"She is a first-year high school student."

"According to the law, you are not entitled to a scholarship because your monthly income is slightly over the limit. If the income were under the standard amount, then your complaint would be taken into consideration," the official said, gently scratching the top of his head with his little finger.

"Excuse me, but we also have to support our grandmother. Actually, she is my father's aunt. But since she was living all by herself, father brought her home to live with us. With her in the household, our income comes to less than the legal norm."

The deputy director cleared his throat as he began to speak.

"However, she is not a member of the family," he remarked.

"She has been living with us for forty years. She is an old woman now, over eighty years old. She raised us. She is a grandmother to us, and in fact that's what we call her."

"You need to appeal to the university. This matter comes under their jurisdiction. They will look at your documents and proof of income, and then make a decision in accordance with the guidelines."

"But I appealed to them a long time ago," Dardan explained. "I submitted all the relevant documents, along with a letter in which I explained the specific situation. I've knocked on their door several times for an answer, but all in vain...."

Dardan looked closely at the face across the desk, hoping to detect the slightest nuance of understanding or emotion. But Comrade Kaptelli remained serious, impassive and cold, just like an expressionless plaster mask.

"Take your case to your district!" The student watched the lips of the director move but only moments later realized that the voice he had heard came from them.

"But a week after father died, I went over to the Bureau of Education and informed them. In fact, they already knew about my misfortune, since our town is small and news gets around quickly. They told me that they had done their duty when they allowed me to go to college. When I said that now I was entitled to a scholarship, they replied that they had filled their quota for granting scholarships in September, and that scholarships in mid-year are granted by the university, not by the district. I then appealed again to the university. The Dean told me that, unfortunately, without the approval of the district, they couldn't grant any scholarships. As a result, I went back to the district, and the matter is still pending there."

"What was your father's profession?"

"He was a pharmacist. He always worked in the smaller districts."

All of a sudden, the official's eyes gleamed.

"Pharmacists have money. Your father must have left you something." The observation smacked of a joke or a hint of sarcasm.

"The pharmacy was government-owned right after liberation, and since that time, father received only a salary."

The director rested his chin once again on his crossed fingers. His look turned icy immediately.

"I don't understand what you want from me. I mean, from us," he said, coldly.

What was so obscure and incomprehensible about Dardan's complaint? Had he failed to express himself clearly? For a moment, the student felt a sense of guilt, but got over it quickly and said:

"I'm asking for my rights. They refused to give me the scholarship I'm entitled to...."

"We don't have anything to do with scholarships. You have come to the wrong office."

The remark pierced him through and through like a cold arrow. For an instant, he couldn't breathe.

"I have come here to complain about an injustice. I was given the runaround by both the district bureau and the university. That's why I'm here...." He looked at the marble slab, the telephones, the lamp, the director's torso behind the desk, and in back of him the white plaster sculpture of the Leader looking forward to a happy future.

"Please, help me! I cannot complete my studies. Must I quit medical school in my fourth year?"

The official raised an eyebrow, as if to say: "That's your business."

"My family has pinned all its hopes on me. They can hardly wait for me to finish my studies and get my diploma."

The functionary seemed annoyed by Dardan's stubbornness. He lifted his elbows from the desk and shifted slightly in his chair as if trying to slide into the background of his own office.

"Think back to the time when you yourself were a student," Dardan said, trying to appeal to the sentimental side of Comrade Kaptelli in the hope that he would gain a better appreciation of the problem. "I'm not asking for money to spend in a disco, or to go wining and dining. I want only to be given the chance to continue my studies. Had my father died in the summer, I would have been given the scholarship in September, right? I have come to ask for your help, because I don't know where else to turn to...."

"I believe you know that with us everything is planned and scheduled beforehand, and you know very well that the scholarship quota for the current year has been met. Therefore…." his lips closed tightly and resolutely.

"As a citizen, I'm asking for my rights, in accordance with the law and regulations. I'm only asking to get what I'm entitled to, no more, no less."

The person across from him moved neither his hands, nor head, nor lips. Only his eyelashes maintained their rhythmic motion.

"I have only one year left; actually only seven months. Wouldn't it be a shame to interrupt my studies and fail to graduate? That would be a loss not only to the family and me personally, but also to society. After I graduate, you can send me to the most remote godforsaken district there is, and I swear, I'll work with every bit of my strength. I'm ready to put that in writing, and file that pledge with the Office of the University, or the Ministry if necessary. Just give me the chance to complete my studies."

Everything in the room: the telephones, the lamp on the desk, the bookshelves, the deputy director and the sculpture were all enveloped by a light gray fog, making Dardan think that the window had been left open, and that steam had been let in. From the window the sky looked the same as before, lead-like and silent. He understood then that the hazy appearance of the objects around him had come from his emotions veiling his eyes. He felt embarrassed to succumb to such a weakness at his age, and quickly fluttering his eyelashes so as to conceal the mist of tears, he got up on his feet.

"Please, help me! I'm not asking for a favor, only justice. You are my last hope."

The face of the official preserved its eternal silence. Not one muscle stirred upon it. Even its gaze became fixed. Dardan looked more closely, leaning slightly towards the director whose face was now the same color as the plaster bust behind the desk. Then instinctively Dardan looked up.

"Aren't you even listening to me?"

No answer. Suddenly it appeared that there were now two busts in the office, and he just didn't know how to account for it. Doubt began to overcome him: "Who have I been talking to all this time? There is no one here. Just these two busts." The student began to rub his forehead nervously, and sensed that his fingertips were moist. Searching for an explanation, he looked around the office. Everything there was so clean, immovable and totally alien.

"Excuse me. I'm leaving," he said to the bust at the desk, as he eyed it with trepidation.

He waited for a response, a word, or even a nod. Not a sound. Complete silence. Walking backwards, he began to withdraw from the office, and the last image he had was that of a frozen man dressed in a beige jacket and a black tie with red polka dots. He opened the door and closed it quietly behind him so he would not disturb the two sculptures in the office. As he walked down the corridor, the image of the stolid, shirt-and-tie official who had turned to stone hovered over him. In the long and dusky corridor, lit up only by ceiling lights, a reflection of the cherry-colored carpet gave the walls a reddish hue. On both sides of the hallway, there were heavy wooden doors with bronze knobs of a blood-red tint. Suddenly he felt the urge to hear his own footsteps, but the paths of red had absorbed every sound with an unquenchable thirst. In the long corridors there was not a living soul except for the guards motionless at every corner as if they too had turned to stone. Though they eyed him surreptitiously, it did not faze him. All he wanted now was to get out of there as soon as possible, and encounter living people once again.

The pavement was still wet in some places from the rain. The light gray flagstones alternated with dark gray ones. Geometric figures in wavy patterns formed absurd and erratic designs of beasts and demoniacal creatures that grappled with one another. Fearing he would tread on them, Dardan zigzagged around them like a man possessed.

"If I step on them, they might start to howl and come after me... I must be delirious. What am I doing on this street? Where have I been…? I just can't remember."

Feeling the need to hear his own voice, he let out a scream. But, it was swallowed up by the city's drab gray buildings and downcast sky. It appeared that some inexplicable phenomenon of the rain the night before had turned everything to stone. Wishing he were back at his dorm, Dardan started walking faster and faster, and then began to run. Ahead of him, the street rose and fell in waves.

ꕥ The Investigation ꕥ

"Is that you Ali?" the secretary of the Minister of Internal Affairs asked on the phone, to make sure he was speaking to the right person.

"Yes, that's me."

"Come quickly to the Minister's office. It's urgent!" he informed him, and promptly hung up.

Emergencies in the Ministry of Internal Affairs were daily occurrences. In fact, the word "urgent" usually made no impression. However, when the call came from the top man, the matter had to be taken seriously. Ali Kapllani got on his feet at once; unconsciously tugged the corners of his jacket and buttoned it, then locked the office door and went quickly up the stairs. Many of the older government employees in the Ministry of Internal Affairs went around dressed in civilian clothes, but not the Director of Investigations. He could not conceive of someone walking into a security institution without a uniform. To him, the police officer's uniform meant more attention, dignity, as well as more importance in the eyes of the public. His close relatives and friends agreed. Section heads like him were only one-step below vice ministers. He could not understand why some people, especially young people, looked down on the police. Actually, very few young people in the cities bothered to put on the blue uniform worn by the police. Not surprisingly, the ranks of the police force were filled with country people from the hinterlands who had only a junior high or grade school education. In the mind of Ali Kapllani, contempt for the police was understandable in the anti-popular regimes of the past. The law enforcement officers of the new government deserved to be respected and honored for their valuable services. Then, the police jokes were ugly manifestations that the reactionary circles sought to incite hatred for the people's police. Deep in his subconscious, Ali felt bad about one thing, only. Copying the Chinese model, the Albanian Party did away with military ranks, viewing that step as a revolutionary measure, which would make citizens value merits, rather than bow down blindly before rank. Though he accepted the elimination of ranks, without ever expressing his irritation to anyone, whenever he looked at himself in the mirror, he imagined how graceful he would look with a colonel's gold epaulettes on his shoulders, with two stripes and three stars. At any rate, he had held the post of Director of Investigations for years, thanks to his ability and superb chameleon-like maneuverings, despite his limited education.

As soon as he entered the office of the Minister, Ali gave the war-time soldier's salute. The Minister nodded, but did not reciprocate with a military salute. He pointed at a chair for him to sit in.

"We've received an anonymous letter," the Minister said, getting to the point right away.

Ali's face darkened at once upon hearing this unexpected news.

"About me?" he inquired, recalling the headaches he had had, with two such letters that were sent from his birth town. Seeing that he was shaken up, the Minister hastened to calm him down.

"No, no, they're not about you," he said, with a hint of a smile.

The Minister got up from his desk, opened the safe box and pulled out a thin file. His boots crackled on the parquet floor, as if he were stepping on frozen snow. As always, from the waist down the Minister wore military attire and civilian clothing from the waist up, to make clear the dual nature of his duties.

"According to my information, there has been a dramatic increase in anonymous letters in recent times. The situation calls for an immediate investigation, since the matter pertains much more to us than to others." He stressed the pronoun "us," then waited for Ali's reaction, which contained a head nod.

"In my opinion, there are two possible reasons. Either our officials violate the regulations for reasons having to do with pull, friendships, etc., or we are dealing with an increase in hostile activity."

"No doubt about it. This is the result of stepped-up enemy activity at a delicate moment." The Director of Investigations knew from experience that the tougher he was with the class enemies, the greater the Minister's respect for him.

"Don't be rash. Haste can harm your profession," the Minister rebuked him.

He did not expect such a remark that hit him like a cold shower.

"We know that most of the letters come from the class enemies," the Minister continued. "They write to discredit our officials, the policies of the Party and its correct line. Some are written by those who vent their fury and personal grudges and animosities, by making political accusations to discredit new executives who move on to higher positions. Their aim is to bury them with half-truths or mere gossip. In the meantime, we cannot deny that others who have nothing against the system write some of the letters; because they are too timid to come out in the open and feel defenseless against the vengeance of officials vested with power. Albanians do not take open criticism graciously, no matter what we say in our podiums and newspapers."

The Director of Investigations was somewhat surprised by the reasoning of his Minister. He had never before heard him explain issues in such detail. Only, he was not sure whether his deductions were his own, or whether he had picked them up at some convention. At any rate, they expressed undeniable truths, which are why Ali tried to memorize them and repeat them to his subordinates, to astound them.

The Minister opened the file.

"The letter is addressed personally to the Minister of Internal Affairs. The anonymous writer in this particular case denounces the 'Chief of Police' of the locality of Kurore," – he stopped looking at the letter – "someone by the name of Aziz Diku. Allegedly he has beaten up a villager in his own office. For whatever reason, the letter has indicated the name of the villager only by his initials. The author explains that he did not dare reveal the name, for fear of the Chief of Police. I find this particularly upsetting because the anonymous writer might address the same identical letter elsewhere" – and he pointed to the headquarters across the street. "They will ask whether we know anything about this, and might criticize our Ministry for incompetence. I trust you appreciate what trouble this letter can cause us..."

He tapped the letter with his finger several times, as if the blame lay with that puny hand-written letter.

"This letter has upset me a great deal and made me think," the Minister said, raising his voice. "The laws have to be respected at all times, and it is the duty of the police to protect the citizens, not pass judgment on them and punish them. There are other bodies for adjudicating the citizens. Those who use the stick, whether they mean to or not, discredit the government of the people." Exasperated, he stretched his arm toward the detailed map of the country hanging on the wall, as if to emphasize those defiant actions like that, were taking place elsewhere.

"Some of our policemen find it easier to use their fists, instead of their tongue," the Director of Investigations was quick to agree.

"No, no, no!" thundered the Minister. "We cannot allow that. There is no reason why our police should be feared by the people, and still less reason to be hated. They should be the most cherished of all people. What's going on out there? We have more than a few police officers in our ranks that are plain ignorant, without much schooling. Does he believe that 'Chief of Police' implies that he has full power to do as he pleases. Definitely not!" the head of the Ministry said decisively. "As a government department, we too," – the Minister lowered his voice – "have our faults. Many times, when we've received reports of official misconduct, we have been soft on the culprits and made excuses for them, saying: he is a good chap, or he comes from a low-income bracket...and other nonsense like that. We went no further than to give them a word of advice, or transfer them somewhere. From now on, they will be relieved of their posts, fired on the spot! It's the only way to deal with blockheads and put an end to their arrogance. The time has come to rid the police of unqualified personnel. You have full authority to dig up the facts on location. I expect a full and accurate report, as soon as you get back." With a brisk motion of his hand, he drew an invisible vertical line in the air, then handed him the anonymous letter.

Ali folded the letter and put it in his portfolio.

"This is urgent!" were the final words of the Minister.

* * *

As an experienced investigator, Ali Kapllani was well aware of how difficult it was to verify anonymous letters. It's like looking for a spider's thread, which is visible only when lit up by the rays of the sun; or a rill of water that is seen one moment, then disappears in the sand. There was a good chance that the victimized villager would deny that he was beaten up, to save himself from embarrassment, or out of fear that the matter might get even messier, if he spoke up. The Investigator would not even be surprised, if the beaten villager praised the police officer that had given him a thrashing.

Incidents of this sort were commonplace. The mentality of the people in the northeastern part of the country was such that a bullet wound was shown with pride, as if it were an act of heroism, while a beating was shameful. They would try to hide the scars and bruises, and never reported them to the police. Sadly, they didn't even go to a doctor to get a medical report for time off from work, or a prescription. Striking a man in public was formerly avenged with a bullet, since it was seen as the gravest humiliation. It resulted in a blood feud between families that lasted for generations, just as the Unwritten Law of the land prescribed. Times had changed, and nobody dared to antagonize the authorities over a slap in the face, or a kick in the pants from a public official. Instead, they kept their mouth shut, as if nothing had happened. However, the investigator did not know what stand the victim was going to take. If he was going to deny the beating, Ali Kapllani had no other option than to obtain a written statement from him, saying that the whole affair was fabricated, and there were no complaints against the Chief of Police and the case would be closed. If he were to admit the beating, then the Chief of Police was going to pay for it.

The wheels of the car rolled down the asphalt road, and the monotonous hum of the engine plunged Ali into thought. From the car radio, there came sounds of light music.

"Let's have some folk music!" the Director ordered.

"Can't get a good signal out here," the driver said in self-defense. "Besides, music is something to delight the ear, isn't that so?"

"No, no, because that's how alien influences infiltrate," Ali objected. "First, you have a liking for the music, then for the fashions, then for the ideology. We know about these things. Did you read the recent speech on youth?"

"Oh, yes," replied the driver, who never took the trouble to read anything, since he picked up all the news he needed from the comments he heard from officials, while driving them around. However, he was well informed about the conservative viewpoints of the Director of Investigations, so he thought the best thing to do was to turn the radio off and keep quiet.

Among the hills, the steel frames of high-tension wires seemed like fabled giants proudly holding up the power lines. Shortly, they would arrive in the new miners' town built twenty years earlier, in the wake of the chrome ore discovered by a team of Soviet geologists. It was said that the Soviets were false friends, who tried to conceal the mining site, but the vigilance of the Party scuttled their devilish plans. Ali recalled that chrome topped the list of export items, and was a good source of foreign currency. The town spread out in the wretched open space, without a speck of beauty. On the slope of the hill across, Ali's eyes met the popular slogan in glimmering white stone, hailing Albania's top leader.

Again, he thought that the members of the Politburo that he knew did not have the authority, the political acumen and the leadership qualities of the Chief. He was the helmsman of the Party's ship, which sailed successfully amid the treacherous waves of politics. Ali adored him, and worried that after his death, the country would plunge into disorder, since no one could take his place.

Reaching over his shoulder, the driver offered the Director a cigarette from his pack. Ali wondered whether he should pollute the air around him, which he called the "microclimate." Seeing that the chauffeur was going to light one up, he figured it made sense to keep him company.

Down in the valley below, could be seen the little houses of a village. They were widely separated from one another, and each one had a little garden, cultivated fields and meadows. In the middle of a green plot of ground, there was the building of a new school. Some kids were playing ball in the yard. Two girls in gray pants, and a young man in a blue jumper, were waiting by the side of the road for a passing automobile to take them to the city. As soon as they spotted the approaching vehicle, one of the girls tried to attract their attention by waving her arm and smiling with a pleading look on her face. The driver turned to the Director to hand him his cigarette lighter, and directed his attention to the people standing by the road. Ali only frowned, and the car sped by without slowing down, just as if nobody were there.

"Don't waste your time to ask for my approval," Ali chastised him. "One never knows about hitchhikers."

The driver glanced at the side mirror, and noticed that the young woman was still waving, though her smile was becoming faint. The Director was cautious, as he did not want to be criticized for riding with anyone with a politically undesirable past. To the driver, the chance passengers presented a possibility to compensate for his small wages. He stepped on the gas pedal, to vent his anger at the Director for depriving him of some extra income.

"It's hot!" said the chauffeur, as he rolled down the window on his side. Even in the highlands, one felt the sweltering heat of August.

The Director did not bother to continue the futile chat. A week before, Ali Kapllani had investigated the death of a forest ranger. It was not a political matter, so the investigation ended quickly. For two days, the guardian of the law hunted pheasants and wild pigeons in the forest, even though it was not yet open season for hunting. Usually, in August he took time off from work, and made arrangements to stay in one of the villas at the beach. He would get his family there, in a comfortable minibus of the Ministry free of charge, on the pretext that he was on duty. To those who complained that the beaches were overcrowded, Ali's response was that the congestion was the clearest evidence that the government of the people had created conditions for all citizens to relax and amuse themselves by the sea, which formerly was the privilege only of the rich. Still, there were some who abused their noble duty, as, for example, the "Chief of Police" of Kurore, who had beaten up a villager in an office of the state. Whether he realized it or not, by that action he drove a wedge between the people and the security apparatus in a state where 'the police were the guardian angels of the common people'. The Director recalled the popular saying about a bad apple. If the Chief of Police was to going to suffer the consequences of his irresponsible deed, he had no one to blame but himself. It was up to the investigator to cut off all avenues of escape, by confronting him with the facts and incontestable proofs.

In town, the Director of Investigations met with the chairman of the local Internal Affairs office, a tall, suave man who looked like a physical trainer. Ali did not tell him the purpose of his visit. Intentionally, he held back, thinking that the chairman might by chance have friendly ties with the Chief of Police, which could cloud the trail of the investigation. He just told him that he had to go to the locality of Kurore.

"Would you like us to escort you?" the chairman asked, showing understanding of the nature of their work. "Or at least let us show you the way there," he added jokingly.

"It's enough that I meet the Chief of Police," Ali retorted.

"The Chief is a good man," said the other. Then lowering the esteem for the Chief a notch or two, went on with a smile, "All things considered. Frankly, he is somewhat repulsive in manners, but you have no idea how transparent he is. He will never let honored guests sleep in that dump of a hotel, but I suppose you'll be back tonight. Shall we have dinner here?"

The Director did not want to commit himself definitely, so he said merely, "We shall see."

* * *

Not wanting to attract the attention of the farmers, Ali left the car and his driver in the shade of some sycamore trees, over by a meadow, and set out on foot for the center of the local town. "Just like a detective," he grinned.

He met with the local party secretary in the hope that the Party functionary would help him out. In truth, he was disillusioned and was not able to draw out anything of interest. Relations between the two were not friendly. The Party secretary complained that the Chief of Police did as he pleased, without consulting the Party, on the pretext that his tasks were confidential. Ali jotted down in his notebook that the Chief of Police did not coordinate his actions with the local Party officials. In his judgment, this situation had its roots in the clannish attitudes that were evident in the northern regions. While the clan chiefs were gone along with the old regime, the new clan chiefs had emerged from the ranks of the Party and state functionaries, who disregarded the laws. The secretary told him that nobody had complained to him about getting beat up.

Ali thought that he might get more accurate information from that the People's local Council. Its chairman, whose body was shaped like an egg, projected instantly the image of a sluggish man. Even inside his office, he had his shirt unbuttoned down to his belly button, and continuously kept soaking up the sweat of his body with a towel. The Director of Investigations introduced himself and explained the purpose of his visit. The local council chairman looked at him sideways, with suspicion.

"Do you have any identification document with you? All kinds of people profess to be officials, you know."

Rather astounded that the official in a forgotten town would be so vigilant in implementing regulations, Ali showed him the identification papers from the Ministry of Internal Affairs. In fact, the chairman had been played for a fool by a visiting journalist who posed as a senior government official and gave orders of hiring and firing people at the council. The incident was a re-enactment on a small scale, more than a century later, of Gogol's comedy, *The Inspector General.*

"Well, now, let's hear what brings you here," the council chairman said.

"I believe you know all the villagers by name. I want to know who is this L.K., who allegedly was mistreated by the Chief of Police," he said, as he reached into his pocket for the anonymous letter.

"Elkay?" remarked the chairman with a frown. To nudge his memory, he shut one eye and began to scratch his ear. "We don't have any such person around here. The name does not ring a bell with me."

The Director of Investigation tried to explain that L. and K. were the initials of the first and last name of the villager. "How can we find this person?"

The Chairman remained indifferent, as if he had not heard anything. The investigator started to suspect that perhaps the Chairman was trying to keep the person in question out of sight. Ali continued to suggest likely names, but was unable to break the Chairman's stoical silence.

A man with a thick mustache walked into the office without knocking. He had a careless air about him, but the moment he noticed Ali he greeted him with a military salute.

"Oh, Mark! Do you know who the Chief of Police has beaten up lately?" asked the Chairman.

"What an ass!" Ali said to himself. "Who gave him permission to bring up the subject?" He definitely did not want to broaden the scope of the investigation beyond the official staff, but was unable to head the Chairman off. Nevertheless, the question implied that the Chief of Police used that method of education frequently.

Mark squinted as he tried to bring to mind all the sinners who had the misfortune to run the gauntlet of Chief's blows.

"By golly, it's kind of hard to remember..." Mark grinned, as if to absolve himself in front of the stranger. Suddenly, his face lit up. "Ah, yes; he beat up that Vuksan Ndreu. Son of a gun!"

"He drubbed Vuksan in the spring, when we were mowing the grasslands," the Chairman corrected him. "Before spring, before...."

"Mehdi Imeri was beaten so badly that his false teeth flew out the window."

The Director of Investigations drew him in his turf, by repeating the initials of the victim's name.

Mark raised his eyes toward the ceiling, as if he were meditating. Just then, he seemed to see a light in the darkness and declared:

"I got it! Liman Kazani. He beat him within an inch of his life," he said, making no effort to hide his enthusiasm for Chief Aziz.

"Well, well, it seems we found who 'Mr. Elkay' is."

"Mark, go and fetch him here, will you?" the Chairman told him.

"No, no!" objected Ali. "All I need is for Mark to show me his house."

"As you wish," said the Chairman.

Just ahead lay the most delicate phase of the investigation, and he did not want the villager to be intimidated by the shadow of offices and officials. He was going to conduct the investigation face to face with him, in as friendly and intimate a setting as possible.

He had to wait a bit in the yard, because the head of the house was watering the garden. Seeing that someone had come to his home, Liman looked upon him as a friend of the family, even though his face did not seem familiar. Ali noticed that, unlike other men, he had not tied his head piece around his cap, but below it, apparently to conceal the bruises from the beating. The Director began by asking indirect questions. To his surprise, Liman came right to the point. He took his cap off, unwrapped the head kerchief and triumphantly showed him the bump he had received from his skirmish with the Chief of Police, twelve days earlier.

"What did he hit you with?" Ali asked like a professional, so as to get his hands on indisputable facts about the recent brawl.

"With just anything. With his hands, his fists, his feet.... He also had something hard in his hand, but I couldn't tell what it was. Everything went dark."

Ali examined the size, location, form and color of the bump, and made the appropriate notations in his notebook.

"What was the cause of it all?" he asked, in the end.

"I do not know. He came at me like a wild boar, and all he said was 'Shut your trap or I'll beat the life out of you,' and kept hitting me right and left, like I was a punching bag."

The indignation of the Director reached its peak.

"Look here," he said to Liman in a friendly manner. "The police are not permitted to engage in violent actions of that kind, and he must answer for what he did. Only, you got to issue a statement about what happened in the office of the Chief of Police." Seeing however that Liman was hesitant, he added, "Or, more simply, repeat what you told me in the presence of Chief Aziz Diku. Do you understand?"

Ali waited nervously for his answer. He knew that this was not easy for a man without any protection.

"Any time," Liman replied decisively, without fear of the consequences of such a confrontation.

"Great!" Ali said, congratulating him. "You are doing the right thing as a law binding citizen. Have no fear. Nothing will happen to you, believe me," he said, to reassure him. He felt that the highlands still had strong men of character and this simple villager, Liman Kazani, was an example of their dignity, virtue and honor.

In a little while, the arrogant Aziz Diku was not going to be Chief of Police, but a villager like all the rest, who bend down and work with the hoe. The investigator had all the facts at hand to deal him a decisive blow, when he confronted him. He had checkmated him, leaving him no opening to weasel his way out. There was no need either for paper work, or for involving other courts. The testimonies and especially the bump on the head of Liman Kazani were sufficient evidence to fire him on the spot, in accordance with the instructions of the Minister himself. Ali was curious to see what this police officer looked like. Perhaps a career officer who had worked his way up cunningly like a fox, or a beast who had badly abused his authority, and brought discredit to the security agency and the police. His conduct was unacceptable and was in extreme violation of the rules. It was time to draft an Internal Memo at the Ministry, concerning the reasons for the immediate dismissal of the Chief of Police of Kurore.

* * *

Aziz Diku was polishing the buttons of his jacket with cleaning paste, when the Director of Investigations walked into his office. The face of the Chief of Police lit up, as soon as he learned of his visitor's identity. Guests of such a high position had never set foot in the region of Kurore.

At once, he put on his jacket with the shining buttons, and stood at attention. First, Ali took note of his big, fleshy nose, which made him look peculiar, while his eyes surprisingly were small and cunning. His hands were huge and full of knots, the hands of a villager who had done heavy work, from the time he was a child. His office was so plain, with hardly any furniture. Its bare and dreary appearance, made one feel deeply sad. There was a desk, two crooked chairs, and a niche with a black, cube-shaped telephone, which had to be cranked by hand, before one could dial with it.

The Chief of Police offered him a cheap cigarette, of the kind he smoked himself. Ali declined which wiped the least social bond between them. He opened his briefcase, took out a hand-written letter, and carefully dropped it on his desk.

"Chief Aziz," he said seriously. "The Ministry has received a letter, in which someone makes the accusation that you beat up a citizen in your office."

"A villager!" protested Aziz.

"A citizen!" insisted the investigator. "The law specifies that all residents are citizens," he said, clarifying the terminology.

"I am glad I did," Chief Aziz declared firmly.

"What a blockhead! Instead of denying it, or finding some sort of excuse, he is confirming it openly," Ali said to himself. He walked up to the window, signaled someone with his head, and then opened the door. In came Liman Kazani, his eyebrows lowered and ready to confront the guardian of law and order.

"What are you doing here?" roared the Chief of Police. "Who asked you to come here?"

Needing help, Liman turned toward the man who had come from the Capital. Ali motioned to him to sit down in the chair beside him, face to face with Chief Aziz.

"Was it here, in this office that he struck you?" the Investigator asked him.

The Chief of Police snorted angry blasts of air through his huge nose.

"Here…," stuttered the villager, not daring to look anyone in the eye.

"It looks like the beating didn't do him any good...," Aziz declared, shaking his head angrily, which showed that he had not gotten over his feelings of hostility toward him.

Shocked by the remark of the Chief of Police, which was as conceited as it was incriminating, the Director decided to bring the confrontation to a head.

"How dare you talk like this?" he rebuked the police officer. "No one has given you the right to inflict physical punishment on citizens. You have violated the code of the law enforcement forces, abused your authority and have dishonored the name of the police officers."

The Chief of Police could hardly keep still. He struggled to control himself, until the investigator from Tirana finished spouting those long and convoluted phrases of his.

"Ask him, ask him why I smashed him," Chief Aziz went on, pointing his finger closer and closer to the head of Liman Kazani, and bringing the matter down to a practical level.

"Whatever wrongs are committed by the citizens, our legal system prescribes punishment as set forth in statutory articles and provisions, and determined by the People's Courts."

"He has said...."

"Excuse me," the Director interrupted. "The citizen enjoys freedom of speech, freedom of thought, freedom of assembly, freedom of the press, all of which are sanctioned by the Constitution. You must understand this."

Above the Chief's head, the portrait of the top leader seemed to follow with particular interest the debate that was taking place in the office.

"Even if the 'constitution' allows him, I do not," thundered Chief Aziz Diku. "The idea of him going around talking nonsense...."

"What has he said?" Ali asked off-handedly. "Whatever it was, you have no right to beat him up."

"No right?" Aziz shot back, astounded and offended. "Is it all right for this swine to say in front of other men that the top leader stripped the villagers of their land, their livestock, their pastures and left them out to dry?"

The Director's eyes nearly popped out of their sockets, when he heard those blasphemous and hostile comments about the Party leader.

"How is that? Tell me once more," he implored him, as he could not believe his own ears.

The Chief of Police asserted once more the grave verbal delinquency and added that his information was correct, since it had come to him from two different sources.

Had his chair been equipped with a catapult device, the Director would not have jumped on his feet any faster. He had never heard such spoken blasphemy from anyone. It was a monstrous fabrication, designed to sow discontent among the villagers. His eyes flashed with anger, as he looked upon the villager who was crouching on the floor, as if he were praying.

"This one here said that, huh?" Ali said, wanting to make sure.

"That's him, all right!" confirmed Aziz, as he pointed his fat finger like a lance at the head of Liman.

"You filthy mutt," exploded the Director of Investigations, "you scum, ragged moron! Idiot! Do you realize who gave you freedom?" Drops of spit spewed from his mouth like shotgun pellets. He started to strike him with his fists, as if he wanted to create a certain symmetry in the bumps on his head.

Chief Aziz was watching with special pleasure much impressed by the Investigator's rapid-fire blows, as the villager huddled down to the floor. To ward off a cloudburst of blows, he crawled on his hands and knees and made a dash for the door. His burst through the door was accelerated by a kick in the pants, as he made his escape. The Chief picked up Liman's cap, which had dropped on the floor, and hurled it out through the open window.

"You should have killed the shit-head," Ali said, foaming in the mouth. His hands were trembling. "This guy deserves to be handcuffed!" Turning to the Chief of Police, he ordered: "Draft a report for the district attorney, charging him with a felony crime."

Chief Aziz did not budge.

"Did you hear what I said?" blurted the high official from the Ministry.

"Let the poor devil go. He has a flock of kids to care for…."

The Director insisted that, under the circumstances, Liman Kazani had to be tried and sentenced, to prevent the spread of such reactionary ideas among the villagers.

"If it were only him...," Chief said, casually. "Others talk like that in narrower circles."

"In my opinion, they should be prosecuted," the Director of Investigations insisted.

"In court? No, never!" objected Aziz. "Such accusations do more harm than good."

Just then, the Director recalled a secret memo that advised judges and prosecutors that the name of the top party leader were never to be mentioned in court. The Chief of Police had done the right thing to close that delicate incident, with a few "educational" punches. Good for him! Ali Kapllani gave points to the Chief of Police for his cleverness.

Strapping a huge revolver, Chief Aziz tightened his belt and headed for the door.

"Well, shall we go to my house?" he invited Ali as if he had known him for years. "We've completed our work here, I believe. We do have a hotel here, but it's crawling with bugs so badly, they can lift you off your bed at night. Besides, the joint is a stop for truck drivers and the mattresses reek of gasoline," Aziz said, scornfully putting down the hotel.

"I'm thinking of getting back to town," Ali said, unsure of himself.

"What's the hurry, my friend? The town isn't going anywhere." Then, he added casually, "I have a fine goat at home, ready to roast. Resmia will cook it in the time it takes us to have a cup of coffee and a smoke."

The goat tipped the scales in favor of staying in Kurore. The Director remembered what the local chairman of Internal Affairs had told him about the Chief of Police. The investigation was complete and he could well dine in those refreshing highlands.

"Well, I made a semi-commitment to the chairman about tonight," the Director of Investigations remarked obliquely.

"Don't worry! We can invite him to join us," Aziz said to reassure him. "He is an old buddy of mine."

It was obvious which chairman he was referring to. Chief Aziz picked up the handset and started to dial locally on the rotary phone.

"Hello? Internal Affairs Office? The chairman, please.... Who is calling? The Chief of Police of Kurore."

ꟸ It's in the Statute ꟹ

Up until the third year in college, neither his classmates, nor his experienced instructors could detect any special talent or ability in him. As far as one could see, Adrian Mekshi had no talent for science, art or sport. He was one of those students who helter-skelter out of classes and muddle through school. He did not stand out in any area. No passions, no caprices.

In the fourth year, however, as if shaking off his lethargy, Adrian astounded everyone with the zeal he showed for a course that everybody else shunned; namely, "The Statute of the Agricultural Cooperatives." Being fully aware that knowledge about the Statute was pure theory and would never be of any use to them in practice, students of agronomy paid little attention to it. Perhaps the stark contrast between Adrian's attitude and theirs, regarding the Statute, was the reason that his zeal seemed so eccentric. Could it be that he had taken to heart the words of Professor Daka, who began the course by stressing that unless one mastered the Statute, no agronomist could expect to succeed in life? One hears nonsense of that sort at the beginning of lectures as each teacher tries to impose attention on the students. At any rate, Adrian impressed his professor by learning the Statute inside out. In return, Professor Daka promised to advise the Ministry of Agriculture to assign Adrian to some administrative institution.

His fellow students did not appreciate Adrian's belated rise to recognition. They started to tease him by saying that Adrian should have enrolled in Law School, where Statutes are studied and memorized.

The staff at the Ministry of Agriculture did not bother at all to assess Adrian Mekshi's knowledge of the Statute. Instead they promptly assigned him to the Institute for Agricultural Research in small town. It turned out that the Institute had a vacancy. Adrian was given a chance to specialize on alfalfa seeds and the cultivation of alfalfa fields. The appointment incited his fellow students to tease him again, saying that it was a pity his vast knowledge of the Statute was going to be wasted. But life has unexpected turns, and Adrian's passion for the Statute was not going to waste.

Thanks to the recommendation of Keti Kokona, a college classmate who worked at the Bureau of Agricultural Cooperatives, Adrian joined a team that was going to conduct an evaluation and assistance mission at a farm, in the south. Believing that the team would need an alfalfa specialist—since this particular plant was very important for the local economy —she thought of Adrian. The institute accepted her suggestion. Also Keti had compassion for this classmate with a heart of gold, and the looks of a horse. Adrian's face did have proportions that were surprisingly similar to those of a horse.

Two years earlier, as third-year college students, they happened to seat on a bench shaded by an acacia tree, outside the main building. As the white acacia petals fell on their shoulders, Adrian told Keti that he loved her dearly and if she...He did not finish, as Keti looked at him with astonishment and began to laugh loudly and uncontrollably. Surprised and jolted by her reaction, Adrian thought that she must have taken it as a joke, so he persisted, saying: "I am serious. I mean it!" He had never heard of any girl bursting out laughing when someone proposed to her. At a moment like that, a slap in the face would have been preferable to that peal of endless laughter. He wanted to know the reason for her unrestrained outburst, and she let him have it.

"My, oh, my! How could you think of proposing? And not expect me to laugh?"

Again, she started laughing and her breasts were bouncing all over the place. She could never imagine Adrian as a lover with whom to take a walk, go to the movies or to the park. Even after the incident, whenever she thought of it, she could not help but smile. A year later, Keti married a renowned doctor, and Adrian sent her a wedding card, along with a symbolic present. Keti was pleased because this showed that Adrian had a big heart and could not hold a grudge. Ever since then acacia trees in bloom and their white petals reminded her of Adrian.

"I don't know how to thank you for thinking of me," Adrian said to her, the moment he met Keti in her office. "You know why? Because it boosts my prestige a bit, in the eyes of the fellows at the Institute. I will be seen as someone who is appreciated by the Ministry. You know how these provincials are," Adrian said. As always, he was transparent and utterly sincere.

"Have you ever been in the southern town of Korce?" Keti asked.

"No. But I know that Manol Kristi, the actor in the film, 'Songs of Spring' lives there. We were close friend when he was in Tirana. Maybe I will see him when I go there."

* * *

As soon as they arrived in Korce, team leader Nastas Dumani held a brief session and asked each member to share where were they employed, and what kind of work they did. As an experienced civil servant, he divided the team into three groups, to exercise "vertical" control over the three kinds of terrain, in the lowlands zone, the hills, and the mountains. As for himself, he assumed the position of director and coordinator of operations. He assigned Adrian Mekshi, Vaso Tabaku and Agneza Domi to the lowlands perhaps on account of Agneza, who was a beautiful blonde. He told them that the best approach was to begin the inspection with the farm cooperative of Dorian, where—according to reports from the Ministry—production had dropped. The first task of the team was to identify the shortcomings, and hopefully the means to solve the problem and forge ahead.

After a week of intensive work with the ledgers of the cooperative, Agneza drew up a chart showing the annual balance. It appeared that while the production line or index on the chart veered downward, the index of expenditures kept climbing upward. The team's work was frequently interrupted by the farm's Chairman Luftar Gorani who kept stepping into the bookkeeping office.

"So, what's the good word from this young lady? Is she of any help? Down here we can use some help," said Luftar trying to sound as a man of modest manners.

After a few days, he asked Agneza if she cared to go horseback riding with him. She answered that she had never ridden a horse and was afraid she might fall. He said that she could ride in front of him, or in the back, whatever she pleased. Agneza frowned upon hearing such a crazy proposal. How could she ride with him? What would people think, when they saw her riding horseback with the Chairman?

"I was merely joking," said Luftar. "But one of these days, I will ask my assistant to mount you on a horse and show you the sights."

Adrian and the local agronomist inspected the farms, the meadows, and a few of the alfalfa fields. Evidently the agro-technical code was an unknown term there. The agronomist was a capable and well-trained young man, but without authority. Next, Adrian began to interview the supervisors, the elderly and the teachers. Informally and without taking any notes, he spoke to them in a simple, conversational manner. Soon he noticed why things were not going well. Indirectly, the object of criticism was the Chairman, though he was not mentioned by name. An old man said that Luftar was willing to work, but "others" wouldn't let him; that everyday someone would ask the Chairman to go to town and that he couldn't say 'No!' Adrian was not sure if the old man was speaking with tongue-in-cheek or was being serious?

Adrian made friends quickly with the bookkeeper, Bestar. They bonded so well, it seemed like they had known each other a long time ago and were reunited by chance.

"I've heard that the Chairman has invited you to dinner," Bestar said, smiling enigmatically, when they stepped in the office of the management.

"I know nothing about it," Adrian replied.

"That's what I heard. But even if he hasn't, he will. He never fails to invite guests to his house. You got to hand it to him, he is generous that way."

"Who takes over when the Chairman travels to town?"

"Is there anyone who can fill in for him?" Bestar replied with sarcasm.

"I'm not joking, because it looks like there is no leadership around here."

"As long as we have this Chairman, we are sure to go downhill," Bestar continued in a sarcastic vein.

"Why did you elect him, if you didn't think he was qualified?" Adrian asked in all sincerity.

"Elect him?" grinned Bestar. "Nobody asked us. He was delivered to us from the town."

Adrian was interested to know a little more about the Chairman.

"Just so you understand, Luftar was one of the 'nine thousand men' when he was discharged from the army with the rank of Major. Do you know how they got their ranks? By seniority! Two years in service would get you the rank of Lieutenant; three years, you are upgraded to Captain and so on. No tests to take, no leafing through the Bylaws.

That's how Luftar got to be a Major. He would have been a Colonel or General, if he was not discharged."

Adrian recalled that the action to discharge those 9,000 officers at the time, was proclaimed by the government as a contribution to world peace.

"First," Bestar continued, "he was appointed county supervisor. Before six months were up, he made a mess of things and was removed from his post. Then he was manager of a brick factory. There matters got worse, because he beat up a Gypsy. The Gypsy clan vowed to burn him alive. Therefore, his bosses kicked him out of there, and dumped him on us, since they couldn't leave him without a position. As a man with a peasant background, he should have managed well enough out here. Sadly for us, he comes from a God-forsaken highland region, and has no grasp of agriculture or livestock. Every morning he jumps on his horse and rides into town, supposedly to attend some important meeting. Actually, he spends his time hanging around coffee houses and rotisseries. Have you seen that skinny kid that sweeps the offices? Well, the Chairman makes him work thirty days a month, because the poor boy has to feed and groom the Chairman's horse. In a word, we are stuck with Luftar."

Bestar also said that the lunches and dinners the Chairman served to delegates and district authorities meaning the cow and poultry meat consumed by them, amounted to twice the figure sold to the members of the cooperative. These out-of-town guests wined and dined and naturally praised the Chairman as a man who respected the old traditions of hospitality, even though he didn't spend a penny out of his own pocket, but like them enjoyed the benefits of the collective wealth.

"Why don't you oust him, then?" Adrian asked, all upset, after hearing that scandalous story.

"He has connections that reach way up."

"The right to elect or dismiss staff personnel belongs only to the Assembly," explained Adrian. "Neither the Party office, nor the Executive Committee can intervene. If two-thirds of the Assembly does not want the current Chairman, a new Chairman can be elected in his place. It's that simple."

"Oho...," exclaimed Bestar, shaking his head in doubt.

"You doubt it?" Adrian asked. "It's sanctioned by the Statute. You want me to read it to you?" He took the Statute out of his pocket, quickly found the chapter on the rights of the Assembly members and recited it to him.

"I've never heard of such thing," the bookkeeper said still unsure.

"You know what your problem is?" asked Adrian while putting his hand on Bestar's shoulder, "—And I don't mean 'you personally' —You just don't know the Statute."

Aware that the local administration and the personnel were not familiar with the Statute, Adrian decided to include this point as a subject for discussion, in the final report. Content to have this opportunity to take action, Adrian went on to outline the bylaws of the Statute, stressing that the document was approved by the Congress of the Agricultural Cooperatives, and it would take a congress to amend or abrogate it. Hearing him speak with such confidence about the Statute, the bookkeeper felt somewhat embarrassed that he had not taken the trouble to read it.

"The Statute is never mentioned in our meetings," Bestar observed.

"And as a result, nobody objects when the Statute is violated," pointed out Adrian. "Of course, since it's not known...."

"When are we going to hold the Assembly meeting? Tomorrow?" he asked.

"I believe we left it for the day after tomorrow," Adrian informed him. "Our team will present its conclusions, and you can bring up the matter of the Chairman. After all, chairpersons do not fall from the sky, right? If you don't like your Chairman, you can elect another one. This is your right."

Bestar shook Adrian's hand more firmly than usual, as if by that gesture he wanted to express his words of gratitude. As a member of the team sent over by the Ministry, Adrian was well informed; that's why he spoke with such conviction. Why shouldn't the farm relieve Luftar Gorani, seeing that he was unfit as a Chairman? For a moment, Bestar envisioned the Chairman without a horse or a chair, a rather simple member of the cooperative, with the shopworn name of Luftar. He would have to go down to the plains, hold a broad-bladed hoe, and plant the corn crop, like the rest of them. The supervisor would tell him what his norm was for the day, and if Luftar failed to meet his quota, the supervisor would lash out at him and take out points from his chart. Hard to imagine that the district authorities were going to let the Chairman be just an ordinary farm worker, much less a discredited one in the very place where he held sway as a Chief.

Bestar started to elaborate on the causes of this phenomenon, and came to the conclusion that society had undergone a change that divided the people into privileged and commoners. Moreover, the privileged had their own strata within the state hierarchy. Their change of positions, appointments and transfers were always horizontal; that is, roughly equivalent to the position they held previously. This concept was expressed openly by the Party loyal members with such oft-heard terms as "he is one of ours," "trustworthy," "a person of merit." Those, on the other side of the tracks, were presumed to be suspect, a potential contingent of the enemy, even if this was not expressed openly. It was nearly incredible that the harshest opponents of the Nazi ideology were practically mimicking the way the Gestapo had divided the Germans in Hitler's time into the trusted versus the mistrusted. None of the officials—with the exception of those who were labeled enemies at a later point—were sent to do physical work. Seemingly, those who did manual labor all their lives were the condemned ones. Wasn't it paradoxical that the "vanguard detachment" of the working class—as the Communist leaders called themselves—should come to regard physical labor as punishment? Was the Party paying any attention to the split, which was deepening as time went on, with catastrophic consequences to the national unity? Bestar thought it best to abandon such maverick ideas and get back to the daily routine of working with numbers.

* * *

Two days later, by majority vote, which exceeded two-thirds of the total, the meeting of the Assembly removed Luftar Gorani from the post of Chairman. In fact it seemed as if the entire constituency in the Assembly Hall had voted unanimously against the Chairman. The motion was so unexpected that Luftar, who was seated at the Podium kept shaking his head and looking at his cohorts, as his mind was buzzing with questions, "What is going on here? Why wasn't he informed beforehand? Why had district officials failed to give him the slightest hint? Who took the decision to put the matter to a vote, and who had given the order to expel him? Why didn't the District Committee Chairman say anything over lunch in town earlier that day? Could it be that the order was given by the local Party Committee?" He fixed an angry look on the Secretary of the local Party office but was ignored. Even the crony of Luftar did not dare to defend him, or to contest the vote, since everyone present believed that the Chairman's dismissal was suggested from above. Most people there thought that some damaging evidence in Luftar's service record as an army Major might have been uncovered. And no one could say what was in store for the Chairman. The sudden dismissal implied surprise. It was prudent to remain quiet, so that nobody could risk being blamed for supporting an enemy the next day. Luftar's rancor was directed toward the district authorities. He could have never dreamed that the instigator was a member of the visiting team. Generally the evaluators were not competent in matters involving staff personnel or management. Luftar thought that the whole thing was due to a misunderstanding, intrigue or fabrication. He was determined to get to the bottom of it, and had faith that the Party would correct the error, as he put it.

The Assembly proposed Agron Toshku as new Chairman. As an educated agro-technician he would know how to rescue the cooperative and set it on the right path.

At the conclusion of the meeting, while people began to disperse Adrian approached Bestar and said:

"Do you see now how simple it is to elect a new Chairman?"

"I still think that the district authorities will not go along with this." Bestar expressed his misgivings.

"Come on, now! They have no business getting mixed up in this matter. It's in the Statute!" Adrian said to reassure him. "It was voted upon, so it's all settled."

That evening, Adrian and the other team members of the evaluation mission traveled to town for their final meeting that was to be held the next day.

* * *

"Is it true?" a team member named Spartak asked him at the hotel lobby. His eyes expressed astonishment and admiration.

Adrian didn't know what the other meant and did not respond. Spartak wondered whether Adrian was pretending ignorance.

"It's rumored that you brought down a powerful chairman."

Adrian laughed when he discovered what the big surprise had been.

"Wow! How did you get wind of it so soon?"

"I happened to be by the farm's offices. What a buzz…."

"How come? What's so extraordinary?" Adrian asked.

Just then, the team leader, Nastas appeared at the door. Spartak whispered to Adrian, "I'll tell you later."

The face of the team leader looked like a dark cloud. Nastas looked at them and scowled:

"Urgent meeting in my room, this instant!"

And he charged upstairs first. Unsure of what the urgency was all about Adrian and Spartak made their way to the staircase. After they got to the Nastas' hotel room, two other members of the team came in and just stood there reluctant to sit down.

"To the hall," ordered Nastas.

As soon as everyone took their seats in the hall, Nastas opened his briefcase nervously.

"The entire team of the Ministry is put in a difficult position. A member of the team, Adrian Mekshi, has committed a grave error and has compromised the entire mission."

Some angry looks zeroed in on Adrian, who sat there as if he were not the subject of the discussion.

"He has removed from his post the Chairman of the Dorian cooperative."

The members of the team had thought about some scandal of a grave nature. To them, the Chairman's dismissal did not sound as scandalous as the team leader made it out to be. So what, if a chairperson of a farm was fired?

Adrian got up to clarify the matter.

"Excuse me, but you are somewhat hasty in your judgment about what really happened. The a-sse-mb-ly ousted the chairman, not I." He pronounced the word "assembly" slowly to remove doubts in anyone's minds as to who did what.

"I don't understand what business it was of yours to get involved in matters that don't pertain to you," Nastas said menacingly.

"Isn't it the task of the inspection team to suggest ways to remedy a situation? Isn't that the orientation you gave us in the beginning?" said Adrian to remind him.

Nastas looked skyward as if appealing for help to a higher authority.

"Are you saying that I advised you to dismiss the Chairman?"

"No, not at all. But you did tell us to do all we can to straighten things out, and this was one of those things." Adrian looked at his teammates seeking their support. It was a sincere appeal not to leave him alone, in the face of a storm of criticism. Seeing the mood of the team leader, both Agneza and Vaso remained silent.

"Are you naive, or just playing the fool?" the team leader asked angrily.

"No need for insults," Adrian implored him.

Instead of apologizing, the team leader put his hands over his head and said,

"How could you do such a thing? I can't begin to grasp it...."

"Why? What did I do wrong? It's in the Statute," Adrian argued.

This time the team leader let his eyes meander, as if to say that he was dealing with an uncommon specimen.

A phone ring interrupted the debate. On the telephone, Nastas kept saying, "yes, yes, yes, right away." The moment he put the handset down, he ordered Adrian Mekshi to go at once to see the local Chairman of the District Committee.

Without saying a word, Adrian walked to his briefcase, opened it and took out the report of the inspection team.

"Beg your pardon, but the report is not typed yet."

With a dismissing gesture of his hand, the team leader indicated that he did not need nor cared about the report. As soon as Adrian walked out, Nastas burst out saying:

"Who brought this ass into the team? You have no idea how the First Secretary turned on me. He was beside himself and kept yelling at me. 'As the team leader,' he said, 'you are responsible for everything that happens.' And he is right. This guy has put us all in a big mess, and it's not likely that we'll come out of this clean." Nastas sighed deeply, as he thought of the consequences he might have to deal with on account of an immature sapling.

* * *

Adrian thought that common courtesy called for a handshake with the Committee Chairman but the official pretended not to see Adrian's extended hand. Instead, he continued to leaf through the pages of a calendar on his desk. Adrian noted that the face of the local authority was pale as if smeared over with kaolin. The Committee Chairman, Kalam Iftari, had wavy black hair, bushy eyebrows; all in all, a man of imposing demeanor. Since Adrian had never seen such a washed-out face, he figured that Kalam Iftari must be suffering from a hemoglobin deficiency, and maybe even anemia. Feeling compassionate Adrian thought of advising the official to step outdoors more often to take long strolls, swim, sunbathe.

The Committee Chairman shoved a file to the side, crossed his fingers and eye measured the agronomist with the stare of an interrogator.

"So, you are...." His eyes rested on an index card on his desk. "Adrian...."

"Mekshi," said the agronomist, to round off the name.

"Adrian Mekshi. Why have you come here?" The look of those dark eyes in that anemic face was fierce and penetrating. "I don't mean to my office, since I called you here myself, I mean why did you come to our district?"

This police-type question perplexed Adrian so much, he could barely murmur,

"Member of the Ministry team."

"What are the duties of your team?" he asked, closing one eye, while the other eye pierced through Adrian like a drill.

"Inspection and assistance," said Adrian, but then remembered that the way he put it, was not liked by the authorities. "Excuse me, I meant assistance and inspection," he corrected himself.

"How do you render assistance?" the Committee Chairman continued with the line of questioning. "By deposing appointed chairmen? Have you come to teach us how to implement policy regarding staff personnel?" Sarcasm and contempt mingled with large doses of anger in his voice, as he went on, all the while clenching his jaws, as if he were biting on something hard.

"Excuse me, ... It was not I who deposed Luftar Gorani. There was a meeting of the Assembly, and the decision was taken to...."

"Who suggested the meeting of the Assembly?" he questioned impetuously, rising on his feet.

"The Assembly meets whenever there are important matters to discuss. It's in the Statute," Adrian said in self-defense, while reaching for the booklet in his pocket.

"That's where you and those simpletons in Dorian are wrong. The Assembly cannot meet without our prior consent!" the district official snorted shaking a fist in the air.

"The Statute says no such thing," observed Adrian. "If you don't believe me, we can look at it together."

This reply, *a la Schweick*, lowered the official's blood pressure, as if he had gulped down a whole bottle of sedatives. He plopped into his armchair and gazed suspiciously at the creature in front of him. Could it be that this fellow didn't understand a thing about the administrative set-up, or could he be hiding cunningly behind the Statute?

"How many chairmen have you brought down until now?" the Committee Chairman was interested to know.

"This is the first time I participate as a team member," Adrian said in all modesty.

"You are not an inspector or instructor of the Ministry of Agriculture?"

"I am an agronomist at the Research Institute specializing in alfalfa," Adrian informed him.

Upon hearing the position, the Chairman's estimation of Adrian's importance plunged swiftly. He felt that he had just found an explanation for the unusual behavior.

"Those who brought you into the team shall be called to account," thundered the Chairman thrusting his finger upward.

Adrian thought at once of Keti. Under no circumstances did he want her to suffer because of him.

"Do you realize what bloody mess you got us into? Do you realize your gross error?" the Chairman asked.

"Frankly, no," Adrian retorted with customary sincerity. "I merely informed the cooperative members about the contents of the Statute, because they had not bothered to read it...."

"Get out of my office, you blockhead," roared the Chairman. "Scram before I kick you out," he threatened, and his face turned whiter than chalk, causing Adrian to wonder how such an abundance of energy could suddenly come out of the official's anemic frame.

As soon as he stepped out into the corridor, Adrian noticed that his shirt was glued to his body. Out on the street, he went over the conversation with the Committee Chairman. Partly, Adrian was angry with himself for failing to fully express all his thoughts. The Chairman arbitrarily interrupted him every time he tried to clarify the issue rationally, and unfortunately, the Statute was not discussed, at all. He was thinking of requesting a meeting with him the next day. With a cool head, the Chairman would listen to the main argument that was logical and principled. Also if the farm fairs well under the new Chairman, then the removal of Luftar Gorani will be justified. Faced with this argument, the official was going to admit that he had rebuked Adrian unfairly and could even ask for pardon.

These reflections lasted about as long as it took him to walk from the Committee building to the hotel. A new surprise was in store for him there. The team was called to an urgent meeting and the team leader had asked those present to unanimously condemn Adrian's action. Before letting anyone speak, Nastas called Adrian's conduct unbecoming, then went on to escalate the attacks, saying he had exceeded the scope of his duties and had even manifested "anarchist tendencies." Adrian waited in vain for someone to come to his aid, by standing up for the truth by upholding the Statute. When the issue was put to a vote, whether to keep or expel Adrian from the team, all voted him out.

In silence, Adrian opened his briefcase, reached for a folder and pulled out a few hand-written pages.

"To whom shall I give the report?" he asked innocently.

"Get out! I don't need your report!" the team leader said menacingly.

"I'm afraid you will repent and ask for it later on," Adrian said quietly, as he put the report back in the briefcase.

After dinner, Agneza said to Adrian that the expulsion vote was meaningless, since in three or four days the team was going to return to Tirana and disband. She suggested that when they return, he meet with the Deputy Minister of Agriculture, who was respected by everyone there.

* * *

"Someone is asking for you downstairs," Agneza told Adrian, when he opened the door of his hotel room.

Adrian thought that more trouble was coming his way.

"Did you get the name?" he asked.

"Yes, Manol, a friend of yours," replied Agneza.

Adrian's face brightened.

"You want to come along?" he asked her.

"But I don't know him," she said, pulling back.

"Come along! You'll have a good time, I'm sure," Adrian said. "Manol is delightful company."

The two of them went down to the hotel lobby.

"Long time, stranger." Manol chided him in a friendly way. "You've been here a week, and have not called on us." He then added: "Oh, I get it. You forget your old friends, when you have pretty chicks around," he said, glancing at Agneza.

Agneza blushed and regretted that she came down with Adrian.

"Be careful now. She is an agronomist, and a member of the team, too," observed Adrian.

"Did I say something bad?" he asked, looking at Agneza.

"Don't pay any attention to him. That's just the way he talks," Adrian remarked, to reassure her.

"Where shall we go? I mean where do you want to dine?" Manol asked them.

"We're out-of-towners," Agneza noted.

"Well, there is Panda, and there is the Old Tourism. Panda has a good ambiance. And it is under the shade of trees; but the appetizers are pitiful. The food in the Old Tourism is quite good."

"To the Old Tourism, then," commanded Adrian.

As soon as they sat down, Manol asked:

"Adrian, you're not your usual self. What's happened?"

"I have been accused of wrong-doings for no good reason, and without justification, in my opinion. Frankly, I don't even understand the reasoning," Adrian complained, and then related briefly what had happened.

Manol was so moved by the story that he got up and hugged Adrian.

"Bravo! Some big shots around here don't even like that fellow but dared not topple him. He is just too well connected. Seeing him trot down the boulevard with his horse was too much to bare."

"It's rumored that he has friends in high places," Adrian said, thoughtfully.

"You know what they say, 'A friend keeps you company up to the edge of the lake. Then he stops and lets you jump in by yourself!'"

Manol said. Then looking with a man's desire at Agneza, he remarked, "Where does this beauty come from?"

"From Gjirokaster," said Agneza.

"I had a close friend from there, but I don't know what happened to him. Some say he died," Manol said sorrowfully. "Others say he fled the country, and still others say that the Secret Police sent him abroad on a mission." Manol's face darkened, as he recalled his friend.

"Are you referring to Mane?" Agneza asked him.

"Yes. You know him?"

"He was my neighbor," Agneza said, smiling. "Our families got along well. And he is alive."

Manol felt like jumping up with joy.

"Really?!"

"Yes. And guess where he is now. In New Zealand!"

"How did he end up there, in the world down under?" asked Manol.

"Well, it's a long story and kind of complicated."

Agneza said that the Secret Police botched her neighbor's "disappearance." Word went out that Mane's clothes had been found by a brook and that he had drowned there. But that brook doesn't have enough water for a drink, let alone enough to drown in. Since the body did not turn up anywhere, people began to doubt that he had drowned accidentally or voluntarily.

"I've never known a more peculiar and more nimble human being," Manol remarked. "One day penniless, begging to bum a cigarette, while the next day, rolling in money. I suspected he had a shadowy source of income from the Internal Affairs. In college, he was the most disobedient and disorderly of students, yet he was not without talent. He was not allowed to take exams, because of too many inexcusable absences from class. Brimming with anger and sarcasm, directed to his instructors, he signed off 'the talented expellee, Mane.' His fellow students split their sides laughing, when they read his papers. It was rumored that Mane signed himself with the secret service. Afterward, Mane went home to his family, and then the news spread that he had drowned. But Mane was not the type to commit suicide."

"His family wanted him to marry my older sister," Agneza said. "One day Mane stopped my sister in the street and said to her: 'If you were not as nice as you are, I would get engaged with you. The one good thing about engagements is that you make love legally. But let's just leave it at that....' My sister was shocked. She could make no sense of his conversation. If he had said to her, you are ugly, unschooled and so forth..., then she could have understood, but to tell her you are nice, and that's why I don't care to be with you.... Later she learned that Mane had gone abroad and that made her realize what he had meant. First he wound up in Canada. Soon after he got to like his new life there, he decided to turn his back on Albania's secret service. Mane went to the authorities and confessed that he was an agent, sent to spy on the Albanian immigrants in Canada. He also revealed the names of his superiors, and thereby exposed and compromised Albania's secret service network in Canada. In turn, the secret police here put pressure on his father to bring his son home. His father said: 'It is up to those who sent him abroad to bring him back here. As far as I know, he drowned, and I wept for him when I heard the news'."

"Wasn't Mane afraid they might 'do away' with him?" Adrian inquired.

"Of course. That's why he went to New Zealand, to hide his tracks," replied Agneza.

"Clever and devious. He put one over *them*!" Manol said with admiration. "Let's have a toast, to Mane!" he proposed, raising his glass.

Adrian held his glass hesitantly.

"Well, he accomplished some mission, didn't he?" Manol remarked.

Adrian raised his glass and grinned slyly.

* * *

On their way back to Tirana, Adrian decided to take Agneza's suggestion and meet with the. Deputy Minister of Agriculture, Mentor Pernaska. He was known as a sober and reasonable man. Adrian hoped that by relating the incident to him exactly as it happened, the Deputy Minister would commend him for standing on principle.

The inspectors of the Agricultural Section welcomed Adrian as the "hero of the day" for his daring knockout blow to Luftar Gorani. They said that the Chairman' s boastful attitude and ignorance were grist for derisive anecdotes about him in the hallways and offices of the Ministry. Also, Adrian was the first to apply in practice the democratic content of the Statute. In their words, Adrian's initiative had strengthen the authority of inspectors overnight, who until then were ignored simply because they were seen as ineffective. The farms could no longer go forward with illiterate chairmen like Luftar who had been appointed for reasons of favoritism or war merits. The times called for capable managers and there were plenty of them around.

"I'm not worried about myself, but I don't want Keti to get in trouble on my account." Once again, he showed his sincere altruistic nature.

"Why should I get in trouble?" Keti asked as she blushed.

"Cause the District Committee Chairman screamed 'Who brought this knucklehead into the team'?" explained Adrian.

"Let him scream. Other people make those decisions," said a colleague.

Then the authoritative voice of the secretary called Adrian Mekshi to rush over to the office of the Minister. Adrian was somewhat dumbfounded to be accorded such honor, since he had asked to meet with the Deputy Minister. Instinctively, Adrian thrust his hand into his pocket, to make sure he had the Statute on him, as one looks for the best weapon of defense.

* * *

The eyes of the Minister followed Adrian from the padded door all the way to the desk.

"Are you 'the one'?" he asked.

The question did not bode well in Adrian's mind. A nickname like that would set him apart from everybody else. "The One" meant the weird, the rebel.

"What was that 'miracle' you pulled out there, young man?" The Minister spoke with a clear south dialect even though anyone know that he had been living away from his hometown for a quarter of a century.

"I did ask…."

"You didn't ask anybody, you acted on your own," the Minister cut in. "The team leader knew nothing of this. You removed from office an honored Chairman, a meritorious war veteran, compared to whom you are nobody. That is nothing to you? What have you got against Luftar? Has he done something to you? When did you have a confrontation with him? What has happened between you two?"

The Minister was talking about the matter as if it were a personal conflict. Embarrassed by what he was hearing, Adrian looked down. How could a public official, with a head full of gray hair, reason like a gossiper? Seeing Adrian with his head bent down, led Minister to believe that he was thinking things over, and this encouraged him to press more vigorously.

"Come out with it, young man, and make it easy on yourself, because the truth is going to come to light very soon." The warning was at once friendly and fierce.

"I…don't even know him. I mean, I did not know him, before going down there…on duty," Adrian said in all sincerity.

"Then, why did you remove him?"

Adrian didn't know how to answer. The Minister viewed the young man with a horse-like face as a sneaky youth.

"Who put you up to it?" The Minister wanted to get to the bottom of things. Waiting for Adrian's answer, he started tapping on the desk with the knuckle of his finger. "Who was behind it?"

"Who was behind it?" repeated Adrian, as if he wasn't sure he heard right.

"Precisely. That's what I want you to tell me. With whom did you discuss the matter? You started saying that you asked…."

"The farm's bookkeeper said that the Chairman takes off and goes to town every day, and the work…."

"That's one!" the Minister said, counting on the fingers of his hand. "Who else?"

"Pardon me, but you are talking about this matter as if I carried out a plot…."

"Close enough. Let us say instead, that you acted in a behind-the-back-fashion," the Minister ventured to elucidate.

"Pursuant to the norms of the Statute, the People's Assembly, by majority vote…."

"Well, well! Did you come all this way to educate us about the Statute?" the Minister intervened sarcastically. "Are you in your right mind? Do you see whose signature is on the Statute? Yours or mine?"

"Well, then…." Unexpectedly, Adrian paused.

"Well then, what? Go on, finish what you started to say!" ordered the Minister.

"I'd like to know…is the Statute still in force?"

"I swear you are an utter...." He let the word "utter" dangling in the air, but it was easy to imagine that he meant an utter ass. "Sure, it's in force. Why are you so worked up about the Statute? What business is it of an agronomist to stick his nose where it doesn't belong?" The Minister reached out and grabbed Adrian by the collar. "Because of your bravado initiative, I had my ears pulled by the Prime Minister, who charged that our department had set itself in opposition to the Party's policy on management.... Do you realize that you have smeared us? You have disgraced us...damn you!"

There is no telling how this tirade of insults might have ended, nor how long it might have lasted, had not the telephone rung. The Minister grabbed the handset at once, and in a very different tone of voice said, in clipped replies: "yes, I personally," "right away," "we don't have any data, either," "yes, it is fine," "yes, right away."

Adrian wondered if they were talking about him. It was not likely that this issue had gone beyond the Minister of Agriculture.

Suddenly the Minister turned toward Adrian who was straightening out his rumpled collar.

"You know what I can do to you? I can take that agronomist's diploma of yours, tear it to pieces, throw it in your face and send you to work on the farm. Get ready to see the Secretary tomorrow at ten o'clock. We will worry about other matters later...."

"Who?" Adrian asked.

"Le-lo, Secretary of the Party's Central Committee," enunciated the Minister.

Adrian was so bewildered, he felt the need to lean against something.

"What are you waiting for?" the Minister commanded, showing him the door.

* * *

That evening Keti and Viktor decided to go out with Adrian. They headed for the restaurant in the midst of an evergreen park with stately trees.

After they had a drink, Viktor asked Adrian whether he was feeling nervous.

"Why should I feel nervous?" he asked.

"The meeting tomorrow, that's why."

"I think it's a good sign that he called the meeting not I.... The Party looks at such matters calmly."

Viktor and Keti exchanged meaningful glances with each other.

"If you want my opinion, put on a show of vigorous self-criticism," advised Keti.

"Why? I don't feel guilty," Adrian said in self-defense.

Viktor was of the opinion that Adrian's imprudent, but courageous action did him some good, since it propelled him out of the abyss of anonymous agronomists. To bring the thorny subject to a close, Viktor asked Adrian to tell them a funny story from the life of his own family.

"I had an uncle," he began. Quickly he corrected himself by saying, "I beg your pardon he is still around. His name is Tuni. An old-timer, sharp and full of fire, he will grab you by the throat, if you ever criticize the administration. It so happened, however, that four or five years after the war, somebody dug up something on Tuni and there were calls to expel him from the Party ranks. My uncle was so upset he was pacing up and down his room like a caged bear. On the day of the meeting called to expel him, Tuni put a revolver to his head and fired. The bullet went clear across his skull and came out on the other side, with a few bone splinters. There was a pool of blood, and he was rushed urgently to the hospital. For three days, he hovered between life and death. On the fourth day, he opened his eyes and asked where he was. 'In the hospital,' his wife told him. 'How come?' he asked. He did not remember what had happened. 'For a check-up,' his wife said. Finally Tuni recovered and was back on his feet."

Viktor looked at him with a skeptical eye.

"You mean to say that the bullet went clean through his head, and yet he recovered?"

"That's right. I have seen the wound with my own eyes, because it's visible to this day," Adrian insisted.

"How is that possible?" Keti asked.

"He is an air-head," replied Adrian. "There was nothing in it to damage."

The explanation was funny yet convincing and all three of them laughed uproariously.

* * *

A guard in military uniform walked Adrian Mekshi from the reception in the lobby to the third floor, at the office of the Secretary of the Party's Central Committee.

The Secretary greeted him and invited him to sit down. Then, he began to ask him some questions, in a purely casual manner, about his occupation, his sector, the perspective of alfalfa, the work experience and the increase of the milk production. Adrian answered in a relaxed manner, not intimidated by the high authority and the lofty office. While in school, Adrian and his classmates had held the portrait of the secretary along with the paintings of the Party leaders in the big parade of May 1. Adrian remembered that the portrait was not heavy but it was a pain to hold it up right, while chanting slogans along with hundreds marching that day on the Main Boulevard. Adrian was used to seeing the top leaders from afar. The secretary seemed older in person, thought Adrian, who could hardly believe that he was standing right before the Statesman himself.

"Tell the story just as it occurred, with all the details. Open your heart without any reservations to the Party. Do not hold out. I assure you that you shall suffer no consequences," he vowed insidiously.

While listening to Adrian the secretary kept biting his lower lip. Every now and then he scribbled briefly on a note card on his desk. After asking a number of questions, he was convinced that there were no dangerous ideas in Adrian's mind. A "victim of the Statute"!

"Listen here, the farm chairmen are not part of the Committee's nomenclature," the secretary explained. "They are appointed and discharged by the district office and nobody has the right to intervene."

"That's not what it says here," observed Adrian pointing to the Statute.

Secretary Lelo smiled.

"Not everything is written there," he stressed, "but you should know that officials everywhere are a monopoly of the Party. Remember that!" In an instant, his face took on a fierce expression, and his eyes turned red with anger. "No one will be allowed to trouble the waters, in the name of democracy. Are you affiliated with any agency?"

"No," replied Adrian, like a guilty soul.

"If you were, this oversight would have been very serious. You and your friends convened the Assembly and dismissed the Chairman. Not only did you fail to consult the Party you also embarrassed it terribly. Your reckless action is a discredit to the Party; that's why adequate steps must be taken to deal with the situation."

"You're done for, Adrian Mekshi," Adrian thought to himself, as he waited to hear what the Party was going to do to him.

"We could annul that unlawful meeting of the Assembly, which you called, and reinstall chairman Luftar, an honorable officer and well-known figure in the district. But after the way he was disgraced, he can no longer remain there. Instead, we shall appoint him to an equally suitable post. You have caused much trouble and that is unforgivable to an highly educated young man, like yourself."

"I did not remove anyone. The Assembly voted...."

The Secretary could barely restrain himself. To keep from calling Adrian an idiot, he rounded his lips and let out a big "poof" of air.

"Our particular brand of democracy is regulated by the Dictatorship of the Proletariat. Citizens do not do as they please. And one more thing. If you don't want to be the laughing stock of the town do not mention the Statute everywhere you go. Agreed?"

"Completely!"

"I shall let you go with an advisory note to the Institute to investigate your scandalous demeanor and take appropriate action," the Secretary said, looking at Adrian with contempt.

Secretary Lelo rang the bell and an officer walked in.

"See him out!" he ordered.

The officer clicked his heels and gave a military salute.

After walking a good distance Adrian felt an incredibly strong urge to smoke and reached into his pocket. Next to the pack of cigarettes, his hand got hold of the booklet *The Statute of the Agricultural Cooperatives.*

There on the little bridge he took his time tearing the brochure into two pieces, then four, then eight grinding it to smaller pieces, that he flung in the stream. Adrian stood there following the flow of the scraps.

ꕤ Monika Has Her Own God ꕤ

Like all important government offices, the office of the Deputy Prime Minister, Rim Pepa had two entrances: one through the main hall, the other through the waiting room. He kept the key to the main door fastened to a chrome chain to be used on rare occasions such as visits of the high-ranking officials, whom he could not bring in through the back door. He preferred the entrance through the waiting room, since that way he could pick up the mail, fax and telephone messages, along with the cheerful smile of Monika. His secretary always came to work several minutes before the office hours to put in order the items on the agenda for the day. Monika radiated warmth and youthful ardor, enlivening the young and newly appointed Deputy Prime Minister, so he could deal better with the tiresome affairs of state. As she talked, Rim felt that she caressed him with the way she moved her eyes. He enjoyed watching her as she from afar granted him a taste of the boundless joy that bubbled up inside her. The oval shape of Monika's face, her clear skin, her dark slanted eyes, as if she were a blend of Euro-Japanese beauty, graced the office far more than the vases and the original paintings.

That morning in May, the Deputy Prime Minister walked into the anteroom briskly, as usual. Monika got up at once to greet him even though he motioned her to stay put. Conscious of her feminine graces, she took care to dress elegantly, so as to best reveal the curves of her body. She had picked from her wardrobe a blouse with dark red and grayish white roses, as if she wanted to invite the spring season prematurely into the offices of the Prime Ministry. The cut of her blouse exposed slightly the cleavage between her breasts.

After taking the folder that Monika handed him, he complimented her lovely blouse with rose petals, which seemed to give off a real scent.

"Can I have a whiff of your roses?" he teased her, taking a step toward her.

"They smell better in the afternoon," she said suggestively, pleased that her superior took notice of her outfit.

Those who walked in there for the first time looked at the pretty secretary with admiration and amazement. As a rule, in such places, one found women who had a clean biography, but were gloomy like prison guards, and if not downright ugly, at least not at all attractive. When it came to staffing such offices or hiring employees for jobs in important institutions, looks were not a criterion. Ordinarily, beautiful women are not thought to be adept at keeping their mouth shut about state secrets, even when they are seriously instructed in advance. Unlike other secretaries, Monika was very attractive and flattering to the point that everyone viewed her as an exception to the rule. She got her position on account of her father's connections with the chief of the cabinet of the Prime Ministry. Rim Pepa was aware of the envious looks of his close friends, who seemed eager to find out whether he had more than a work relationship with Monika.

"What's new?" he asked her.

"Requests for funds, requests for materials, complaints about jobs and appointments," she replied.

He pursed his lips, as if to say that she did not exactly get the drift of his question.

"How do you feel?" he asked, smiling faintly, and giving her to understand that the previous question had nothing to do with official business.

"Grand!" she said.

"I'm glad, because when you are upbeat, the whole office brightens up." The caressing look of Deputy that morning glided from her face to the blouse strewn with roses. "You know how you look today? Like your bosom is covered up with rose petals," he complimented her.

"I think Van Gogh did a painting of a girl with bare bosom on a tray covered with roses," Monika said.

"How do you know that?" asked the chief.

"It is a classic painting," Monika said and fluttered her eyelashes like a saintly woman.

The Deputy Prime Minister went into his office, determined to perform his official duties with the youthful energy and devotion of a newly promoted executive. After he took off his jacket and out it on the hanger, he sat down in the comfy armchair. Appointed to his high post only a few months earlier, Rim Pepa felt good every time he walked into his luxurious office with parquet flooring, glittering furniture, blinds to reduce sunlight, a T-shaped desk, and several armchairs for intimate social conversations. He had catapulted from the post of supervisor of a construction team to the highest Party level. His chubby face could be seen in the postures at party conventions along with those of the senior members of the Politburo. His portrait was carried on the shoulders of marchers in parades, the way Christians used to carry their icons. Since he had risen from the ranks, Rim was regarded as an official who was familiar with the problems at hand, and who knew from experience how to solve them. And Rim was aware of the advantage he enjoyed over his older government members. There was a time when they seemed to him like experts with special talents to administer the complicated machinery of the state. After he came to know them, and saw that they were ordinary functionaries, without any special skills, he lost all respect for them. Most of the government officials were stifled from working in offices for lengthy periods of time, and made decisions or proposals that deserved to be called 'bureaucratic'. There were complaints that institutions and government agencies had become "bureaucratized," isolated from their base. Most of the Politburo and Cabinet members had grown old and had neither the zeal, nor the requisite energy for work. At the end of World War II, some visiting journalists had noted that Albanian leadership had the youngest median age of all governments in Europe. Four decades later, it was ranked among the oldest. The shuffling of officials from the top down and vice-versa didn't help matters much. In intellectual circles, a new word began to be whispered about, 'gerontocracy' or the rule by the old men. In the foreign press, the international experts described Albania's leadership as the most dogmatic of the communist governments in Eastern Europe and as the most loyal to Stalin's dethroned regime. Although there were no indications of any change, Albania's leader took steps to bring in new blood. While none of the old-timers was removed, the total number of the Politburo members and appointees went up from nine to thirteen. The clever maneuver preserved the Party's united front! Rim Pepa was one of the lucky candidates whose credentials were screened carefully by the personnel. The finger of the top leader ran down the list of candidates and stopped next to Rim's name and just like that an unknown construction supervisor was mounted to the highest level of the government hierarchy. Soon afterwards Rim moved from a modest apartment to a three-story villa with luxurious furnishings, in the exclusive residential block of the Party leadership. In addition, he had a BMW with a driver, a Peugeot for the family and a jeep for driving over rugged terrain or hunting. Rim was provided with bodyguards who quickly satisfied every whim of his. A delivery man brought groceries to the doorstep of his villa. The grocery list was drawn up by his wife, Juliana, with the help of the children.

As soon as he sat down in the armchair, his eye fell on some typed sheets, fastened with a clip, and a note saying, "Internal Memo"—a formula that had displaced the intriguing term "classified" or "top secret" used by the old Administration. He knew that those sheets contained the report of the Government Commission on the technical safety conditions of the depots and warehouses of the state reserves. He leafed through the sheets with unrestrained nervousness, since the subject brought back memories of unpleasant associations. Just as Rim expected, the report dealt superficially with the main issues. It recommended half-baked actions such as chimneys for aeration, importing suitable ventilators, dehydrators, and anti-rust pain to prevent corrosion, which wreaked havoc on the machinery. This meant that more funds would be spent, and all in vain. For a poor country like Albania, state reserves were an obsession imported from countries with powerful economies. All indications were that it had become a chronic disease. Rim Pepa believed this sincerely, but would never admit it publicly, or even privately, after what happened at the last meeting of the Politburo. Fortunately, his candidness with the Party and his colleagues had bruised him only slightly. Again, he recalled the words of a friend who came to congratulate him on his new post:

"Be careful, Rim. Keep your eyes open. Those who give you a chair can just as easily give you a shove. Remember, the bigger they are, the harder they fall…."

He threw the report away with disgust then looked through the agenda of that day: 8:00 – Meeting with the director of the brick factory. 9:30–10:40 – Meeting with the legal advisor of the Prime Ministry. Draft law for packaging. He never imagined that a Deputy Prime Minister would have to deal with idiotic matters like boxes for tomatoes and cucumbers, corn husks, saplings of willow trees, marsh plants, the quality of bricks, sage, junipers…. His eyes moved down on the sheet of the appointments. 11:30 – Meeting with Professor Alfons Morena. Nervously, he pressed the call button. The anteroom door opened up, and in walked Monika with pen and notebook at hand. She drew close to his desk, ready to take dictation.

"Monika, what is the meeting with Professor Morena about?" The tone of his question was more like a criticism than a request for clarification.

"You told me to schedule a meeting since last week you were unable to see him. Professor Morena waited in the anteroom two full hours, and left only when the office closed," explained Monika.

Suddenly the tone of his voice and the gloomy look on his face indicated an almost visible rift between them. Monika knew well that he could have received the professor any other day of the previous week, since there were plenty of blank slots in his appointment calendar. Suddenly he looked interested in a less official matter.

"Did you like his company?" Rim teased her.

"He kept mum the whole time," she said openly. "I don't know how his wife can stand him," she added.

"Perhaps he is good in bed…" he teased.

"Who can go to bed with a bear like him? Not me, not even if he were the brightest man in the world."

The Deputy Minister smiled and let her go, all the while watching the sway of her skirt between her legs.

He recalled his surprise the day he walked in his office and the personnel manager, whether on purpose or out of ignorance, disregarded protocol and introduced her by saying, "Monika Ferri, the secretary of your office." As they shook hands, Rim wondered how long it was going to take him to conquer a beauty like her. He envied the executives of institutions in Western countries, who hire their own secretaries and as gossip had it, had them as mistresses. A beautiful woman like Monika could not be without a lover, and that, of course, presented a serious obstacle to the romantic visions of the new Deputy Prime Minister.

After a couple of weeks, he decided to take the offensive, but in a slightly indirect fashion, without risking anything, and without provoking her verbally. It was a stratagem that had paid off when he was construction supervisor.

One afternoon, a little before the end of office hours, he pressed the call button. Monika stepped inside and stood before him, ready to take orders. Holding some sheets of paper in his hand, Rim said that he was tired. Then, he began to stretch his limbs and to moan lightly, as if he had a stiff neck.

"Is your neck stiff?" Monika asked politely. "Looks like someone slept without covers last night," she teased him craftily.

"No, no, not what you think. Last night I was at the Hunter's Hotel, and I think the window in my room was open, and I didn't pay any attention. A massage would help at this time…." The implication was obvious. "Do you know anything about massage?"

"I have never tried it…."

"You can try it on me, if you like," he said, and promptly loosened his tie, ready to surrender to the inexperienced masseuse.

Monika unbuttoned the collar of his shirt, and with delicate motions and gentle fingers, began to soothe his rigid muscles. At first, he let out soft sounds of pain, then exclamations of pleasure, giggling and shifting his body as if someone was tickling him.

"Shall we shut the door?" he suggested. "Someone might walk in, you know…."

"Let them come," she retorted. "Why should we care?" It looked like she was serious about the massage as a remedy, which made Rim fear that his plan was foundering.

"We are duty-bound to look after the health of our supervisors," she went on after a while, which again raised doubts in his mind, as he tried to figure out when the little shrew was serious, and when was she joking.

This was a lateral maneuver to explore the secretary's emotional terrain. Rim was exploiting the notion of a psychologist, that contact with the male body entices sexual ideas for the female. He grasped her arm and began to caress it with both hands to show his appreciation for her service. Monika did not protest. Then he made another advance. He lifted her hand to his lips and kissed it. Again, Monika interpreted that as an intimate expression of his thanks. Then he got up from his chair and facing Monika began to return the favor of the massage by caressing lightly her cheeks, the lobes of her ears, and her throat. Then his hands slid from her throat to her shoulders, to her waist, to her hips, which he grasped tightly, as he drew her close to him and kissed her lips with fervent passion. It was clear where he wanted to go. Monika held him off, saying gently, "Not now, not now." The Deputy Prime Minister was exhilarated by the promise of future pleasures. "Not now" meant "Yes" later.

A few days later, Rim called the secretary to his office, to put the finishing touches to a report. It was a job they started on the large work desk, and finished on the three-seat sofa in the back of his office. The sofa was quite long, but not very wide, which required them to put some creativity to work. Monika did not pretend to be a virgin. She used all of her experience to please the chief, believing that it was her duty to put the charms of her body in the service of the Party, as was expected of a devout Communist. Meanwhile, allured by the massage he had the other day, Rim liked to have his joints limbered up and fondled by her hands. That way, he got into a good mood faster. Two or three times a week, he stayed with Monika after office hours to work on some "classified" jobs, which they always finished on the three-seat sofa, with subdues cries of pleasure.

Rim Pepa let a sigh out and turned his attention to the possible purpose of the appointment with Professor Morena. Their previous meeting was still fresh in his mind.

He had come to his office with a grimy black briefcase, out of which he pulled out a few sheets of paper, and then began to set forth his request.

"You know as well as I do, that our printing presses are carrying a heavy load. The printing of books, especially books of literature and science, has been delayed owing to the weakness of the printing sector. The delay has created serious anomalies in some sectors. Last year, quite a few school textbooks got into the hands of students, only after a three or four months delay, which hampers severely the teaching process. Since this matter pertains to the propaganda sector, we think that if the new printing press—which is expected to be imported during the current six-month period—is put into operation, the printing delays would be reduced substantially."

"What's stopping you?" asked the Deputy Prime Minister, even though he knew what the Professor was driving at. "Lack of space, funds, or labor?"

"No, none of that. The printing plant has sufficient free space, labor and fund reserves. The problem lies elsewhere, in the bureaucracy. This press has been tagged as a state reserve item, at a time when we are confronted with pressing needs. In my view, it is a luxury, if not an anomaly, not to make use of it for an indefinite period. Can you help us?" Professor Morena asked him.

"You are asking for a change of plan, right?" he summarized.

"The administration will profit economically, since it will recoup the money it invested—if not all, certainly some of it," the Professor said, continuing his argument.

"Now, listen to me, my dear Professor Morena. If it were up to me, I'd issue the order right now to put the press to use, as soon as it arrives. However," he digressed, with a smile, "the problem is somewhat different. Changes in plans cannot be made without the approval of the Politburo. Believe me when I say that, as a government, we have no right either to change or to supersede the prerogatives of the Politburo. We can, however, submit our own proposals, and hopefully the matter will be settled soon since in a couple of days we will have the Politburo meeting. I shall bring up the matter, and I am sure that it will win the approval of all the Politburo members."

Afterward, the meeting changed into an informal social chat, as they reminisced about the college years at the University of Tirana. They laughed when they recalled what a heavy load they thought they were carrying as students, when in fact they had more free time than ever.

"By the way, what do you think of state reserves?" Rim asked.

"Grandma used to say, a good housewife always stocks up." He thought for a brief moment and added: "Grandpa's favorite proverb was: 'When you have no light at home, it is pointless to take a candle to the mosque.'"

Both of them laughed heartily. Logically, Rim knew that the notion to have lathe factories, radio stations, and medical operating rooms underground, to make them totally safe from air raids in case of an imposed warfare—was ideal from one standpoint, but a catastrophe from another. That which enemy bombs could not reach, was fully vulnerable to rust and the crippling humidity of tunnels, which put out of action, even before they were used, lathes, costly machines for boring holes, and sophisticated equipment of inestimable value. There were constant orders for supplementary expenditures, ventilation chimneys, packaging of merchandise with sheets of polyethylene, and rubberized raincoats. None of these measures proved effective. Even the importation of tons of dehydrators and anti-rust products, which for a time seemed to offer the surest form of protection, did not meet expectations. The dehydrators saturated with moisture, had to be changed constantly. The use of anti-rust materials on delicate parts of the machinery was not recommended. As a result, the corrosion continued unabated. Rim wisely called it, "The whirlpool that sucks up our impoverished budget." Why should expensive machines be 'buried' underground, as soon as they are imported? Not even a rustproof product could resist for long the dampness of the tunnels. The more sophisticated the machines were, the sooner they became inoperative. The modern equipment they brought in turned into useless scrap iron after a few years. Wheat turned color and spoiled, corn flour turned bitter, sugar hardened like rock, potatoes sprouted. In spite of it all, hundreds of trucks, year in and year out hauled in the same kind of freight to the remote depots in the mountains, so as to maintain the reserves at the prescribed level.

Rim told the Professor about the notorious incident involving a military depot that housed 700 tons of gasoline. The depot was located on a mountainous slope, not far from his construction site. It was guarded night and day by armed guards. The cap of the fuel tank could not be opened, even to fill a cigarette lighter with fluid, without the order of the Minister of Defense and the Chief-of-Staff. The depot was to serve as a source of supply in case of war, since it was considered by experts to be invulnerable even to bombardments from the air, in case enemy planes detected the site. After three years, an official commission that was appointed to assess how well prepared the reserve depots were, discovered unexpectedly that the fuel reserve tank didn't have a drop of gasoline. How could 700 tons of gasoline disappear or be squandered? Surely, the depot manager was indicted and tried in court. What had the guards watched on their tours of duty during those three years? Since the manager came from a family loyal to the party, the likelihood of sabotage or contraband was ruled out. The accused in his defense put the blame on the constructors of the depot. The construction company maintained that throughout its operations it had applied the blueprint, but could not answer for the welding job on the tank. The welding engineer submitted signed and sealed reports certifying that the tank met all welding specifications when it was delivered. One investigating commission after another was appointed to establish fault, and finally the blame was placed on an earthquake that had occurred several months prior, and the case was closed. The gasoline evaporated in thin air, along with the money spent for the construction of the depot.

Both broke out laughing. Rim invited the Professor to get together socially sometime. They said they should meet soon for a cup of coffee on a Sunday or any off day.

* * *

Following that meeting, Rim had gotten himself in serious trouble when he approved with enthusiasm professor's viewpoints on state reserves. The Deputy Minister had believed that it was an ideal occasion to come to the Party's aid with fresh thoughts and bold ideas. He had thought that in meetings of the Politburo, discussions were sincere and without reservations, as befitted the forum of the ideal democracy. It was the second or third meeting that he had attended as a Politburo appointee. The reasonable proposal to change the destination of the new printing plant could win him the respect and admiration of the senior members. He would have not taken the initiative to introduce the suggestion if Professor Morena had not come to him.

Rim raised the issue of the printing press at the Politburo meeting. He tied the ideological and economic arguments to demonstrate that his proposal to revise the standing plan was unquestionably profitable. The old members of the Politburo paid close attention to his suggestion, which seemed to them both valuable and unacceptable. The Deputy Prime Minister presented his case in words that even members of the Politburo with a grade school education could understand. However, none of them spoke. No praise, no criticism. Experience had taught them to be cautious and not hasty. The Sphinx-like expression on the top leader did not give them any single clue. They were ready to act on either one of two extreme options; approve it enthusiastically, or bury it under a barrage of criticism. Then the 'Pharaoh' took a deep breath and said that 'Albania's encirclement' had not been well understood and the Party had much work to do to educate the masses on this priority issue. The top leader pointed that some of the highest representatives were insufficiently sensitive to 'the blockade' and inadequately involved with the situation at hand. In the end, he added that politics always takes priority over the economy,

Every word spoken by the top of the pyramid made Rim's head reel. The comments were serious: indifference to the encirclement, out of touch with reality, and unworthy of the Party's trust. He could face expulsion from the Politburo and demotion from Deputy Prime Minister to a lower position than the one he had previously. The Party could evict him from his luxurious villa, take away his Mercedes-Benz, his family's Peugeot and the jeep car. He rested his elbows on the desk to give more support to his body as he felt his blood pressure shoot up. In a few seconds, his pressure plunged quickly and he felt cold sweat dripping down his forehead. Then his face turned pale, like the masks on Chinese actors. He feared that he was going to faint and be carried out of the meeting in a stretcher.

However, the top leader was content merely to point out that political myopia should be taken very seriously. Perhaps going as far as expelling the new Deputy Minister would have implied that the Politburo had been hasty in selecting the new appointee.

After throwing his knockout punch with the first blow, the Party Chief believed that there was a valuable lesson to be taught to the inexperienced new blood. In a congenial tone, the foremost leader affirmed that he was not talking about a particular individual or individuals. Instead he meant to highlight the Party's policy. The pressure of domestic and foreign enemies, the military forces of the Warsaw Pact as well as a possible NATO invasion of Albania's lowlands was a real danger, he said. But the Party would never capitulate. It would launch a clandestine war in the cities and guerrilla warfare in the mountains. That meant that the Party press, the newspapers, magazines, brochures and leaflets had to continue printing without letup. That is why the printing press had to be on stand by within the state reserves. The Party Chief was the mastermind behind the idea of leading the struggle against the enemies from an underground tunnel, in a secret hideaway. Rim could see how at the end of that much-talked-about war, as Chief-of-Staff, the leader would march triumphantly into the capital for the second time—the first victorious entrance was recorded in 1944!—and be welcomed with flowers and ovations.

After that meeting Rim was on his toes. Those who showed no regard and those who befriended him warned him to be careful. The Prime Minister called him to his office and started yelling at him derisively:

"Just what did you hope to accomplish, with that proposal against reserves? Do you realize how far you went with your criticism? You have set yourself up in opposition to the directives of the Party. That was very immature. Why didn't you come to talk with me first? What do you think I'm here for?"

Within a week Rim's hair turned gray around the temples, giving him a more imposing and more mature look. He realized that it was more prudent to keep his mouth shut, than to stand out for expressing original and daring thoughts. Contrary to what he had believed, the Politburo was not a forum where ideas brewed and suggestions were aired freely. It was no place for 'internal democracy." There, visions were the monopoly of the Leader and throughout the years ideas came only from his brain. The free expression of ideas in that environment was even more dangerous than any other setting.

Monika Ferri alone stood apart from everyone else around the Deputy Minister. Not only did she like his gray hair around the temples, she said that his new look was more dignified and manly. Then she kissed both of his temples and said, "You are adorable!"

Like certain people who always blame others, Rim Pepa was quick to excuse himself. If Professor Morena had not come to his office, he would not have submitted that proposal to the Politburo meeting. After that incident, he couldn't even bear to hear the professor's name or mention of his title, because he associated them with the blows dealt him by the Party leader. He felt like kicking himself, when he recalled that he had entertained the same viewpoints as Professor Morena.

Rim decided to keep quiet at home about the recent meeting of the Politburo. But the secret was let out by the fellow members, who told their wives about it, who in turn whispered it into the ears of his wife, advising her to teach her husband how to behave in the new circumstances. Juliana could hardly wait for him to come home from work, so as to get all the details and call him to account. However much he tried to downplay the incident, she blasted him with a volley of insults, without any regard for his respectable post. In the end, she said to him: "We're going to go down because of you." As a practical wife, she had no consideration for the fact that all the enjoyable privileges for her and the family were tied to her husband's new position.

* * *

The last time Rim fondled her breasts, he had told Monika that everything about her was lovely, gracious, and perfect except her last name. "Ferri," he said with disapproval, putting the stress on the 'r.'

"What business have you with my last name?" she retorted jokingly. Then added:

"I've changed it, mind you, but I keep it a secret."

"Even from me?"

"You've never asked me," she said flirtatiously.

"Could you whisper it in my ear?" he pleaded.

"Monika Ferrari. Pretty modern, huh?"

His face darkened at once and hastened to reject it.

"No! No! Let no one hear of it! Or they will accuse you of being infected with bourgeois ideas."

"My girl friends like it," she said.

"How do you mean?"

"They like it, the way we like anything that's 'forbidden'," she explained. "Yesterday, I was at the beach and I saw some Moslem youth wearing gold crosses around the neck. Can you believe it?"

"Hush!" he whispered, placing his fingers gently over her lips.

She turned her head aside, and freed her mouth.

"I know some of them. They have no religious feelings. They don't know anything about religion. They just want to rebel."

Monika smiled at him.

"To them, it's some sort of game…."

"What about you, Monika? Do you believe…?" he asked her suddenly.

She wondered for a moment whether she should answer him sincerely. She did not want to upset him but was curious to know his thoughts.

"What does it matter to anybody, whether I do or don't? Don't all religions preach precepts that make sense and are good?"

"Vain prejudices…," he said, sticking out his tongue.

"I don't know, but I felt sad when religion was banned," Monika went on. "They didn't have to shut down the churches and the mosques. No harm in preserving them. What did it matter if some old men and women went there to pray? Judging by the way things were, religion was on its way out. Young people showed no interest. Do you know that my Moslem neighbor used to come and light a candle in church? When I was little, my grandma took me to the village. Every so often she went to some ruins to light a candle. 'Why are you lighting these candles?' I asked her once. 'There is nothing but stones here.' 'It's a good place,' grandma said. Only later I learned that those were the ruins of a church."

"Useless expenses," he said.

"Even so, religious gatherings had their own charm. My sister-in-law used to dress up every Sunday to go to church. Now she stays home on Sundays, and prays secretly in to some icons. 'Whoever casts stones at the Lord, is going to pay for it,' grandma used to say," reflected Monika.

"Nothing happened to us," he contested. "We have made history as the first atheist state in the world."

"Well, when a delegation from Iran visited our College, they put up inscriptions from the Koran in the hallways, and drove female journalists out of the press conference, supposedly because Ayatollah's diplomats did not want to see uncovered women. I heard it from my friend, Leila, who is a radio journalist." Monika felt offended by the unsavory incident.

"No, I didn't know that," Rim said, and a gleam of anger flashed in his eyes the moment he realized that his mistress was flouting religious morality. "You are not exactly practicing what religion preaches," he needled her, as he fondled her tender breasts.

"I am not cheating nor betraying anyone. I believe in my own way," she replied calmly. "My God allows me to enjoy my life, as long as I don't harm anybody. What about you? Do you really think that you are true to the regulations of your statute?" she burst out.

The exchange had taken an adversarial tone, and he thought it was prudent to change direction.

"You don't know everything," he chided her.

"I don't care to," Monika said in self-defense. "I know my beliefs and I am true to them." A moment later she regretted that she had spoken her mind so categorically. She turned back to pillow talk. "You know something? When you first came to the office, you seemed very serious to me."

"You don't think I'm serious?" he prodded her.

"I meant to say 'principled'," she said, trying to straighten things out.

"You don't think I'm principled?" he again prodded her.

"You know what I mean," she said explosively.

Both burst out laughing.

"I wondered, how long was it going to take me, to have my chief into my arms?"

"Really?" exclaimed Rim. "Do you realize that we've had the same thought?"

"We're the same type," she said, without sounding cynical, or labeling the type.

"That's enough philosophizing," he said, as he slid his hand under her slip, until he reached the elastic band of her panties. With a brisk movement, he yanked them off her legs, buried his nose into them, and inhaling with ardor, sighed, "The scent of Spring!" A moment later, he flung them away, and embraced her tightly.

Each time they finished making love, Monika took out her handkerchief, dipped a corner of it into a bottle of alcohol, then cleaned any tell-tale spots on the sofa, and all remnants of lipstick on his neck, cheeks and chest, so as to wipe off all traces of sinful behavior. She could not wipe off all of them, since Rim went home with his batteries burned out, and delayed as best he could going to the conjugal bed. Often he shut himself up in his study, and gave notice that he did not want to be disturbed, as he had to read some materials of great importance.

* * *

Juliana was worried about the physiological condition of her husband. He didn't seem to have the energy anymore for a normal sexual life. Gone were those happy times when he returned home from the construction site, took a quick shower, slipped into bed, and waited for her to join him. He was as restrained now, as he was impatient then. Lately, he returned from the office, ate a bit of supper, secluded himself in the study with a stack of papers, then went to bed complaining, "I'm so tired!" and promptly fell asleep. This was not something that happened just over the past week. It had started earlier. These days, she was paying for Rim's prestigious Party post, with lower levels of pleasure in the matrimonial bed. Was his job so exhausting that it drained him of all physical energy? On the advice of a midwife, she began secretly to add

Vitamin B12 tablets to his food, but they did nothing to augment her partner's sexual zeal. She began to search for other remedies. She went to a fortuneteller, then to an old woman who knew how to break spells and the curse of the "evil eye." She talked about her problem indirectly to some of the women "in the block," with whom she was close, and was relieved to learn that they had the same problem with their husbands. It was a syndrome that the majority of young Party and state leaders shared.

"Keep quiet! Daddy is very busy!" This admonition rang out throughout the house, whenever the children screamed in fun, chased one another, shouted insults and complained, without caring at all how the affairs of government were going. They were much too young to understand that for the past several months, their father was not solely the husband of their mother, but a man who was wedded, so to speak, to the state, as well.

It distressed Rim that, despite his current position, he was not appreciated by the family, anymore than he was appreciated when he was supervisor of the construction project. Outside the family, his words were listened to with close attention, jotted down on paper, copied, repeated and quoted by his subordinates. He felt good especially when he showed up at podiums and reviewing stands, when there was no other official to outrank him. Then, all the people fixed their eyes on him, while those near him smiled humbly.

* * *

Monika informed the Deputy Prime Minister that Professor Morena was waiting in the reception. Rim looked at his wristwatch.

"Show him in," he commanded.

The Professor walked in, holding a briefcase in his hand. Since Rim made no move to shake his hand, he refrained from giving him his hand.

"What is it?" the Deputy Prime Minister asked him, even before he sat down. He was not sure anymore what Professor's Morena's official position was, nor did he bother to inquire.

The Professor put his leather briefcase on his lap, opened it, and took out a typewritten sheet of paper.

"Formal papers should be submitted to the Secretariat of the Prime Ministry," Rim said, to head him off. "The rules must be respected by everyone," he said as if to apologize that he could not make any exceptions.

"We have sent it to the secretariat, as called for by protocol, whereas this is a reminder regarding the matter for which I requested a meeting with you," the Professor elucidated.

"So, what's this all about?" His tone expressed his impatience more than his interest. To show Morena that he was pressed for time, he looked long at his wristwatch.

"Near the hill where the machine plant is being built, there is an old church, dating from the XII century. It's one of the oldest in our country, and perhaps in the Balkans, as well," Professor Morena explained. "But...."

"For matters of this sort, you must address yourself to the Deputy Prime Minister in charge of the cultural sector. You've come to the wrong person," Rim chided him. "You should have known this much...."

"It was he who directed me to you, since the church at present is administered by the construction project. As such, it comes under your sector...."

"Yes," Rim interrupted him. "I'm aware of that. It seems to me, however, that this place of worship has nothing of interest. No iconostasis, no frescoes or mural icons, as they are called."

"Experts of Christian art affirm that its extraordinary architecture has enabled it to resist the wear and tear of the centuries."

"An old ruin," observed Rim disparagingly, with an ironic smile.

"Sure, it's a Pre-Christian structure," the Professor noted. "I can't understand why a unique building such as this, did not make the list of state monuments of culture. We are of the opinion that we can redeem this oversight, by proposing to the government to designate the edifice a monument of culture, and allow it to become a part of our inventory. As it is, the project management is using the church as a warehouse for cement, dynamite, etc., even though we are willing to build a warehouse specifically for the benefit of the project, at our own expense."

"Can't you wait until the construction of the plant is completed? Since you've put up with this situation for twenty years, you can wait for a few more months," Rim said, sardonically.

"From all indications, this structure is being abused, and is on the way to ruin. Moreover, we fear that someone might get it into his head to make off with its stones."

"What are you saying? Those stones do not figure at all in the construction of the plant...."

"Tourists will marvel at its architecture," the Professor mused, as if talking to himself.

"Is that what you think?" The question was more of a rebuke, than an expression of wonder.

"We take pride in our factories and hydroelectric plants, because we started from nothing," Professor Morena said, pursuing his train of thought. "Yet they make no impression at all on international visitors. The old church testifies to our building traditions, style, antiquity, and at the same time, serves as a point of contact between the culture of its day and our culture, which are separated by seven centuries."

Rim gave a push to his armchair, the way children do, widening the distance between himself and Morena.

"Still harping on religious cults and temples? Don't you know, or have you forgotten that we are an atheist state?" He purposely sidetracked his remarks to show him how shortsighted he was in the political arena.

"They are a part of our history. Permit me to remind you that religious sentiments are not exclusively connected with one's respect for Medieval art and architecture. The written Albanian language begins with religious writings. Lastly, the Party has entrusted to our Institute the task of protecting both religious and secular monuments."

The Deputy Prime Minister gritted his teeth with anger, and repented getting into this discussion.

"All right, then. What exactly do you want?" he asked, looking at the hills across the window.

"That the church become a part of our monuments."

"Fine! Send me the request. Ah, you've already submitted your request. Have we finished, then?"

The Professor walked out of the office.

As soon as he left, Rim Pepa began to distill the essence of the meeting. A Deputy Prime Minister who would issue an order to protect a certain church by some river as a cultural monument? Such a request—were he to submit it to the Politburo—would be seen as political myopia, contrariness, madness even, considering that the top leader only recently called to the attention of the Politburo plenum that religious feelings had revived in central Albania; hence, the Party's struggle in this area was not over. It was the Party's duty not only to scrutinize sporadic manifestations of religious sentiments, but also to uproot them without mercy. By now, Rim Pepa, too, had gained sufficient experience to view phenomena with a political eye, like all the members of the Politburo. He was in a position to demonstrate how much, and in what manner he was serving the revolution. This was the only correct stand for a revolutionary who had faith in the line of the Party. How could he propose that another church be added to the fund of monuments of culture? He couldn't stand the sight of the mosque in the center of Tirana. The religious temples were the basis of religious sentiments, and the sooner they disappeared, the sooner would full-fledged atheism be enthroned. Why should people believe in mystical beings like God, and not in the Party? He knew that the mentality of the Albanian people had placed God above the Party, and no amount of propaganda had been able to reverse that relationship. In their worldview, there is a God somewhere, who sees and judges everything that happens in the world, including the deeds of the Party, and one day He shall punish it for its transgressions. Even without thinking deeply about the matter, they thought that God was eternal, while the Party was temporary, and like all ephemeral things, it was not worthy of worship. Perhaps this was the main reason why the Party had dethroned God for good. After all this philosophical meditation, Rim was somewhat surprised that from time to time, such bright ideas suddenly flashed into his head.

Professor Morena lived in a world of fantasy to think that tourists would be fascinated by the ancient church. This was a grave political error. By making such a statement, he had in effect written off all of the majestic constructions of the Socialist Epoch in the country. He had to be denounced and be made into an example. Rim came frightfully close to losing his position on account of Professor's views regarding the state reserves.

What if Morena had reported somewhere, concerning their discussion? How naïve he had been.... Could he afford to endanger his position again, for the sake of a crummy old church? He had to come up with a revolutionary solution that would suit both the Party and himself.

* * *

"Yes, blow it up with dynamite," Rim ordered. Monika picked up the command, just as she was walking into his office to deliver an urgent message.

On the other end of the line, there must have been a certain perplexity or hesitation, since Rim went on to say:

"It's the order of the Deputy Prime Minister," after which he put the handset down.

"Don't!" a voice within Monika cried out. She was aware of the issue, and yet hoped with all her heart that she heard wrong.

Soon after she heard that the ancient church had been dynamited. She felt that something had collapsed inside her, as if she also had crumbled into a pile of rocks and become a ruin.

Rumors were heard that a cultural monument of historic significance had been destroyed, word went out that the explosion was accidental, allegedly due to the dynamite that was stored in the church. The gross lie was swallowed by the naïve, but not by Monika, who had heard the order that went out from the office of the Deputy Prime Minister. Neither did those who had seen miners with jackhammers, boring holes into the walls of the church, and placing sticks of dynamite in them. It troubled her that the handsome man, with an angelic face, could issue such a monstrous order

"We're going to stay around a little longer, to have a look at the report," Rim said and smiled at her.

She tried to avoid eye contact with him but for a fleeting moment their eyes met. Behind the desk she did not see the face of the man she loved. Rim's features resembled a cow's udder with bulging eyes, like those of the Gorgon. She knew that her feelings for him had been blown away and leveled like the old church by the river.

"Not tonight," she said, without hesitation. "I have made other plans."

Instantly sensing the sudden drift, he asked in a threatening tone:

"Have you decided to quit your job?"

She closed the door behind her without answering.

ꕤ The New Display of the Local Museum ꕤ

While putting the finishing touches to the refurbished local Museum, Director Vullnet Marko, learned by chance that during the liberation war the army's highest-ranking command had passed through the village of Verrishte. This important discovery was certain to upgrade the museum, as well as the man who made the discovery, namely the Director of the Museum, Vullnet Marko. Filled with so much joy, he felt compelled to share his enthusiasm with Kola, Principal of the Agricultural High School, who a few years earlier, had taken the initiative for the construction of the local museum. Although a newcomer to the region, Kola knew the history of the village and the country better than anyone else. No one could appreciate historical facts like him.

The school was nearby, yet Vullnet ran over there so fast that by the time he reached the principal's office, he was out of breath and emotionally all worked up.

"I have discovered…a stupendous…fact…about…the history of… the village," he spouted.

"Huh?" exclaimed Kola, as he stood up.

"The Joint Chiefs of Staff …passed…through here….during the war…and even slept here...one night…"

"No!" said Kola, in an obviously contradicting tone, so as to draw him out and hear more persuasive arguments.

"Yes!" insisted Vullnet.

"Who told you?" Kola asked.

"Isak, Isak Idrizi."

"Wow! Wow! Wow!" he exclaimed, standing beside Vullnet.

"A very lucky coincidence. And the timing! Just one week before the reopening of the museum after renovation."

"Isak, you say, huh?" Kola asked to reassure himself. "How is it he never told me? I've talked to him who knows how many times, yet he never mentioned this incident," the school principal remarked, dissatisfied.

"You know how some villagers are," Vullnet said to calm him down. "You got to pull it out of them with a pair of pliers. Also, something must bring the subject up, otherwise forget it."

Indeed, as history has shown, quite a few of the great scientific discoveries of science have been the caprice of chance: Newton's apple, the teakettle of James Watt, the invention of the blotter, etc. The most recent example was the discovery of Vullnet Marko. Had he not stepped out of the museum to stretch his limbs, and had he not met Isak there, the startling event would have been buried in the grave.

"We must inform Faik at the Village Council," Kola suggested.

"Certainly," Vullnet said, backing him up. "Send a student over to invite him."

Faik Balla, President of the Village Council, was a grey-haired veteran whose hair stood up like the tufts of a brush. Surprisingly, he received the big news coolly.

"I've not heard of such a thing, either during the war, or later," he said. Then quickly inquired about the source.

"Isak told us," revealed the Director of the Museum.

"Isak who?" asked the veteran, since there were four people in the village who were named after the honored biblical patriarch Isaac.

"Isak Idrizi," Vullnet informed him.

"Ohooo!" he exclaimed disdainfully. "Isak is not credible. Why, that man can't be trusted to give you the time of the day."

The Museum Director went on to say that Mustafa Topuzi from Lushaj, had told the same story.

"Maybe, maybe," he murmured thoughtfully.

Vullnet thought that he had to share the circumstances of the discovery in great detail. He had seen Isak walk in the museum, holding a bowl behind his back. Then he watched him make the rounds of the exhibits, and then exit without making any comments. Curious to get his first impression, he followed Isak outside.

"'How did you like the new look of the museum?'

"'So-so,' he said grudgingly.

"'You didn't like it? Keep in mind that we are not finished with it, yet, so we are open to suggestions and criticisms from visitors.'

"'No, no, you're doing fine,' Isak said mockingly.

"'The museum is not ours. It's for you, I mean the people of the region.'

"'Are you hurt because you didn't see your name on display?' I teased him. Typically, those who did not see their name exhibited, got sore. 'We are not the Census Bureau, you understand. It is common sense that not everyone will be featured in a museum,' Then Isak retorted with a maxim from the wellspring of popular wisdom.

"'If people valued the worth of the ox, they wouldn't slaughter it for pastrami when it grows old.'

"Just then, a dark-complexioned man, with a finely-chiseled face and thick eyebrows, whom I had not seen before, showed up by the cafeteria."

"'What! The cafeteria beans are not cooked the beans, yet?' he asked.

"As soon as he saw Isak, who was looking at the sun, and me standing alongside him, he said tartly, 'What is Isak up to? This guy will have you believe in fairy tales, if you let him.'

"Isak frowned, and as if talking to himself, said that I was new around here, and didn't know about things that happened in the past. Then, I said to him, 'No offense, Isak, but I have not seen your name anywhere, either for good or bad, even though I've leafed through many documents and memoirs about the Liberation War.'

"'Well, let's hear what this guy, who knows me, has to say,' Isak said. The swarthy fellow revealed to me that Isak was a familiar figure to the army's highest ranking officers, because he delivered mail to them and received communications. He added that both of them had served as guides to the Staff."

"Let's hear them," said Faik, "but I have my doubts."

The Museum Director, the School Principal and the Village Council Chairman walked back to the cafeteria, where Isak and Mustafa were waiting for them. Kola, the School Principle was quite upset that Isak did not confide to him the glorious exploit, while he was writing the history of the village, and instead dropped it unto the lap of the Museum Director.

"How come you didn't tell us this story before?" Kola reprimanded him.

"Did anyone ask me?" replied Isak, taking the offensive. "Nobody!"

"We issued a call to all those who had photographs, documents or other items relating to the war, to bring them to the museum," the School Principal explained. "We even advised the children to remind their parents."

Isak nudged his buddy with his elbow, as if to say, look what I have to deal with.

"You want me to give it to you straight? Well, it's not easy for a self-respecting man to come forward and say, 'Look what I have done,' because that would be bragging. We were waiting for you to call us, because everybody knows about it," Mustafa said.

"Excuse me, but are you from this village?" Vullnet asked him.

"We're from Lushaj. They call me Mustafa Topuzi," he said proudly, as if his were an academic title.

"Since I have no knowledge of it—and I'm the village historian—I assure you that nobody else is aware of this fact. I think this should be featured in our museum. Sensational," remarked the school principal.

"By all means! We shall highlight it with a special stand, with the names and photographs of these comrades," concurred the Museum Director.

A new Isak was coming to the fore now, quite different from the one they had known until then.

"I tell you frankly, I never imagined that you, Isak, could be involved in something like this," Faik told him. "After all, when we were fighting, you used to go to town to sell wood."

"With all due respect, you're not a good judge of people," Isak rebuked him. "You go along with the opinion of the crowd."

Isak then absolved the Chairman of the Village Council of any guilt, saying that he had a good heart, but unfortunately had been misled by those who were out to blacken his reputation. He heaved a long sigh to show how much he suffered that others did not believe him.

"Let's not get away from the subject," Vullnet intervened tactfully. "Tell us about the itinerary of the Joint Forces Command, how you traveled there, where did you take them and who did you meet?"

The questions of the Museum Director made Isak stop and think.

"We need some details," said the school principal. "You understand that…."

"Details? Here goes," replied Isak, right off the bat. He began by saying that he delivered highly confidential letters and communiqués in town. Then he pointed his finger at Faik, who had accused him of selling wood in the market.

"We had designated Zeke as our liaison to the Staff," intervened Faik.

"Well, who led Zeke to the forest?" Isak asked those present, with an air of triumph. "Who stood guard over him?"

"Fine," said Vullnet, granting him the point. "Can you tell us who informed you that the Staff needed a guide?"

Isak closed one eye and plunged into thought.

"What do you mean 'Who informed me?'" he asked, as if offended. "It was I who informed the others. If the father of this man here were alive today," he continued, indicating with his hand the Chairman of the Village Council, "you'd hear what he would say about me. The poor man died young. And he asked for me even as he was breathing his last breath. What last wish he had in mind, I do not know. Isn't that the truth, Faik?"

"Yes, yes," Faik replied hurriedly, backing him up, even though he could not recall his father asking for Isak in his last moments. Maybe he was too shaken up at the time to have noticed.

Isak said that he took his mule and went to cut wood in the forest. The snow was up to his waist. He saw several men walking toward him. As soon as they recognized him, they embraced him warmly. Then he led them to the village.

The Director of the Museum scratched his neck, and tried to picture the scene.

"You say you met them in the forest, fine. But who brought them over there? Because it had to be someone who knew the way...."

"It was me," Mustafa joined in at once.

"Go on!" the school principal urged him.

Isak reached toward Vullnet, and took out a cigarette from his pack.

"I had gone to see a friend in Balldren. 'We're going to recruit you for a secret mission,' my host said. 'You must not whisper a word to anyone. You will guide these men to Zalleger and from there onto Letaj, which is on the way of the destination. You are the most trusted man we know.'"

"We set out with three pack mules. I walked about fifty meters in front; the others followed. I kept my eyes wide open. Big responsibility, you know. What if we were ambushed? It's not that I was worried about my own skin. In some situations, a man doesn't give a damn about the risks he takes. As for the roads, I knew them blindfolded."

"Which way did you go?" Vullnet asked.

"From Balldren, we headed to Stojan Gorge, and then to the White Grill. I have to tell you, the snow up the hill was very deep. It nearly killed us. We stopped at the Gorge. I handed out a bit of tobacco to each one. But I had no paper to roll the tobacco. Then, in a flash, a tall man with a round face opened his briefcase. Talk about a charming fellow!" Mustafa and Isak winked at each other, giving one to understand that they knew he was the Commander in Chief.

"'I have paper,' he said. So, each of us rolled a cigarette. But the wind was so strong, you couldn't light it. My friend had given me cheese and warm bread baked on an earthen pan. I wanted to give a chunk to each of them. They refused to take it. 'That's your bread,' they said to me. 'Don't worry about me,' I said. 'I'm going back home, but you—you better eat what you can here.' 'Give it to your kids,' said the tall man, and his eyes filled with tears. I swore to them that I would not put that bread back into my sack. 'Either you take the bread, or I throw it into the brook.' Finally, they took it. There was enough there for a platoon, or more...."

"Didn't the Staff carry any food with them?" asked Faik.

"I don't know what the Staff had. I can only tell you about the food I gave them."

"Go on!" Vullnet pleaded.

"As soon as we got down to this side of the forest, I heard the sound of a hatchet. I got worried. Quickly I motioned to them to hide into a cave, while I continued to go forward."

"What about the horses?" asked Faik.

"Them, too, went into the cave," Mustafa continued. "I came down the slope, hiding behind the trees when I saw Isak's horse."

"Mule," Isak corrected him.

"From a distance, it looked like a horse," Mustafa said in self-defense. "However, I couldn't tell if it was him, or whether he had given his horse to somebody else. Isak was seated on a rock, cleaning the snow off his shoes."

"By golly, you recall things so well," Isak said in admiration.

"'Are you alone?' I asked him.

"'Yes,' he replied.

"I signaled to the staff to come down. They came and Isak met them. I could see that they knew each other."

"Excuse me, didn't you say you were going to Letaj?" Vullnet reminded him.

"We changed the plan, after we heard gunshots coming from that direction. So then, Isak became their guide. The next day, I met them again in the forest. Where did we meet, Isak?"

"At the Spata brook, right in the middle," answered Isak, coming to his aid. "You were sitting on top of a rock, and you had lit your pipe. As soon as I saw the smoke rising from your pipe, I knew it was you."

"Where did you take them, the night they came here?" asked Faik.

"Where could I take them?" Isak paused a while, so as to recall once again those difficult moments. "I thought about it and decided to take them to my place. Kind of tight but it was just one night. Firewood? I had a whole stack. Food? There was cornmeal mush, and fried eggs with minced meat. Who could you trust in those days? Besides, it was late. I figured, rather than trigger an alarm, or risk being spied on by someone, it was better to bring them home...."

"You did not even inform the Village Council, or anyone in the District?" Faik wanted to know.

"Nobody. It was orders," Isak said curtly.

"It is proper that we place a commemorative plaque on the house," remarked Vullnet.

"When they left," continued Isak, "the tall fellow unbuttoned the holster of his revolver, took the gun out and handed it to me."

"'Here, take it,' he said, 'and keep it as a souvenir from me.'

"What a revolver! What can I say? It had an ivory handle and a cylinder, too. My heart skipped a beat when I laid eyes on it."

"Did you take it?" Vullnet asked, hoping to get his hands on a precious relic, and a valuable material object.

Taking his time deliberately, Isak lit up a cigarette, and felt that his listeners were playing close attention, after their curiosity was aroused by the story of the revolver.

"Let's see now, where were we? Ah, yes, the revolver. For sure, it was worth twenty gold coins. I asked myself: Should I, or should I not take it? In some situations, a man just doesn't know which way to go."

"You didn't take it?" Kola asked.

"No," said Isak.

Everyone let out a sigh of disappointment.

"'No,' I said, 'I'm only going back to the village, you—you might need it on the road. It's wartime.' He laughed, put his hand on my shoulder and patted me two-three times, like a friend. I felt like hugging him. Just the same, he didn't leave me empty-handed. He reached into his briefcase, took out a notebook with red covers and handed it to me.

"'This, you have to take,' he said. And so I did."

"Do you have it?" Vullnet asked him.

"I had it until two or three years ago. But when the children grew up, they tossed it around here and there, and who knows where it ended up? It's too bad. I didn't have the wits to keep it," Isak said, sorrowfully.

"Did he write anything in the notebook?" asked Kola.

"Of course. He wrote my name, his signature, the date and who knows what else. I was blown away when he handed it to me. 'Jot down your memories, Isak, because we will need them some day,' he advised me. He was right of course, but I.... Well, we didn't think then like we do today...."

"What pack of lies!" grunted Faik. "Get the hell out of here! I don't believe a word you say, anymore."

Isak looked hard at those present, and swore:

"It's true, I swear by my children!"

Faik's outburst and Isak's oath were followed by silence that was broken by Mustafa.

"Well, I kept it," he said, with a gracious smile that lit up his swarthy face.

"What! He gave you a notebook, too?" Vullnet inquired.

"He offered me with a round of ammunition and a custom made cartridge belt. To be more exact, we exchanged belts, because I gave him mine, in turn!"

"You'd do the museum a great honor, if you can bring the belt over," Vullnet suggested.

Mustafa stared at him with a scolding look.

"There's nothing to think about," Vullnet remarked. "Next week we will have the re-opening of the museum, and will invite the Joint Staff here. We will put the cartridge belt on a special display stand, along with your name as the donor."

"If you only knew how many people have asked me for that cartridge belt," he said, and as he spoke, he kept raising his arm higher and higher. "Up to now, I have held on to it. Believe it or not, I hate to part with it. It's a cherished souvenir, you know."

"Don't think we want the belt for nothing," Vullnet elucidated. "Happily, the museum has not spent all its funds, and as soon as the Acquisitions Committee apprises the belt, I shall put the money right here," he said, patting Mustafa's pocket with his hand.

"Money is not an issue," Mustafa said disdainfully.

"Of course," joined the school principal, "but our society knows how to show its appreciation of relics."

After a series of passionate pleas, Mustafa Topuzi half-promised to surrender the belt, provided he succeeded in persuading his family to go along.

Faik got up and paced up and down a bit to relieve tension. Turning to Isak, he said:

"You're a devil, that's what you are, Isak. You chatter all day long here and there, yet you say nothing about things that really matter."

"Well, now, I'm not like some people who will do anything to get at Certificate and a war pension," Isak said, to justify his behavior. "You know, I had forgotten all about it. But this guy here," he said, as he nudged Mustafa with his elbow, "he has a sharp noodle. Remembers everything down to the last detail."

"How can one forget such things?" remarked Mustafa, speaking like someone who understood the value of historical encounters.

"Well, let's not waste any time," said Vullnet, who had a reputation as a practical man who knew how to get things done. "Now we know the itinerary of the army's highest ranking officers, the place where they slept, and their guides. You will bring your photograph...say, the size of a picture postcard, for the display."

"That's not necessary," Isak said with an air of modesty, after remembering that he didn't have a single half-decent photo of himself, and to get a new one cost money.

"On a second thought, let me have your identification papers" proposed Vullnet, "and our artist will draw your portraits."

Neither Isak, nor Mustafa had their identification papers with them. So, the Museum Director asked them to bring the papers in the afternoon. The cafeteria had opened. Without saying a word, Isak and Mustafa went inside.

"A double serving of beans for me," Mustafa ordered.

Isak stood there, and without saying a word, put his empty bowl in front of the cook.

"Are you paying for it, or eating on credit again?" asked the cook.

"You know what to do," Isak said smiling.

Mustafa signaled to Isak to draw near.

"Don't forget to get the Certificates from the Village Council," he commanded.

"Today?" Isak said, disconcerted. He didn't think it was proper to rush things.

"Strike while the iron is hot!" said Mustafa firmly.

* * *

Isak walked home with a bowl full of beans, and a Certificate in his pocket. As soon as he stepped in, he flung his hat into a corner and called out:

"Did you hear me, woman?" He was embarrassed to call his wife by her name.

"What got into you? Why are you hollering?" she turned on him.

"We are no longer poor folks!" said Isak. "We're through living on beans." He took the Certificate out of his pocket, and waved it in the air as if it were a bank check. "War pension, month after month." Then he started dancing solo, waving the Certificate in the air like a handkerchief.

"Have you gone loco?" his wife tore into him. "Since when do those who did not fight in the war, get a pension?"

"I was a guide," Isak explained.

"You?" There was such sarcasm and distrust in that single word that for a moment Isak lost his bearings.

"Why can't you believe?" he asked, after he collected himself.

"They had to depend on you to show them the way?" his wife asked, sneeringly.

In Isak's imagination, the monthly pension gleamed bright, and he swore to his wife that he was going to spend that money only to buy meat, chickens, turkeys, goats and lambs.

"Nobody gives you money for nothing these days!" remarked his wife, as she removed the corn bread from the earthen pan. "Eat your beans, and keep your mouth shut," she commanded.

* * *

"We put our heart in presenting the history of the town into this museum," Vullnet said to the Chairman. He felt disappointed that the museum was deep in the hinterlands, where few people traveled and government authorities rarely set foot. Still, their discovery will be appreciated by the descendants and the war veterans, he thought. "Did you notify comrade Zamir at the headquarters?"

"Yes. I told him to come a day earlier, to see the museum at a leisurely pace.'"

"And what did he say?" Vullnet was interested to know.

"He said that he will be here."

"Did you mention anything about the newest stand and the guides to the Chiefs-of-Staff?"

"No."

"Just as well. Let him see for himself."

* * *

As soon as the 'Volvo' of the highly positioned veteran came to a halt in the main square across from the renovated museum and the Cafeteria, Faik and Vullnet ran toward him, followed by the local secretary of the party's office, the school principal, and the in-house museum decorator.

They all greeted Zamir as a respectable official.

"You are the first visitor of our renovated museum. And when we go inside, you will see how much work and dedication we have put.... We are especially proud of an amazing display.... You will see it soon enough!" said Vullnet while pushing open the doors of the museum.

Accustomed to inspections prior to official openings of little town museums, Zamir walked quickly past the exhibits on Antiquity and the Middle Ages that had little value, apart from some reproductions of maps.

"We have given priority to the National Liberation War," Vullnet told him.

"Naturally," he concurred.

The entourage that followed heard him say from time to time, "nice, nice." They wondered with anticipation about Zamir's words of appreciation on the special display that commemorated the night that the Army's Commanders had stayed in Verrishte.

"Here it is! We saved the best for last!" Vullnet announced rather solemnly.

The visitor gawked at the display. He noticed the portraits of Isak and Mustafa and turned nervously towards Vullnet:

"What are these two doing here?"

"They were guides to the Joint Chiefs of Staff," Vullnet tried to explain.

"Who? Isak Idrizi?" questioned the visitor with scorn.

"Didn't I tell you?" the Chairman of the Village Council said quickly to Vullnet. "Isak can't be trusted."

"Everything Isak said was backed up point by point by Mustafa Topuzi from Lushaj," observed the school principal.

"Isak is capable of making up stories on the spot," Zamir said. "He sent a stack of petitions to grant him a war pension. Now he is claiming he was a guide, because he knows that guides are entitled to a pension."

"I began to have my doubts when Isak said that he had taken the Chiefs of Staff to his home," the school principal said.

"You had doubts, but you kept your mouth shut.... You said nothing to us," Faik said, rebuking him.

"Their stories were full of details. Anybody could have been confused," Vullnet said in his own defense.

The idea of making a one-of-a-kind 'discovery' about the Highest Military Authority's sleepover in the little town had carried away the men-in-charge of the museum. All the details about the notebook, the cartridge belt, the home-made bread were sheer nonsense!

"There is no greater fool than the one who wants to be fooled!" concluded the visitor.

"We still need to find out how the Chiefs of Staff got here and who were the real guides," intervened the ever-practical Vullnet.

"You're still in the woods? They never set foot in this area!" responded Zamir walking towards the Museum's exit.

The Sweetest Death

In the office of the Health Minister entered Kanan holding a telegram in his hand.

"We have just been informed that Servet Joni has died," he related, looking again at the telegram with the death notice.

"We're all going to die someday," the Minister said jokingly. Then, with a serious demeanor, he asked, "Who is Servet Joni? I have never heard that name before. I mean, what does the Ministry have to do with him? Is there some complaint about the health care, the hospital, some particular physician, the first-aid treatment?"

"No, nothing like that," the Director of medical care assured him.

"What is it, then?" the Minister asked, irritated.

"Since you have advised us to inform you, upon the death of a close relative of the senior party officials, I thought I should let you know…."

The Minister suddenly awoke from his stupor, and asked: "Did you say his name was Joni? Any connection with Arsen Joni?"

"It's his brother, or more exactly, he was…" Kanan said.

"One can only imagine how devastated his family must be. You did well to inform me. I must without fail express condolences to Arsen, in my own behalf and in behalf of my department."

For his part, the minister was not clear about what one was supposed to do on such an occasion. Should he wait for a notice from the protocol office of the Prime Minister, advising that the office pay a formal visit to the member of the Politburo or perhaps express sympathy to the family individually? He concluded that the best thing for him was to pay respect ahead of the others. Then he realized that Arsen must be off to attend the funeral of his brother. Clearly, both options had their pluses and minuses. It was difficult to choose, even for a Minister.

Even after smoking three cigarettes, he was unable to make a decision, so he picked up the phone and called the Minister of Agriculture, who had served in that post for a long time, and had more experience in such matters. Recently, Mirush had been promoted to a candidate member of the Politburo, practically he was on the threshold of the highest position that a Party member could aspire to.

Replying to Mentor's question about what to do, Mirush said without hesitation that the honor and duty dictated that they stay close to comrade Arsen at this time of great loss; otherwise, he might be offended.

"Do you think we should attend the funeral of...?" the Minister froze up for he could not recall the name of the deceased.

"Of course. As for myself, I have to go to bid him 'good-bye,' first of all because we come from the same region, and secondly because we grew up together," he said decisively.

"We don't know when the services will be held," observed the Health Minister.

"I shall inquire and let you know at once," came the response from the other end of the phone line.

* * *

The next day, as they were driving south, seated comfortably in the Mercedes-Benz of the Politburo candidate, the Minister of Health said off-handedly:

"I have not been aware that Arsen had a brother in the south."

"He chose to live there, himself," Mirush responded.

"Did you know Servet?" Mentor asked.

"Yeeees, I knew him since I was young. Knew him quite well. A man of stature!" said Mirush, with admiration. "For a time during the war, we were in the same battalion. He was a brave fellow. Nobody could slow him down. He had put his head on the block, so to speak, the moment he took up the arms. A man of rare qualities, soft-spoken, friendly, sociable. After the liberation, he was an officer for a while. Later, he went to the Soviet Union for advanced studies in the military field, but I believe he returned home, after the break up in with Moscow. Yet, even in civilian life, he never took off his army boots. He was an elegant dresser. Man, what a splendid sight he was, all dressed up! He went about with his vest unbuttoned, so he could show off his tie. He wore fine jackets, as well, and hats that he tilted slightly to one side. Real *chic*!"

As soon as they got to the city, the chauffeur asked for directions to the home of the deceased, then steered the black sedan in the proper route. A line of cars and jeeps of different types and colors, were parked along a good stretch of the street, near the house of the departed.

The candidate of the Politburo and the Minister of Health got out of the car and started to go up the stairs, hats in hand. Both leaves of the door to the apartment of the deceased were wide open, so that visitors could walk in without knocking. Upon entering the reception room, they spotted Arsen, who seemed shattered by sorrow and the stifling heat. To his right, there was a woman with a black headscarf, evidently the lady of the house. Further away there were several women, all dressed in black. The minister was somewhat relieved to see that the old tradition did not hold here, since both men and women were received in the same room. He did not have to go to another room, and put on a look of grief before the casket, for the sake of appearances. He noticed that his companion shook hands first with the wife of the departed, then with comrade Arsen. Carefully, he repeated the ritual.

Like one who was familiar with the customs of the region, Mirush asked "Did he suffer much?"

The widow raised her eyebrows with a hint of nervousness, but said nothing, as if to indicate that it didn't matter anymore.

"It was totally unexpected," answered the brother of the deceased, which is to say, the member of the Politburo. "I was getting ready to go to work, when the telephone rang, at about half past six. They said to come over, because Servet was ill and had been rushed over to the emergency ward. In fact, he had expired overnight, but you understand, they did not want to tell me right away...."

"Sudden deaths are harder to take, because one is not prepared for them psychologically," observed Mirush, and all agreed. "A dear one slips through your fingers, and you cannot believe it. You feel like you're in a bad dream."

"The doctors ascertained that it was a severe heart attack," Arsen explained.

The Minister of Health, being a specialist who understood the bitter blows of fate, shook his head sorrowfully and said:

"The heart is the most delicate organ in the body," Mirush elaborated. "Out of the blue, it takes stops beating, and you drop dead. It's the best way to go, because you don't feel anything. But it's a terrible blow to close survivors."

He was voicing age-old truths, and everybody was in agreement.

"Did he have heart trouble?" Mentor was interested to know, as a health professional.

"Actually, he never complained. Isn't that right, Neriman?" Arsen said, seeking support from the widow, his sister-in-law.

She shook her head, to indicate he hadn't.

"Maybe he did, but wouldn't say," said the Minister of Health. "It all depends on the character of the individual."

"He did not tell. He was a restrained man," Mirush noted. "You are aware that I knew him since the war. He was a patient man because he had faith that we were going to win. What's more, he was soft-spoken and cheerful. When you went with Servet to someone's home, you made friends with the man of the house, within half an hour. He communicated with everybody. In this respect, he was outstanding. As for loyalty to the Party, he was top-notch. He has also received several honors, I think."

"Yes, the medal of bravery, and, and...I can't recall them all, now," Arsen said, to excuse himself. "We've ordered five or six red satin pillows, to display them at the funeral ceremony."

Just then, Shahin, the party secretary of the district entered the room. He walked past the members of the family, which meant that he had been there earlier. He went directly to the two ministers, who had arrived from the capital. He only shook hands with Mirush, whereas opened his arms wide and embraced Mentor warmly.

"Where did Servet work lately?" Mirush asked.

Arsen didn't know what to say, so he sought the aid of Neriman, by turning toward her. She, however, continued to maintain her mournful silence.

"Manager," intervened Shahin. But since that post seemed rather modest, he up scaled it. "That is to say, director of the pension's office."

"How old was he?"

"Fifty-nine," answered Shahin.

"Shame, didn't even reach retirement age," an old man broke in, "even though he worked in the pension's office."

"Life is strange," observed Mirush. "Servet doled out pension money to others, but didn't live long enough to receive a pension himself."

"Several times we offered him positions of responsibility, but he refused," informed Shahin. "He was content where he was, year in, year out."

"He was a modest man," said Mirush. "Modesty is a big plus in life. It's the most prized value in a communist, Lenin has declared."

In truth, the citation pertains to Marx, but none of those present questioned it, either because they did not know the source, or because they did not want to offend the high-ranking Party official who was ignorant of Marxism, even though he was seated in its Red Pantheon.

Then the conversation shifted to the ten moral qualities that defined the New Age Man, inscribed on the membership card of every communist, so they could be aware of them constantly. Mirush noted that every Party member had assimilated those qualities, and then some.

With positive conviction, Mirush said that Servet lived his life honorably, and in our time, such a life has exceptional merits.

"He left behind a respected name," he said, in a burst of poetic inspiration, which caused Shahin to look at him with admiration.

"A family man, decent, hard worker, loyal to Marxist principles – these values are paramount today. Yet, death doesn't care, and is doing away with our best fellow…."

Neriman, who, all along, had remained silent as a sphinx, gave him an angry look, and immediately rushed out of the room.

"Yesterday afternoon, he and I were together," intervened Shahin. "We joked, had some drinks – I mean a glass, since at our age the body needs 75 grams of whiskey, because it lowers the blood pressure, they say…."

The titled figure in the field of health was in agreement. He thought Ruci's statement embodied scientific truth.

Someone at the door signaled to Arsen and he got up at once and walked over there. He returned promptly with a stack of telegrams in his hand.

"A telegram of sympathy from the Prime Minister," announced Arsen to those present. His face lit up with joy, almost as if his brother had come back to life. "He says, 'we share your deep sorrow.'"

The telegram passed from hand to hand, as if the mourners wanted to glean something more from the one-line inscription on the tape glued to the surface of the telegram.

"Neriman, a telegram from the Prime Minister," Arsen said, reaching out toward her with the telegram, as soon as she appeared at the door.

"That means he is not coming," she said, while refusing to take the telegram.

"The newspaper, I believe, will print his obituary, with a photo," someone said.

"He deserves it," Mirush added, to put a lid on the matter. "He was a fine comrade, loyal to the end."

The funeral was scheduled for three o'clock in the afternoon. Since visitors kept coming to express their condolences, the two officials from Tirana saw fit to step out, so as to make room for others. The District Secretary went out with them.

* * *

"How is it, that no one bothered to serve us a cup of coffee?" Mentor complained.

"After the funeral, not before. That's the custom around here," explained Mirush.

"We can have a good cup of coffee at the club," Shahin proposed. "We have plenty of time."

"How is the winery doing?" Mentor asked. "Is it going to produce sweet Riesling again this year? Last year they sent me a whole case of it, for wine tasting, you know. It was excellent so I'm ready to order a case."

"Wasn't Servet, the head of that plant for a while?" inquired Mirush, not knowing for sure.

"He was, indeed," Shahin assured him, with a grin.

"Why are you grinning?" queried Mentor.

"He became notorious there. The inspectors discovered that, over the course of a year, Servet had put in 404 days of work. Astronomical! Even if he had gone to work out of the city every day in the year, he would have had a total of 365 days to his credit. He kept filling out work-forms, turning them over to the bookkeeper, and pocketing the money. That's not all. He called female employees to his office and pressured them to give in or lose their job. We had to transfer him. However, the winery got a bad name, and since that time, nobody dares to send a young woman there, whether she is single or married."

"Did he hit the bottle a little, like in the old days?" Mirush asked him, and simultaneously brought his hand close to his lips, as if he were downing a shot.

"Not just a little," observed Shahin. "Servet drank every kind of alcohol, with or without color, till he got groggy. All day long, he was like a boat bouncing with the waves."

"You said earlier that he was a supervisor over at...." Mentor squirmed as he tried to recall Servet's place of work.

"You mean the pension's office? That was a joke. He showed up there, only to get a good salary. What could we do? He was, after all, the brother of comrade Arsen. We have capable young people: economists and well-educated finance specialists, who wait anxiously for job openings. It was useless to try to look up Servet in his office. He didn't even spend an hour there. 'I'm off to do field inspection,' he would say, then made the rounds from one bar to another...."

"You're going a bit too far, or perhaps you are just joking," the Minister rebuked him gently.

"I swear, I'm not," Shahin said, in self-defense. "Everybody around here knows these things. What happened last night tops them all. I suppose you know about the scandal.... I mean, do you know where he died?" Shahin asked, to whet their curiosity.

"In some restaurant or on the road?" Mirush ventured to guess.

"That would have been peachy.... Servet died in the arms of his mistress."

Mirush looked grim, seeing that the name of his old-time friend was being sullied. True, his conduct was unbecoming and clashed directly with the norms of public morality. Nevertheless, it was not in good taste to gossip about him like this. That didn't stop Shahin from continuing with his revelations.

"We all knew that he went to her regularly, to top her two or three times a week, and he made no effort to keep it a secret. We tried to advise him a number of times, but he told us we were behind the times. We said to him that people were talking. 'I don't care if others talk. They will get tired of talking, and then they will stop,' Servet said, in self-defense."

"How did his wife put up with him?" asked Mentor.

"As if he cared about Neriman. He had hot pants. His mistress... what a beauty; a lovely widow that can steal a man's heart. She had such a shapely figure that, when she walked down the street, she attracted men's eyes like a magnet. He turned around to see if anybody was listening, but fortunately, there was no one in the lounge. "Servet had good taste, you got to hand it to him," Shahin noted with admiration.

"Well, well!" grumbled Mentor, indirectly scolding him for sympathizing with a libertine.

"Anyway, she was his 'official' liaison," the Party secretary continued.

"What do you mean by 'official'?" protested Mirush Kajtazi. "The law forbids polygamy."

"I mean that his amorous relations were common knowledge. What's more, the mistress was proud of Servet's company. Whenever she shopped for meat or wine, she said she was expecting Servet. It was in her bed that our comrade breathed his last breath." One could detect both mockery and esteem in Shahin's voice. "She called up emergency. The doctor who showed up could do nothing, except to confirm the death of 'her husband.' Then she informed him that he was not her husband, but a visitor and close friend. We had to keep this under wraps. We had to get him out of there, without anybody noticing. Neriman and the family had to be notified. We did not know whether to tell the truth, or lie to them. We were in a tough spot, either way."

"Did you get personally involved?" Mentor asked.

"Of course! Only my authority could coat over the grimy mess...," the secretary said.

"Tell us," Mirush commanded.

"I called up the doctor who pronounced him dead, and told him to return to the companion's home, put Servet on a stretcher, take him to the hospital and declare that he died there. The doctor objected saying that the emergency ward does not admit corpses. I said to him, 'Do whatever you want. Take him to the morgue, if you wish, or to the autopsy clinic; just, get him out of there.' Then I sent the second-ranking secretary – together with another comrade, to give the bad news to Servet's wife. Neriman didn't shed a tear. She said she did not want that philanderer back in her house. 'Let the other woman tend to him,' she said, screaming at the top of her voice. I had to go over there myself. I took her aside, and tried to convince her that the way she was taking this, was not good either for her, or for the children. She was not convinced. To put pressure on her, I told her that we were going to dump the corpse on her doorstep, without her permission. 'If you bring him here,' she said, 'I'll leave the house and won't come back until after the funeral.' Then I softened my tone. 'Please, Neriman,' I said, 'all of us praise you for your patience and self-restraint....' She replied, 'I put up with him as long as he was alive, for the sake of the children. I can't do it anymore. Why do you ask me to keep mum about his shameless ways, which went on and on during years? He got what he deserved.... I shall never forgive him for the shame he brought on the family.' I have never seen a more indignant woman. We had to find an acceptable solution. Did you notice how she received visitors who came to express sympathy?"

"I thought she was stone-faced on account of the pain she felt," Mentor said.

"You know what else she said to me? She said, 'You expect me to foot the bill for the funeral expenses of a rake that expired in the arms of another woman? He didn't bring home even a quarter of his salary.' I tried to impress on her how this would look to the outside world. She said, 'Let those who don't know the story, learn all about it now. I don't care.' I told her that our committee would cover the funeral expenses, since Servet was a war veteran. Truly, a tragic-comedy," commented Shahin.

Clearly, Mirush looked upset, not so much, because of Servet's suddenly eventful death, but because of all those fine words, he had said about him earlier. If the Party leaders were to learn about the interesting circumstances surrounding Servet's death, what would they think of those who attended the funeral? He looked angrily at the Minister of Health. It is his fault that Mirush had to attend the funeral of a knave, who died in the bed of his mistress. Instinctively, he felt that he had to inquire if there was another personality there of equal rank with him. That way, he would not give the impression that he paid no attention to the moral equation of things. There was only one other personality at the funeral – Arsen Joni, the brother of Servet.

"Has comrade Arsen heard of the incident?" Mirush asked.

"Certainly! When he arrived from Tirana, I was, talking to Neriman at Servet's home. Comrade Arsen walked into the room with a desolate look on his face and eyes full of sorrow. He opened his arms wide and rushed over to his sister-in-law, and said with overwhelming sadness,

'Neriman, he is gone! How could you let him go, so soon? Where are you, dear brother? Let me look at you one more time....' Since he did not see the body there, he headed for the bedroom. Neriman grabbed his shoulder and said bluntly, 'Now that he is dead you found your way here? Where have you been until now? You didn't invite him, or us, even when you married your daughter.' She talked to him as if he were a nobody. 'Let's forget about those things now, and let me see my brother,' he begged her. 'Sit down. You will see your brother, in due time,' she said. Her mocking, icy tone of voice shattered comrade Arsen. He slumped into the armchair, curled up and waited to hear what dreadful thing had happened.

" 'We took him over to the hospital, to do an autopsy on him,' I broke in."

"He fixed his eyes on me and said, 'Come out with it! What happened? Was he killed? Did he commit suicide, or what?' 'He died a natural death,' I said, to calm him. 'He suffered a heart attack during the night, and died on the way to the hospital.'

"'Natural, totally natural,' followed up Neriman, in a sarcastic tone. She got up in a hurry, took her brother-in-law by the arm, and the two of them went into the adjoining room. When comrade Arsen came back, he looked more despondent that when he first showed up.

"It's a pity for a man of merits like Servet Joni to end up like this," Shahin said in ending his story.

"Indeed, you told us that he was a brave warrior. Fought standing up...."

The Minister of Agriculture eyed him with an angry look.

"Brave?! You call brave someone who fires behind a rock and sprays the sky with bullets? Enough, for heaven's sake! We know what he was like...a big fart and wisecracker. We almost shot him for making advances to a female comrade. If she hadn't begged us to forgive him, we would have shot him, and been spared the trouble he has caused us."

"His friends say that he was expelled from the Military Academy in Moscow, as well," Shahin added, "although he went around saying that he returned home on account of our break-up with the Soviet Union. It was funny how he kept saying, 'I don't depend on anybody!' As if people didn't know that he was Arsen's brother. Who knows how many other villainies of his they ignored?"

"I don't feel like going to the funeral," Mirush declared.

"We have no choice, we got to go for the sake of comrade Arsen," Shahin said, emphatically.

* * *

All three hopped into the Party secretary's car, and joined the long procession of cars that accompanied Servet to his last home. At the cemetery, Mirush was the first one to get out of the car. He lifted his pants up, so they would not get all dirty from the mud, and proceeded toward the throng of mourners. He looked very calm, and surveyed the landscape with pleasure, like someone taking a stroll, while the other two followed. The mourners gathered around the newly dug grave. On the smooth and shiny fabric of the pillows in the casket, trophies, decorations and medals glinted in the sunlight. Mirush could hardly wait to hear the end of the speech about the exemplary life and lofty deeds of Servet Joni. While the eulogy was being delivered, Mirush whispered to the Secretary:

"It seems to me that there is a spirit of liberalism in these funeral orations, which runs counter to the teachings of the Party. What's the meaning of these boundless words of praise? Do you look at the speeches, before they are delivered? I think they should be looked at."

"You are right. We should be more reserved," Shahin said, with deep conviction.

After placing the wreaths on the fresh soil over the grave, the members of the family lined up to receive condolences. Arsen Joni was first in line. Mirush, Mentor, and Shahin joined the long line of mourners. "Come and join us at the dinner for the deceased," said a voice that came from the group of family members.

Walking back to the car of the secretary, the Minister of Health commented:

"Big crowd at the funeral. Just like an open-air meeting."

"If you ask me, he was worth less than the funeral expenses," snorted Mirush, not caring in the least to hide his contempt for the departed. "They should say: Mud to mud."

"Funerals have their lighter side," Shahin said. "On our way here, I heard an old man say to his buddy: 'That's what I call a sweet death. I wish I could go like Servet'."

Mirush did not appreciate the humor that expressed approval for the violation of moral norms and marital fidelity.

"The restaurant where the funeral dinner will be served is nearby. Custom requires that we have a bite to eat, drink the custom-honored coffee of the occasion – which, by the way, we were not served at his home – and shake hands with the members of the family," advised Shahin.

"We already shook hands with them at the cemetery. I see no reason to go through that again," protested Mirush. "Besides, I have a seven o'clock appointment in Tirana."

The Minister of Health backed him up. They had come together; they should go back together.

The secretary leaned over and whispered:

"To say nothing of his other follies, Servet put the top leaders in a predicament. However, I do have an obligation to show up at the restaurant. I can't afford to be absent."

The car engine started with a pleasant hum and took off, leaving behind a trail of thin blue smoke, which gradually dispersed in the afternoon air.

℘ Made in Albania ☙

Last week, the widely circulated newspaper *Zëri i popullit* published a long article about Albania's foreign trade. Among other things, the article pointed out that we, Albanians are duty-bound to think seriously about our exports, to expand the range of traditional articles, keeping in mind that "without exports, there cannot be imports." To say that unless we sell, we cannot buy, was an open threat to the citizens, and it did plunge me into deep thought. As a responsible citizen, I am sensitive to problems that concern the country. Seeing the worried look on my face, my wife asked what was bothering me. I should have kept my mouth shut, for as soon as I told her, she began to scold me.

"You got no reason to worry about exports and imports. That's the responsibility of those who get paid for it, and spend their earnings roaming all over Europe like perennial tourists."

The target of her outburst are the scores of government employees in the Department of Foreign Trade, and firms with names ending with "Imp" and "Ex," like "Agroexport" and "Mineralimpex" and many others. The wise guys go on trips out of the country to sell our products, and return with their suitcases full of household goods for themselves and presents for their bosses.

Personally, I think that we should not take a narrow view of the problem, as my wife does. It is a good thing that the government officials buy foreign goods. This way they help boost international trade, and also make it possible for us to look at some elegant merchandise. Let evil tongues rail that foreign trade took a nosedive when those positions were taken over by the nomenclature clan, and that most of them are incompetent. Take my word for it they are wrong. You have no idea how clever and resourceful they are.... I'll give you just one recent example. When the government specified that one must know a foreign language to get a job in the foreign trade sector, they obtained their certificates and diplomas within a week, all signed and stamped by the accredited institutes and school departments. What's more they got them without taking so much as a single course or even walking through the doors of a language school. Who can say that this is not evidence of ability?

Indeed, even those who know foreign languages take care, not to communicate well with representatives of foreign firms, when they travel abroad, since such a tactic opens doors for them to travel abroad one again. Travel abroad is the best business today.

Evidently our exports have suffered a notable decline even in articles like chrome, tobacco and petroleum, which kept our export trade afloat, it is our duty as devoted citizens to help our export specialists with concrete proposals and suggestions.

The field of foreign trade is limitless; only it requires some imagination. The trick is to impose ourselves on the capitalist market, with the high quality of our goods, and packaging that is so attractive they will take our crates without the tomatoes, and our glass jars without the pickled peppers. And the main thing, in my opinion, is to offer unique products, which cannot be purchased anywhere else in the world, even if they were to climb up and down the latitude lines of the five continents, like the steps of an apartment.

Inspired by the article, I have the pleasure to recommend such a rare commodity, which the international market needs today, and will need even more in the future.

We could export, at very handsome returns, acclamations, ovations, frenzied hand-clapping and especially rhythmic applause, which is by far our supreme specialty in the realm of sound. This genial idea came to me the other night quite by chance, while watching a movie by a famous French film director. As waves of a massive demonstration passed by on the screen, I had the feeling that all of Place de la Concorde in Paris was shouting in unison our best-known slogan in this half-century, "a-e-e-e, -u-e-u-e-e-e-e!" I was stunned. Why were they shouting in Albanian, instead of their own language? I solved the mystery yesterday, while chatting with a friend of mine, a TV editor. He told me that the French director had been in Albania for a visit the year before, and was astonished by... what do you think? The style of the socialist architecture? The beauty of the landscape? The blue waters of the Riviera? No. The acclamations! Captivated by their perfection, he wanted to acquire several meters of massive rhythmic applause, to use them for his latest film. Eager to seem generous, the directors of Albanian Radio/TV gave them to him gratis!!! What rank idiocy! What folly! How can you such a gem be given gratis? Think of the dollars the Albanian Film Studio would have paid to purchase similar sounds from Cinecittta or Hollywood, or any other international film studio?

Do you think it is easy to gather twelve hundred government representatives in one place and have them shout in unison -a-i-e-e, -u-e-u-e-e-e-e? Or to order thousands upon thousands of citizens to cheer all at once in the Skanderbeg Square? Even if the film producer paid the 'shouters' just five dollars apiece, which is a peanut, he would have had to shell out two hundred thousand dollars. Not to mention that the young generation of Europeans doesn't even know how to shout, no matter what you pay them, while the Americans can only howl.

Truthfully, it was no easy job even for us to master this particular art. It took God knows how many meetings, conventions and Congresses, as well as numerous years of training. Thanks to our caring Communist Party, which identified shouts with patriotism, rhythmic applause with unity, yelling with devotion and acclamations with enthusiasm, we learned to applaud indoors and outdoors; in flat, hilly or mountainous terrain; in momentum. In time, our acclamations became a reflex action. As soon as we spotted people on a reviewing stand, or a gathering of high officials, or even a Mercedes-Benz with curtained windows, we started to applaud either singly or in chorus. In fact, this mentality became so ingrained in us that even at weddings or evenings with the family, we could not eat or drink without shouting in unison some ovations and acclamations for the Party.

Nobody has applauded longer, more vigorously, or with as much style as we have. Our credentials in the field of acclamations reached such a high level, that we can lay claim to this discipline as a specialty of ours. The rich experience we have accumulated is enough to make us the envy of every country in the world. Maybe we are not perceptive about the latest developments in science, and we generally don't stand out for our work ethic but when it comes to enthusiastic clapping, standing ovations and rhythmic round of applause, nobody can beat us. We are invincible! We are champions!

Since we have accrued this rare treasure, starting with kindergartens and on to colleges, factories, military bases, town squares, all the way up to the halls of Party Congresses, why should not we market a portion of this wealth. And the best part, no matter how much we sell, there will still be plenty left over to meet our needs.

To advertise this rare commodity, I think we need to have a catalog with appropriate classifications of the shouts, the ovations and the rounds of applause. It must be complied by sound technicians and music experts, and should feature classifications that perhaps could follow musical terminology such as *moderato, andante, allegro, allegretto, crescendo, allegro vivace, marciale* all the way to *maestoso*. A widely unlimited selection of applauding sounds and styles without any possible match will surely put Albania on the world map of the trading business. Endless variations such as angelic rhythmic applause with children's voices, lyrical acclamations by young girls and women, martial rounds by soldiers and students, acclamations by people in marches and parades. Excited handclapping and hysterical, I mean, historical– rounds of applause from the Party Conventions throughout the years. Trust me, enough applause to drive anyone wild: furious, stormy, wall penetrating, sensational, majestic, riveting, electrifying! The export sector will soon be selling applauses 'Made in Albania' across the seas all over the globe!

Ovations for a variety of occasions! Albania's exporting goods industry will be proud of such an item! The demand for this peculiar article will be inexhaustible! What a product! Admittedly, acclamations signify a great accomplishment scored by the Party! It does not take a mastermind to realize that such ovations represent a precious product created by the socialist system!

I am confident that the one-of-a-kind-item of export is going to be a sensation in the international market. Here is a headline that is sure to draw a crowd: Buy acclamations 'Made in Albania'! No other country can supply such a line of production for export!

꧁ Daydreaming ꧂

Gole's face brightened up when his nephew visited him unexpectedly. Seeing him wearing a suit and tie, a married man with children, Gole asked himself whether his visitor from the capital was ever that little boy in short pants who returned from the playing field all sweated up and ate a bowl of breadcrumbs swirling in milk, after endless hours of playing outside. Gole tried to recall the boy's last visit.

"How many years is it, since we last saw you?" the uncle asked in a nice way.

"I don't remember," Kleo replied, without feeling any regret about the infrequent visits.

Although the town of Fier was not even a three hour drive from Tirana, the capital, his nephew stopped by only rarely. The uncle believed that only the most competent and brightest economists were hired to work in the State Planning Commission, since it was there that the future of the country was charted.

"It's a position of responsibility. You have to have a lot in your noodle to work there," Gole would say to his fellow pensioners.

"Look, Uncle, we go wherever they order us to go, not where we want to," Kleo said, to clarify the point.

"Don't give me that.... If you want to, you can fix it," his uncle declared, with a smile on his lips. "Even when you visit us, you're gone in a jiffy."

"You want to know the truth?" Kleo retorted. "I don't have the heart to stay here." He turned around and looked at the kitchen. Two straw-padded mattresses spread tight on the floor, leaving barely enough room for a small table between them. "It is really cramped!"

"No doubt about it," Gole conceded. "For three years straight, I've been going around from office to office to ask for a bigger apartment. My feet are killing me." The housing issue dispersed all the excitement of seeing his sister's boy. "If I had laid just one brick a day in all that time, I could have built my own house by now. No matter who I talk to, I hear the same story: 'We'll look into it', 'It's in the works', 'don't you worry about it', and what did I get? Nothing! And to make matters worse, she dogs my footsteps at every turn," he said, pointing to his wife. "Wherever I go, she follows. What's the matter with you?" he hollered at her, menacingly. "You didn't hang on to me like this, even when I was a young man."

"It's his high blood pressure," Sofika explained to the nephew. "We know a lot of old men who have died on the waiting lines. That's why I don't leave him alone," she said, resolutely.

There was something comical about their relationship. They argued and mocked each other because of some whim or quirk of one or the other, quarreled and traded insults loudly, and then, all of a sudden, lowered their voices as if they were some other couple altogether.

"Do you know the Mayor?" Kleo asked him.

"You bet, I do! I've known Masar since the war.... We were buddies," Gole elucidated. One could tell from the tone of his voice that he was unhappy over the stagnation of their comradeship.

"What Masar are you talking about?" his nephew asked, since the name rang a bell for him.

"Masar Veizi, who else...?"

"You mean he is still alive?" Kleo exclaimed with astonishment, as if the Biblical story of Methuselah who lived to be 969 was recurring before his eyes.

"Alive and well, stout and rosy-cheeked like a mountain shepherd. Why should he get old? He has a palace for a home, he gorges on meat and baklava, and he has a couple of cars always at his doorstep, one to take him to the highlands, the other to the lowlands. Then there are receptions to go to, and dinners, and...in a word, he's having a hell of a good time!" the simple war veteran burst out.

"I remember him, because he tied the Pioneer's Scarf around my neck, at the memorial monument thirty years ago. He must be in his seventies by now," observed Kleo.

"He is past the 70's. We are the same age," Gole Meta said, to set the record straight. "Me, I'm a victim...because I didn't have any schooling, while they decided to keep him...."

"Why?" the nephew cut in. "You finished the elementary."

"True enough. He didn't have more schooling than me, but he had connections. That's the difference. And only a few years ago, to everyone's surprise, they made him Mayor. In the old days, they used to say that 'he who sits beneath the pear tree, gets to eat pears,' while today, it's the guy on top who eats the pears, while those below take whatever those on top throw them," Gole complained.

"Hush!" his wife yelled at him, as she pressed her lips with her fingers.

"Have you gone to see the Mayor?" the nephew asked. "Why don't you ask for an appointment, seeing that he is a friend of yours? Go to his office and explain the situation. After all, it's not as if you'll be asking him a favor—only what you're entitled to by law."

"Nobody pays any attention to veterans," Gole continued with his complaints.

"No, Uncle, you're wrong. Who is running the country today? The elderly!" retorted the nephew.

In the course of four decades, the state administration went from one extremely young age to the exceedingly old. In 1945, youngsters without any experience were given titles and held ministerial positions in the government. According to the Soviet journalist, Ilya Ehrenburg, the median age of the Albanian government officials at the time was the youngest in the world. Forty years later, old men sat as the heads of every government office. As in all communist countries, gerontocracy held sway. The postwar youth had grown old, moving vertically from one post to another or horizontally from one armchair to the other, and leaving no openings for young people. A close friend of Kleo used to say that their generation was condemned to vegetate in the shadow of authoritarian old men.

"We are the 'shadow generation' or the 'scorched generation'," he confided, likening his peers to the "Lost Generation" of Europe. "To them, it seemed quite normal to hold positions of power in their youth days. But, now that they are pushing seventies, they do not trust college educated young people in government positions. The old generation alleges that the young ones are 'immature' and 'without experience', forgetting that back in the days when they took the reins of government into their hands, they were semi-illiterate."

Aged Ministers and supervisors, men who are ill with infection of the prostate gland, or who pea in their pants and chairs because they can't hold their water, or doze off in their offices and during official meetings are in charge of the administration. There was some talk about reforms but the country kept sinking deeper and deeper into the quagmire of conservatism and conformity. Not a single ray of hope could be seen on the horizon, which made Kleo and his friends think that nothing would change, until the old generation died off and relieved the political scene.

"Do you know comrade Masar well?" asked the nephew.

"That womanizer!" Sofika burst out, all of a sudden. "He keeps after women teachers who want to transfer to the city.... That's why I don't let Marlena file a complaint with his office or even ask for a job there. God forbid!" she swore.

"He is a big womanizer," Gole added. "He doesn't change. As the old saying goes, Habits die three days after the soul leaves the body. Ever since he is the in-law of a Politburo member, he is enjoying the good life."

Kleo smiled when he heard Gole call the mayor "a womanizer."

"Just be brief," Kleo advised. "Tell the Mayor that you have two problems: One, housing; the other a job for Marlena. As a single mother, divorced from her husband, she has priority over others, you follow me? There is a clear government guideline about that."

"Don't the officials at the employment office know the guidelines?" asked Gole.

"Knowing them and applying them, are two different things," Kleo remarked.

"My application for housing is the oldest of them all," Gole added. "And yet, the others, who applied after me, got their apartments, while I have nothing. I took this up with Sali, the head at the local office and asked him: 'Why did you provide housing for Minella, Andrea and Isak? Is it because they bend over to please you?'" Gole began to go over the bill of complaints, as if he was talking face to face with the local official.

"You are wrong to bring in other people," noted his nephew with disapproval.

Gole listened intently.

"You're right! Sali told me the same thing last year. 'Just tend to your own affairs. What business is it of yours to complain about others? Have you come here to tell us how to do our job? We make our decisions based on our data and recommendations…'."

"What more do you need? He gave it to you straight."

Gole Meta surveyed his surroundings with scorn.

"Since we married off our son, we turned our bedroom over to the newly-weds, and moved to the kitchen. As for Marlena and our granddaughter, we could not kick them out of their room. The trouble is that now I have to wait until the TV is turned off, before I can go to sleep. Then I have to put up with the clatter of the dishes in the dishwasher. My ears are buzzing. Seven souls in just two rooms and a kitchen!"

"There are three couples in one household. So, legally you are entitled to four rooms and a kitchen," his nephew explained.

"We're not asking for four. We'd be satisfied with just three. But when I told the secretary at the housing office, that we are three families, the witch lifted up two fingers and waved them before my eyes, and laughed. In other words, I don't qualify as a couple. Me and my wife are much too old, in her book...."

"I wish you had a stroke, so we can be rid of you and the housing problem!" his wife cursed him.

"In the appointment sheet at the Mayor's office, don't mention the word 'housing'; otherwise the form will end up in the waste basket," advised Kleo as an experienced civil servant.

Smart boy! He takes after our side of the family, reflected Gole.

* * *

Gole Meta believed that the Mayor would walk him around the office, as soon as he would hear Gole's name be called in. The Mayor would not let his wartime chump wait at the door. He would probably say to him:

"You are right, comrade Gole; you're absolutely right! Why didn't you come to see me sooner? After all, why do we have government offices? Why did our citizens give us the vote, and entrust us with responsibilities? Just so we can deal with their problems, and help them as best we can.... You should have come to me as soon as your son Meta got married; indeed, even before he wed. You've been sluggish, comrade Gole, admit it! Did you expect us to call you and tell you: 'Here's the authorization for the room you're entitled to! This is a wedding present for your son!' Do you suppose they inform me about the troubles of my army-days fellowmen? I'm only one man. You should have come straight to my home with your problem. Imagine, a man of your age sleeping on a straw-padded mattress! And your niece sleeping on a portable bed! As far as obtaining employment for your daughter, I will advice that she start work in education as early as tomorrow. No, no, you need not thank me! She deserves it, as a highly educated head-of-household. There is no need to bring in other arguments."

Gole set off with Sofika for the office of the Town Hall. Upon arriving there, he let Sofika at the door, while he himself went inside. The receptionist at the cubicle motioned to him to approach.

"What do you want?" he asked him.

"Would you tell the Mayor that Gole Meta wants to see him?"

The receptionist smiled derisively and pointed at the appointment hours on the glass pane. The Mayor received visitors only on Fridays from 12 to 2:00 p.m.

"You mean I should come back on Friday?" Gole asked to make sure.

"First, you need to fill out the form and to state the reason for the visit…."

"He is my wartime comrade," asserted Gole Meta, his feelings hurt by the civil servant's show of disrespect.

"Well, since he is your friend, go to his home. Here we have rules."

The rascal did not care to hear him out. He closed the window of his cubicle, shut himself inside and began to read the paper. Gole filled out the form and, recalling the advice of his nephew, Kleo, noted as the reason for the visit: "To talk about certain family problems." He handed the form to the civil servant at the cubicle, and begged him to deliver it to the Mayor at once.

"I know my job," he answered, as he took the form and put it on top of a stack of written pleas. "Come back on Thursday to see if your name is on the list of persons the Mayor will see on Friday."

"He didn't see you?" Sofika asked, as soon as he came out, with a gloomy face.

Downhearted, Gole quoted to her the words of the receptionist.

Slowly, the two of them dragged their feet home.

* * *

On Thursday, a notice on the window of the receptionist's cubicle said that the Mayor was to attend the Assembly's meeting in the capital. The following week, the visitors' session was cancelled without giving any reason. Afterward, the Mayor met with a visiting Chinese Delegation, and so Gole did not see his name on the visitors' list until four weeks later.

"All things come to those who wait," he said as soon as he returned home. "Tomorrow, at one o'clock, we shall see the Mayor. Have you had your coffee, yet?"

"It's brewing right now. I figured I better wait for you. So, what does that noodle of yours tell you? Is the Mayor going to give us a home?" she asked.

"Since he is willing to see us, he will take care of one of our problems at least."

* * *

Friday rolled in. And Gole and Sofika walked hand to hand to the city's offices.

An elegant young woman came out into the hall, holding a sheet in her hand.

"You will walk into the reception room when your name comes up on the list," she announced.

Gole Meta was the third in line. He went in holding Sofika's hand. The retirees, like engaged couples, went to see the Mayor as a twosome. Sofika looked attentively at the bright secretary, seated at a desk with three telephones. Dressed neatly and with light makeup, she lit up the entire office.

"I wish my Marlena had a job like that...," she said, enviously.

The door to the office of the Mayor opened up, and on the threshold there appeared a middle-aged woman, red in the face, all sweated up, with eyebrows lowered, and eyes gleaming with deep emotion. Gole feared that his plea had gone awry. The secretary invited him and Sofika to go inside.

On a high-backed, black leather armchair, there sat Masar with his grey-haired head and sideburns. A man with a face of swollen veins, he radiated authority, warmth and self-confidence. He was healthy and full of vigor, yet could not hide the furrows on his forehead or the bags under his eyes. He stood up, greeted them, offered them cigarettes, lit up Gole's with a cigarette lighter, and sat down in his armchair.

"How have you been, health-wise, comrade..." pretending to be looking for his cigarette lighter, he glanced at the list of the people seeking to see him "…comrade Gole? We see each other so rarely these days…."

Gole turned to his wife.

"Didn't I tell you that comrade Masar knows me?"

"This poor man has run himself ragged, knocking on the doors of all the Town Hall offices," said Sofika.

The Mayor dealt easily with Sofika's remark.

"It's just that we are so busy, not because we don't care. I have meetings to attend and assignments to go. I rush here and there, because the work load keeps getting heavier, and I'm not getting any younger, you know…the years take their toll." After this pathetic introduction, he added sorrowfully, "Old age is catching up with us, Gole!"

"You're holding up well, comrade Masar. Not a wrinkle on your face, just like a young man," Gole complimented him.

"I am past the double sixes," said the Mayor.

"Oh, that's nothing. My father married for the third time at the age of 73, and increased the size of the family by fathering a son," jumped in Gole, while asking himself: Did he say the double sixes?

The Mayor smiled, to signal approval, but then went on to say:

"In the old days, people married at any age, while today the Bureau of Vital Statistics considers the big age differences. You recall comrade Sefer Janina? They refused to issue a marriage certificate, even though the young woman put her foot down, saying, 'What do you care if I want to marry an old man?' But they ignored her. The old timers knew how to live life and how to enjoy it, forget what we say that they suffered and had a tough life."

The Mayor talked as if neither age nor his position separated them. Gole felt a little uppity in front of Sofika.

"A young bride rejuvenates an old man or sends him sooner to the other world? What do you think?" the Mayor asked him.

Gole told him the opposite of what he really believed, because he was aware of the Mayor's weaknesses.

"She renews him," he affirmed, and involuntarily looked at Sofika. "If I had a young bride, instead of this one, you would see how young and lively I would be."

Sofika pursed her lips scornfully.

The Mayor was interested to know what the retired people in his neighborhood were doing. Had they embarked on any community activity? Were they paying attention to the education of the new generation? He stressed that young people honor and love the retirees, envy their decorations and medals, listen with glee to their tales about the war, and need their counsel….

"True enough," said Gole, although inwardly he believed that the Mayor did not really know either the young people, or the city. The youth avoided the elderly like the plague, let alone listen to their drivel.

"The children are full of praise for the Party," Gole said, thinking that such flattering words would please him.

The Mayor showed his approval with a nod of the head.

"I have two boys and a girl. I raised them, sent them to school, either College or High School, and married them off."

The Mayor leaned back on his armchair.

"One of them has a boy. I'm crazy about that little rascal…. 'You made me a Grandpa', I say to him to tease him, while he pulls my moustache. The other son is in the next town. His wife is expecting any day now. Actually I'm twice a grandfather, because Marlena, too, has a daughter."

The Mayor began to rub his forehead ever so softly.

The caressing warm rays of the springtime sun, streamed from the windows, along with the honeyed aroma of the acacias. Red apple blossoms, white pear blossoms and clusters of lilac that intertwined outside in the courtyard, enticing the Mayor to recall a meeting he had with a female teacher the day before at a farm. He was astonished by her eyes, for they had the same color and the same seductive and challenging look as Veronika's, the woman he had loved in his youth. The teacher had asked him if he could give her a ride to the town. "If it's possible, of course," she added. The Mayor let her hop in, at once. As the chauffer-driven car rolled down a verdant plain, the Mayor leaped over to the back seat, so as not to leave her alone. Seating alongside her, he put his hand on her shoulders, and asked what her name was, what she was doing, and what her dreams were. What a sweet voice she had, and what a captivating look! What was her name?

"Marlena divorced from her husband, and for no fault of hers," Gole said.

Marlena? I thought her name was Mariana, or Marietta…and she was not married. But even if she was, it didn't matter…. Lunch was more delicious when the cook brought over a bottle of muscatel wine.

We split our sides listening to his jokes. And the lamb he had baked was so good, it melted in the mouth. What is this guy prattling about?

"Her in-laws kicked her out, even before the trial began. They threw her clothes out the door, and wouldn't let her in. All her complaints fell on deaf ears. Legally she was entitled to a room in their apartment. However, they did not have a single vacant room, so Marlena and her daughter came back to us. We couldn't leave them out in the streets.... So, now we are three couples in the house...."

Couples...what couples? We were talking about the time...for our rendezvous. Was it three, or four o'clock? The hours just fled away.... The Mayor put his elbow on the desk, and then rested his head on his arm. He half-closed his eyes, the better to focus on the visitor.

"Our daughter, an unemployed teacher," Sofika intervened.

I thought she asked for a transfer not employment. She has a child, too. Great! Good reason to transfer her. It is the issue of housing...an extra room.... She is coming to the office. We can put in a portable bed.... A portable bed is too small....

Drifting into drowsiness, the Mayor's face relaxed making the wrinkles and the hollows more visible. Gole kept gabbing about his family troubles.

The door opened slowly, and the cleats of the pretty secretary clattered on the parquet like the notes of a xylophone. She approached the Mayor's desk holding a letter in her hand. She took a look at his posture, and exclaimed with astonishment:

"Good grief! Is he dozing off again?"

Fearing that she would embarrass the Mayor if she woke him up, the secretary did not disturb him. Fortunately, just at that moment, one of the telephones rang, and the startled Mayor opened his eyes, coughed and grabbed the receptor.

"Hello!" he said, then turned to his secretary and asked, "What happened to that teacher?" In front of him there was Gole Meta and an old woman. What were they doing in the office? What did they want there?

"We are going to look into your problem," he promised them. "Don't worry! And don't lose any sleep over it!"

And just like that the meeting was over. The Mayor shook hands with them as the secretary stood by to walk the old couple to the door.

꧁ An Instructor's Journal ꧂

SPY NEEDED
-INQUIRE WITHIN-

My grandfather used to say to me "Evil finds you without any efforts; the Good hardly comes by even when you search for it." I recalled his words years later after the meeting I had with Basri Bedati. Correction! After the meeting Basri had with me. Since then, I feel that I have been sucked into the whirlpool of misfortune and I do not know if I can ever deliver myself from certain calamity.

It all began after the dismissal of the Minister of Education from his post.

In the latest convention of the Party, Minister was harshly criticized. The repercussions, as might be expected, were first felt in the Department of Education, where I work. By analogy with similar incidents in the history of the Party, some felt that the Minister's career was over. Others did not go along with that conclusion. Even I was one of the skeptics, since such verbal attacks are not an uncommon occurrence with us. But a week later, all doubts dissipated. The decree issued by the Presidium of the People's Assembly, confirmed the dismissal of the Minister of Education on grounds of incompetence. The same decree noted the appointment of Arian Tartari as the new Minister.

How could the fallen Minister be called incapable when he ran the affairs and headed the Ministry for fifteen years in succession? That is a tough charge to comprehend even for those who did not know him. And it is a specially 'hard ingestion' for the Ministry staff who had attended a number of ceremonies, where the dismissed Minister had received orders and medals for his leadership skills and devotion to Marxist principles. Also, dismissing the Minister on the motive of 'incompetence' after fifteen consecutive years on a ministerial post does not really honor the head of the government.

* * *

As one of the 54 instructors at the Ministry, I am neither a sociologist, nor a historian. A common civil servant! I just like to 'toy' with ideas and scrutinize the phenomena of our life on earth. More often than not, I'm the one who is being judged for my critical and unconventional thoughts, but in the meantime I have the pleasure of passing judgment on the government policies that I do not like. I am opposed to the narrow concepts of the Party, its restrictive decisions and the fabrications about the recent years' initiatives that are supposed to serve the Revolution. I have not an iota of respect for our ideologists, who have made a cult of poverty. In my view, whoever thinks that poverty brings the people closer to the Party and heightens their political consciousness, is mistaken the whole blessed day. How can anyone who is stripped of any possession be content? The recent 'public' initiative to take away the private livestock of the villagers, and put them in a reservation, supposedly for their benefit was hailed as a revolutionary action. I think it was shameful to snatch the milk and bread from the mouths of children in the country. Our Marxist ideologists claimed that the 'livestock collectivization' initiative was going to free many working hands and increase production. But, in fact, there was neither an increase in production, nor an improvement of the economy numbers. My heart ached when I saw the villagers make their way to the town to buy a loaf of bread, and stand like guilty souls at the doors of bakeries, because the orders were not to sell bread to the farmers. First of all, it doesn't make sense for farmers to buy bread in the city, when they are supposed to produce and sell grains they don't use; and secondly, those villagers fed the Partisans during the war, without asking even so much as a nickel! As long as these farmers buy bread and cheese in the city, the government's propaganda that it is mindful of the country people's welfare rings hollow to the ear.

I try to preserve my independence as a "homo sapiens," but when it comes to my personality..., well, I just think that it went down south a long time ago. I am not lame-brained, nor crazy enough to confide to others the thoughts that brew in my head. Does that make me a hypocrite? No. The fault lies with "those" who force me to conceal my thoughts and refrain from saying what I think. At the same time, I just know that I am not alone, and that other people have similar thoughts, or perhaps even more extreme ideas, even though they do not voice them. That's to be expected! It was insistently and continuously demanded that people conform to any initiative originating from above. Throughout the years, despite of what citizens really thought of such initiatives, they went along and applauded them. I too cheered the initiatives that were meant to tighten the screws on us because we could sense that the government wanted to be deceived. Years of constant pressure to achieve conformity in a grand scale resulted in a formidably formal submission. Not inconsequentially we live in one of the most conformist society history has ever known. Our theoreticians call the people's formal compliance a "monolithic unification" around the state's leadership. In my opinion, the term is a blatant fabrication, since the subordination is neither monolithic nor unifying. Who are we fooling? Every year scores of people are sentenced and imprisoned for alleged anti-government propaganda, or for engaging in reported hostile operations. It seems to me the ceaseless efforts to brainwash everyone did not produce the expected results. Instead the tendentious indoctrination raised doubts among citizens and set off an ideal defensive mechanism.

I feel that I have a lot to say about our political establishment. But in the meantime, I serve a system that's not to my liking to feed my family and myself. There are no other options available. Private sector was vanished for good, and all jobs, whether manual or mental, are government jobs or dependent on the government.

I cannot feel like a free citizen, as long as I am denied freedom of thought. No, that's not the correct way to put it. I mean, as long as I'm denied the freedom to *express* my own thoughts, since fortunately the government has not been able to take away my ability to think. I doubt that any establishment or machinery for that matter will be able to take full control of a people. The human brain, with its complex biochemical processes – the greatest miracle of nature and evolution, the memory bank of many generations, – is a million times superior to the most advanced computer. The machines have fantastic computing speeds, but no imagination, no powers of abstraction and most certainly no feelings. I also believe in telepathic powers. I think that brainwaves are the most mysterious and most powerful force of nature. What is it that distinguishes geniuses from ordinary people? Definitely not the limbs, the proportions of the body, or the size of the skull. Rather, it's the imaginative and creative capacity of their brain. Nowadays, I read and hear about UFOs, interplanetary spaceships and visits from extra-terrestrial beings. In my view, that's only journalistic poppycock and the fantasies of myth-maniacs. I don't believe that aliens have ever come to planet

Earth. But their brainwaves powerful enough to travel through galactic space, have reached us since long ago.

* * *

The newly appointed Minister of Education, Arian Tartari, had been a local Party Secretary. Up until then he was 'a nobody' that had made no contribution to either education or culture. Why was he selected when right in the capital, the university of Tirana had plenty of respected professors, estheticians and pedagogues to choose from? It was not the first case of 'sudden rise to power'. Frankly I wondered about the overnight escalation of cab drivers or lumberjacks to the highest levels of the Party. In light of the new appointment, I began to see the Ministers as "liaison officers," a sort of "transmission belts," if you would, between government agencies and the top leadership.

Two years ago at the beach, my family's cabin and that of Arian Tartari were next to each other. He was vacationing with his wife, their only daughter and his mother from a distant region. We became acquainted and parted at the end of that summer vacation. Our relationship began on the seashore and ended there, leaving no trace behind. We were bound neither by our work, nor by our interests. As far as I recall, at the time, he was a High School principal. To my great surprise, when he took up office in the Ministry, he asked whether I still worked in the same place. When the new Minister learned that I was still there, he asked to meet me. I went to his office and congratulated him on his new post. That was enough for my co-workers to refer to me as 'the Minister's friend'. Strangely, their attitude influenced me, as well, for I began to see myself as a respected and privileged instructor, just because I was acquainted with the Minister. Vain self-flattery of the petty civil servant. In retrospect, I think that my pettiness was precisely the reason why Evil came knocking on my door. And it was not alone….

A former High School mate, Basri Bedati, an operative at the Ministry of the Exterior, or the Interior – I'm not sure which – began to recurrently stop by the Ministry. I thought that he was calling in favors to help someone he knew get in a sought-after college. Basri knew all the VIPs and went to every office. He was a smooth talker and made jokes easily with people. Very casually Basri walked into my office without any misgivings. One time he recalled when he and I walked out of the boarding school without permission and later got grounded by the custodian. After thirty years my memory was not as good as his since I could not remember any such incident. Naturally I did not tell Basri that he talking through his hat or that maybe he confused me with someone else. Thinking back in High School he had his circle of friends and I had mine. At the end of the High School I learned that Basri had failed all his classes, except physical education. I heard that he returned to his birth town, while I continued with my higher education. Later on, I heard quite by chance that Basri had donned a policeman's uniform. The news was amusing and surprising for it never occurred to us that someone we knew from our school days might become a policeman. As young men, we were prone to rebel to the law enforcement and generally despised uniformed police. Gradually, the news of Basri's joining the police force wore off. In time thoughts about him sank further and further from my mind.

Then a few years later I ran into Basri unexpectedly at the Square downtown. He was dressed in a honey-colored suit with stripes, flowered beige tie, white shirt with dark blue collars, and shiny black patent leather shoes. He seemed as if he had just come off a fashion parade shown on the 'banned' TV programs. His chic look was flawed slightly only by his hairdo, with its rebellious strands that shot out in different directions, just like in his youth. Both his behavior and manner of speech gave me to understand that he enjoyed some kind of official post.

"Where are you working now?" I asked him.

His lips parted, revealing two rows of white teeth, while his eyes shone with glee.

"I just got back from New York, on leave," he said with a jaunty smile.

"From New York?"

I would have found it more credible if he had said "The cover of 'Moda Magazine'."

"I've been working at our Mission in New York for some years," he explained.

Spellbinding! He was a career diplomat? The school flunky was representing our country and meeting with diplomats of the East and the West. The wonders of communism have no end. The foreman of the construction it goes to bed and wakes up a Minister overnight, while the Minister does the day's work and goes to bed a shepherd. Then suddenly

I remembered that as a policeman, maybe Basri was doing guard duty for the Mission in New York. But our embassies and consulates do not have police in their staff, or doormen, or guards. I wondered in which language did Basri communicate, since he didn't master even the standard Albanian. Perhaps no foreign language knowledge is required, since he had no business with diplomats in the metropolis of the world. It could be that he was a detailed security service with a special mission. I had heard that *Sigurimi* had opened files on every Albanian abroad, which needed to be updated every so often. I guessed that he had to recruit agents and collaborators from the community to survey Albanian postwar political exiles and immigrants in America to obtain reliable information. The task of surveillance was a permanent and sensitive operation. But I could not help feeling astounded at how and why Basri Bedati was appointed to work in America? I couldn't possibly believe that he had obtained his position on the strength of his rare skills as an investigator or detective. The enigma could only be explained as the workings of the hand of the blind fates or friends in really high places....

They say that education paves the road to success. If Basri had finished High School, he would have languished in the countryside and never would have found his way to America, much less join our Mission at the United Nations in New York.

I recalled the surprise encounter after I saw him in the Ministry's hallways. Even though I was not sure of his place of employment after New York, I saw him come in at the offices where I worked, walking into anyone's desk with ease, as if he belonged there, smiling and greeting people in the hallways.

Since the shake-up in our Ministry, Basri dropped in more frequently. He even called me at home, waited for me when I got off work, walked with me all the way to the bus station and sometimes dragged me to some bar to have a drink. "It's to renew our old friendship," he would say. As I think back, I never telephoned him. Indeed, I didn't even know his number. It was clear that he was trying to befriend me. I just was unsure of his motives. Once he asked me casually how I felt about the new Minister. I told him frankly that the changes in the top brass didn't matter much.

"Well, it helps that you are a friend of the Minister," he remarked.

"Acquaintance," I retorted, "a chance acquaintance, at that."

"So, you have zero emotional involvement with him," he commented. Then, as if talking to himself, he added: "So much the better."

I couldn't see why he took an interest in the feelings of a simple government employee for a high official. What did it matter to him?

Yesterday morning the mystery of those conversations I had with him cleared up. Basri invited me to step out for a stroll. We walked along the Boulevard, and up the road to the buffet-bar of the Big Park. Although the place was nearly empty, he walked to the farthest corner table to sit down. He seemed in good humor, which made me think that he had some good news to share. Two or three times he patted my hand in a friendly manner with a gleam in his eyes.

"I have no doubt that you will welcome my proposal. We've known each other since High School, and even though we've met only occasionally in recent years, we have mutual respect for each other." He paused briefly, while searching for the best way to press on. "First of all, you should understand that even telling this to you means that we appreciate your skills and honesty, and above all your loyalty."

I noticed that he was speaking in the plural, but did not interrupt his talking.

"Believe me," he said firmly, as if taking an oath, and then paused again, while fluttering his eyes, "we went over the list of candidates with a fine-toothed comb.... And after careful screening, you were found to be the most suitable."

His phrases remained mysterious. I had the easy feeling that someone was setting a trap for me. Seeing that I did not react to his opening, he asked me in a nice way:

"Did you follow me?"

"No, frankly, no. Why all these riddles? If we are friends, or you view me as a friend, why don't you come out with it?"

He granted my point, at once.

"It's my own fault," he said. "I should have started in a different way. Look, we need a trustworthy man...."

"There you go again, mouthing enigmas," I rebuked him, raising my voice a bit that time. "What do you mean by 'we'?"

"Darn it...!" he laughed out loud. "That's the way I talk," he said, confessing his weakness. Then, losing no time, he added, "You know where I work, there's no need for details...."

"I know that you worked at the UN for some years, but right now, I don't know for sure, where you work right now, I swear."

"Well, I do perform the same functions, only now I am stationed here," he said, without specifying anything. "So, to go back to what I was saying before. Of all the employees in your sector, including males and females, you are the most suitable."

"Most suitable for what?" I asked, in all seriousness, as I still could not grasp what he wanted from me.

He looked at me with skepticism, which gave me a hint.

"Are you proposing a new assignment for me, with higher pay?" I inquired, without asking about the implied duties the position entailed.

"No," he assured me. "You are not going to change your place of work, or your job." At this point, he motioned to the waiter, and said to him "*Repete*" while pointing to refreshments and appetizers. Clearly Basri wanted to impress upon me that I was eating and drinking with someone who was savvy about the etiquette of fashionable dining. Turning his attention to our table, he said: "The appetizers were good. Did you see how he loaded up our plates? The chef is a friend of mine."

"I can't," I said tactfully.

"It's a big day. We're starting a new phase. Do you remember our High School? How many years has it been since then? We are old friends and we are going to become even closer, because we are both sons of the people who are devoted to the Party. Your duty is both easy and simple. You will keep an eye on a certain person, and you will inform us about the company that person keeps, the people who visit him in his office, the fellows that he takes with him on out-of-town assignments...and so on. Do you understand me now?"

I did understand. My first reaction was to bolt out there without even looking at him. Now his broad jawbones seemed like a vicious clamp ready to crush me. In his face those huge jaws gave him the appearance of a Mastodon that could pulverize bones like pieces of candy. All this time his agenda was to recruit me as an informant. Sitting there, I began to rethink my conduct toward him. What gave him the idea that I was a suitable candidate for a snitch? Where could he possibly get such a perverse idea? How had I impressed him as the right man for such an impertinent mission? Do I even look like I could be an informer? That's nonsense. People with all kinds of looks engage in espionage, and some of them are quite likeable. I could not recall discussing politics with him at any time. Our conversations never exceeded the boundaries of formal etiquette. I knew not to share my ideas except with a very few confidantes, who had similar views. Such talks were somewhat therapeutic since they helped me to let off steam and release some of the psychological pressure; otherwise I would have burst like chestnuts over a fire. While Basri was waiting for me to respond, my self-defense mechanism kicked in. Should I turn him down right now? But curiosity got the better of me and I felt like digging in deeper. How was I expected to watch "X" as an *incognito*, from afar or by deploying a different tactic? I assumed from the hints he had dropped earlier that the 'target' was in our department at the Ministry. Could it be one of my friends at the office?

"May I ask who is the subject, or rather the object of the surveillance?" I asked.

He pondered for a moment, as if he hesitated to tell me.

"Well, of course you should know. It's a friend of yours," he replied smiling, "or better yet, an acquaintance of yours."

"Who do you mean?" I persisted.

"Arian," he whispered, "Arian Tartari."

"The Minister?" I felt my eyes were ready to pop out with astonishment.

He nodded.

I took a sip of water as my mouth felt completely dry. The new Minister was 'the suspect'? Could it be that he had made some wrong move already? It was hard to imagine since the Minister was just recently appointed to that position. I expressed these questions to Basri openly.

"Nobody has any doubts about him," Basri Bedati explained. "He is a Minister, after all, and a member of the Cabinet. He represents the government."

I could not help feeling a strong contradiction! How could a ranking official be trustworthy and simultaneously distrusted to the point of being 'shadowed' by rookie informants?

Anticipating my next question Basri said: "No doubt, you are asking yourself, why didn't the establishment pick out a trustworthy Minister? You know that every branch of government performs its own duties. No position no matter how high is above our sensitive radar.... The job that I am proposing here requires tactfulness. You will continue to work in the same office as usual, drawing the least amount of anyone's attention. But you will start to mention the Minister casually from time to time when talking with your colleagues. You know, many people have a narrow concept of vigilance, it entails not just keeping your eyes peeled, but also having your ears opened, as well."

I wondered how many moles there were crawling around in every department at any institution at all levels of the government. Suddenly I thought of a billboard by Sara Komani showing the face of a border guard whose human eye appeared like that of the eagle. It came to my mind because it got a load of praise as a graphic work of powerful symbolic significance and won first prize in a national competition. Despite its original analogy, the fierce look of the guard eagle eyes filled me with anxiety. Ironically, a few years later, the only son of that billboard's artist was arrested and sent to prison for telling politically sensitive jokes to a close circle of 'vigilant' friends. The eagle's eye watched the enemy and its beak pecked at the flesh. I thought of the artist Sara Komeni and my heart filled with despair. I wonder what went on inside her artistic soul? Had she considered denying her own blood ties, or did she feel like ripping instead the work of her artistic hands?

Well, I am certain that if Basri knew even one percent of the thoughts in my head, I would have been in real trouble and he would have never zeroed in on me. My mind went back to the new Minister. Could it be that he had a different view on the so-called revolution's triangle: "Learning – Military training – Physical exercising" After all, it was plain to see that it had torn down our system of education. Which lunatic had the idea of wasting one-third of the school year doing physical labor and military training? Practically the academic year dwindled to six months of studying extreme politicizing of textbooks. I am sure that the Minister was greatly devoted to the Party. Imbued with the Communist ideology since his youth, he also regarded with nostalgia the wartime generation, which believed that the Communism was going to bring heaven down to earth. I have read that a French philosopher has said that revolutions eat their own offspring like Saturn. The first display of that morbid phenomenon in Albania's political history occurred in 1948. Even earlier since a good number of Communists were killed by their own fellow comrades during the war. Some were shot to set an example but most took a bullet in the back. After the war, almost every five years, people who were honored for their patriotic deeds in the past, were labeled as enemies, deviators, saboteurs. Like a monster from some dark cave, the dictatorship tears apart its victims making sure its teeth never get dull. The steady erosion reveals the continuous crisis and power struggle within the Party ranks. The panic of being the next one to take the fall makes everyone tremble with fear, regardless of the position in the hierarchy.

Trying to pull my thoughts together on the mater at hand, I considered Basri's point of view. Believing that I was in agreement with him, he then continued to explain the complex mechanism for the surveillance of top officials. The recruited informer included personal chauffeurs, bodyguards, office secretaries, receptionist, or anyone else who got in the net. Until then, it was widely believed that the waiters at International Dajti Hotel were secret agents of the Ministry of the Internal Affairs, but not everyone could grasp the gigantic scope of surveillance. As far as I was concerned, Dajti Hotel was a "foreign territory," where a citizen was scrutinized by hidden eyes and the hotel personnel right from the beginning to the end of the stay there.

"Practically your job is delicate in nature, but also easy," Basri went on. "Because you have only one object under your surveillance." Consciously or unconsciously, the agent Basri reduced the Minister to a mere object. "You are part of a select list which is no small achievement. The 'top secret' list" – he said that in English – "is known to only three people, whom I need not mention by name. It is a special honor, and I assure you that you will enjoy other favors, as well."

So, that's it. I was automatically advanced to an elite agent. Then I thought back at the period of my life when I worked in a southern town. The security operative in the region entrusted a close friend of mine to snitch on me and even coached him on how to provoke me. Being naïve like a child, my friend told me about it and also revealed the "secret code" used by agents. The dark discovery was a blow to my purest feelings and beliefs. Why was I a target? What suspicions did the security sector have on me? I was terribly hurt and decided to quit my job and never again go back to that area where I was viewed as a suspect without any grounds. I told the nerving incident in just a few words to a confidante who made light of my indignation. "I thought you were smarter than that," he said, "I tell you frankly that you disappoint me. Every one of us is shadowed by an agent especially the well educated and the artists. You got the chance to know who is trailing you, while I have no idea who is watching me," he added raising his eyes toward the ceiling, as if he were looking for help from above. "I am astounded that your informer revealed the secret code to you. Either he is a fool, or he fully trusts you. But if the *Sigurimi* finds out about this, the guy will be in hot water."

That episode that came to mind in the new circumstances chilled me. Once a target, and now a potential surveillance man! At what point had I made the jump from the list of suspicious citizens to the list of most trusted operatives? I felt nauseated. One way or the other, no one is 'above' surveillance. Also, not inconsequentially, we are all links of a long and intertwined chain.

"Let's meet once every two weeks. I will tell you the place and the time. If I am unable to show up or tied by some unexpected duty calls, then a colleague of mine will come in my place. The password will be: 'Do you like the Dajti Park?' and your reply 'I like the Big Park better.' That is just in case you meet with one of the guys, because I am your contact, and you and I have no need for codes and passwords."

He was talking as if I had already agreed which infuriated me. Despite the flattery that I was in the category of the select few, 'the mission' seemed to me quite despicable. Why turn into a hired hypocrite who smiles at the Minister and on the other hand spies on him just to boost credentials with the security chiefs? That kind of asset is like poison that gradually intoxicates and decays its own host. Much like the cancer's metastasis that spreads aggressively into every organ and when it reaches the climax of its destructive work, perishes along with the body.

"Shall we consider this matter closed?" I suggested, as calmly as I possibly could.

"You mean call it a day?" asked Basri. "We understand each other, right?"

"I mean that you should find someone else...."

Basri scowled and looked at me with both disappointment and sorrow. Then pressing his lips together in a tight line, he advised me:

"Try to be reasonable. Opportunities like this don't come by often. Think about it."

Along with the friendly advice, his words implied a threat. I knew that it was in my interest to give him some explanation.

"I have no gift for this sort of thing.... That's it, in a nutshell."

His forehead became wrinkled with angry lines.

"Is there some reason?" he asked anxious to dispel my objection quickly. "We can help you out...," he suggested.

Right away I thought of the compensations that the *Sigurimi* agents received, also known as "the second payroll." *Sigurimi* also gave its active operatives supplementary funds to entertain 'the target'. Maybe Basri was spending money from that special fund to recruit me over lunch. He was eyeing me with contempt, as if I were a foolish child who turns down a precious gift, out of caprice.

"Think it over again, calmly. Consider all angles!" he advised for the second time.

The silence that ensued grew tense. I thought I sensed a swampy smell.

"This is not your final answer," he said with confidence in his opinion.

"Yes, it is!" I said firmly.

"You need to relax!" he urged me. "We'll meet again here or somewhere else." He thought for a moment, as to consider the following step and continued: "I confided in you sensitive information that nobody should know."

Basri was chagrined to have trusted me excessively. He didn't know what to do next. His behavior prompted me to feel that he was as thick-headed now as he was in High School. I had qualms about releasing some of his stress by promising him that I would not divulge his secrets. But I thought it best to remain silent and leave him hanging, so he would get a taste of what is like to be a prey to anxiety. I could hardly wait to step out into the open and escape the mugginess I felt when looking at the square-like jaws of his. There was hardly any talk on our way back. The fueling source of our conversations until then had suddenly dried up.

Later, lying down in bed, I fell to thinking about why I was swept into this whirlpool. Why was Basri looking for a new agent, instead of assigning one of their agents to spy on the new Minister? Then I thought of a possible answer. After the dismissal of the former Minister, some of the instructors were dispatched to other jobs. It could be that his 'spy' was one of those instructors. Talk about tying up loose ends or cutting off loose tails, in this case. Why didn't *Sigurimi* protect its own agent instead of casting him off, too, like an old rag?

"Think it over," had said Basri again when they finally parted.

To take my mind off that thorny subject, I began to leaf through the volume, *Legends of Ancient Greece,* an amusing and instructive reading. After reading again the legend of Actaeon, I arrived to a novel conclusion that day. In this version of the legend, Actaeon was the faithful servant of Artemis. One day he rushed into the house looking for the stableman to ready the coach. Hurriedly he flung open every door on that hot day. At that point, Artemis, the maiden Goddess of the Hunt was cooing with pleasure and cooling off as she was bathing. As soon as Actaeon opened the door to Artemis' bathing chamber, he froze with embarrassment. His still stance was interpreted by Artemis as a determination to deliberately stand there and ogle the charms of her lovely form, which she kept hidden from the gods and lustful mortals. The angry Artemis took him to court. Nobody believed Actaeon's honest testimony. The connivers said that he entered Artemis's chamber on purpose, while the judges whispered among themselves that if they had the luck to gaze upon the naked goddess, they would have gladly accepted any punishment.

In my mind, Actaeon's legend was a great metaphor for the senseless punishment of innocence. I had always believed that staying out of trouble was a matter of keeping clear of any wrongdoings by using logic, willpower and especially self-control. But I began to see that wholesome traits of character were not sufficient to keep evil away. As long as your actions were subject to the other's people's judgment your moral qualities were of no avail. You could be at fault for hearing or seeing what you were not supposed to hear or see. The legend of Actaeon proved that virtue can be faulted without cause. Regrettably I felt that the modern-time-Actaeon like myself would have to endure a much severe experience. At least the predecessor had the pleasure of witnessing the nudity of a goddess and being astounded by the charms of Artemis as water streamed down her petal-soft skin, her curvy breasts and shapely legs. I always thought that such images accompanied Actaeon in the solitude of his prison, whereas I faced the dim prospect of seeing over and over in my mind Basri's square-shaped jaws. I was disgusted by his sneer and his persistence to recruit me as a mole. Each time his advice to "think it over" echoed in my head, a resolute voice inside me resonated "No! No! No!" I could not serve the cause of evil and live to wither with self-pity.

* * *

I had an appointment with my cousin, Teme at the Sopoti coffee house, across from the Ministry of Foreign Affairs. It is the best coffee house in our part of town. I knew that tradition called upon me to invite him for dinner at home. However, my wife told me bluntly that she does not want me to meet with anyone whose have been released from prison, including friends and relatives. She believed that I was not careful and got mixed up with 'scumbags' for no good reason. It was useless for me to try to explain. And I cannot really blame her. Our society has made some of our moral norms quite inflexible. The stigma of imprisonment is permanent even for minor offenses. Most people including my wife neither knew nor cared to differentiate between 'political prisoners' and common depraved criminals. My cousin who used to be a supervisor at a tailors' workshop in the town of Permet fell victim of the bottle. He liked the bottle and knocked back four to five double shots of whiskey or any alcoholic drinks daily. At some point he started helping himself at the cash register. The financial inspectors discovered a deficit that amounted to thousands of leks.* The Court sentenced him to six months in a prison facility in the south. There the inmates also did some digging work on the bare slopes of the mountain at a beautiful spot, even ideal, one could say, on the shores of the Ionian Sea. They planted orange, lemon, citrus and olive trees in the new plantation. Every time I drove by that facility, fenced with barbed wire and tended by armed guards, I was disconsolate that such a beautiful place was nothing but hell for the inmates.

My cousin was ensconced at the bar when I arrived. He was in the company of some of his friends. The cognac glasses glittered in front of them. They invited me to join them without interrupting the guy who was talking. As I sat with them, I heard the fellow say that informers are the most privileged group, because they are taken care of and paid well by *Sigurimi.* On a whim it made me upset, but I restrained from commenting. Life is full of amazing chance happenings.

"A good neighbor of mine," he added, "would disappear from time to time. I later found out by chance that she was a professional provocateur. Can you believe it? I guess there actually is such a profession. She was a blue-eyed blonde of clear skin who looked good, even though she was past forty. Attracting men was a cinch for her. While on an assign-

* The *lek* is Albania's monetary unit.

ment out-of town, I walked with a relative into a club and I spotted a familiar face. She walked by us with pride, like women of standing. At that point, she pretended not to see me, and I hesitated to greet her."

"Do you know her?" asked my relative.

"Yes, we're neighbors," I replied.

"She has helped us a lot. You have no idea how clever she is. A first-rate provocateur. Every time a female detainee keeps her mouth shut, we call on Merita. As soon as she comes in, we make her up to look like a tortured woman and put her in the detainee's cell. After a few days, Merita finds out everything about her. Very smart," he said with admiration.

The guy at the opposite side of the table shared the story of an informer that barely escaped alive from his cellmate. His anecdote began some years ago when one informer was placed in the same cell with a 'suspect'. Believing that the newcomer was also a victim, the detainee opened up to him. The provocateur ratted on him and the poor fellow was sentenced to eight years in prison. Years later, after the convict was released, he and his family moved to another town. But again he ran into trouble with the system. Charged with propaganda against the government, he was taken in detention in another prison facility. Coincidentally, the authorities put the same provocateur in the cell with him. The detainee recognized the 'rat' from the previous sentencing. As soon as 'the operative' began his 'chat' about the regime, the other fellow snapped:

"How dare you insult the people's regime, you scum? You think I'm a dirt bag like you? I'll rip out your filthy guts and eat 'em!" He knocked the snitch down by throwing angry punches at him. The informer began to yelp in pain battered by a storm of blows. The police snatched the rat but not before the detainee beat him black and blue. As the police dragged away his beat-up body, the other guy kept yelling, "Let me finish him!" The provocateur was sent to the hospital, and the incident was closed.

"I think no operative has paid more dearly than Ylber," continued my cousin. "In prisons and internment camps, there are organized bands which will tear you apart, if you disobey them. At the Lukove camp, there was a fierce ogre-like man by the name of Xhagai whom was feared even by the guards and the police. When packages with food and cigarettes for inmates came in, he was given his share apart from the others. One day, he asked me why I was busted and I told him straight 'misappropriation.'

" 'How much did you steal?' he asked me.

" 'Twenty-five thousand.'

" 'That's nothing. A very modest swindle,' he said.

" 'No, it wasn't "the stealing." I took the money to spend it on booze.'

"Xhagai introduced me to his gang as 'a rare species'. I gave him a bottle of whiskey and we became friends. He had a nickname, which he had borrowed from the gangster in the Indian film 'The Vagabond'. It's common knowledge that *Sigurimi* recruited moles among the inmates. And it so happened that the Gypsy convict at Lukove found out from a policeman that Ylber Mata was the 'mole' in our group. Ylber, a man in his forties, was known as a quiet, well-behaved fellow with rosy cheeks and broad hips. The Gypsy passed on the news to Xhagai, who whispered 'Ylber, huh?....' He started thinking hard to find an exemplary form of punishment, which Ylber would remember for the rest of his life. Upon devising his plan, Xhagai instructed the Gypsy fellow to call a group meeting at a secret spot to discuss a sensitive plan. Ylber came to the meeting believing that he was about to uncover a big secret. The meeting spot was on a hill, located in a terrain of briars and thornbushes, away from the camp, and hidden from the highway and the barracks. As soon as we gathered at the designated spot, Xhagai declared forthrightly:

" 'We have a mole in our group. Let him come forward now and confess; otherwise, I will shame him right here and now.'

"There was dead silence. The inmates looked at one another.

" 'Come on, you coward. Why don't you speak up?' Xhagai walked up to Ylber and yelled, 'Filthy rat! You thought we were never going to unmask you? Don't you know that there are moles who spy on spies?'

"Ylber was trembling and couldn't utter a word.

" 'Tie him up,' ordered Xhagai and after pushing Ylber to the ground, lowered his pants and shorts and got on top of him. Ylber whined like a pig, all the while screaming, 'Don't, I beg you! I'm a married man!'

"No one dared to move. We heard Xhagai say to Ylber, 'Don't tighten up your asshole, you idiot, or it will hurt even more!'

"There was a burst of loud laughter. Ylber thought that by tightening up, he would ride out the ordeal.

" 'Bring me a pointed stake,' ordered Xhagai. 'I'm going to ram his asshole so bad, he will scream every time he takes a shit.'

"We saw the Gypsy sharpen the point of the stake on a stone, just like in the Stone Age. The moment Ylber saw the stake, he surrendered. In the absence of Vaseline, Xhagai used some toothpaste to lubricate his ass. We heard some oh-oh-oh exclamations mixed in with sighs of pleasure. When he finished, Xhagai got up and invited the rest of us to take turns with Ylber. Nobody in the group accepted, with the exception of the Gypsy, who said that this was probably his only chance to enjoy a white ass. As soon as he got on top of him, the crowd began to sing, 'How lovely is our bride!' At last, Xhagai straightened up, tightened the belt of his pants and said, 'You are now a dirty hole.'

"The crowd laughed loudly. Ylber was on the verge of tears. He seemed shattered, and one had the feeling that he would give up the ghost, if you so much as tweaked his nose.

" 'Go and tell your prison guards that you've been raped, and are no longer a virgin…' Chief chided him. 'If I get more prison time for this, I will be sure to tell the judges how I topped you.'

"After that, Ylber disappeared without a trace. No one saw him even at the emergency room in the prison camp. We don't know what happened to him. There was talk that they hid him in an isolated cell, and later transferred him to another camp.

" 'No matter where he goes, the scandal will dog his steps,' Xhagai told us, speaking like one who had long experience in prisons and detention camps."

As the stories grew gruesome, a part of me felt at ease that I met my cousin at the coffee house instead of home. The words of my grandfather rang in my ears again. I felt that Evil was somewhere listening and marveling at his own doing….

Tirana 1987 – New York 2004

☙ The Skull Crusher ❧

1

He picked up the telephone handset, placed it to his ear, and after saying three times "yes, yes, yes," and then, "as you please, of course," he set it down on the hook. His face radiated joy, so much so that his wife became curious, and wanted to know the reason for the sudden change in his looks.

"Good news?" Lindita asked him.

"Stupendous!" replied Fation, without going into details, so as to make her even more curious.

"Well, come out with it, will you?" she said, impatiently.

"I shall take part in the execution," he enunciated, in a manner that gave each word its proper emotional weight. "My supervisor just gave me the news."

"Aha! Big news, indeed," remarked Lindita, downplaying the news as if it were nothing out of the ordinary. "Is that what got you so excited?" she asked with sarcasm. "I thought they had invited you to be a part of some delegation that's going abroad...."

"You don't understand," he rebuked her. "To be more exact, you don't understand the significance of a telephone call like that. Do you think that executions of Ministers and Politburo members happen every week? This is a rare occasion, never to be repeated. It's an event that can never be forgotten. Just picture for a moment a man trembling with fear, as he faces the firing squad, the very man whose portrait we have held in our hands like an icon, for years and years in every parade, and every festival."

"The execution of a man doesn't seem to me like an amusing scene," his wife continued.

"A man, you call him?" he mocked her. "You still don't get it. He is an enemy and deserves to be punished. No one should feel sorry for him."

"Not even his wife and children?" she asked.

Her unexpected question left him tongue-tied. He didn't know how to reply. He had never imagined the ex-Minister as a father, a husband, or maybe even a grandfather.

"Give it a rest," he said curtly, in a nervous tone. "No pity for the enemies. They were unfaithful to the Party and got what they deserved."

"You sound just like the old timers," Lindita went on, as she placed a tablecloth. There was anger in her voice. Fation tried to take a more sentimental approach.

"What's gotten into you tonight?" he asked hoping to calm her down and make up before they sat down to dinner. "We've always understood each other. We used to agree on just about everything. How come tonight we don't see eye to eye?"

"How come you don't think of going to a concert or a show.... Do you know that summer is just about over? It's been months since the last time we set foot in a café," complained Lindita.

"You know how busy I've been this year," he replied in self-defense. "How many Sundays did I have off this summer? No more than two or three."

Fation was coming home from work later than usual, feeling tired, distressed and aggravated. He complained more often about his headaches and lack of sound sleep. His wife understood that the job of the investigator at a time of political disturbances and the imprisonment of high-ranking Party officials required extra work hours. Lindita recalled with nostalgia the family's Sunday picnics at the Big Park, on the hills of the city. They packed their lunches and just enjoyed a day out with the children. In the evening they went to a café to listen to music. She wondered if the tensions brought on by official responsibilities would end soon. Lindita feared that witnessing an execution might strain her husband's nerves.

"You know what? Don't go!" The tone of her voice was a sincere plea, devoid of any trace of anger she felt earlier. "Find some kind of an excuse and don't be a part of it," she begged him.

Fation gave her a disapproving look, but kept his mouth shut.

"I think it will spoil your mood...," Lindita said, continuing to unfurl her train of thought. "I get all shook up just picturing the execution!" Her shoulders shuddered with revulsion.

"First of all, I am duty bound as one of the investigators of this case," Fation said softly, finding an opening in the debate. "And secondly, orders can't be questioned. What makes you think that this ordeal will make me grouchy? You think I will feel sorry for him? On the contrary...."

"When will the hour strike for the poor wretch?" she asked.

"You're driving me up the wall tonight," he scowled. "Why do you say 'the poor wretch'? He is an enemy of the Party, an enemy of the people. Get it?"

"Didn't you just say that you used to hold up his picture like an icon?" she sneered. "If it were up to me, I would dismiss him from his post, take away his car and his bodyguards, expel him from the government residences and send him to do community work. That will teach him."

Fation grinned as he pictured the former General and ranking government official in the trenches with the Gypsies and some scumbags. How naïve!

"You have great imagination, no doubt about that!" he complimented her.

"Have they set the day yet?" Lindita was interested to know.

"Tonight!"

"Tonight?" she said with astonishment, as if such a thing were inconceivable.

"At four in the morning, I have to be at the New Prison building. I don't know where will be going from there, the east or the west side cemetery."

An Executive Order of the City Hall had decreed that Tirana's main boulevard located at the center would also be the zonal line between the two cemeteries of the capital. Since then the deceased from the eastern side of the city were buried in the cemetery of Shtish-Tufine, while the departed of the western area were put to rest at the Sharre graveyard. Fation had no idea where those who were sentenced to die were executed, nor did he know where they were buried. Then again, it could be that, for security reasons, the burial site was changed constantly.

"They're not going to send a car to pick you up?" Lindita challenged him. It was customary for the Investigation Office to dispatch a car to the home of its employees, whenever they were called for duty on urgent business.

"I forgot to ask. But I can walk there, too. It's not far," he answered.

"Does he know that he will be shot tonight?" she inquired.

"I don't think so. As a rule, they don't tell them…nor is that necessary. I guess once they shove him into the prison van before dawn, he knows where he is going."

"Poor Sabrie and the children who will have to live with this…," she said, as she thought of the Minister's wife, whom she had met by chance. She had impressed Lindita as a simple and reserved woman, not at all conceited, despite her husband's position.

Fation raised his hand impetuously, as if to say, "Enough!" His tense face showed his exasperation. Why should he feel sorry for the wife and children of a traitor?

"Did I tell you that Uncle stopped by?" she asked. She didn't have to mention Pleurat by name, since he was Fation's only uncle.

"What did he want?" Fation wanted to know.

"Nothing. 'I just dropped in to see you,' he said."

"Did he spout any nonsense?" he asked, with a certain pent-up fury.

"If you ask me, what he has to say is not nonsense, at all," she remarked.

"Oh would you stop it!" he snapped at her.

Shortly after, it occurred to him to ask if uncle left any message.

"No. He didn't even stay for coffee as much as I invited him. I meant to ask him to wait for you here, but I didn't know when you were coming home. You didn't tell me," she said in a mildly scolding voice.

"There was no way I could let you know, since I did not know myself," said Fation in self-defense. "I'll try to be more considerate next time," he said jokingly.

Uncle and nephew exchanged barbs with each other whenever they discussed politics. In a heated debate, Fation had said to his uncle once that he sounded like "The Voice of America." The mockery was very hard on Lindita, whereas Uncle Pleurat started to laugh, and noted that sometimes "The Voice of America" expressed opinions that were not to the liking of Albania's government. He had advised Fation to quit working "at that office," not to besmirch his character. His nephew retorted that moral considerations had nothing to do with his line of work.

Lindita set the table and motioned to him to come over. They began to eat without saying a word. Only the clanking sounds of spoons and forks on the porcelain dishes were heard. Fation broke the silence and asked about her day. Lindita only shrugged, which he took to mean that she didn't care to answer.

Later Fation put on his pajamas, and as soon as he lay down in bed, he asked her gently not to take too long with the dishes, the pots and pans. He knew that the matrimonial bed was the ideal place to forget about the confrontations and storms of the day.

"I can't leave the dirty dishes in the dishwasher. But you go ahead and sleep. You don't have any dishes to clean, or clothes to iron, or curtains to put up," she replied with scorn, signaling that she was not inclined to take his advice. The agitation that was tearing her inside was far removed from any desire for bodily pleasures.

Shortly after Fation fell asleep, and wasn't even aware when his wife got into bed. How could he? She took care not to make the slightest sound, as she stretched out close to the edge of the bed.

At half past three in the morning, the telephone rang. Fation grabbed the handset at once. He had expected that call with anticipation.

"Jovan is sending the office car to pick me up," he said joyfully to his wife, reminding her indirectly of their earlier conversation on the subject. This meant recognition of his rank. "Where is my ironed shirt?" he asked.

"On the chair," she replied sluggishly.

"And my suit?"

"In your wardrobe, where else? Why wear your best suit there, anyway?" The question implied a certain reprimand.

"I don't know who is going to be there," he retorted.

"All right, do as you like," Lindita said, turning her head the other way.

Usually she advised her husband on what to wear, to help him look presentable. But that night she couldn't care less.

"You're not going to help me?" he needled her.

"Why, you're not a baby. Even the kids get dressed by themselves.... Walk softly, so you don't wake them up," she cautioned him.

They had a girl and a boy, Suela and Dritan. Suela was a high school student and spent more time than ever in front of the mirror, trying out different hair styles, and matching outfits. Literature was her passion. Even in grade school, she stood out for her recitations. She was one of the best students in her school. If only she could become an artist some day! As a father, Fation was concerned over the sudden blossoming of her bodily charms. He thought she was somewhat spoiled and even provocative, and feared that she was going to slip out of his hands quite soon. Dritan spent all his afternoons in the sports field playing soccer. His parents hoped that his passion for sports was a mere whim of his youth, and would not become an obstacle that would prevent him from pursuing a serious profession.

"You know that Suela's school benefit recital is in two days?" Lindita reminded him.

"I have no time for that," Fation said curtly.

"You cannot take two hours off from work?"

"Since you are going, then...," he mumbled the rest of the answer.

A car honked outside, and Fation rushed over to the window at once. He returned to his wardrobe to decide what tie to wear.

"Should I put on the red tie with the black polka dots?" he asked her.

Lindita had mentioned that the tie went well with his blue suit, and brightened up his somewhat dark complexion.

Yet all she said that night was "As you wish!"

2

His supervisor was waiting for him across from the iron gate of the State Archives, puffing on a cigarette. With his stout built and the cheap Stetson hat he wore to protect his bald head from the sun, he was easy to spot. His clumsy body, fleshy face and likable demeanor, did not agree with his position as Chief Investigator in the country's capital. He looked more like a prewar retail grocer, than a top investigator. His career background was simple. He left his job as a shopkeeper's apprentice and joined the guerrilla forces. After the war, he held no responsible position or official rank. In 1945 Jovan Katroshi was assigned to the People's Defense Bureau, which happened to determine the course of his professional life. For several months, the Bureau operated in the northern regions of the country swiping "reactionary individuals," and collecting illegal guns. Later, he worked as an instructor at the Ministry of Internal Affairs for several years. In the mid sixties, he was appointed Chief Investigator. A quiet and restrained man, he carried out the duties assigned to him by his superiors without questions or reservations. His staff liked him because he did not show a descending attitude towards them.

Fation walked up to Jovan and offered him a cigarette.

"Thank you, but I'm still puffing mine," Jovan said.

"This time I really got my work cut out for me." Jovan complained. "You have no idea how I labored to do the 'list of participants.' The Minister sent the list back to me three times. The first time, he said that it was too long. I put the names of all the colleagues who wanted to witness the execution of comrade Ta…," he stopped and corrected himself angrily "the shit-face, I mean." Then trying to explain his lapse, he said, "I am so used to saying his name because he was a top dog for a long time." He took a long puff on his cigarette then threw it away. "The second version of the list was returned to me with a marginal note, 'Reduce to a minimum!' In his office the Minister said to include 'only those who have to be there, no one else!' I trimmed the list again and showed it to him. Next to each of the names, the Minister noted the position, signed and gave me the list with the notation, 'to be shredded, after the execution.' I have it in my safe box and will tear it as soon as I get back to the office."

Fation thanked him for his thoughtfulness.

"You earned it. I didn't do you any favors," his supervisor said.

The previous investigator of the ex-Minister was dismissed quickly on the pretext that he lacked experience. Yet everyone knew that the investigation of former members of the Politburo was considered a great opportunity to move up. At any rate, Fation got on the short list of those who would attend the execution of the ex-Minister. The make-up of the judicial body, and the place and time of the trial, was kept secret even from the people involved in the investigation. The whole process resembled a mafia trial. On one side, there were the district attorney and the magistrates; while on the other side was the defendant, all by himself. The defense attorneys withdrew from the case, arguing that the defendant was educated and quite capable of representing himself. Behind closed doors, no one was supposed to know what the defendant said, his arguments in his own defense or attacks against the Party leadership at the trial. It was rumored in confidence that the trials resembled a farce, since there was already a verdict before the defendant ever stepped in the courtroom. And no, the verdict could not be appealed.

Fation had heard that after the sentencing the former Minister appealed to the People's Assembly to spare his life. His appeal startled some and made others grin with scorn, for it was well known that the

Parliament acted on orders of the Party, even on matters of less importance. The head of the Assembly whom some people called "President," either to make fun of him or simply to flatter him, each day signed a stack of certificates of merits, assigned medals, various orders and decorations. According to regulations, the signature on them had to be authentic and original. Stamped signatures or initials were not acceptable. Neither he nor the Presidium had the authority to spare the life of anyone who was condemned by the Party as a traitor. Petitions for pardon were put in the file cabinets with a marginal note, "Petition rejected," without even a formal glance.

To get to the prison gate on that day Fation counted four cordons of police and armed civilians. Along the way, a close inspection of documents and passes! Since the police knew his boss, Jovan, they let them fawningly. Contrary to Fation's expectations, outside the prison gate there was only a small car, with curtains drawn and no lights inside. It seemed like an abandoned vehicle.

After a while, another car, with only the parking lights on, drove up furtively and braked just behind the small car. From its rear door, there slid out a man with an odd-shaped face, narrow forehead, thin beard and high cheekbones. Strangely enough, his face bore a resemblance to the caskets used by Orthodox Christians, and the association with death nauseated Fation. He found himself wondering whether any woman could possibly accept to be embraced by a man with such a hellish face. Fation recalled seeing him at the coffeehouse in the Internal Affairs Ministry. His name was Jashar Elmazi. His heavy Southern dialect was a definite giveaway of his origin. His creepy looks and lead-colored eyes made Fation uneasy every time. No one seemed to be sure about Jashar's profession or specialty in the Ministry. Overcome by curiosity, Fation asked his supervisor about Jashar's position. His response was a gentle caution, "Why don't you let his employer worry about that." Fation kept quiet and felt like kicking himself for yielding to his inquisitive nature. Curiosity was not encouraged among employees in the administration.

A man wearing a cape knocked on the iron gate of the prison. A small window of crisscrossed iron bars opened up, and behind it could be seen the face of the night guard. As soon as he saw the man with the cape, the guard withdrew. The bolts on the lock of the gate scraped and groaned in the murky silence of the night, the gate swung open and the van drove inside. A second gate with iron bars separated the courtyard from tunnel entrance. Knowing the regulations, the van driver came to a stop in front of the gate. He knew that the front gate did not open before the gate in the back was closed and secured. After going past the grid-iron gate, the van glided into the prison courtyard, and after several maneuvers halted before the main entrance to the prison, a heavy iron gate covered with rust.

The man with the cape entered the prison building. A few moments later, one heard the rasping sounds of keys and padlocks, bars and hinges, followed by the thud of shoes and boots on the steps.

At the prison gate, a trio of people showed up: a hunched man, and two police who were holding him up, so he could stand on his feet. Under the faint lights, Fation was barely able to recognize the former General. His mouth was plugged with a wad of polyester, to prevent him from screaming with rage or from terror. He walked like a cripple, with his hands hanging down. For a moment, a gleam of light glanced off the chrome metal of his handcuffs below his legs. Fation knew that the ill-fated high-ranking officials and dangerous criminals were shackled in such a fashion: one hand behind the back, the other in front, and both of them clasped with chains below the thighs. This way the prisoner was forced to stoop like a cripple and to step lamely as if afflicted with hernia, instead of being able to walk tall or even appear remotely defiant.

Tied up however as he was, the General could not climb the four iron steps of the door to the van, and the police were forced to pick him up bodily and to heave him face down on the dirty floor of the van. The polyester on his mouth swept the dust along the way, as he slid on the floor. The felon wailed with terrible pain, without articulating any words.

The motorcade consisted of two jeeps – one in front, the other in back of the prison-van – three cars and two trucks, headed east on the highway that ringed the capital. "The ex-General is headed for the east side cemetery," reasoned Fation. Apparently, the graveyard to the east of the city was preferred, because it was in a quieter area and with less human traffic in the morning hours. The cars kept moving on the road, keeping a greater distance one from the other, so as not to give the impression that they were all part of a motorcade.

Up above the stars began to abate, as a sliver of light appeared on the crests of the mountains. A night bird winged its way in the sky like the shade of an evil spirit. The motorcade took the Dibra road and continued toward the Dajti Mountain, bypassing the east side cemetery. It could be that the execution site was on the other side of the city's mountain. However, a little past Gurore, the first jeep turned to the right and drove on an unpaved road that zigzagged among thickets and a strawberry grove. The massive murk presence of the Dajti Mountain and the obscure shade of the night formed a dark cloud that forecast a storm. Looking out the car window, Fation could barely make out prairies of shrunken oaks, mastic trees and bushes.

The prison-van halted in front of an abandoned hanger, without a roof or door. It seemed like the structure was intended for a barrack or warehouse, but owing to lack of funds or strategic considerations, it was abandoned and left to the mercy of the elements.

The silhouettes of people that moved in the bluish predawn light seemed to be waltzing silently, without music or vocals, not unlike an ancient rite of sacrifice. The police stationed themselves at different points around the hangar, to secure the area against a sudden, last minute attack. The cautionary step seemed futile and even ludicrous to Fation. Evidently, the former Minister had no friends and no allies. His former loyal comrades were terrified and fearful for their own lives.

The front door of the prison-van opened, and out came, the longish, casket-like face of Jashar. He slammed the door to let everyone know that he had traveled in comfort seated alongside the driver. From outside the car, a policeman pulled the bolt that secured the van. The doors of the van were locked from the outside, to prevent any attempt of the prisoner to escape. The convict, the armed police and internal security, were all locked inside, as a precautionary measure to forestall any possible derailing of the schedule. The guards took their places on both sides of the rear door of the van, with arms cocked, as if the ex-General was going to try to flee as soon as the door opened.

One wing of the door opened easily, while the other wailed as iron brushed against iron. The wail rent the crisp air like a sharp knife. The hunched former General emerged from the side of the car and stopped, as he sought to locate the steps of the van. If he had jumped from where he stood, he risked falling down and getting hurt badly. The instinct of self-preservation prevented him from taking a step, even now when he knew that in a few minutes he was going to be shot. The police gave him a hard push from behind, and the General fell on his face flat on the ground. The plug of polyester flew from his mouth, and he snarled angrily:

"Pigs!"

Those around him laughed with scorn, taking pleasure in seeing him fall on his face.

"He is used to name calling, the rotten skunk...doesn't understand his situation."

The two civilians, who accompanied him in the van, jumped on the ground, grabbed him by the arms and lifted him to his feet.

"You squashed me, jackass!" he yelped.

"Shut up," yelled back the policeman on his left. He swung with his elbow to strike him hard on the face, but only hit his ear, as the convict bent his head down below the shoulders.

"Move your feet! Don't make us drag you like a coward. Now is the time to show what you got, not in your office!" the other policeman roared menacingly, as he gave him a kick.

Jashar Elmazi led the procession, followed by the police. Fation and other civilians walked in back as they went into the hangar. Jashar headed toward the southern wall of the structure. On that side, the plaster was chipped off and full of holes, while on the other walls it was smooth and even, although it looked dingy from the wear and tear of time.

"Here!" said Jashar, placing his foot on the spot where the condemned was to be brought, about two meters away from the wall, so that the bricks on the wall would not be spattered with blood. Otherwise, they would have to be cleaned with a washrag. The guidelines specified that no trace of the shooting should remain. "Hold him there!" he told the escorts, the moment they arrived at a certain line. "Take off the chains and tie his hands behind his back!" was Jashar's next command. Judging by his manners, it seemed that he was the master of the morbid ceremony.

Then Jashar drew close to the prison's director and whispered something to him. On orders of the director, three policemen with weapons, moved away from the gate without doors.

A keen-faced man with a yellowish complexion like dried up tobacco leaves, took out of his pocket a typed note, and read it out loud. It informed that the petition for pardon had been rejected by the Presidium of the People's Assembly. The verdict of the trial remained in force, as well as the sentence for high treason and for plotting with foreign intelligence to bring down the people's government. Fation recognized the man who was reading the official note. He was one of the army's prosecutors known for his arrogance in trial hearings. He could have been the head of the judicial body of this case, or maybe a jury member at the military court. After reading, he folded the letter, put it back in his pocket. Then he buttoned the pocket and patted it twice to make doubly sure it was safe there.

The chilling metallic friction caused by the bolt when loading the weapon with bullets, ripped the silence. The bylaws state that during the loading, the barrels must point downward, in order to avoid accidents or firing without orders.

A security officer in plain clothes draw near the convict and informed him that the law grants the right to speak before being shot.

The former General looked at him with void eyes without understanding what was being said.

"Your last words!" the security man shouted as if speaking to a hard-of-hearing.

The condemned still didn't understand what was being asked of him. The security man stepped back, after making a gesture of contempt, as if to say: "Fine. We can do without them. We don't need your last words." He signaled to the guards who were still holding the convict up by his arms, to get away from him. They walked away hurriedly, leaving the former Minister alone in front of the execution squad. At that moment the former member of the Politburo remembered to utter his last words. He gathered all his strength and yelled:

"Long Live the Party of Labor! Long Live the Central Committee of the Pa...."

Bang! Bang! Bang! Three shots cut off his last words. His open mouth was then distorted from the pain he felt, and he let out a prolonged "ooof" sound that rose skyward, while his body collapsed feebly on the ground, resting on his side. The pierced heart and aorta had rapidly interrupted the circulation of the blood to the vital organs.

Fation had thought about the final moment of execution, the "the merciful blow." Since his college days, he had been impressed by the term *colpo di grazia,* and one day he asked his professor about the origin and historical circumstances surrounding the expression. His professor defined it as a kind of euphemism invented by the bourgeoisie, an upper class 'sugarcoating' of "a death blow." Fation wondered about that last ritual of the execution and the man entrusted with such a task.

A swarthy man with big eyes, dark brows, bald, with a bulky torso and short legs, approached the executed. From his gander-like manner of walking, Fation knew that it was the doctor of the prison hospital, Dr. Gogeni. To deal with those who simulated illness, but were not actually sick, Dr. Gogeni resorted to the Dark Ages' practice of making injections with *rubrum,* "red-colored water," which neither harmed nor benefited the patient. It only caused a burning sensation, like chili peppers. Now he had to confirm the death of the former Minister, and sign the death certificate. The hands of the executed were sprinkled with blood, and the doctor felt sick to the stomach and was reluctant to take the pulse. He deliberated for a moment, and then pressed the tip of his finger on the carotid artery. After looking at the pupils of his eyes, which had no sparkle in them, the doctor announced:

"He is dead, the scum!"

The doctor articulated the words loudly, to let everyone know that he hated the common enemy. His zeal ran counter to his humanitarian profession.

The prison director and Jashar walked over to the dead body.

"Let me have the handcuffs. They are part of my inventory," the director said.

"Of course!" replied the man with the hexagonal face. "Damn it! They are sprinkled with blood, and need to be washed," he snorted, as if that was not part of his job.

"Very well; let me have them later," the director said.

Nobody else went close to the body to fire the last shot. Suddenly, Fation began to wander that perhaps the guidelines had changed recently for the sake of saving one bullet.

As those present started to come out of the hangar, here and there cigarette lighters and matches flared up. There were sounds of bolts clanking and car doors slamming, and then all was quiet. Three or four policemen scurried behind the bushes, and a little later the flow and splash of urine could be heard. Two of the police took a waterproof canvas from the van, and ran toward the hangar. Curious to see the final act of the execution, Fation hung around the hangar. He noticed that Jashar collected the three spent cartridges and put them in his coat pocket. The police spread the canvas alongside the body, and stood there waiting for new orders. Then, one of them said:

"Jashar doesn't need any helpers. Let's go outside."

Jashar eyed him with such a scolding look. They did not dare to move.

"Are you waiting for me to pick him up?" he yelled at them.

Dawn had slightly pushed darkness aside the little hills to the west of Tirana. The undulating hills, touched by the morning sunrays were magnificent to behold from afar.

Drawn by an unknown force, Fation neared the corpse. The man turned around and his hexagonal face had a grimace on. Then Fation heard him say:

"Almost done! "Don't get bored!"

There was something enigmatic about those words. Fation imagined that the body would be wrapped in the waterproof canvas to be buried. That canvas would be a shroud and a casket. The body would probably be buried in some hole dug up nearby for that purpose or in some unmarked spot by the cemetery. Fation could not help thinking that had the ex-Minister died of any illness a few months earlier, the government would have proclaimed a period of national mourning, the flags would flown at half-mast, and his coffin would have been transported to the cemetery on top of a cannon. There would have been wreaths, speeches, tears and distress over the great loss, newspaper articles, praise to the skies for the deeds of the departed, whereas now they were dumping him in a pit wrapped up in a dirty old canvas.

Jashar bent over the body to remove the handcuffs. As soon as he pried them loose, he turned and looked at Fation.

"He won't need them in that world," he said, trying to be funny. He threw them away from the body and then thrust the tip of his boot on the flank of the corpse to turn it face up. But the corpse kept sliding face down, and his boot got stained with blood.

"Turn around, you pig!" snarled Jashar, and using his hands, he rolled the body face up.

With the mouth open, the corpse seemed to still be making a failing effort to utter the last words, "Long live the Party!" while the lifeless eyes gazed at the sky.

"Still with your eyes open? Oh-ho! You want to go on seeing, huh? Do you see me? Do you know who I am? I am Jashar. You don't recognize me? You'll find out right now!"

He reached underneath his jacket, and pulled out a cleaver that had a blunt side like an adz. He ran his finger over the cutting edge, to check its sharpness, then lifted it up and struck the dead man's face just below the nose. Wham! The blade buried deep, as it sliced the flesh. The crack was so wide, it seemed that the corpse had gotten hold of the cleaver with its teeth, and did not want to let go. Jashar bore down on the handle, yanked the blade out and struck again, this time a little higher. The blade came out spattered with bits of brains, all mushy and whitish in color. He struck again with a slanting blow, and a round ball jumped out of the eye socket, and rolled on the grass like a glass marble.

"Where do you think you're going?" Jashar addressed the eyeball. "I got you!" he said, and he grabbed the eyeball and put it in the mouth of the executed man.

Then his hand began to strike quickly. Wham! Wham! Wham! On the cheekbones, on the other eye, on the forehead, the jaws, the mouth, faster and faster. Fation's stomach tightened up like a knot as he watched Jashar at work.

"Look at me, you scoundrel! Look! You see what I did to you?" he ranted over the body of the deceased. "I crushed your skull so that even your own mother won't be able to recognize you, even if she scraped the dirt over your grave with her own fingers, fifty years from this day." Using the dull side of the cleaver, he crushed every bone in his face, until all parts were reduced to a mush of blood, flesh, skin and brains.

Fation started seeing yellow, green and blue sparks dancing before his eyes. His sight grew dim and his legs barely held him up, and he leaned against the wall. He began vomiting and gasping for breath. A few drops of vomit fell on his red tie with the black polka dots. He took out his handkerchief, and began to wipe off the vomit. Lindita's pleading words rang in his ears: "Don't go. Find an excuse of some sort." Fearing that he might collapse, as his limbs were trembling, he walked slowly, leaning against the wall. The loud sounds of his vomiting attracted attention, and the prison director sent over a policeman to check out the site.

"It's that new guy," the policeman told the prison director. "He was vomiting."

"Fation, the investigator?" Jovan asked.

"I think so."

"That's all right. He will get used to it," the director said.

Feeling somewhat let-down by the weakness shown by his subordinate, Jovan got out of the car and headed straight for the hangar. He found Fation holding his stomach with his hands, and looking pale as a lemon.

"What happened?" he asked.

"I feel like my belly has turned upside down."

"Why did you hang around there?" his supervisor asked in a warning tone.

"I wanted to see what was happening to the very end," Fation explained.

"Come on, get in the car!" his boss said. "You will catch a cold here. A cup of black coffee will settle your stomach, only there is no bar or restaurant around here."

Jovan asked if by chance someone had a bottle of cognac or brandy, but no one seemed to pay attention. It could be that they were annoyed and irritated that the investigator had lost his nerve.

An hour later, they were back in town. Fation was not riding in the prison van so he did not see whether the corpse wrapped up in the dirty waterproof canvas was dumped into a pit on the slopes of the Dajti Mountain, or carried back in the van for burial on the other side of the city.

"Don't come to the office today," Jovan told him. "Go home and get some sleep, if you can, because sleep is relaxing."

3

The apartment was totally quiet. The sofa bed, the curtains, the TV set; the chairs were just as he had left them a few hours before, only he felt that he was returning there after a long absence. He had a void as if being hollowed from within. Hoping that sleep was going to relax him, he took off his jacket and pants, untied his tie and put it on a hanger. Lying down on his back, he closed his eyes, expecting to fall asleep at once. But suddenly, on the ceiling there appeared the vision of a smashed skull, with the mouth open, and one eye rolling on the grass like a marble, and the bloodied cleaver. Between fits of sleep, he saw the ex-Minister standing before the gate of the other world. He had been stopped there by the gatekeeper who informed him that anyone without identification, or with heads hollowed out like a ladle, were not permitted to enter. The ex-Minister returned to the hangar and pleaded with Jashar to fix his head, but the man with the coffin face was chasing him and threatening to crush the other parts of his body with the cleaver. The crushed skull and the hexagon-shaped face glided on the ceiling as if performing a macabre dance in a perverted show. Eager to return to the world of the living, Fation opened his eyes. The gate of the other world and the Last Judgment in his nightmare were just like his grandmother had described them when he was a child. "Nonsense! There is no after-life," he said to himself, with the conviction of an atheist. He got up, poured a glass of whiskey and downed it in a single gulp. He followed that with another shot, to numb his nerves a little. But it didn't work. The disfigured face of the executed and that of the executioner went on with their mad dance on the ceiling, the walls, the kitchen counter, everywhere he turned his eyes. Did the convict really say, "Long live the Party!" or was that his imagination? It would have been more logical if he had cursed the Party that took his life. The convict's dying words kept coming back to Fation's mind.

He put on a shirt and reached for the tie when he noticed a few white spots on it. Looking at it more closely, he recalled that those were droplets of vomit. His face drooped. He decided to give the tie to Lindita to clean. But what could he say to her, if she asked where and how the spots got there? Better to take out the traces of the unpleasant incident himself. He went to the bathroom, took a towel, moistened it a bit and rubbed the tie until he was convinced that no tell-tale trace remained on it. Afterwards, he hung it up in the closet to dry, and keep it out of Lindita's sight.

Fation stepped out of his home, not knowing where he wanted to go. He walked the street that led downtown and as usual his feet willy-nilly took him to the bar of the Ministry of the Internal Affairs. Through the window he thought he saw Jashar in, eating and drinking with his buddies, as if nothing had happened that morning at the roofless hangar. There was no mercy killing, no final blow. The bashing-of-the-skull scene flashed in his head like lightning. Instead of looking at Jashar's nauseating face, he decided to take himself out for a walk in the Big Park and seek comfort in the bosom of nature. He sat down on the steps of the City' Opera and Ballet, across the Archeological Museum. Students walked to and fro carrying mimeographed materials and textbooks. Some young couples were also sitting at the steps studying or chatting intimately. He thought that one day his daughter Suela would probably study there at the Acting School. Department . Hobbled by prejudice against artists, Fation hoped that Suela would want to go to a different school. In the eyes of the Department of State Security, artists were hopeless liberals.

Seated on the steps, Fation looked vacantly at the pedestrians who walked by him. "Do these people know that this morning, the former Minister was executed on the hills of Tirana? Do they know that Jashar Elmazi crushed his skull with a cleaver, while now he is drinking and feasting on appetizers? Damn it! My mind keeps going back there. I got to erase that bleak scene from my memory."

A middle-aged brunette with dark eyebrows walked by. She resembled Dizi, his former girlfriend in the days when their families lived in the southern town of Delvine. She ran over to him, her face beaming with joy. Her dark eyes still glistened with life and lust, just as they did when she was a young. She asked him about Lindita and the children, as if she were family and without a trace of jealousy or spite.

Some twenty years ago, Fation and his buddy, Gogo, walked around town as teenagers almost every afternoon in the summer. Their town had no boulevard and no public park. But that didn't stop them from roaming in the alleys until dusk. One afternoon in August, Fation was waiting for Gogo to finish stacking up some logs outside the house, when Dizi walked into the front yard. As a relative, she went to Donka, Gogo's sister, whenever she needed help with her stitching or knitting. Donka, was about four years older, and was more experienced in handy work. Since Donka had gone to the fountain to draw water, Dizi said that she would wait for her and then walked over to Fation, beneath the arch of the gate.

In the courtyard near the kitchen, the cherries glistened among the green leaves, while above them hung branches of juicy, golden plums. Dizi was curious to know what kind of a career he was going to choose, after he graduated from High School. He revealed to her a long-cherished secret that he was going to be a pilot, and fly over their town with his head sticking out, so as to amaze his friends, his teachers and his relatives. "Would you take me with you?" Dizi asked, right away. "Of course," he promised quickly. She thanked him by throwing her arms around his neck and kissing him. Fation was left speechless. But her daring act encouraged him to reward her by kissing her back. He drew her close to his chest, and began to kiss her on the neck, intoxicated by the aroma of her hair and the heat of feminine passion, which he had never known before. Dizi welcomed the kisses with her eyes half-closed, and her head resting on his shoulder. Even without flying high in an airplane, the two of them were above the clouds.

They started meeting in the courtyard shack, supposedly to hide from Gogo, who pretended not to know anything about their relations. Dizi did not wear a brassiere. Her breasts, which bounced like two doves ready to fly away into space, incited Fation to unbutton her blouse, slide his hand underneath and fondle her teats. Dizi welcomed the caresses with pleasure, curiosity and restraint. "From the waist up, do whatever you like; from the waist down 'No.' That's what my aunt taught me," she said to him. Their fling which did not go beyond kisses and sweet embraces, lasted until the end of summer. In September, Fation's father was transferred to the town of Berat, and the family moved there. He and Dizi separated as friends, without tears, without sighs, and without promises to be faithful. Each cherished in their hearts the sweet memories of their secret rendezvous in Gogo's shanty place. Years later Fation heard that she had married a shoemaker, but three years later he was consumed with jealousy and divorced her. Gossip had it that she flirted with her bosses in the carpet workshop. In a small town like Delvina, it was impossible to keep secret extra-marital relations. After the divorce, Dizi went on weaving carpets in Delvina, until her daughter graduated from High School. She then decided to move to Tirana. Putting her physical charms at work, Dizi was able to get residence permit, relocate, as well as obtain housing in the capital. Her experience had taught her not to surrender to government officials, before securing the favors she had asked for. Whenever they winked at her, intimating that they meet for quick act of passion, she smiled coyly and said, "First the papers, then the fun. We have lots of time. I'm not going anywhere."

"You look tired," Dizi said.

"I stayed up late," Fation replied.

The blue apron she was wearing was a clear indication that she worked as a cleaning woman at the University or the Museum of Archeology.

"We will get together sometime...," Fation started to say.

"Whenever you like," she said. "I'm always here."

4

It was close to four o'clock, when he began to walk home slowly. As soon as he stepped inside, Lindita eyed him reproachfully, as if she had unearthed something sinister.

"How did you make out?" she asked.

"Fine," replied Fation, confident that she had not detected anything.

"Where did you soil your tie so badly?" Lindita inquired.

Her question was so sudden that he was forced to pretend he didn't understand.

"My tie?" he turned her question around.

"Yes, the red tie with the black polka dots. I tried to clean it, but couldn't. The tie was discolored in some spots, maybe by acid; that's what it looks like. What a shame! You ruined your best tie," Lindita said with regret.

"Could be that vinegar drops got on it, when I was having breakfast," he said, in self-defense.

"And the pants? Why are you so careless? You're worse than a kid."

"I'll have a look at them," Fation said. It was merely an excuse to get away from his wife and the acerbic discussion.

Lindita set the table and called him to lunch.

"The children ate in a hurry and went out. They were going to the movies," she informed him.

Fation had no appetite, but decided just the same to sit down at the table, in order not to add to the suspicions of his wife.

"By the way, how did the execution go?" Lindita asked.

The question took him by surprise, so much so that he exploded and dropped his fork on the plate.

"Can't we have a bite to eat in peace, damn it?"

"There is no need to get upset!" she said, to calm him down. "Finish your lunch and then tell me about it, if you want."

Fation's mood changed quickly. It made sense that his wife should ask to hear what happened especially since she had advised him not to attend the execution.

"I should have listened to you...shouldn't have gone. I get sick to my stomach whenever I think of the execution," he said, without trying to conceal his disgust. He granted that she was right, and hoped that by making that concession, she was going to drop the pesky subject.

"Did he say anything when they shot him? What were his last words?" she wanted to know.

Fation heaved a big sorrowful sigh. No, it was not possible to side-step the scene that shattered his nerves.

"You don't want to talk about it? Then don't," his wife said curtly. "As if I really care to know what his dying words were.... He probably said 'Long live the Party!'"

"Well, I'll be darned!" observed Fation, all excited. "How did you know? Did someone tell you?"

"Why should anyone tell me? Didn't the generals who were shot a few years ago, shout the same slogans?" Linda observed quietly.

"Frankly, I didn't believe my ears, when I heard him. I never thought he would.... How is it possible?" Fation wondered.

"He has cheered like that all his life. He doesn't know anything else...."

Her explanation that this was a mere force of habit seemed too simple and superficial. However, he had no desire to continue the debate.

"Do you really think the dark suit is ruined?" he asked, to change the subject.

"I don't know. I'm going to take it to the cleaners. If they can clean it, fine. Otherwise, we'll do without it."

"I am a lucky man to have you, believe me!" Fation emoted, and reached out to embrace his wife.

In the afternoon, he suggested that they go out for ice cream. Lindita thought about it for a moment, but then decided she had better go to the cleaners instead, knowing that spots are more easily removed while they are still fresh.

"Go and see your uncle," she suggested. "I believe he is troubled about something."

"I'll think about it," he said.

"Still mad at him, huh? You should at least respect him for his age," Lindita remarked.

"Age doesn't count in certain cases," countered Fation.

"I might go with you, if I come back early. It's been months since I last saw Aunt Miriam.

5

Since the senior investigator was hospitalized in the intensive care unit, and there was no telling when he was going to recover, the board assigned Fation Bashkurti to take over the investigation of Milazim Gruda. Fation tried not to show his delight over the assignment. Indeed, he asked his chief to grant him four or five days, at most a week, to wrap up the investigation of a frail young man with the foxy eyes, who related his adventures in robbing train coaches as if they were heroic deeds.

"As for that pickpocket," the chief said casually, "that will be Mark Puleshi's job, whereas you understand, we are trusting you with a different case."

The Ministry officials called the prison for minors "Correction Facility" while the public labeled it "The school of vagabonds." Fation was not enthusiastic about the much acclaimed "Makarenko method of education," which included teaching different crafts to the kids in these institutions. Makarenko was a Soviet pedagogue known for his progressive or liberal educational philosophy. Experience showed that even those few who completed the training and were released, once they got out they went back to their old ways, and ended up in the hands of the police, who brought them back to the institution. The young man that Fation was investigation was an escapee from that kind of school, but this time he was headed for prison, because he was past sixteen, and therefore no longer a minor.

"If you can loosen up the screws in the Gruda case, the stock of our sector will go up, and so will yours. I have faith in you," the chief concluded.

Fation Bashkurti was keen to believe that after a careful screening of all the investigators, he was picked as the most competent, most able, and best prepared. In fact, he considered the recent ill health of the senior investigator a gift from heaven. Life is so capricious! One man's meat is another man's poison. His strongest rival was out, and he had the opportunity to unfurl his skills and climb one step higher on the narrow staircase of the bureaucracy. Fation's father, who was one of the oldest war veterans in the region, never had any ambition, and remained a provincial government employee all his life. Fation, on the other hand, had his eyes fixed on prestigious positions like Judicial Counsel of the Prime Minister, University Lecturer of Political Science, Member of the Supreme Court. If you are nobody, no one pays any attention.

"I am ready," he told his chief, as he simulated a military salute.

Jovan nodded.

"That's what I expected from you," his chief said, in a gesture of congratulations.

"If you will permit me, I have a question," Fation said, somewhat hesitantly.

"Certainly, go right ahead!" the chief said.

"I tried to figure it out myself, but ran into a brick wall, as they say around here." He stopped, not knowing how to continue.

"Come out with it!" Jovan prodded him, smiling feebly.

"Did the ex-Minister really shout, 'Long live the Party!' just before they shot him?"

The chief confirmed it by nodding.

"How is that possible? If you ask me, he should have expressed rage, instead."

The last words of the defendant were a legacy of 'bourgeois jurisprudence,' which had no value whatsoever for Jovan's simplistic reasoning.

"Good question," he said, as if talking to himself. "It just came to me that the saboteurs of the economy sector said exactly the same words in their final moments some years ago." Then he came up with a quick explanation. "You know why? Because they are politically savvy. They profess loyalty to the Party at their last moments, when actually their aim is to get our sympathy for allegedly being victimized through no fault of their own."

"Political hypocrisy," Fation called it. It could not be anything other than a devilish tactic, an evil trick. He thanked Jovan, and walked out of the office.

6

"Good day, Uncle! Lindita told me that you had asked for me. What did you want?" Fation asked him, as soon as he stepped into his uncle's studio.

"If I told you that I just missed you, would you believe it?" Pleurat retorted, raising his eyebrows.

"No," Fation replied dryly.

"You're smart! It is a pity your intelligence works for the devil," he said, berating him.

"You have prejudice against my bureau and the whole administration, even though you yourself have worked in this sector," his nephew noted, chastising him.

"Exactly! I know them inside out…."

Pleurat Dardha had worked in the diplomatic sector from 1946 to 1948. His staff gathered intelligence on political exiles in Greece, Italy and Germany, where the leaders of an anti-government group were located. Alert, energetic and easy to get along with, he quickly won the sympathy of his superiors, and that cost him dearly. After the decent of Minister Koci Xoxe, on espionage charges, Pleurat was out in the cold. He was demoted and was employed at a Collection Agency.

"This is not 1947," observed Fation, alluding to the period of rank abuse of government authority by the secret service known as *Sigurimi.*

"The content hasn't changed," his uncle retorted. "Do you know any other country that brags about dictatorship?"

"I don't follow you," remarked Fation.

"Next to the mosque in the center of the city, there is a billboard in red letters on a blue background that reads: *Dictatorship is the Best Democracy.*"

"I have not seen it," objected Fation.

"I have and I was speechless. In my opinion, it is a perfectly self-incriminating statement. How can a dictatorship be a democracy, when the two systems exclude each other? People like you don't even notice that billboard. However, it got the attention of an international visitor, who stopped to photograph it. I happened to know that the photo of the billboard was shown on TV overseas with the comment, 'Here is the Albanian leadership's understanding of democracy. Take a look at how the dictatorship is presented there.' You can imagine what havoc was caused here. The city's Party officials' got hammered for political myopia and the poster was removed. That is an amusing story, don't you agree?"

Fation decided to move away from the political subject:

"Why were you looking for me? Any reason?"

"Yes. And unfortunately, this time I need your help...."

"At your service."

"I want to read the official court transcripts from the 1947 'Trial of the Assemblymen.' Where can I find them?"

"At the Ministry of Justice, I believe."

"Do you think I don't know the address of the Ministry?" he said sarcastically. "They told me that they don't have any files on trials. Do you think they really don't have them or they simply didn't want to give them to me? The transcripts have to have been filed and stored in the archives somewhere, isn't that so?"

"I'll look into it," promised his nephew. "Do you think your name has popped up somewhere?" Fation needled him, to get more details.

"No, that doesn't worry me," his uncle said. "The 1947 trial wiped out most of our prominent scholars. Worst of all, we rubbed our hands with glee, thinking that the deck was cleared; no barriers left to hamper the revolution. How naïve! As I recall there was no evidence presented in court against them. The prosecution's case was pure propaganda. Anyway, do you think you can get the files for me?" he asked.

"No," replied Fation, curtly. "I don't want to get mixed up in matters that don't concern me, or can raise doubts about me."

"I like people who know how to protect their ass," his uncle said.

"I thought you were going to get angry," the nephew said quietly.

"No! And you know why?"

"I know," replied Fation. "It's the sign of our times. Isn't that what you were going to say?"

Pleurat's wife, Miriam, came in with two cups of coffee and two glasses of water. She asked Fation about Lindita and the children, and said that she missed them, and regretted that they hardly ever visited.

While sipping coffee, Fation watched his uncle's eyes, which gleamed from time to time, as he brewed ideas in his head. Looking straight into those eyes, Fation asked the question that was spinning in his head.

"What would you say if I told you that the former Minister's dying words were 'Long live the Party'?" He expected his uncle to be somewhat surprised. Instead, Pleurat observed quietly,

"Perfectly normal!"

"Paradoxical, you mean. Political truculence and devilish deception." The argument of his supervisor seemed more reasonable than Lindita's suggestion that it was merely 'force of habit.'

"Did you hear that nonsense somewhere or did you come up with it on your own?" blasted Pleurat.

Fation lowered his eyes and his uncle knew that they were not his nephew's thoughts.

"You do not suspect phony behavior or hypocrisy?" asked Fation with considerable misgivings.

"No. Sad to say the former Minister meant every last one of those words," Pleurat replied decisively. "You were disappointed because he remained loyal to the Party until the end. A man has no reason to be phony in his last moments. You have to understand that he served the dictatorship with zeal. Ironically that system took his life. It is paradoxical if not absurd! Forgive me if I raised my voice and got emotional. But as far as I'm concerned, he was neither a traitor, nor a hero. He was just the unfortunate victim of our failings," Pleurat said, winding up his argument. "I trust you understand that."

"I understand that you cannot bring yourself up to see him for what he really was," Fation argued on a more practical level.

"Then tell me whom did he betray? I would hold him up as a champ, if he had attempted to overthrow the regime. But I assure you that such a thought never crossed his mind. The question is: Why should the former Minister have wanted a change of regime? He had power, glory, a villa, a Mercedes-Benz, personal bodyguards, paid servants, and a shining future for the children. He had all of these. What more could he possibly want?

His uncle's point made him think about Voltaire's observation that revolutions in the end consume their own offspring. Was that happening already, he wondered? Roughly every five years, ranking party officials had been charged and tried for political deviations.

Fation ended his visit by telling his uncle that he had to go to see a friend. As soon as he stepped out, he began to rethink his uncle's reasoning. How can traitors be unfortunate victims of political and economic failings? Uncle lives his life in a chrysalis, which, as everybody knows, lacks eyes and is unable to see. Isolated in his studio, he has nothing better to do other than to scribble his stuff and make up theories. Who could deny that those who fled the country, formed contingents that served the enemy of the country? They endangered the socialist future of the nation, and that called for increasing vigilance both at the borders and within the country. And that's why Milazim Gruda's case is so critical, Fation thought.

7

After midnight, Fation woke up suddenly and sat on the bed, staring at the window across the bedroom. A breeze swayed the curtain gently, while beyond the window, there was the azure sky. He was breathing fast, unevenly and with difficulty, then began moaning and talking as if he were delirious. "He came back…his bloody face was on the window…. What do you want from me? I am not the guilty one…. It's your own fault!"

Lindita heard something in her sleep. At first she thought he was talking in a dream, and turned her head the other way. But when she heard them again, she woke up. She sensed that fear and terror had taken hold of her husband.

"Who were you talking to?" she asked calmly. But he didn't or couldn't hear her. "Hey, it's me. Who were you talking to?" Lindita insisted.

He turned toward her, and looked at her intensely.

"Did you see anything?" he asked.

"See what?" she asked, startled by the question.

"The…that came to the window…."

"We are on the second floor, remember?" she teased him, but ever so gently, and grabbed him by the arm, as if to shake him up. "You've had a bad dream. Don't worry, it will pass."

"It was not a dream. I saw it, just as I see you," he insisted, his eyes fixed on the window, as if some unexpected menace was going to jump in from there.

"Wake up, dear, please" she pleaded in fear. She slid off the bed and went around, so she could look him straight in the face. "Calm down! Would you like a drink of water, or coffee? Maybe lemonade...." And without waiting to hear what he preferred, she headed for the kitchen. The door of the refrigerator opened, and shortly after she returned with a glass of lemonade in her hand.

The look of terror had gone from Fation's face. He drank some lemonade, set the glass down on the bedside table and laid his head on the pillow.

"He scared me out of my wits! I felt as if he came to see...."

"Who?" inquired Lindita.

He did not want to reveal the name, and said briefly,

"Just a foolish dream...."

"We all have bad dreams. But you scared me because you were talking to yourself. Good thing the children did not hear you," she said, as she stretched out suggestively alongside him. Perhaps intimacy was the best way to relax him.

However, he placed his hands beneath his head and closed his eyes, and seemed to have fallen back to sleep.

8

When he woke up, he saw Lindita walk in the apartment holding his black pants and a bag of vegetables from the market.

"What did the experts at the Cleaners say?" he asked. His tone of voice was tinged more with sarcasm than with curiosity.

"Terrible," replied Lindita. "First they put me on hold for three days, because the senior chemist was away. Today I talked with him and he said that the discoloring cannot be restored with chemical treatments. The only thing left to do is to dye them black. I asked him whether the pants would not hold the dye in the rain. He said that there is no guarantee. So, it is up to you. What do you want to do with them? It's a shame, a fine suit like that...."

"I ran into Dr. Dragush. He sends his regards."

"Who?" Fation asked.

"The doctor, your cousin."

"The chap who works in the Psychiatric Hospital? Can't say I envy him," he teased. "Do you know what he says to me when I run into him occasionally?"

"What?" she asked.

Suddenly Fation changed his mind.

"Oh, never mind him," he said. He did not want to tell his wife that whenever he ran into his cousin, the doctor said half jokingly that one day Fation was going to be in his care. "Don't bet on it!" Fation responded to him. Then Dr. Dragush argued that a number of Fation's new and former colleagues undergo treatment. He shared with Fation that some sensitive statistics show that the Secret Service employees are increasingly suffering from psychological illnesses, neuroses and depression. Fation remembered visiting a classmate in the mental institution and had never forgotten how miserable he was.

9

Although the case of Milazim Gruda seemed quite straightforward, the investigation was not going as expected. The charge was 'attempted flight from the country,' even though Milazim Gruda had been arrested in his own house in Tirana.

Over a period of twenty years, the article on the illegal border crossings had undergone drastic changes for the worse, with flagrant "deprivations of liberty" to offenders. The incarceration for such a serious offense increased from eight to fifteen years. Also the areas of territorial restriction within the country grew larger with time, while the area of free movement grew narrower. To visit a relative or even your own family around the restricted areas the authorities demanded a special pass. Used to be that the offender who was caught attempting to flee the country via the borders was arrested and jailed. Afterward, the borderline expanded to the "soft belt,"—a cultivated strip of land about three four meters in width, running parallel to the border. The "soft belt" preserved the "footprints of escapees," as well as those of enemies who tried to get in the country. Still later, the restricted zone included all the villages near the borders. This area was called "Zone-A" and all the identification papers of the locals had a special seal on them. In the mid-seventies the charges for attempted flights became so frequent and illogical, that apprehensions and arrests took place in towns far removed from the borders of the country. How could anyone living in Tirana or Elbasan escape, short of using a balloon or zeppelin, whose construction would have been detected, of course, from the very beginning? One count in Milazim Gruda's case was 'planning to flee the country with two associates,' who worked in the mechanical workshop. He denied the charge vehemently, saying it was a groundless and malicious intrigue.

Fation Bashkurti began his interrogation confidently with the customary assertion that *Sigurimi* knew everything. Consequently, the psychological pressure wore down the suspect to the point where a confession seemed like a relief. The nebulous threat was effective with those who believed that *Sigurimi* was aware of everything that happened above and below ground, much like the eye of God that sees the visible and the invisible. At that point in the investigation, Milazim answered calmly that if *Sigurimi* knew everything, they would have no reason to arrest him. The keen logic of his remark chilled the investigator like a cold shower.

"Do you mean to say that you didn't try to flee? Do you deny it? I'm warning you! You will make it harder on yourself, because we have the evidence at hand," Fation screamed.

After a week of intensive interrogations, Fation stepped up the pressure on Milazim Gruda, to break him at all costs. But the suspect did not budge from his position. Later Fation changed his tactic, by being gentle with him. He offered him a cigarette, and said that the suspects' associates had maybe pushed him on the wrong path. It would help if the name of the real instigator was revealed. In fact, Milazim had no idea who else was under investigation on the same charge. He knew however that a cousin of his wife was being questioned by police in the port town of Durres.

Two days later, Fation interrogated the suspect for sixteen hours straight, asking him over and over again to tell him his name, his family name, the names of his father and mother, his birthday, his birthplace, the schools he attended, the places where he worked, as if he did not have his file in front of him. Whenever Milazim refused to answer, or looked sleepy, Fation struck him with a broad leather strap that left no marks on the body.

Fation spelled out the penal code acts for a serious offense such as "crossing the border illegally" and advised the suspect to confess, if he wanted to receive a lighter sentence. Milazim said that the years spent in confinement were not as important as the name of his family and his reputation. He continued to affirm that, in his view, any proposal to flee the country is a provocation or senseless joke. He could not possibly abandon his new wife, who hopefully was pregnant with their first child, two years after they were married.

10

The state TV was replaying a film, which Fation was watching without interest from the sofa. Lindita noticed that his eyes were burning, as if he had a fever. She knew that they had not been intimate since that night when she refused to go to bed with him earlier than usual. She should not continue to capriciously reject his advances, because that might push any husband into the arms of some other woman, and mainly because she loved him. Lindita was an old-fashioned woman who did not believe in embarrassing or teasing her husband in bed. She was taught to wait until her husband took the initiative to make love. That night, without words or gestures she tried to excite him in a round about way. She took a bath, dried her hair, perfumed herself and went straight to her wardrobe to pick a dress that showed her shapes suggestively. Fation liked best the silk dress with roses, which clung to her body and brightened her face with a mauve-tinted light. The local shops were supplied with Chinese silk fabrics. The translucent flower designs and color-coordination, which revealed the aristocratic taste and venerable traditions of the Chinese, satisfied the buyers. To weave fabrics from the fine strands of silkworms was like catching the rainbow in the sky and weaving it into the loom. Lindita became animated every time Fation drew her close to himself and his hand started to play with the silk fabric on her thighs. Under the silk, her thighs seemed prettier and more enticing. She picked a rose-colored shirt, on which the flowers on her dress looked like real petals. The care she had taken to dress well was rewarded immediately by Fation.

"This dress makes you look younger," he complemented her.

"I thought you weren't going to notice...."

"How could I help it? You look ravishing. Where are you going? It's a little late for visiting," he remarked.

"I wanted to see how it looks on me...since I haven't put it on for quite a while."

"Too bad you're going to take it off in bed," he said, with a suggestive grin.

"If you like, I'll keep it on," she retorted, with a coquettish look.

"You're not afraid it will rip?"

"Big deal! I'll get another one. They're not expensive."

Perfect communication, and much easier than she had thought. As usual the bedroom act began with petting and kisses and caresses, until he rolled her skirt up to her neck, and then in a dash pushed her brassiere up. Lindita waited for the next move, when he put his hand on the elastic hem of her panties. Fation had told her that he enjoyed taking her panties off with his own hands. The segments of the night action, all of them familiar to Lindita, unfolded one after another. She did the right thing to arouse him herself. Why should she deprive herself of the joys of marriage after seventeen years?

Fation was breathing somewhat hard, and now and then moaned with pain. Why was he taking so long, after all that petting? He kept reaching down with one hand and then the other. His sweat became so bothersome that Lindita finally yelled at him:

"Get away from me!"

He drew back, and suddenly covered his face with his hands.

"Forgive me, please! This has never happened to me before...."

His flaccid face showed the outrage he felt for being unable to complete the act.

"I caused you pain, I know. I was not able to satisfy you...." He covered his face, ashamed to look her in the eye.

"It happens," his wife said, to comfort him.

The expression, "It happens to everybody," hurt him, and immediately a suspicion crawled in his head.

"How do you know that?" he asked with annoyance and suspicions.

"I had heard that from grandma," Lindita replied, without being aware of his suspicions. "Someone had put 'a curse' on the husband of her cousin, and the poor woman suffered for God knows how long. 'There is no worse fate than to be a widow, with a live husband,' grandma used to say. They found a Gypsy woman, who was able to break the spell. Why, haven't you heard of husbands bedeviled by 'a curse'?"

"So, that's it!" he said, mockingly. "You believe that someone has put a curse on me?" He sounded hurt.

"There is no reason to drag it further," she complained.

Fation got out of bed and sat in a chair by the desk. He put his head in the palms of his hands. He seemed seriously disturbed by his lack of manliness. The word "impotent" hit him like a hammer on the head. How long was it going to last? What if he did not recover?

"Do you care for something hot or cold to drink?" Lindita asked, as she threw her dressing gown over her shoulders, ready to wait on him.

"Some poison," he said angrily. "Do you have any strychnine? That's what I need now."

"Why do you dramatize the matter like this?" his wife said, good-naturedly. "Nowadays there is medicine for everything. There are specialists, as well."

"Oh, yes! So everybody can find out about my impotence," he retorted, cynically.

"There's no point talking to you. You distort everything I say. Okay, do as you please; you're smart enough," she said, and headed straight for the kitchen, to avoid making things worse.

It was only toward the break of day, when Fation managed to get some troubled sleep. He tossed and turned and moaned, as if he had fallen into the clutches of a new nightmare.

The frigidity brought on by his emotional imbalance did not last long, and after some days everything was normal in their matrimonial bed.

11

Lindita Sofroni had worked as a typist in the Ministry of the Internal Affairs. Well behaved and timid, she flushed up to her ears over the slightest rebuff. Unlike her female co-workers, she did not patronize the cafeteria at the Ministry. To avoid going there, she packed her own breakfast at home, and brought it with her to work in a paper bag. Her clear features, the rosy tint of her skin, the soft brown eyes filled with sincerity and civility, had drawn Fation to her. Lindita had accepted Fation's marriage proposal and said it was all right with her, as long as her family approved. The custom of checking with the family had been abandoned by the new generation, and Fation did not know how to explain her behavior. Was she a slave of patriarchal traditions, or did she simply not want to oppose her family? At any rate, her sincerity and naïveté dispersed those doubts. The engagement was announced and two weeks later, they celebrated the occasion with drinks and appetizers.

After their marriage Lindita was transferred to a different job since the policy did not allow for a husband and wife to work in the same institution. Fation objected saying that the Investigation Sector work is focused on the field sites. Then after Lindita's transfer to the Institute of Natural Sciences, he tactfully asked how she liked her new workplace.

"It's all the same," she said. "I keep hitting the typewriter keys. Do you think I am sorry that I am not at the Ministry? The Ministry wears you down with its urgent assignments. Everything was 'Urgent.' Nothing could wait. Here I am more relaxed, and my salary is the same as before."

Lindita was not impulsive or ambitious, and Fation had no reason not to believe her.

12

While Fation was presenting a progress report on the investigation in his chief's office, there was a light knock on the door and in came a stocky man. Fation's chief got up, embraced him like an old friend and called out 'Selami, my old buddy.' The visitor greeted Fation with cordiality.

"Are you busy?" the visitor asked with pretended casually.

"No, no, we're finished," answered Jovan.

"May I be excused?" Fation asked, and after saying goodbye, left the office.

"What do you think of this young man?"

"Tops," replied Jovan. "He is one of the most competent investigators we have. I like his alertness and determination. If an investigator lacks sharpness, he is not worth a wooden nickel."

"How do you feel now that we are nearing retirement age?"

"Time takes its toll, whether we like it or not. What matters is that we leave the banner in good hands." As always, the chief had his feet on the ground.

Then suddenly the visitor asked:

"Were you 'there'?"

Jovan nodded "Yes."

"I heard that someone felt sorry for the former Minister, and began to whimper."

Jovan frowned that his subordinate was the object of malicious gossip.

"That's not what really happened," Jovan observed. "Nobody wept or sighed. The investigator guy was upset when he saw Jashar's work with the cleaver. That was all," Jovan explained.

"Oh, so that's how it was," noted the visitor with surprise. "It is bad enough hearing about Jashar's work, let alone seeing it. But why did he hang around there, in the first place?"

"Curiosity, that's all...," responded Jovan, who then moved on to make a point about the hearsay. "I tell you what, the distortion of evidence proves that there is internal intrigue, jealousy, petty grudges and personal ambitions," Jovan said as if he were reading a report.

"There is something else that should concern us," remarked the visitor as he took out a folder from his briefcase. "The enemy has stepped up the game."

"Well, we've never been short of work," Jovan said, quietly. Like old friends, they allowed themselves the luxury of a jest.

Quietly Selami handed him a list of names, which read 'Suspects under surveillance.'

"Look at it carefully, and if you have anything in your files about the suspects in this list, make a note. We need some evidence before we take appropriate action."

Looking over the list, he put his finger on one name.

"I was wondering if Pleurat Dardha is Fation's uncle?" he asked.

"Well their last names don't match," observed Jovan.

"A maternal uncle, perhaps?" Selami questioned inquisitively.

"As far as I know, Fation does not have an uncle," Jovan assured him.

"Don't take too long with the list," was Selami's final instruction.

13

Fation went to Durres to meet the investigator who had taken into questioning the cousin of Milazim Gruda's wife. The report said that the suspect named Luan, a notorious bandit and smuggler, had attempted to get hold of three tires from a driver in the trailer park. The driver had issued a signed statement that was solid evidence without any doubt. However, the suspect was lost for words when the interrogator asked him at which point had they planned to cross the border. "At the straits between Ksamil and Corfu, over Lake Ohrid going to Macedonia, or over Lake Shkodra into Montenegro?" The local interrogator noticed that the suspect was a crook who could not be trusted, no matter what and filled in the gap by noting in the court record that the crossing point was going to be determined later in the proceedings.

They continued the meeting at the bar where the local interrogator could treat his colleague from Tirana to a cup of coffee spiked with cognac, or a *boze,* a refreshing corn flower drink. At the counter there was a middle-aged woman, with salt and pepper hair, and whose face was dreary like a rainy day.

"Wasn't there a gorgeous bartender working here at the counter?" Fation said.

"Rozi?"

"I don't know her name but she was a knockout," continued Fation.

"You don't know the trouble she caused us?"

"No, I haven't heard anything. It's been a while since I was here last – weeks, maybe months."

"Rozi robbed the cafeteria blind. Only she knows how much she pocketed from stealing left and right. Beautiful and bright like an enchantress! Man oh man! She was a hell of a sweet woman. The police, the investigators, the district attorneys, I mean, our clients, crammed the counter when she was around. They enjoyed the food a lot more with their eyes glued on her. Just to seem like big sports, or simply to get her to smile, they never picked up the change, when she waited on them."

"Taking tips is not stealing," said Fation, cutting in.

"Quite right. Well, we thought she was single, but in fact she had married once, and divorced two times. The second time around, she did not take the vows. For two or three years, not a single inspector bothered to come over to check on the inventory. Apart from stealing coffee, by cheating on coffee stocks – which is common – she brought in bottles of cognac and brandy from outside and sold the stuff here by the glass. Big money-making scheme! She was trapped quite by chance, because of a silly slip. She was serving appetizers with olives here, at a time when the government warehouse and suppliers didn't have one blessed olive. All at once, inspectors charged in. The deficit was huge! The deputy chief assigned her case to me. I called Rozi to the office. She came all dolled up, rouge on her lips, like she was going to a wedding. I burst out saying that she had appropriated socialist property. The slut began to laugh.

" 'No,' she said. 'If you care to know, there was nothing to steal there. I only ate cake and cookies whenever I had the urge.' "

" 'Then, how do you explain the deficit?'" I asked.

" 'I lost the receipts,' she said. 'I didn't know I was supposed to keep them.' "

"She did not admit to robbing the clients.

"'Did I slip my hand into anyone's pockets? Did I threaten them physically or verbally? No. They tipped me out of their own free will.'"

"There was talk that some of the guys from the office had slept with her. So I told her what were the penal acts for that kind of offense. All of a sudden, she got angry and protested.

"'You should prosecute the chiefs. Do you think I was burning with love for them? I had a boyfriend and I still do. I will tell the court everything. I'll spare no one, not even your chief.' "

"As soon as she mentioned the chief, I knew that my neck was in jeopardy. I asked her to tell me what kind of relations did she have with him, and for how long. She said she did it just once with the chief. "He behaved like a gentleman. He reserved a room in the Adriatic Hotel, where the respectable crowd stays, and for two days I lived like a princess. The food bills and the drinks were all prepaid," she said. "Ironically, it happened that on those very days, Prince Sihanuk of Cambodia and her beautiful spouse Monica checked into the hotel, and the staff thought that Rozi was an agent on a mission. Who could have thought that our counter girl had turned into a Mata Hari? As I drove her home that night, I asked Rozi to make no reference to any investigation. Afterward I went straight to the chief, to take his pulse on the matter. The chief jumped to his feet and asked who was 'the ass' that initiated court proceedings against her. I said that 'the ass' was the deputy chief.

"'Jackass!' fumed the chief. 'If word of this gets out, it will be a scandal. We are the investigators who collect evidence, investigate corruption and misconduct, but we were robbed in daylight right at home. Just under the noses of the operatives, the chiefs, the police.'"

"I asked him indirectly whether he intended to take any actions against her."

"'She was good because she tricked us all,'" he declared firmly.

"Then he suggested giving Rozi her leave and severance pay, terminating the investigation and authorizing the supply sector to transfer her to another place. Instead of the beautiful Rozi, here works an ugly broad with a clean biography."

"And do you know where is Rozi?" asked Fation.

"At the restaurant by the beach. Are you thinking of looking her up?" he prodded him.

"Why not?" He bit down his lip when he thought of himself equal to a discredited bartender. "Actually, I have some urgent business to attend to. Another time," he added.

14

Since that fateful morning Fation tried to stay away from the Ministry's cafeteria to avoid seeing the "skull-crusher" and revive the horrid visions. He had known about stone crushers, glass and nut crushers and even metal crushers. He was amused by the variety of "crushers" that came to his mind. But no matter how hard he tried, the images of the skull-crusher and the bashed skull persisted.

He had taken a walk out of the office and had come to the Square. The Scanderbeg's statue, the flower garden behind it, the 15-story Hotel, the Culture Center with its white marble stairs and columns and above the columns, a huge billboard, Long Live the Party of Labor! Hard to imagine those were the last words of the ex-Minister. He knew that he was going to die in a few seconds and he could have very well expressed his rage and disappointment, Fation reasoned as he walked on.

Close to the park was the Ministry of Defense, and right across from it the Ministry of the Internal Affairs. Some people were enjoying the refreshing evening air of Tirana, the greatest gift of the city's climate. Fation wondered again if anyone there knew that Jashar smashed the skull of the former Minister, who was executed at a hangar near the Dajti mountain? He became upset that his mind scurried again to that horrible scene. In the veranda of the Bar-Buffet groups of young and old enjoyed cold beers and fried appetizers in earthen casseroles. The original name of that restaurant at the park was no longer remembered. Since it stood in isolation amid the greenery of the park, resembling an island in the middle of the ocean, its more appropriate 'namesake,' Taiwan, gained instant popularity. The apparent likeliness of the Bar-Buffet with the island on the other side of the world, in the middle of the blue Pacific, was always amusing to him.

Walking on the pathways of the park, he saw a face he had not seen for years. By now, however, his hair had grown completely gray.

"Is it you, Bujar?" Fation asked, just to be sure.

"It's me, from head to toe," he replied.

"I almost didn't recognize you. Your hair is completely gray."

"Those who say that gray hairs come with wisdom are so wrong. A lot of stupid people also get gray heir. And I am one of them," he chuckled.

"You haven't changed, at all," Fation complimented him.

"You have got to have brains to change," Bujar answered and then introduced as 'friends' the two men who were with him.

Bujar was a former colleague who had quit *Sigurimi* on his own initiative, two years after he was recruited as an agent. His decision shocked the operatives and alarmed the supervisors in the Ministry especially his recruiter, Selami, who called him to his office several times, and put pressure on Bujar to withdraw his request to retire. But when Bujar did not bend down, Selami advised him to keep quiet about the agency's methods of operation, otherwise he was going to pay dearly. Afterwards, knowing that he was under surveillance, Bujar locked down the dial of his radio to the government broadcast. Bujar's radio turned into a loudspeaker for Radio Tirana. "A preventive self-defense measure," Bujar would say jokingly to friends who came to visit him at home. Everyone knew the story of the radio, so Fation asked him:

"Is the dial still locked?"

"No, I don't have a radio anymore. I sold it," he said, laughing uproariously.

A woman who passed by greeted Bujar with a gracious smile.

"Moza! If you should happen to run into my wife, please tell her that I ran into some friends and will be running a little late," he said. Then, turning to Fation, he said: "We send word to each other like in the old days, because I am still on the waiting list to get a telephone."

As they parted they promised to meet again, each knowing full well that they were not going to willingly get together.

15

The clickety-clack of the prewar 'Olivetti' typewriter could be heard all day long at uncle Pleurat's. Fation called those writings "The scribbling of an amateur," and was never curious to read even one paragraph. Yet, he envied his uncle's inexhaustible energy, although he called it 'psychopathic zeal.'

As soon as the door opened, Pleurat stopped typing. The unexpected visit of his nephew pleased him. They had been closer when Fation was in High School. His young imagination filled uncle Pleurat with hope that one day his nephew would reach the pinnacles of science, and do honor to his country, to himself, and to his family. Back then Fation would say with conviction that other planets were inhabited with human beings, or living creatures, because life was the result of the transformation of solar energy, and could sprout wherever the sun's rays could reach. Also, the young Fation imagined that a few thousand years from now, our descendents would not have the pleasure of seeing meteors fall from the dark blue skies at night, because they were getting progressively fewer, and one day there would be no more meteors. But above all, uncle Pleurat was struck by Fation's idea that a new source of energy could be obtained from the earth's rotation by mounting gigantic wings at different points of the globe. Uncle had asked him whether that was his own original idea, or whether he had borrowed it from someone. "Mine," had answered Fation, calmly. It seemed that his nephew had the spark of great scientists, and in the future was going to make a name for himself.

However, uncle Pleurat was profoundly disappointed when Fation decided to go to Law School. What could his nephew possibly like about a school where students were fed data that were doubly uncertain, and half-baked blocs, in the context of the ideological split of the Communist world? Apparently, his nephew was enticed by considerations of practical gains.

"I have a question, Uncle Pleurat. Do you know when and how the term *colpo di grazia* originated?"

"Do you think that an '*ignoramus*' like me could enlighten a college graduate like you?"

"Enough of that!" Then he softened his tone, and added, "Tell me, if you can."

Pleurat's dark eyes suddenly lit up.

"All right, only keep in mind that I know this from my readings. *Colpo di grazia* emerged in Italy in the XIV Century, shortly after the invention of firearms. The great humanists of the Renaissance stigmatized torture especially to those who got the death penalty. They called such practice 'a relapse of the human society to the age of barbarism.' If a person is sentenced to die, then execution should be administered, without resorting to torture. But it was not easy to break with tradition. Generally, the masses viewed execution as a show, a form of public entertainment. In France, the prisoner was tied to a wheel and after having the limbs and ribs all broken, was wheeled on the road to his death.

"How horrible!" exclaimed Fation.

"In Spain, the Inquisition burned heretics alive, on a pile of wood, in the name of Christ, who, ironically, proclaimed equality of all men, and who opposed fighting evil with violence. Incredible! Do you know that the guillotine was invented to lessen the pain of the condemned, since the knife severed the head in two-three seconds? Its inventor was a French physician named Guillotine, and so the execution tool was named after him."

Although fascinated by the history, Fation was curios whether the expression "merciful blow" appeared in legal documents and the Albanian law in King Zog's time, before the war.

"I have no idea," replied Pleurat. "I do know that after the war, the Public Trials acts specified two kinds of capital punishments: 'death by hanging' or 'the firing squad.' Hanging was regarded as more painful, and for that reason was 'reserved' for the 'big fish,' while the firing squad was a relief by comparison. After the execution, one shot was fired at the head of the corpse, not to lessen the torment, but to make sure they were dead. I suppose the same procedure continues today."

"No," said Fation. "Now after the execution comes 'skull-crushing by cleaver.'

Fation looked at the floor.

"You mean to say there is no longer a 'merciful blow' procedure?"

"The face of the former Minister was smashed to a mush with a cleaver…I saw it myself." Unsure how to go on with the story, he stopped. Then asked: "Why, I wonder?"

Pleurat's dark eyes glowed with astonishment.

"What, what? They crushed his skull, you say?"

Fation nodded.

"That means that the system is coming to an end. Its end is already near. The end!" he emphasized. "You deserve a treat. That is some news!"

"You are not making sense, you know that?" the nephew scolded him.

"Not at all. I know that Gasper, the trombone virtuoso with the Vaudeville ensemble, was shot and then 'crushed.' I heard it from a good source. The crushing of skulls must be an order from above, to erase identification. Someone fears that thirty or fifty years from now, those who are wrongly condemned, will be reburied with honors, and commemorated. And someone wants to make sure today's dead won't be recognized tomorrow. That someone is sadly mistaken since forensics tells us that every attempt to wipe off prints and evidence leaves new prints and new evidence," concluded uncle Pleurat.

Disbelief could be read in his nephew's eyes.

"You don't believe me?" asked uncle.

Fation signaled "No" with his head.

"Experts of Anthropology are able to reconstruct the skull with amazing accuracy, even after several centuries. If I'm not mistaken, a Soviet scientist by the name of Gerasimov reconstructed the portrait of Ghengis Khan from studying his skull."

At that moment, Fation recalled what Jashar said about the ex-Minister's mother not being able to recognize her son.

Pleurat left the room and came back holding a bottle of cognac. He filled two glasses and took a sip from his glass. Fation did not move.

"You don't care for a drink? It doesn't change anything, believe me."

The conversation had deeply confused Fation, who walked out without saying anything to his uncle.

16

Hidden behind stacks of files and papers on his desk and around the office, Fation was surprised when Bujar walked in and interrupted his work:

"And what brings you here?" he asked him.

"The troubles of other people," he answered, smiling as always.

"I thought that maybe you were in some kind of trouble," Fation needled him.

"Fortunately, no. I'm not going to keep you long, because I know how busy…."

"Cut out the polite remarks," Fation said, interrupting him.

"I don't like them any more than you do, but they still pop out," Bujar said, in self-defense. "Worst of all, people take them for innuendos even when I'm serious."

"I'm listening."

"My neighbor wants to see you, and she asked me to intervene on her behalf. She knows that you are investigating her husband, who is charged with attempting to flee the country. Her name is Lila. If you want to see her, fine; if not, that's okay, too. Just pretend I never spoke to you about her request."

It was an unexpected move and Fation had to give it some thought. He tapped his pen on the desk, as if he were sending out messages by Morse code.

"If you want my opinion, I told her, 'Forget it.' But she insisted, and I decided to come and see you," Bujar said, coming straight to the point.

"What is your connection with her?" Fation asked, winking at him craftily.

"No connection, apart from being neighbors, I swear," he said.

"Please forgive me for asking, but how did she find out that you and I know each other?" Fation asked.

"She saw us talking by the park the other day."

Fation thought that he might be able to get some details from her, about her husband's preparations to escape. This could be 'the big break' in the tiresome investigation.

"Fine, she can come in tomorrow at eleven," he said, after consulting his calendar.

"I will tell her," Bujar said.

"What do you think? Does she want to see me to make it easier for her husband, or to make it worse?" inquired the investigator.

There had been instances when close relatives of suspects driven by anxiety went voluntarily to the local investigator's office to confess the "faults" of the detainee.

"I don't bother my head with stuff that doesn't concern me," Bujar answered curtly.

"Why did Milazim Gruda want to flee? What were his motives, in your opinion? I am asking you as a friend, no strings attached."

"Look, I don't know and cannot know, what he had in mind. I am not a fortune teller. We say 'Hello!' when we see each other going in and out of the same building. Other than that, we keep no company, let alone share secrets. I really don't know anything."

Fation listened quietly and offered him a cigarette.

"I've quit smoking," said Bujar, placing his hand over his heart, in a gesture of thanks.

Walking the visitor to the door, Fation asked tactfully if he sees any "old friends" after his resignation.

"Oh, you want to know if I have any regrets for quitting the Secret Service? Not really!" Bujar said calmly. "When I put my head on the pillow at night, I know that I have not wronged anyone, willingly or unwillingly. I sleep well and I feel well."

Fation believed him and for a moment could not help feeling a spark of envy.

17

Running out of breath, he burst into the bedroom, locked the door and said to her in a thundering voice:

"Take your clothes off!"

His tone more than his words caused Lindita to look at him as if she didn't believe her ears. Her eyes asked silently about the meaning of that order.

"Can't you wait until dusk?" she asked in a scoffing tone.

"I said, take off your clothes now," Fation's voice boomed once again.

Ordinarily, he went to bed after taking a shower, sprinkling a bit of cologne and set the mood with a little foreplay just to please his wife. That afternoon, however, the rage in his voice was chilling, and contrary to what he was asking her to do, the erotic mood was not there.

Linda noticed that Fation's eyes were burning with anger, however much he tried to conceal it. Even so, not wanting to make matters worse, she obeyed and took off her skirt and shirt.

"Take them all off. I don't want to see a scrap of clothing on you." His words and tone of voice were infused with sharp-edged anger.

"Very well! If that's what you want," she consented though after seventeen years of marriage, she felt embarrassed to appear before him naked. She stood there, with her eyes on the floor.

Fation approached her and she couldn't help wondering if he was trying a new bedroom routine. She sensed that he was examining her from behind, without touching her.

"What's this scratch here?" he asked.

"You just noticed that? I've had that since grade school," she said, in a reproving voice.

She was still not sure about what was going on.

"What is it you are looking for?" Linda asked.

"You know what," he replied harshly.

He walked around in front of her, leaned forward close to her breasts, and began to feel them Instantly Lindita sensed that he suspected marital infidelity, and was now looking for the evidence left on her body by the other man. Shocked by the crude inspection, and insulted she picked up her clothes, got dressed quickly, covered her face with her hands, and started crying.

"Tears and pleas don't work on me," he shouted. "Who was here a few minutes ago?" he asked, shaking her up.

"So, that's it! You suspect that I…." She was unable to go on, being overwhelmed by the anger that boiled inside her.

"What was he doing here? You better speak up."

"Who?"

"Ja-shar, that's who," he said, pronouncing his name slowly, and gritting his teeth.

"I don't know anyone called Jashar. I've never even heard that name," retorted Linda.

"You don't know that casket-face? You've never seen him?"

"Never!" she replied.

"Don't lie to me. I saw him coming out of our apartment building," he roared.

"Maybe, but there are eight apartments in the building. How do I know where he went, and whom he met?"

Fation recalled what was said at the Ministry's bar about Jashar's 'big gun," and his notorious affairs with the wives of officers, who went away on duty. As soon as he saw Jashar walk around his apartment complex, he became furious, thinking that the 'casket-face' had been to his own apartment. After he settled down, he began to think clearly. How could his wife get him into the apartment? How could she lock herself with him in the bedroom? The very sight of Jashar's ugly face was enough to make her shudder. "I was mad to think he was here," he scolded himself. "I got jealous over a freak." Then he went to Lindita to ask for forgiveness.

"Please forgive me. I had no reason to doubt you."

Offended by this late eruption of jealousy in their married life she refused to make up with him. Why all those doubts, when she had not given him any grounds? She decided she would do better to busy herself with house chores, than to dwell on dark thoughts.

18

Later Lindita 'replayed' Fation's state of mind quietly and without asking him any questions. The fear he felt almost constantly, the unexpectedly jumping from his armchair to get to the window, and look outside, the staring at the door, as if someone was going to rush in. Not knowing what to do to help him, she went over to her mother to unload the cares that were troubling her, and relieve the stress. If it's true that daughters are the depositories of their mothers' complaints, it is also true that they often feel the need to be mothered, even when they are grown up.

"Did he beat you up?" her mother asked.

"Beat me? What are you saying, mother?" Lindita turned on her, feeling offended by the question.

"Does he come home drunk?"

"No, I've never seen him drunk."

"Does he bring home his salary?"

"Yes, he does."

"Then you got no reason to complain. The world is full of women who get beaten up by their husbands, but still they keep their mouth shut, for the sake of the children."

"Mother, you don't understand," Lindita pressed on with her complaint.

"Bear with him! It's his job." That simple woman, relying on her intuition, hit the nail on the head with her remark. Raised in the countryside in the patriarchal setting, her mother believed that it was better to endure a bad husband, than to be without one.

Lindita went on saying that for several months he 'was torturing her and the kids.'

Fation is making life miserable for the boy. Just last week he refused to buy for him a pair of running shoes that all the boys' friends in school are wearing already. Lindita also complained that he watches over their teenage girl, Suela, like a hawk. He finds fault with her clothes, saying her skirt is too short, or too long.

"Let him keep a tight rein on the kids. It will do them no harm," she said. When she saw that Lindita bent down her head, with no desire to talk anymore, she told her not to worry. The young ones will do their things, no matter what mom and dad tell her. "Do what you can to humor him, and if he is bothered about something, get out of his way, because that's the way men are. They want things done their way."

19

At the mezzanine of the National Library, Fation was coming out of Social Studies' hall, while uncle Pleurat was going upstairs for a cup of coffee.

"I congratulate you for entering in the Temple of Knowledge," he joked.

"I came to meet Judge Stavri if you know him, but I couldn't find him," Fation said.

Uncle Pleurat's disappointment with that answer was visible. He suggested to go upstairs for a cup of coffee and Fation agreed.

They sat down at the table silently, as if they were strangers. Fation thought that their relations had long cooled off, because they held opposing political views. But wondered why those differences would affect relations within the family. Uncle Pleurat did not understand reality, or to be more accurate, he did not want to understand it. Fation referred to his uncle scornfully as "my antidote." Yet, he respected him, because he was neither a hypocrite, nor a conformist.

"Can you tell me if you still blame the investigation profession because of some corrupted investigators?" he was content with the way he worded the question, and waited for his reply.

"I have changed my opinion on that," uncle Pleurat said.

"Good! You see things more realistically now," Fation remarked, seeking to compliment him.

"Not the way you mean it. The investigators make up only a thin slice of the moral breakdown of our society. Do not think that that I am just being stubborn or difficult. I see everyday that the agencies and offices that should serve as a model of virtue have become the most corrupted of all."

"For example?"

"The District Attorney's office, the Courts, *Sigurimi*, the Party committees, and on and on…."

"You're saying that I should abandon the investigation profession."

"I think by now, you know how much or how little you have compromised yourself," uncle Pleurat said.

"You can think what you like. But as far as I'm concerned, I see no connection whatsoever between individual character and profession," Fation argued.

"Well, he who steps into a mud pond is not going to come out clean," uncle Pleurat declared bitterly. "Soot and filth collect gradually, like flour on the miller's hair."

"Do you know where such ideas will put you?" his nephew asked, immediately regretting the warning sound of his words.

"I know. But I am not shouting them from the City Hall's rooftop, am I?" Suddenly, uncle Pleurat began to smile. "Yesterday, I witnessed a funny scene. Between nine and ten in the evening, I was coming down the steps of this coffee shop, and I saw a kid, who had climbed up the Scanderbeg statue, and was talking and waving his arms. A few pedestrians, who happened to be around started running toward the monument from the square. I got a little closer, but couldn't make out what he was saying. The police came over and ordered him to get down, but he did not care for them. Upset that this kid was going to cause some sort of public protest, two policemen climbed up and dragged the kid down, put him in a jeep and drove away. Do you suppose they will jail him?"

"Certainly; for desecrating the national symbol, and disturbing the public."

"Poor crackbrained kid," said uncle Pleurat sorrowfully. "Do you think that prison will help restore his sanity? I want to ask you something, but you don't have to answer, if you don't want to. Suppose your boy, Dritan, got mixed up with a band of robbers, and he came home with bundles of banknotes. Would you have him arrested? I'm speaking hypothetically, because I know this will never happen," he added.

Called to choose between his professional obligations and his feelings as a parent, Fation hesitated and then decided to dodge the answer.

"I don't believe I'll ever face such a situation. But I will say this to you, blood is thicker than water."

20

"So, we meet here, as agreed," he said to Liliana when she opened the door, with number 17 painted on it with a thin brush. Her upper lip was slightly shorter than the lower one, which gave her whole face a coquettish appearance.

"Well, I gave you my word," she said, giving him a seductive side glance, as she opened her handbag, and took out a flask of liquor and two small glasses. "I figured we can use these."

"Cognac? To warm up?" he remarked.

The giggling sounds she made pleased him.

"Did you drink with your husband, too?" he asked her.

"Sometimes."

"Do you have a nickname. Liliana sounds a little long," inquired Fation.

"Lili," she said.

"Lili? That's prettier than Liliana," Fation said.

He took off his jacket, hung it in the closet, approached Lili from behind, put his hand on her shoulder, massaged her neck, and kissed her behind the ear. Tickled by her black hair, and dazed by the scent of her perfume, he said:

"Shall we go to bed?"

Liliana took off her shoes and stockings, removed her dress, got into bed and pulled the bed sheet over her, all the while smiling at him coyly.

"Why didn't you take off your undergarments too?" he asked her.

"I prefer to take it off in bed," she chuckled.

Fation got excited as soon as he slipped into bed alongside her. He seemed intoxicated by the aroma of her perfume and her ravishing feminine charms.

"Fantastic perfume. Where did you get it?" he asked.

"From the sailors, at the port," Lili replied. "You can find anything, if you have money."

Fation lost all restraint as he went after her small breasts, pressing them hard with his hands.

"You're hurting me!" she complained, in a mild tone. "Take it easy."

He apologized over and over again, and then caressed her breasts gently and covered them with tender kisses. The bed scene continued with the entwining of their bodies and mutual sighs of pleasure.

His encounter with Liliana turned out well. And they had reached a common understanding. Fation walked out of the hotel satisfied. He thought that the Italian expression *Donna di leto,* best described her formidable qualities in bed.

He walked briskly between the marble columns at the square before heading for the Ministry. Although reluctant about the meeting place, he walked in there to meet with judge Stavri. He looked around and when he did not see the judge him anywhere, went to the counter, ordered a cup of coffee with a shot of brandy, and sat down at a table across from the entrance. While waiting, he began to go over some thoughts that swarmed in his head. He had promised Lili that he was going to do all he could to lessen the charges against her husband. "I am turning into a hypocrite. She doesn't know that I am trying hard to find "evidence" to convict her husband, Milazim Gruda. I should not have gotten into bed with her. I have become 'a dirt-bag' like some of the faces in the office, like the scumbags that make promises just to get women into their clutches, then turn their backs on them." In his own defense, he argued with himself that she had taken the initiative to go to him to help her husband. Fation recalled how she lowered her eyes in his office, as she told him that she would give "anything" for the sake of her husband. Then, she suggested that they discuss the matter quietly, somewhere outside, where they would not be interrupted. In his mind, he began reading a report on himself: "The investigator started out with the intention of obtaining information from her about the suspect's alleged plan to flee the country, and instead he ended up by compromising the investigation with a sexual escapade."

With a growing sense of disappointment, Fation brought to mind once again the conversations he had with Lili at the hotel bed. She swore that her husband, Milazim had never mentioned "fleeing" and that he wouldn't think of abandoning her. Could it be that the suspect kept his plan secret even from his loving wife or was she lying? Fation was unable to shake these doubts. Lili was so pleasant and playful that he considered arranging another encounter with her, at some other hotel. She was naïve enough to think that, if she gave herself to the investigator, he would lessen the charges against her husband. Generally, the conviction was 'spelled out' from a higher office, and the investigator's job was simply to make every effort to 'find the facts,' the witnesses and the arguments for the file that was going to be sent to the court.

His thoughts were interrupted by Guci known within the Ministry as "Bigmouth." He came and sat at the table uninvited. Guci's cleft mouth reached into the middle of his cheeks, revealing his inmost molars when he laughed. Guci had been kicked out of the investigation department for some moral-related incidents. Fation felt contempt for a scum like Guci, who deceived the wives of the suspects into thinking that he would review their cases just to get his way with them.

"Have you just 'scored' one?" was Guci's opening question. "When I was an investigator, I seduced some chicks that could drive you crazy with their looks."

"Leave me alone. I want to have my drink in peace!" Fation turned on him angrily.

"Damn the reputation! Screw them while you can. Latch on to the chick that lands in your hand, because once it takes off, you won't be able to catch it."

"Not everybody is like you," Fation needled him, feeling qualms about surrendering to the physical pleasures.

Just then Judge Stavri showed at the door. His face resembled the characteristic features on the classical sculpture, with two sunken eyes, thick eyebrows, prominent cheekbones and strong jaws. In contrast to his rough features, he had a mild temperament. If the court should appoint him to preside on the case Fation had investigated, he would feel relieved knowing there would be no hassle with procedural matters, and returned files for further investigation.

Quickly Fation spelled out the problem to the judge. No matter how you cracked it, the suspect was 'a hard nut.'

"I was glad when they assigned this case to me, but now I am in a bind."

"I thought this case was being investigated by the senior investigator? Or am I mistaken?" Judge Stavri asked.

"He was hospitalized due to some heart condition."

"I saw him yesterday. He was fit as a fiddle," commented Stavri.

"Really? He may be out of the hospital, or maybe getting treatment as an outpatient," said Fation, trying to appear calm, when in fact his misgivings intensified.

"I know the old fox well. He has sized up the case and knew he risked failure. Smart bastard has a nose for these things," praising and damning the surviving skills of the senior investigator. "Did he leave any notes in the file?"

"Nothing, just a page of identity information. The rest of the pages are blank. The suspect does not admit anything and insists that his 'attempted fleeing' is only a fabrication. He is driving me crazy. I'm exhausted," fumed Fation.

"Take it easy," Judge Stavri told him, trying to ease his frustration. "If you don't get anything out of him with the classical methods of persuasion, turn your attention to your witnesses. If a couple of people can testify against him, you have met the administrative requirements for the evidence the court needs to process the case."

Obviously, the system had found the way to 'break' the stubborn 'nut' cases. Fation thanked him silently.

"Why do you thing the lawyers were excluded from the judicial process? What does that tell you about Justice?" Judge Stavri asked exhaling tobacco smoke through his mouth and nose.

"I don't know what to say. I haven't thought about that," Fation replied sincerely. "If you ask me, lawyers are liars and manipulators who resort to all kinds of 'legal' arguments to twist justice. I have no respect for them!"

"No, no!" Judge Stavri disagreed. "Their mission is as virtuous as it is humane, they are officers of the court upholding the law both for the defendant and the government. Do you think that the accused can defend themselves?" he asked, questioning once again the administration's decision to keep the lawyers out of the courtroom.

"Well, these days they defend themselves very effectively, if you ask me," babbled Fation.

"Baloney! Three-fourths of the defendants who have been through grade school and at best have finished Junior High School, have no idea about the penal procedure. You know very well that pleading 'not guilty' cannot be considered adequate self-defense. That's why we have lawyers!" Judge Stavri looked Fation in the eye, and then added: "The lawyers are left out since this administration does not want any witnesses in closed-door trials. The Goddess of Justice had left the building."

In Judge Stavri's view, the dissolving of the Ministry of Justice was a huge mistake, because it plainly supported the thesis that where there is no justice and there is no need for such an institution. Judge did not hesitate to share his ideas with his colleagues, and both those who quietly agreed with him, and those who did not, find him trustworthy and pleasant.

21

At the fountain in front of the University Building, Dizi was walking with a young girl, who could have been her daughter. Her oval-shaped eyes and pony tail made her peculiarly charming.

"Wow! It's Fation!" she exclaimed running toward him, and embraced him just like she did long ago, under the arched gate of Gogo's house. Then she kissed him while the girl looked at her with bewilderment.

"Verushka, darling. Don't be surprised. I've loved Fation since I was a young girl, like you. I love him still, and will go on loving him!"

Stunned by this loud show of affection, Fation looked around to see if anyone was watching. There was not much human traffic around the fountain. Like every well-bred hooker, Dizi was big-hearted, loving, full of warmth, and an everlasting admirer of the opposite sex.

All of a sudden and out of nowhere, Liliana passed by them. Her high heels clattered on the stone pavement as she walked proudly, coquettishly, with her beige handbag swinging from her shoulder, quite aware that males were following her with their eyes. She nodded ever so slightly to Fation. But he felt uneasy since he did not want anyone to know about them. Did she greet him on purpose? Was she trying to compromise him? He noticed that Dizi smiled at her warmly.

"Do you know her?" he asked Dizi.

"She is my neighbor," replied Dizi. "We live in the same apartment complex. I feel sorry for Lili, because her husband has been detained. Poor woman!" she said, sorrowfully.

"And do you know why? I mean, the reason he was detained?" he asked struggling to contain his anger. "Her husband tried to flee."

"Who? Milazim? Come on! Silly gossip!"

The last thing Fation needed was to listen to Dizi's trite "defense" of Milazim, so he muttered an excuse and cut the conversation off.

22

"Speak up! Spill your guts! Let's go! Don't make me to drag it out of you, you dog," Fation yelled angrily.

"You got no right to offend me, comrade investigator, " pointed out Milazim Gruda.

"I am not your comrade, nor a buddy of yours," Fation snapped.

"Mister investigator," Milazim said, correcting himself.

After the war, names such as: "Mister," "Your Excellency," "Your Highness," were taken out of common usage and replaced by "comrade," which connoted equality. However, after a decade, an odd transformation took place. It was the judges themselves, along with the prosecutors, the investigators, and even the policemen on the beat who insisted on being addressed as "Mister" by defendants and convicts, in order to draw the clear distinction between them and the felons.

"You're going to teach me how to speak, you who betrayed your country by attempting to flee? I'll pull out your teeth and hand them back to you one by one," threatened Fation.

The desperation to get an admission of guilt from the suspect was building up and Fation's patience was running out. His nerves stretched thin. After four hours of interrogation, he mentioned the name of the cousin of the suspect's wife, Luan Agalliu, who allegedly had to supply the tires.

"I burned my bridges with that clown years ago," replied Milazim. "I can't help it that he is a cousin of my wife. He came to me and asked for cash urgently. He said he would pay it back but he never did. I never cared to talk to him after that. Whatever that scum says about me is bull."

"Naturally, that's very convenient. But the court looks at evidence, not opinions. Speak up, I say!"

Milazim remained silent.

"You don't want to talk? I'll beat you to death, I swear!"

"I shall not confess to what is untrue," he declared resolutely.

"Don't worry, you will sing. I'll make you sing. Sign the confession form, if you don't want me to smash your head against the wall." The fury that took over him drove him to throw himself from the chair to the suspect knocking him down. Then he began to kick him with his boots in the back, on his neck and face.

"Talk, you son of a bitch! Talk, before I bang your wife again at Hotel Vjosa." He was beside himself, and could not stop even after seeing trails of blood on his shoes and on the floor, where Milazim's body had dropped.

"You dog! You will fry, if you refuse to admit your crime!"

Fation continued to hit him, until he felt exhausted. Then, foaming at the mouth, he went to the door to call the guard and asked him to take the suspect back to his cell.

"You beat his brains out," said the guard, as he dragged the body of Milazim Gruda. "I think he is gasping for his last breath."

"Throw a bucket of water on the shit face!" ordered Fation.

He sat down in a chair, lit up a cigarette and began to inhale fervently. "What if he croaks?" he asked himself suddenly. "Who cares? It's his own fault." He pressed the butt of his cigarette with his foot, and stepped out to find the guard.

"How is he?" he asked.

The guard said that the suspect was still unconscious.

The idea that the suspect might have died during the course of his investigation flashed into Fation's head like lightning. "If he dies, then I might be suspended, or even dismissed from the investigation bureau. "A killer-interrogator" – that's what they'll call me," he thought. "Then again, my partners might cover up for me, and call the death an 'unfortunate accident.' The bureau is not going to sacrifice me and help an enemy of the state. What a mess! Maybe uncle Pleurat was right about my quitting this job as an investigator."

Now, more than anything, Fation hoped that Milazim would recover quickly, but he scolded himself for getting sentimental about enemies. For the first time, he questioned whether Milazim Gruda was indeed 'an enemy.' Could the suspect be a victim of an intrigue devised by someone who was after the dark-eyed Liliana? He recalled that a few years earlier, a *Sigurimi* operative put in prison a doctor, out of lust for his beautiful fiancée. Not knowing who had been 'the informant,' the desperate woman asked the same operative to help her. She argued that her betrothed was innocent and uninvolved in any anti-government propaganda. The operative agreed to help provided she would sleep with him and she accepted. Later, the unexpected happened. The doctor's fiancée and the *Sigurimi* man got married.

"I think the suspect should be sent to the hospital. There's no telling what might happen," suggested the guard. "Shall I call the doctor?"

"Do whatever you want," said Fation pretended indifference.

His limbs were giving in and he needed air. He could not remember if an interrogator had ever been accused of murder before. Suddenly the senior investigator's illness seemed more of a ploy to drop out of this case. After all heart problems and high blood pressure were common symptoms in the Bureau. In privacy certain doctors referred to such professional hazards as "illnesses of the profession" like lead poisoning for the typesetters and silicosis with construction workers. At any rate, it would have been easy for a smart investigator to obtain a bogus medical report from a physician friend of his.

23

Later that night he jumped out of bed, pushed the window curtains aside and pointed in the dark, saying he was going to 'kill him' like a stray dog. Lindita woke up and watched him with growing fear. Fation went over to the dresser, opened a small drawer and searched for his handgun. When he didn't find it where he usually kept it, he began to doubt that his son had stolen it. Quite upset, he headed for Dritan's bedroom to get him to say where he had hidden the gun. Lindita cut him off, grabbed him by the arm and said:

"Don't wake up the boy. You took the gun out of the drawer yourself, afraid that Dritan might sell it, after you refused to give him money for the new running shoes. You said that you were going to put it in your office's safe box, remember?"

Thinking back on that day, Fation slowly recalled that he had put the revolver in his safe. Then in the bedroom, he listened intently for sounds beyond the window curtains.

The next morning, on his way to work, he was groggy and moody and by chance did not take the usual shortcut to the office. He thought of it only after he had gone two blocks past the shortcut, and was angry with himself. It just felt like he was walking into a dead end. Wouldn't it be better to ask his supervisor to relieve him of the responsibility of interrogating Milazim Gruda? Wouldn't that put in doubt his competence and shake the board's trust? It could be safer to ask the suspect to forgive him for the incident, and then perhaps offer him a bargain. Apologize? To the suspect? No, never!

It turned out that the "Gruda case" had become problematic already. The moment he stepped in his office, his chief called Fation in.

"How is the interrogation of Gruda going?" the chief started.

"Not so good," replied Fation, without hesitation. "He denies all the allegations. Yesterday he was being so stubborn, I smacked him once in the face."

"You injured his eye, and that does not happen with a slap in the face. Physical injuries are not allowed. You understand?" the chief said coldly.

Fation nodded submissively but then to justify what he had done, he said:

"I believe that we should show no mercy to enemies."

"Do you think I have compassion for them?" the chief asked, angrily.

"No, I did not say that!" replied Fation, stepping back.

"Listen here! If we waste the suspects we would be covering up our tracks, and that is not in our interest, at all. Our job is to dig down to the bottom, find the causes of enemy activity, and then deal them such a blow that will knock them out. In this case, we have to get the names of the collaborators? Why did Gruda and his accomplice want to flee? Who was the instigator? Who was going to meet them on the other side of the border? These are the questions that need answers." The chief's forewarning hit the investigator like a cold shower. "You have tarnished the profession of the investigator. That's all I wanted to say. I'm finished!"

Fation returned to his office more dispirited than ever went through the files. In all likelihood, the interrogation was going to drag out until the suspect was broken down psychologically and physically. Fation thought that getting that point sooner rather than later would help him restore the trust of his superior. The idea of visiting the Mechanical Workshop to meet the Party chief officer and the supervisor came to him at that time. Inspired by the moment, the investigator considered stopping by Gruda's neighborhood and talking to an old friend who happened to be one of Gruda's neighbor, Dizi.

24

Wearing a rose-colored dress, her dark hair flowing over her shoulders, Liliana walked gingerly on her high heels and swayed her hips as always. She was coming out of the main entrance of the Investigation Bureau as Fation walked in the courtyard. Sensing that the investigator had no desire to see her at that particular location, she barely made eye contact with him.

"What was she doing here?" Fation asked himself. "Did she come to seduce someone here? Is she after bigger fish?" A few steps further, he was petrified by the thought that she had stopped by there to file a report on him. "It was a mistake to swallow her bait. Will they believe me that it was she who tempted me? That won't make things any easier for me. I fell into a trap…a victim of erotic passions. What do I do? Put myself out there publicly for getting mixed up with the enemy's partner, or deny her story?" He was going to be badly discredited in the eyes of his supervisor and the office as someone who comprised his principles for sexual pleasures. He had to get out from this whole mess. But then again maybe she had not been there to report him. The pros and cons in the matter were even.

Up to the end of office hours that day, Fation was on pins and needles, fearing that his chief might ask him for details concerning his 'moral degradation.' But neither the chief, nor the personnel office asked for him. Nonetheless, he was not at peace, because as a rule it took several days for an investigation of this nature to be brought up and discussed with the parties. After a tormented week of fears and unrest,

Fation released his suspicions about Lili, but cursed badly whenever he thought of her.

25

Dizi agreed right away the investigator's proposal to testify against her neighbor, Milazim Gruda. Indeed, she felt flattered that Fation had turned to her for help

"Sure," she said. "Just tell me what to say, 'cause I don't know anything about that kind of business."

Exercising caution, Fation asked her if she had seen any old tires in the garage of the museum. Dizi answered that in the piles of junk down there she had seen old car parts, broken seats and tires.

"Should I say that Milazim asked me to get three or four old tires for him? Is that it?" Dizi asked, her eyes shining with joy that her old love had thought of her.

"No, not tires, but tire tubes," he corrected her. "Remember to say those words!"

"I'll do anything to help you, like your own sister," Dizi said. Even though she considered him 'a brother,' she was ready to embrace him passionately in public. Dizi's burning passion and eagerness hinted that she was hoping to rekindle the adolescent flame and just let it burn.

Fation knew from experience that the most difficult part of the investigation was still ahead. He had to press ahead with cunning caution to get the witness to come in. As soon as the witnesses were told that they had to show up and confront the accused, they backed down.

"One of these days, you have to make a deposition. You understand? It's a procedural matter," he said to her with a rather casual attitude, so she could grasp that this was a customary formality.

"I'll go anywhere. Just tell me where to, 'cause I don't know the way," she said, and spun her head around so quickly, the locks of her dark hair went flying into the air.

"I'll pick you up or send the driver to get you," Fation promised her.

"You're so sweet," Dizi flattered him, and like a loving kitten, she nestled close and threw her arms around his neck, like she did years ago when they were teenagers.

26

The moment Milazim saw his neighbor in the room, he rolled his eyes. First, the interrogator asked Dizi if she knew Milazim Gruda, and she answered, "Yes, we're neighbors." Then, with similar casualty, she testified that he had asked her to get three or four used tires for him. Milazim's jaw dropped with astonishment upon hearing such startling testimony. However, he restrained himself and quietly asked her whether she recalled the time of the incident.

Dizi looked a little puzzled but the interrogator motioned to her to reply.

"I don't recall the date, but it's been a few weeks since then," Dizi answered, unsure.

The interrogator looked at her with approval.

"Where? Where did I ask you?" demanded Milazim.

Dizi seemed baffled on that point.

"Where?" continued Milazim. "Was it in your apartment, my apartment, at the dairy store or at the bakery? Where did we have that conversation?"

"Tell him! Don't hold back!" Fation prodded her.

"At the steps of the building," said Dizi, pinpointing the place.

"I asked you to get me three or four tire tubes at the steps of the building?" he asked with sharp sarcasm in his voice.

"Yes" affirmed Dizi, without batting an eyelash.

"Why? Are you the storehouse custodian at the truck depot? Why should I have asked you for tires? To make beds with them?" Milazim said, throwing a barb at her.

"I don't know. I just know that you asked me," Dizi insisted, "and I told you, I'll see what I can find out."

Milazim was silent for a few moments, as if he were debating with himself whether he should blurt out what was boiling inside him.

"Look here, Mr. Interrogator. I did not bother to say 'Hello!' to this sleazy woman, let alone ask her to get me tire tubes or anything else for that matter. The only things she stores are the condoms in her handbag."

Sparks of rage shot from Dizi's eyes.

"Condoms? You can ask Lili for condoms, not me! You hear?" screamed Dizi, in her customary jargon.

"Scram! Everybody, from north to south knows that you are an easy lay," Milazim told her, motioning nervously with a trembling hand, as if he wanted to push her as far away from himself as possible.

Dizi who had lived in the capital for several years, and was well versed in the local dialect, shot back right away:

"You're dirt under my feet, you and your buddies who keep chattering like fishwives.... They can't shut their trap 'cause they don't get what they want from me. You better zip it!"

Just as Fation was about to intervene to calm them down, Milazim muttered under his breath, "Look who is preaching morals, the shameless slut!" That's all Dizi needed to explode:

"The slut is in your own house. It's your Lili who gets picked up from the intercity drivers and is pumped in the back seats of their cars."

The sweet girl of the 'green years' of their adolescence was vanished. This filthy mouthed vulgar woman was the true Dizi. The confrontation between Dizi and Milazim degraded to personal insults, and the investigator had to conclude the session quickly, claiming that it had accomplished its purpose. In the end, the witness had given a statement and had said what was needed. Fation only had to include her testimony in the file for the court.

"I told that mutt off, didn't I?" Dizi asked the investigator, fishing for a compliment, as soon as they stepped out into the courtyard.

"He got what was coming to him!" he said.

Dizi's dark eyes lit up with joy.

27

Miriam, uncle Pleurat's wife, stepped in their apartment looking very distressed. She was pale and could hardly breathe.

"They arrested him," she said in one breath, slumping into the chair, as her hands dropped on her lap. They knew that she meant her husband.

"Why? What did uncle Pleurat do? What did they say?" asked Linda.

"They did not say anything. The officers broke down the door, told him they had an arrest warrant, handcuffed him, shoved him out, put him in a jeep and drove off." Her lower lip trembled as if she were running a fever. The violent scene of the arrest had shattered her emotionally.

"Oh, you poor soul!" cried Lindita.

"He got what was coming to him," Fation blurted with rage.

"Fation!" gasped Lindita.

"He should have seen it coming with all that stuff he said against the government," continued Fation, unable to control himself. "Did you expect *Sigurimi* to put up with him forever?"

"What a pity!" sighed Miriam, striking her thighs with the palms of her hands.

"What about the children?" Lindita asked.

"They were not in.... It is bad enough he was arrested...."

Miriam turned to her nephew, and said to him, prayerfully:

"I beg of you, find out why they arrested him, so that we can, at least...tell our relatives, when they ask us."

"I won't move even my little finger for a... for a... re... react... revisionist," Fation burst out all upset, because he couldn't find the proper name for his arrested uncle.

"He stayed home all day. It was like he had put himself in prison, willingly," Lindita said, in defense of the uncle's defense.

"Apparently, it didn't help, did it?" Fation pressed on with his gripe.

"Oh, bitter fate! ... What will become of me and the children?" Miriam asked herself.

"Could it be a misunderstanding? Maybe they could release him later today or tomorrow?" Lindita wondered.

"Bless your heart, but I doubt it," Miriam said, full of anguish. "The poor man is not well, either...he has an ulcer in his stomach."

"Let him die! And the sooner, the better," raged Fation.

"How can you talk like that about your uncle? Really! It's sinful!" Lindita tore into him, while putting her hands to her cheeks, as if she were going to scratch her face.

"We bear different family names, we are...not related, you know," Fation argued

He was making an effort to renounce his blood ties, despite the fact that both uncle Pleurat and Fation's father had the same mother. His point was to show that Pleurat was only a "half-uncle" to him not a *bona fide* uncle, since his paternal grandmother had married twice. He was pleased with the term "half-uncle." Fation scowled thinking of his grandmother's second marriage, though the marriage had taken place three quarters of a century ago when there were no 'class struggle' and no 'socialist system.' Poor Grandma had been put to rest in peace twenty years ago in the village cemetery. "What lunacy!" he said to himself.

Lindita took out a little coffeepot, put two teaspoonfuls of ground coffee in it, and said to Miriam:

"Have some coffee. It will help to calm your nerves."

"I can't," she said, and promptly got up to leave. She asked them to forgive her for disturbing them.

Lindita saw her out. She returned with a bitter heart, incensed by the cruelty of her husband.

"How could you speak such words against your uncle? Shame on you! Called him a revisionist, too," Lindita said, chastising him.

"I meant to say 'dissident' " Fation said, in self-defense. "Just as well, though. I don't think Miriam knows the meaning of that word."

"She came in here looking for support and kind words. Instead, you shoved her into the pits."

"Are you trying to defend him?" he asked angrily. "I don't think you're on the right track…I think you're sliding into…."

"Whoa! Remember, you're at home here, not in your office," Lindita said, getting back at him. "You're talking like the old-timers in the community. "Suppose you landed in jail, and I went to see your uncle. Do you think he would have behaved like you?"

"I don't want to have anything to do with him, or his family," he declared. "Is that clear?" he asked, then went on to answer his own question, saying, "Perfectly clear!"

"Whether you like it or not, the whole world knows that he is your uncle," said Lindita, pointedly.

"I have no use for such an uncle, no use," he hollered. "Don't you understand that I don't need this right now?"

"So you turn your back on him?"

The renouncing of a convicted fellow by his kinsfolk and even by his own family, as a result of political pressure, had become a common practice. Since 'political excommunication' ran counter to the norms of Albanian tradition, society had come to conform without giving its approval, painfully aware of the propaganda for internal consumption. People smiled cynically when they heard and read in the papers statements of parents who renounced their convicted child, mindful of the extreme pressure that was put on the inflicted families. Ironically, after such public condemnations, their folks were not spared the internment camps. Some believed that the practice of penalizing relatives of the offender had gone too far, when renowned artists and writers were sent away. As a result, the Party drafted a new set of criteria aimed at confining punishment to a closer circle of relatives. Out of curiosity Fation had read them over but could not be sure whether there was a 'half-uncle category' that applied in his case. Yet, now he had to know with certainty to be able to defend himself, if the need aroused.

"There is nothing I can do for him," Fation burst out. "Whether I speak well or ill of him, nobody will believe me." After a short pause, he added: "One thing is clear. He does not like this system. And that's putting it mildly. He despises it…."

"Nonsense! He went to fight for the system," Lindita said, contradicting him.

"He came to regret that," he retorted. "I know that for a fact."

"Really, now, you have a way of beating an argument to death, needlessly," she said, putting an end to the discussion.

Uncle and nephew had not been in agreement on quite a few issues. Fation recalled what his uncle had once said to him: "The *Sigurimi* machine resembles the grindstone that eats away even as it consumes its own substance." That reminiscence gave Fation the idea of jotting down notes about his disagreements with uncle. Feeling a sense of relief, he put pen on paper, but quickly stopped cold, fearing that his disclosures might backfire. He could be accused as a collaborator, because he had withheld information from the Party. "Why haven't you made these disclosures before? As an investigator, it was your duty to come to us right away. It is too late to shut the stable door, after the horse has bolted."

He put the note card aside, picked up the phone and called Judge Stavri. He asked for clarifications on the new criteria, to ascertain whether his half-uncle was listed as a close relative. As soon as Judge Stavri assured him that "a half-uncle was not mentioned in the list of relatives" Fation was not as edgy as before.

"It is interesting you should ask," Judge Stavri added over the phone. "The new criteria indicate that the nephew 'pays' for the uncle's sins, but not the other way around."

Fation could make use of such detailed data to help himself.

28

The visits to the jail had been a flattering occurrence of satisfaction for Fation Bashkurti. He walked about like a lord, interrogated the convicts and gave orders to the guards in a loud and clear voice. As he walked the hallways, he purposely clacked his heels hard to make his presence emphatic. Now, however, he had to step quietly and quickly from fear that he might run into his uncle in the jail corridors. He was determined to walk on without even looking at uncle Pleurat, in case their paths crossed unexpectedly. The rules about walking an inmate out of the cell were strict, and the guards always kept silent, never glancing right or left. But what if uncle greeted him, or expressed gratitude to see his nephew there? What if uncle felt morally superior, following the arrest, and even smile to Fation just to show that had been right all along? What if uncle made an innuendo that would bring down Fation's authority in front of the prison guards?

Despite all his best efforts, he couldn't forget that in one of those cells was his uncle, whom he had cared for deeply as a young man. While Milazim Gruda was being treated at the hospital, Fation kept clear of the jail. But the investigator knew that avoiding the jail visits wouldn't last long and in addition he had been advised to resume the interrogation. Feeling tense Fation climbed the stairs quietly, and when he stepped into the corridor of the second floor, he paused and listened carefully for the sound of some door bolt sliding on a prison cell. The hallway was empty and silent, and he hurried his steps.

After asking the guard to bring in the suspect, Fation lit up a cigarette. A few puffs later, Milazim Gruda was in the room. His right eye was bandaged up with gauze, while his left eye gleamed like before.

"Have you decided to talk?" Fation asked him, without apologizing for beating him.

"I haven't said that I don't want to talk," Milazim replied quietly.

"You have made up your mind to plead guilty?" Fation said, hoping that the beating had lessened his determination to resist.

"I have never admitted to the allegations against me in the past, and I don't admit to them now. That's is where I stand," he declared.

"Then you shall die here," Fation warned him.

Then tried to persuade the convict that his resistance was going to crack as soon as 'the others' admitted that they were preparing to flee the country with him.

"Everyone answers for himself," asserted Milazim Gruda.

That day Fation Bashkurti concluded his interrogation session quickly. As soon as the guard handcuffed Milazim and walked out the office, Fation hurried down the stairs.

29

Just a few month months away from his retirement, the chief of the Investigation Bureau, Jovan had announced that he would not work a single day past his going out day, even if they begged him. Casually chief said that he was tired, and his hernia was worsening. Rumors about 'the new chief' were already in circulation. The Senior Investigator, who was the strongest candidate, was temporarily out of the running, because of his poor health, if indeed he was ill. Fation hoped that his senior colleague was seriously taken ill and would never recover. At the same time, the appointment of the new chief was the purview of the Ministry of the Internal Affairs. It could not be ruled out that 'an outsider' would be the frontrunner, and the current professional investigators would be bypassed.

A few days after the arrest of uncle Pleurat, Fation's supervisor called him to his office, and informed him point blank that he was being transferred from the Investigation sector. The news was very sudden. Fation felt he had slipped into an abyss, and nothing could break his fall. He even thought his body was starting to disintegrate in a sort of a black hole that sucks in lives, whole planets and meteors. Instinctively, he reached out to hold on to something, and it was only when he grabbed a solid object that he managed to stand up. Then he noticed that he was holding tight to a corner of a table.

"Turn your files over to Mark and the office inventory to the administration chief," ordered his supervisor.

"Are you saying that I am being fired?" asked Fation fearfully.

"I don't think I used the word 'fired.' You're being transferred to a position to be decided by the Executive Committee."

"Why?" Fation dared to ask. "Is it permissible to ask for what reason, or reasons?"

"You know why. I don't have to tell you," his chief replied coldly.

He was being dismissed from the Investigation sector, on account of his half-uncle. Referring to the Party's recent memo, Fation quickly argued that his half-uncle did not figure as a close family relative.

"That argument is of no significance, at all," said Jovan, turning thumbs down on it.

"Are you aware that I have opposite views from Pleurat?" he asked, ready to elaborate on the sharp political debates Fation had with his uncle.

"I don't want to hear it," snapped his chief. "This is an order, and it has to be carried out."

Fation's arms went limp. His superior for a number of years did not care to hear any arguments and did not even give a second thought to Fation's 'transferring.' What about the chief's glorious evaluations and boisterous talk about Fation's promising career as an investigator? Such questions and bits of past conversations swarmed his mind at once, not fully aware of what was supposed to be his next move.

Mark Puleshi appeared at the door. With his skinny and bony frame, he looked as if he had escaped from the morgue. Fation gathered that it was his 'cue' to leave the Chief's office. In his last walk to the office, Fation was followed by Mark. As much as he tried to show composure, Fation's hands were shaking so much; he had difficulty opening the file cabinet. Letting out a few deep sighs, he took out several folders, including one with blue covers, which was thicker than the others.

"The file on the defendant Milazim Gruda," Fation said, flinging it at Mark with contempt. "The most stubborn and obstinate man I have ever known."

"You failed, didn't you?" Mark teased maliciously. "You have to admit it."

"And who are you to judge me?" retorted Fation.

"Today, you are the subject of discussion, not me" Mark said, curtly. "It's you who got the heave-ho from the Interrogation unit. Do you think that's small potatoes?"

"At least no one has yet snatched my gun from my belt," lashed out Fation.

Some twenty years earlier, Mark Puleshi signed up to work undercover like a mole, into a secret anti-Communist cell. Such covert mission would have catapulted him into the company of "Unsung Heroes." But the plan along with the dream blew up in his face. The "agent" whom he met at a shack near the Bami graveyard, told Mark that he knew he was working for *Sigurimi.* "No, on my honor," Mark swore. "In that case, why did you come here armed?" the 'informer' asked. Then he stuck his hand into Mark's belt, grabbed his pistol, and shoved him out with a kick in the ass. "Go and tell your partners who disarmed you." That story became an internal joke at the Investigation unit. For ten years after the incident, Mark worked the streets as a policeman. Then he was admitted back to the ranks of investigators, after completing the Adult Continued Education Program in Law School.

Sigurimi officers were blatantly arrogant with their former partners who had lost their positions of power. Fation was whimsically thrown in with the likes of Mark Puleshi. Feeling that he was given the same treatment as some dirt bag irritated Fation even more.

30

The thought that he had been kicked him out into the streets without a cause frayed his nerves. He yearned to meet a friend, even an acquaintance, and sit down at a nook in a café, and indulge in gossip for a while. But where could he go? News about changes in the line-up of personnel, reached the Ministry's coffee shop sooner than anywhere else, and lingered there the longest. Since the dismissal, Fation had the feeling that whatever bar or restaurant he would go to, people would star at him and whisper among themselves about his expel from the Investigation sector, due to the arrest of his uncle on charges of hostile activity. In his mind, Fation went over the standard procedure, once again. The chief of the personnel office was going to note the arrest of the uncle on Fation's personal records and that 'stain' would dog his steps all his life. Until then, Fation had helped put away people with tainted personal biographies who were considered potential enemies of the government. From then on, he too would be an outcast, whipped by the system he had served with loyalty. This thought struck his head like a hammer. He felt like shouting to the world that he had not changed his convictions and remained devoted to the Party. But who would listen to him now? His own supervisor refused to hear him out, and those higher-ups who had ordered his dismissal, wouldn't even let him get near them. Ironically, Fation recalled clearly how he considered hypocrites those relatives with stained family histories who were pushed to the margins and yet professed untouched loyalty to the Party. He thought that Lindita was right when she said that once you loose your foothold, nobody gives you a hand.

With these thoughts in mind, he found himself at the steps of the church-turned-Bar-Buffet, on top of the hill. Uncertain, he went inside and sat down at a side table. When the waiter came over, he ordered a glass of peach juice and a short espresso. "God help me!" he mumbled without even thinking. That prayer welled up from the depths of his soul. But the moment he realized what he had said, he became angry with himself. "What an idiot! I am praying in a Bar-Buffet! There is a counter instead of the altar and there are paintings of still life in place of the saints on the walls." The simple observations fueled his unexpected thoughts about the possible survival of the religious sentiment in the recesses of the soul, after years and years of living in an atheistic state. More and more surprised by his own out-of-place-ideas he wondered whether it would be a sin for a non-Christian like him to pray in an Orthodox church. He remembered that his deceased grandmother believed that every "wholesome place" hears the prayers of believers. Secretly she herself used to light a candle in the ruins of an old Orthodox church.

The mild weather prompted him to take a walk out of the Café and around the lake. He estimated that the perimeter of the lake was approximately five thousand meters. Although it was small in size, the man-made lake in the shape of a grape leaf, added to the beauty of the park and the south side of the capital city, and offered amusement both to those who swam in the designated area and to others who simply contemplated the lake scenery. He walked over the man-made dam and out into the meadows on the south side. This was the barest and least attractive side of the lake. As soon as he arrived at the paved pathways shaded by trees, he felt refreshed and elated. The variegated landscape, croaking frogs, thrushes looking for seeds in the grass, beetles waltzing on flower petals, lizards sunning themselves on fallen tree trunks, made him stop and sit down on the stump of a poplar tree, so as to look at them more leisurely. Every living thing lived as it did the day before, the year before, even thousands of years before. A yellow leaf broke loose from the branch above, spun around in the air, and fell on the surface of the lake. "Her last dance," thought Fation and unconsciously likened it to his condition. The leaf was brought down by autumn, while he was brought down by a set of criteria. No, not even the criteria.... For the first time, it occurred to him that the criteria could serve as sanctions for punishing the innocents simply on the basis of kinship and blood ties. The criteria dealt a knockout blow to the penal code, and indeed to the Constitution itself. He was astounded that the conclusion he had arrived at, drew him close to the ideas of his uncle. He got up and began to walk at a faster pace. Office hours were over by now, and his colleagues at the Investigation unit secured their drawers and closets with red wax and string to protect their secrets. Fation felt that it was a good thing that his boss did not want to listen to him. Otherwise, he would have besmirched himself in vain. His uncle's views did have some points. In his opinion, 'the class struggle' – in a country without classes – was as a devilish invention of the country's leadership to resort to violence and terror at any time and against anyone who opposed it. He thought it was sarcastic that it called itself the people's democracy. Suddenly he asked himself he would be handling the investigation of his uncle? Could Mark Puleshi be assigned this case? It would be an irony of fate to be delivered into the hands of a vicious man like him. At any event, the investigation Mark was handed over was already a handful and was likely to drag on.

He had strolled the lake for about an hour and headed home with a heavy heart. How was Lindita going to take his departure from the Investigation sector? Would she ask for a divorce to protect herself and safeguard the future of the children?

31

"I'm finished! Done for!" he wailed as he slumped into a chair.

Lindita went over to him, put her hand on his forehead, touched his neck and hands, and seeing that he did not have the slightest fever, said to him:

"Are you drunk, or just raving mad? He walks into the house as if death has come calling for him."

"Death is right. They fired me from my post."

Instead of feeling sorry for him, and sighing along with him and expressing sympathy, she coughed slightly and said,

"Losing your job is not the end of the world."

"They will send me as a judicial counselor...some place, I don't yet know."

"Good," said Lindita. "Why do you say 'fired,' when you have been transferred?"

"Imagine! Fation Bashkurti, judicial counselor at a construction company or a garbage collection unit, surrounded by manure and muck and street cleaners...down in the dumps," he groaned.

"You'll still get your salary...."

"It's him. It's that damned soul that has brought this on me," shouted Fation. "I could tear him apart with my hands."

"Keep your voice down. The children will hear you," Lindita scolded him.

"I'm going to file a statement about that evil mind of his."

"Stop talking nonsense!" his wife said. "Do you recall that doctor from Berat who scribbled eight pages of dirt against his army officer brother that had been expelled from the Party? You called him a spineless bastard. Do you think that people who turn against their own relatives are respected? Do you think you will be reappointed to your former position if you denounce your uncle?"

Fation started to rub his temples. He knew that the doctor had smeared his own brother out of fear. Such desperate actions were not a chance occurrence or an exception to the rule in his daily work. Following the arrest of their husbands, quite a few of the wives went over to the local *Sigurimi* office voluntarily, and denounced their partners for anti-government comments and remarks. For their part, their husbands did not hold it against their spouses, since they knew that their wives took that step out of fear of being sent to an internment camp, losing their job, and for the sake of the children. The security officials, too, knew the motives of these statements and they ignored them, telling the wives that they had waited too long to speak out.

Fation decided that it was best not to do anything that might aggravate the case of his uncle, and consequently his own, as well. He hoped that his uncle would be able to ward off the accusations against him, and receive a conditional sentence. He had no doubt that his uncle was arrested on the most common and senseless suspicion, the most ludicrous and serious violation, namely “anti-government propaganda.” In his uncle’s opinion, that particular article of the Penal Code was abused to such an extent that any commonplace criticism about public eateries, any complain about food shortages, any grievance about the lack of fish or onions in the market place was quickly interpreted as a willing act of defiance against the system.

32

The job of the judicial counselor at the Communal Sector was easy. Fation had to make sure that new guidelines sent by the Ministry did not run counter to the laws in force, and the updated regulations were in line with the Ministry’s previous orders. From time to time, he offered stylistic or orthographic suggestions in the materials just to validate his official duties.

“I guess we can make the reservation for the company’s villa on the beach for the summer vacation,” Lindita told him.

“I think the Ministry has already reserved it for next year’s vacation.”

“Already?” Lindita remarked with surprise and disappointment. “They reserve the villa for themselves. If you can’t do that for your own family, I don’t see the point of working there,” she teased him.

She was not aware that despite the unchallenging nature of his job, Fation was struggling to stay focused at work At times he gazed at the office window with an anxious look on his face, or got up and opened the door when nobody knocked. One day he came home before the end of the office hours. He had a haggard look, highlighted by the dark sacks beneath his eyes. He kept silent until the children went to bed, then he confided to his wife the secret that had been torturing him.

“Someone is following me,” he said to her in a low voice, while looking sideways furtively. “Do you believe me?”

“No,” she replied. “Who cares about you? You don’t have any clout.”

“I know when I’m being followed. I have seen a shadow…,” he said slowly, and waited for his wife’s reaction.

“You are followed by a shadow?” she repeated, to make sure she heard right.

He nodded and looked at the door as if afraid of anybody's eavesdropping.

"I thought you meant that someone from the secret service is trailing you.... No harm can come from a shadow, right?" she said, trying to calm him.

He looked at her with annoyance and readable frustration.

"It's torturing me, I tell you. It sneers at me and won't leave me alone. I will try to shoot it...."

"Shoot what? A ghost? Do you hear yourself?" she asked.

Then she rolled her eyes and heaved a deep sigh.

"It's because you're tired and worn out from work," said his wife. "Can I get you a glass of whiskey and a bite to eat?"

"No," he replied.

"Do you want to go out to a restaurant? Or maybe you want to rest...."

"I'm not tired. Sometimes I wonder how it's possible for anyone with such features to walk around, even if it's a ghost."

Intuitively Lindita mentioned to him Dr. Dragush.

"Who?"

"Your cousin, Dragush. He is a medical doctor."

"Never!" he hollered. "You think I'm crazy?"

"I think you should go and talk to a neurologist."

"I got no business with a neurologist." he asserted.

The conversation had taken a downward turn.

"I'm going to bed," he said, and stood up hastily. His face expressed anxiety and boredom.

Sleep is believed to be the most effective sedative, superior to any medicine. But just a few minutes later, Fation was out of bed. He got dressed and stepped outside without saying where he was going. Lindita followed him with her eyes wearily, not daring to ask him anything.

33

However much she tried to seem composed, Lindita felt nervous and somewhat anxious as she entered the office of Dr. Dragush, Luckily, there was nobody else around, apart from the doctor.

"I came to visit a friend of mine, and stopped by to see you," she said, with a sly grin.

"What's the name of your friend?" inquired the doctor politely.

"It is better you don't know," she said timidly while trying to smile.

He offered her a chair to sit down.

"How is my cousin?" Dr. Dragush asked.

Instead of giving an answer, she was silent and contemplative.

"Is there a problem? Doesn't he feel well?" the doctor went on.

"Oh, please help us!" she pleaded urgently.

"What's happened?"

"It's bad enough that the poor wretch is beside himself, but he has made our lives miserable, as well," she complained with tears in her eyes.

"You know you can talk to me."

"Every time I complain to my mother, she tells me: 'You got troubles? Be patient. He is your husband.' And I have put up with him, not knowing if that has helped any."

She mentioned the night when he 'saw somebody' at their bedroom window, and the episode of the ghost that follows him around. Lindita said that her husband suffered from lack of sleep; that sometimes he woke up at night just to go out of the house, and that he kept a gun by his side. She had noticed that her husband's emotional condition changed frequently and without cause and that lately he was in the habit of talking to himself.

Then the doctor asked how Fation was getting along with the children.

She said that he quarreled constantly with the girl. Strangely, however, their daughter was closer to the father whereas their son was distanced and unaffectionate with him.

"It's only recently that I found out that Dritan can't stand to be called 'the cop's kid,' or 'the government's fink.' You know who the kids call 'a fink nowadays'?"

"Yes. The *Sigurimi* agents, or volunteer informants," the doctor told her.

"Anyway, when it comes to the children, Fation vents his anger on me.... 'You pamper them, like they are still little kids,' he screams."

"He says that he is being followed?" the psychiatrist was interested to know. "Has he said at any time who he suspects?"

"No."

"How is his blood pressure?"

"Perfectly normal," said Lindita.

"Would you tell Fation to come and see me? I just want to talk to him," the doctor asked.

"He won't come. If people find out, they will say he is crazy."

"Let him come quietly. If he doesn't want to come here, he can come to my house," Dr. Dragush suggested.

"It could be serious," the psychiatrist noted. But being aware that schizophrenia caused panic among the relatives of the afflicted, he refrained from telling her, especially since he did not have conclusive proof, as yet. "Manifestations of depression, anxiety, fear…."

"At least, give me a medicament that I can put in his food, without him being aware," Lindita pleaded, believing that the doctor had a clear notion about the diagnosis.

Dr. Dragush smiled at her charitably.

"Who is telling these fairy tales? There is no specific medicine for such cases, as there is for the common cold or malaria," the psychiatrist concluded.

34

Following his "transferal," Fation had stayed away from the city's bars and restaurants that were usually frequented by his colleagues at the Investigation sector and *Sigurimi* men. In his relentless attempt to cut all ties with his uncle, Fation had not even asked who was the interrogator on that case, nor did he care to know. Every time he thought of his uncle, geysers of hatred erupted from the depths of his being. Fation believed strongly that uncle was responsible for his removal from the Investigation department and the downfall of both his career and future. Also, lately Fation was seized by a growing fear that he would slip further even below the level of judicial counselor. The uncertainty ate away at him and strained his concentration, while at times it offered a new perspective on certain details. His uncle used to say that the horseman and the footman see the road ahead of them differently, and it's only when the horseman falls off his horse, that he is able to judge the reality of the footman objectively. Fation began to see how difficult, if not impossible, it was for the ordinary citizen to uphold his rights and even defend himself. The plain formulas he had conveniently repeated in his line of duty now started to sound ironic: "Go wherever you are assigned to take your punishment, and then demand justice in accordance with official guidelines!" The denouncing statements of spouses and the letters of siblings after arrests had been made in their household appeared to testify to the moral unraveling of the smallest and most delicate unit of society, namely the family, as a result of extreme political pressure. Terrified by such dark thoughts, he wondered whether his vulnerable mind was simply echoing his uncle's ideas. He still remembered how good it felt to bust the suspects, to be trusted by superiors and above all to have power over people's lives.

Walking usually helped to clear his head, but 'left' him more susceptible to being followed. Fation stepped with hesitation into the hall of the Palace of Culture, and looked behind his back. He noticed a raised hand that was inviting him over.

"I didn't see you at the trial," were the first words judge Stavri said to him.

"Trial?" Fation asked, as if in a daze.

"Your uncle's trial. Or didn't you know the trial date?" judge Stavri asked.

"To tell you the truth, even if I had known, I would not have been there. I know how some of 'our own' would have watched me like a hawk. If I showed anger, they would have interpreted that as hypocrisy. If I were pleased...well, I have no reason to be pleased. It's better this way. How did the trial go?"

Judge Stavri raised his hand upward as if to gesture the heights the trial had reached. .

"Terrific! Your uncle is terrible," he said.

"A sworn enemy, you mean?"

"I mean, sensational. An eloquent speaker, a brilliant analyst, a true thinker. I don't believe anyone, to this day, has dared in our court of law to make the accusations he did. Bless my soul!"

Bedazzled to hear judge Stavri's review, Fation wondered whether there was sarcasm involved. After all, his expressed admiration did not correspond with Fation's sentiments.

"Uncle did not humble himself or show remorse?" asked Fation and gave him a quizzical look.

"Remorse? Pleurat tore the prosecutor to shreds and not just him alone. He called all our prosecutors 'narrow-minded, servants of the regime, and not of justice.' Then pointing his finger at the prosecutor in the courtroom, Pleurat said: 'Here we have a true representative of that species! Of the man who speaks without thinking; the defender of the law who lets go with his accusations the way a cow drops its dung.' "

"And the prosecutor put up with it?" Fation inquired.

"I don't think the prosecutor ever expected such language. The prosecution and the court were dumbfounded. Pleurat called our judges 'worms that feed on the corpses of the murdered.' I don't think such words have ever been heard in a courtroom, since the end of the war. He pounded us," judge Stavri observed.

From the fine points to the tone of the voice, it was clear that judge was more than impressed with the defendant's arguments.

"Powerful analogy, indeed," judge Stavri continued to deliver his impressions, "because worms need ever more corpses to feed on. At a certain point, Pleurat asked: 'How can anyone expect justice from judges who receive ordered verdicts from above? As long as they merely execute orders, our trials are only farces.' "

"Farces? Is that what he said?" asked Fation who could not believe his ears.

"Well, he said a lot more. Pleurat called the system by an ancient Greek term, which I heard there for the first time. He said: 'Tromokratia' – the power of terror has displaced 'democracy' – the governing by the people. It is madness molded into a system. That's why it makes no sense to talk about democratic government, people's government, and similar labels.' He then added that 'power of terror' is coming to an end and illustrated his point with a simple example. 'Some years ago,' he said, 'when we heard that a relative or friend had been jailed by the government, we felt miserable and rushed to give heart to their families, while now that kind of news causes a different reaction, as we all know. Regrettably, imprisonments have become daily occurrences and even more sadly nowadays the number of the innocents inside prison walls is greater than the number of the villains.' But the high point of it all was when he turned to the court and asked 'Is there anyone here who thinks like I do?' Silence. Someone replied, 'No, we don't think so!' Then,

Pleurat simply said: 'You may speak for yourself, but not for everyone. You don't know their thoughts. For I am sure, that there are plenty of people who think like me.' He added that people's ideas cannot be handcuffed, jailed nor killed. And when so simple a thing as this is not understood, hypocrisy and dictatorship rule. It was a jolting trial for the judges, as well as for anyone who heard about it. Pleurat conducted himself like a man. You got to hand it to him, even if you despise him," judge Stavri concluded.

Emotional confusion overcame Fation once again. His uncle, Pleurat, true to his principles, revealed his thoughts in a court of law, knowing beforehand that such act would call for a severe sentencing. His courageous conduct had impressed the conformists and opponents alike, but his powerful verbal indictments to the system could have bitter repercussions for his nephew. Fation was not sure whether he could endure another blow like losing the right to practice his profession or even a second transfer from his position as judicial counselor.

"How many years did uncle get?"

"Twelve. Some thought that was not punishment enough others believed it was too much. I think this trial will be remembered for a very long time," predicted judge Stavri. "I can't help noticing that you don't share my opinion."

"It was because of him, that I got the boot," Fation explained irritably.

"No! Your emotions are clouding your judgment," observed judge Stavri.

Fation felt that someone was watching him and asked judge Stavri's permission to leave. He stepped outside hoping to be alone. The open space usually helped to dissipate the dreary thoughts in his head, but did not make it easier to escape from the 'shadow' that he felt was behind him. It occurred to him that tradition required that he pay a visit to his uncle's family and see how his aunt was doing. But his legs went numb, as soon as he thought that the house was now under surveillance by secret agents. Now he had no wish to go and be seen in his uncle's home. Moreover, he could be 'reported' for harboring sentiments for a declared enemy. Then suddenly he recalled the discussion he had with his uncle about blood ties, and his face drooped. He began to think that those ties were not dear to him, let alone 'sacred.' In a reverse case, his uncle would not have feared to go by Lindita's side. These thoughts made Fation feel like a coward and a conformist. Judge Stavri's last remark about emotions interfering with his judgment swirled in Fation's head with stupefying speed. Since his uncle was paying for his sins with twelve years in prison, why should his nephew be punished too? It would be the same as punishing a man twice for the same crime. The criteria that was practiced for years by the Interrogation unit suddenly seemed to him like the fiendish inventions of fashionably dressed executioners.

Troubled by his unorthodox thoughts, Fation walked wherever his legs took him. He was not going to tell Lindita about judge Stavri's praises for Pleurat's conduct in court, and his terrible indictment of judges. In her simplicity she had believed that uncle Pleurat was right. After a while he noticed that he had walked up to the path that led upward to the lake. The splendor of the autumn foliage and the fragrance from the carpet of decaying leaves on the ground did have their appeal on him.

"It only takes an hour," he said to himself. "One hour. Twelve years…twelve."

Along the path that led up to the hill, Fation walked by a poplar tree, behind it a hexagon-shaped face wearing a cap, smiled at him maliciously. Determined to shoot at it, he reached for his gun but quickly remembered that the pistol was in the safe. Fation turned his head around, not to see and be seen by that grim face. A man was pacing slowly along the road, but his footsteps could not be heard. Fearing that the follower would spring at him and choke him to death, he turned around slowly, and then ran toward the city, panting hard along the way. His suspicions inclined him to be careful. When he got to the sidewalk he stopped to catch his breath somewhat, and then turned his head. He noticed a figure huddled behind the iron bars at the front yard of the Guards Unit. He shuddered, and more anxious to escape, he ran across the square and down the boulevard, until he came to the little stone bridge over the Lana River. Then he hurried his steps toward home, not looking either sideways or behind, walked quickly up the stairs, opened the door to his apartment, locked himself into the bedroom, lay down in bed with his shoes on and pulled the bed sheet over his face.

After knocking uselessly on the door for hours, Lindita called the doctor. In an alarmed state, she said that Fation had locked himself in the bedroom, and was absolutely unresponsive to her pleas to open the door.

Later that evening the ambulance stopped at their apartment building. Its bright lights and the wailing siren pushed aside the night shadows of the city all the way to the psychiatric hospital.